Typewriter Pub, an imprint of Blvnp Incorporated
A Nevada Corporation
1887 Whitney Mesa DR #2002
Henderson, NV 89014
www.typewriterpub.com/info@typewriterpub.com

ISBN: 978-1-64434-219-0

DISCLAIMER

This book is a work of fiction. The characters, incidents, and dialogue are
drawn from the author's imagination and are not to be construed as real.
While references might be made to actual historical events or existing
locations, the names, characters, places, and incidents are either products
of the author's imagination or are used fictitiously, and any resemblance to
actual persons living or dead, business establishments, events or locales is
entirely coincidental.

ALASKA

LOTTE HOLDER

type
writer
pub

To my family and friends.
I love you, thank you for the endless support.

And to Jess. Thank you for reading Alaska on the bus to school.
I wouldn't be here without you.

This story is written with the British spelling of words.

Trigger Warning
The following story contains strong language, violence,
and violence to children.
Reader discretion is advised.

CHAPTER ZERO
Rogue

"When you look death in the eye, and death blinks first, nothing seems impossible."
- The Fifth Wave, Rick Yancey

Rogue. It's a word that's been circulating this world for as long as I can remember. It's the word that haunts children as they sleep, nightmares flashing visions of beasts with bared teeth. It's the word used to describe monsters that are only whispered around an ominous campfire.

Rogues are always portrayed as werewolves who have been stripped of their humanity, so that the pure monster within the werewolf's soul is the only thing that remains.

I have a different opinion.

There are some rogues that are bloodthirsty creatures. They kill for sport. Unless you have a death wish, you never want to go up against one. You will lose, alpha or not.

But there are other rogues that are not the mindless beasts you would imagine. There are those who have fled their packs because of abuse. Others who have run away because they simply don't feel as though they belong. And there are those like me that, well, didn't have a choice.

But I am still a rogue. Packless, to be more precise, yet I'm still classed as a mindless animal, although I'm pretty sure that I'm sane.

I don't particularly like talking about my past, but there's a point in your life when the pain of loss becomes bearable. Of course, the scars on my soul will never truly fade, but with time they will heal.

My history dates back to five years ago, when I was twelve years old. I wasn't a particularly special werewolf—just a young girl who was often looked over. No one saw what was truly inside until my first shift.

Being a female, it was rare for me to be able to shift. At the time, I couldn't believe that I, an average female werewolf, would be able to shift, nor could the rest of my pack. Half wanted to kill me, and the rest wanted protect me. The situation didn't end well.

My mother and father gave their lives to protect me but it wasn't enough. With her dying breath, my mother had pushed me into a river, which had carried me miles down south to a lake in Alaska.

I can't count the number of times I almost died that night. It was a miracle that I was still alive at the end of that traumatic experience, as if fate had pushed me that tiny bit further into the complexity of life.

I blink away my tears, eyes burning and heart in flames. I was stronger than this. I could have always killed myself one way or another; there was no one left who cared about me. But I didn't. I had survived for a reason, and I was going to discover that reason. My parents didn't die for pathetic tears and a daughter who watched life go by like a passing train.

Frustrated, I stand up, almost whacking into a branch above my head. God, why was I so clumsy? Hopefully, I was growing but that didn't mean that my limbs needed a mind of their own.

2

I lean forwards over the river's edge, water gushing against the stones on the bank. The sun is beginning to set, scarlet rays painting the mystical landscape a gentle pigment of crimson. There is no wind, and the only sound is the birds calling for the night. The trees are covered in a soft blanket of fresh snow, frost spiking the bark of long toppled trees. The scene is tranquil, and for once, it feels calming. It feels as though I am home.

The clear and perfectly still water of the river provided the perfect mirror. As I glance into its fathomless depths, I can clearly see the hazel of my eyes glare back at me.

I wouldn't consider myself pretty. Perhaps striking, but not pretty. My rich mocha hair drifts into my face, my angular nose and freckles along the bridge being partially covered up. My lips look somewhat paler than usual but they had never been my most prized feature anyway.

I sit back on my heels and splash water on to my face, clearing the muck and dirt from my skin. The water cascaded down my face, dropping to the floor, my ears able to pick up each patter as they landed. I made sure I didn't get too close—I didn't mix well with water.

Sometimes, being a werewolf is amazing. But life is short; many die from disease in their early years, and those who survive often die in battles for territory or control of a pack. The truth is that demise is inevitable being a werewolf, but some manage to postpone their expiry dates for a little longer.

Sighing, I turn away from the stream and the peace it offered. It was time to head back to my temporary home.

Five years ago, when I hauled myself from the lake, I wandered for miles before finally collapsing and accepting death. That was until they found me. The supposed "rogues" had taken me under their wing, and I have never looked back.

"Ali?" someone asks from within the forest, almost causing me to jump out of my skin. It sounded as though an atomic bomb had been blasted right next to my ear. Sometimes, I hate the sensitive senses you were automatically gifted with when born a werewolf.

Taking my sword in my grasp, I head back along the path and come face to face with Dylan.

"God, you scared me Dylan. Don't you dare do that again, otherwise . . ." I trail off, not knowing what to say. Would I really hurt him? I had always been shy and often closed myself off from people I didn't know. Sure, spurs of confidence had landed me into trouble, but Dylan was the only person I had ever confided in.

Just like me, he is seventeen, and not to mention extremely good looking. It was difficult to not be swayed by his endless brown eyes and matching shade of hair. Despite the cocky look in his eyes, Dylan's tall frame was something many women found attractive. If he wasn't my friend, maybe I would see it too.

Dylan raises an eyebrow. "Otherwise you'll stab me?"

I nod, biting back a smile. "If you insist."

"You wouldn't do that," he argues. Although he was my closest friend in the Rogue pack, he still got on my nerves. I preferred to be alone; it gave me time to think.

"You seem to be underestimating my personality," I state, continuing to trudge up the well-trodden path. The walk to the camp only took two minutes, but it was best to walk and talk rather than waste time.

I hear the sharp snap of a twig as Dylan parades behind me. "You can put your sword away now, Alaska. It's not like anyone's going to jump out from behind a tree."

I roll my eyes. This was the true Dylan—the guy who thought he could save the world with his infamously handsome smile. I had to admit, for a werewolf, he had decent teeth. "Just because you have a bow and arrow and an arrogant personality doesn't mean I'm incapable of protecting myself," I retort, refusing to place the blade back in my belt.

"I am not arrogant," Dylan argues back. I can't see his face, but I can imagine his jaw dropped and features scrunched so that they somewhat resembled a scowl.

I shrug my shoulders. "If you say so." If this was his attempt at flirting with me, he had failed miserably.

"You can be such a b*tch, you know that, righ—" Dylan begins, but the friendly conversation is sliced like a knife as a scream fills the empty air.

"Crap," I murmur as the wails continued to ring through the air like the whistling blade of a hurled axe. I knew that cry. It was Lily, the child of one of the rogue couples. The sound makes the hair on the back of my neck stand on end and my heart hammer like an electric pulse.

Why would she be screaming? It's not like anything in this territory would want to hurt her.

I sniff the air tentatively, and the aroma drifting through the forest is enough to make me shrivel my nose in disgust. This was the one time I let my guard down, and they had to attack?

"No, no, no . . ." I murmur, sprinting down the rest of the path, feet thumping against the compact earth, heart racing so quickly it feels as though it wants to break out of my chest.

Blood rushes through my ears, almost deafening me. Almost. The screams are still as prominent as ever. It was as if I was surrounded by dying bodies, all screeching at me to make it stop—to make the pain stop.

The seconds draw out into a millennia, each agonised breath taking a century to complete. Every footstep takes longer than humanly possible.

When I reach my destination, I almost collapse to my knees. The tents I had called home for the past five years are being hungrily devoured by flames. Werewolves carrying an assortment of weapons are shooting anyone down their path. And the place was alive with people; people screaming; people running; people dying.

A girl runs past me, and all I can do is grab her arm and scream, "What the hell's going on?" Because that's all that I can do.

The girl looks terrified, but I would too if I could see my face right now. Masked with hatred, my features contorted into an unrecognisable creature. The face of a true rogue.

The teenager—whose name I recall to be May—tries to tug away, but it's useless. She is too weak, and my rage is too strong. "T-they told us to move out of their territory, but we refused to. Alaska, we need to go. They'll kill us all."

I release May, her strawberry blonde hair following her like a flowing river. "Run. Find safety. I'll hold them off for as long as I can." May stares at me for a second, but every second wasted is another innocent so-called "Rogue's" death. "Go!" I order, and she does as she's told.

I wasn't the oldest member of the group, but I had gained respect due to my skills with a sword and my background. Many did not know about my ability to shift since it was a secret I didn't like to share around, but they all sensed that I was powerful.

The rogues I had grown up with all run to the north and the cover of the mountains, in the opposite direction of the attacking pack of wolves. All I had to do was buy them as much time as possible; they would never be able to outrun the warriors. If this was the reason as to why I had survived that fateful night, then so be it. I will die, and that will finally be the end. The end of the suffering—the end of the torment.

The grip of my sword is cool to the touch, although it's been nestled in my fist for the past five minutes. I don't care. Nothing burns like the cold, and that scorching heat was the only thing fuelling both my adrenaline and fear.

An arrow glides past my head. Not aimed at me, but aimed at one of the pack members. Dylan. Even I had to admit that he was a good shot.

Another pack wolf falls to the ground, white snow stained scarlet. I didn't have time, but I took those few seconds to study the fallen warrior. Just as suspected, he was a member of a true pack. But we had never threatened them, so why were they attacking us? Why did they want us to move?

Faces that I grew up with glance my way as they attempt to run. That was the thing about our tight-knit community; you never left a soldier behind. But I had to buy them time.

"Run!" I shout, signalling for them to head towards the mountains. They don't hesitate to charge in the direction of my hand.

Dylan comes to stand beside me, arrows flying from his bow every second. I raise my sword, readying myself for battle. The pack members had not noticed me yet, but with Dylan slowly but surely dwindling their population, I would soon be their next target.

"You hold them off," I tell him, the adrenaline pumping through my bloodstream at such a high concentration that I can barely think straight. I can barely even feel fear. "I'll protect the others."

Dylan nods, his supply of arrows dwindling low. I wonder how long it would take for him to run out of arrows and resort to hand-to-hand combat. I don't know the exact number in minutes, but I know that it'll be soon.

Two of the pack wolves break out from the other fifteen werewolves, swords in hands, running so fast that they appear to be a blur.

Without hesitating, I follow the two men, gulping when I realise that both were almost double the size of me, and older too. But that doesn't stop me. When you've already conquered demons in your life, it's easy to conquer them again.

"Hey!" I shout, causing both to turn in my direction, snarls worn on their worthless faces. They growl, but the closest one to me is immediately cut off as I chuck my sword and it embeds itself straight through his chest.

The other wolf, unexpectedly, looks unaffected by the death of his pack member, but his growl begins to grow as he charges towards me, sword in tow.

Crap. Well congratulations, Alaska, you just lost your sword.

I sprint towards the werewolf, reducing the distance between us. He swings out his arm, sword lashing towards me, but at the last second I duck under the blade and slide on my knees, just escaping my head from being decapitated.

I stumble to my feet, grabbing my sword from the chest of the fallen warrior. The man was not yet dead; I had missed his major organ by a few centimetres. Even so, he would be dead soon, and part of me thought that he deserved it, because who in their right mind would have the objective to kill children?

Turning around, I come face to face with my opponent. He was ghastly looking, with a burn across most of his face, and a claw mark running from his eyebrow to his cheek. This werewolf had been through a lot, and I knew that my chances of getting through this battle alive were slim.

The man sniggers at me, his beastly face becoming even more hideous. He doesn't look much older than me—nineteen, perhaps? But I don't care. He wanted to kill me and I wanted to kill him.

"Are you gonna cry, bitch? Because if you do, I might take it easy on you," the man snarls, rage fizzing through my body like wildfire.

I never cried. Yes, I almost did earlier, but I couldn't remember the last time I formed tears.

With a battle cry, I swing my sword around with all my might, hoping that the battle will be short and that I would come out victor. But my opponent smashes my dreams as his sword meets mine, a metallic clang filling the frost-bitten air.

Frustrated, I swing my sword again, but to no avail. Of course, I knew what I was doing with such a weapon but my body was so pumped full of adrenaline that I could barely make sense of the world around me.

For a third time, I slash with my majestic blade, only for it to be knocked out of my hand by the extreme force exerted from the blade of my opponent. That had never happened to me before, and only now does it dawn on me the trouble I'm truly in.

I grit my teeth, not even thinking for one second before ploughing into the man headfirst and arms outstretched, an animalistic cry erupting from my throat.

The man's body is hard, but I manage to knock him back by a few meters and cause him to drop his sword. My head hurts from the impact, but I don't care. I had already lost one family and I wasn't going to lose another.

A fist meets my stomach, and I release my hold of the monster, coughing blood from my mouth. If I wasn't angry already, I was completely and utterly enraged now. My eyesight blurry, my wolf is beginning to show.

I didn't have anger issues; I just used my indignation to fight. It allowed me unleash all of the locked up feelings I had been stowing away for years.

Powerless, I stagger back, the man closing in. He was so close, I could almost smell his breath fanning against my cheeks.

The man smiles, pleased at the situation. His hands were no longer fists, but tensing fingers that could snap my neck at a moment's notice.

And then his fingers slacken. His face becomes as bland as a piece of paper. His body drops to the floor like a stone, an arrow sticking out of his back like a victory flag.

I glance back up to see Dylan smiling at me, and I give him a quick twitch of my lips in return. I probably would have lost the battle, but I wasn't finished with the pack wolf just yet.

I was stronger than he thought. I always had been. Bravery just isn't my forte.

A cold wind blows across the battlefield, chilling me to the bone. The world turns grey, and my heart begins to slow, my body finally relaxing.

That is until the sword rips straight through his body.

He had no chance to say goodbye. No chance to receive my thanks. No chance to even drop the smile from his gorgeous, demised face.

A halo of crimson blood stains the snow around his body, the liquid flowing from his mouth, sword in his back.

Dylan is gone.

And all I can see is red.

CHAPTER ONE
Alpha

"I have a theory that selflessness and bravery aren't all that different."
- Tobias Eaton, Divergent

In that moment of rage and torment, I do what any other rogue in my position would do; blindly run head first into battle.

I hurl myself forwards, picking up my sword on the way, unsure of where I'm going—unsure of what I'm going to do.

The man who stabbed Dylan is still standing there, power and glory emanating off his muscular body as he claims his sword from my comrade's corpse. It's clear to see that even after stripping the life away from my friend, he didn't feel any guilt.

He gazes up at me with enraged eyes, but that's the last thing he does. My sword rips through his body before he can contemplate what's going on.

Like Dylan's, his death was quick. Maybe I should've dragged it out, allowing the pain to rule him for the last few minutes of his tedious, miserable life. I'm not a psychopath, but he killed Dylan. No one kills my best friend and gets away with it.

There aren't many pack wolves left but those that remain stare at me, their hands twitching to use their weapons. That's when I pick him out: the Alpha.

He was like a thorn on a rose, sticking out like a sore thumb. It was obvious he was in charge because of the power that rolled off him in waves. Not literally, but I could still feel his

11

authority engulf me as I charge over the corpse of his fallen comrade.

I collect my sword, now encrusted with blood. The Alpha stares at me, only ten metres away. I could tell by his calculating look that he was trying to find a way to solve the situation. He would kill me—or at least try to—but he had to figure out how to do so. I had already proved that I was a hard target.

I place my feet so that they're shoulder width apart, sword held protectively across my body. There is no escape for me now. If I run, the much faster male wolves would definitely catch up with me. I had no hope. But I wasn't going to die. Not like Dylan had.

"Why?" I ask the pack through gritted teeth. They all stare at me, dumbfounded that I had had the nerve to speak. "We did nothing to you," I spit out.

The Alpha steps forward. I step back.

"We were sent here by the Alpha King to kill any rogues," the Alpha hisses, making the hairs on the back of my neck prickle. There is something ominous about him that I can't quite put my finger on.

His face is handsome, with a sharp jawline that matched with a relatively close-cut mop of mouse-brown tresses, bringing colour to the snowscape. His eyes are a deep blue, almost appearing jet blue due to the distance. There is a scar above his right eyebrow, although it had turned a pastel white over time.

I shake my head, almost tempted to laugh. It was obvious that this group—my group—of werewolves were not rogues or any kind of threat. "We're not rogues."

"You are not a pack under the influence of the Alpha King. Therefore, you are rogues," he snarled, making me want to slap his worthless face. It was a shame that he was too far away. "And ruthless, bloodthirsty beasts like you have no place in this world."

Anger rises in my chest once more, and this time, I can't flush it down. A growl begins to form on my lips but I stop myself.

12

If I growled, they would know that I could shift, and I didn't know what they would do to me if they knew the truth.

In the werewolf world, only a minority of females were granted with the ability to shift. Many said it was a gift, when in reality it was a curse worse than death. Alpha males sought out shifting females for mates, sometimes forcing themselves on a female. Others kept them prisoners because they were different. I had lost my family due to this.

But the growl continues to develop, and I can't stop it.

Don't growl, Alaska. Don't you dare freaking growl.

I can't help it; I growl.

The Alpha raises an eyebrow, but I don't give him any more time to react. It was hard to tell whether they would kill me or keep me alive because of my "gift". Either way, I didn't want to find out.

I rip through the clearing, sword raised above my head as I pounce, swinging it down in a mighty arc. It was stupid of me, fighting an Alpha, but the more time I wasted, the better.

Clang. My blade is met by the Alpha's, except he thrusts it towards me and the force causes me to stagger back, dropping my trusted weapon in the process. He was stronger than he looks, his cobalt eyes sending shivers down my spine.

In the blink of an eye, I punch him square in the face but the blow seems to barely affect him. A single line of blood trickles from his nose, yet his face does not appear to be affected by the pain.

His body rams into mine as he pushes me against a tree, the air forced out of my lungs. Freezing metal meets the side of my throat as he threatens to slit the skin.

His face is now only a few centimetres away from mine, and it's easy to distinguish the strange flecks of silver floating in the sea of cobalt of his pupils. His eyes are beautiful, but they're the haunting kind of beauty that makes the blood in my veins boil like water left on a hob for too long.

13

"Any last words, b*tch?" he snarls at me, showing his almost perfect white teeth.

I spit in his face. The knife presses further.

The rough bark of the tree seems to grate on me as I try to shrink away from my untimely death, but I know that there is nowhere to go. That there's nowhere to hide. Within this clearing of frostbitten land and smouldering ruins, I would die. Just like Lily—just like Dylan.

Everyone was safe, so my death wouldn't be in vain. I guess it was a good thing dying a hero.

Thinking about Dylan, my brain clicks on again, the cogs whirring and spinning as they process my thoughts. Dylan always did the right thing. Even if he isn't here anymore, he always knew what to do.

What would Dylan do? I ask myself.

I would stand here and wait for death, knowing that it was inevitable.

But Dylan? He would save his life at any cost, even if it meant exposing himself.

With as much power I can muster, I push the Alpha off my body. However strong I might be for a female, I am no match for an Alpha. I know that, but my thirst to live outweighs his obligation to end me.

His grip falters for a second, and I grab my chance with both hands.

Bones crackle and snap as my body is consumed by a horrific pain, my skin prickling, my flesh turning into some beast I never asked to be. It was a type of torture that you couldn't imagine; not even in nightmares.

I let out a scream of agony, the air in my lungs suddenly stinging like needles. I close my eyes, going from a bleak world of one to wonder, where every particle of floating frost and each unique crystalline snowflake is visible to the naked eye. With a crunch, my nose elongates into a snout, aromas of disgusting body odour and pine needles hitting me like a wrecking ball.

In a second, the pain is over, but it seems to take centuries. Every click of a bone reverberates for eternity before the agony subsides and another wave sweeps through my body yet again.

A werewolf's body structure was the same as a typical wolf species except slightly larger. We could heal faster than the typical human and were stronger; better.

I glance up from my brown paws, wondering if my hazel eyes are much more vibrant when I'm in my wolf form. The Alpha just glares at me, clenching and unclenching his jaw as he figures out what to do about the situation. The mask of shock contorting his features is enough to tell me he wasn't expecting me to shift. But then again, neither did I.

I growl at my opposition as he sets down his sword, bones bucking until before me stands a much larger brown wolf, the scar still above his eyebrow. It's strange to be facing such a powerful monster, but I can still win this fight. I was faster and swifter than he anticipated. I was gifted that way, but I had never faced an alpha before, and the thought makes my stomach writhe.

"So you can shift," he growls, raising his head as he sizes me up. There was no point; he was already half a metre taller than me. "But that won't save you."

I know it won't. But I was trying to be Dylan, which so far had turned out okay. For starters, I hadn't been stabbed—yet.

I don't reply. Instead, I just growl. It's enough to let him know that I'm not going down without a fight.

The brunet wolf bolts towards me, his speed taking me by surprise. The air makes way for him as he rushes towards my wolf, each fall of his paw sounding like rumbling thunder.

Using my agility, I manage to slide out of his way, but only just. His paw swipes thin air, but if I had been a second later, his claws would have torn their way through my entire left abdomen.

I take a breath, trying to calm down my racing heart. The steady beat doesn't falter for a second.

The Alpha turns, and we begin to circle around the area, challenging each other on who is brave enough to attack first.

"Scared?" he mocks, teeth bared as though he's somewhat smiling.

"Do I look scared?" I snarl back.

The wolf doesn't answer. His hackles rise, and his lips move upwards, exposing his huge yellowed canines. Deep blue eyes glare at me.

And then it all happens at once. In a blur of brown, his figure is in front of me, his weight knocking me to the ground. I roll over in the snow, but his paws have caged me before I even get the chance to stand up. I thump my back leg into his, knocking him temporarily off balance and dash out from under his body. I feel a flood of relief, thinking I've made it out before his claws latch onto my pelt and pull me back.

His claws tear through my flesh, and all I can do is howl powerlessly.

His eyes look directly into mine, neck shielded from my view so I can't tear out his windpipe. What a shame, I would have done it, too.

I feel vulnerable within the enclosure of limbs. I had known that this was a fight I was unlikely to win, but I didn't realise it would be over so quickly. I had expected myself to at least come close to winning, or given the man a decent scar to leave on his body for years to come.

Staring at his darker, chocolate-pigmented underbelly, it was obvious that he had won and I had lost.

Moments tick by. I become more paranoid. When will he deliver the killing blow? Will my death be quick, or torturous?

The Alpha doesn't move in for the kill. Instead, with his brown fur swaying in the zephyr, he barks one word that sends a shiver down my spine, "Shift."

16

He wants me to shift? But why? I was a rogue—he should kill me. That was the law. I would rather he got it over and done with.

I try to writhe my way out of the cage, but it's useless, so I do as he says. Our clothes rip when we transform, but we have found a material that is able to shift with us. Luckily, I was wearing it, otherwise I would have to face a group of men naked.

Bones crack and snap back into place, and I can feel my straight hair run down past my shoulders once more. My warmer winter clothes have been shredded due to the shift, so I stand in the freezing cold wearing tight black leggings and matching T-shirt. The garments are so light it feels like I'm wearing nothing at all.

The Alpha shifts before me, and as soon as I'm about to make a dash for it, he grabs my arm and holds on to it like a vice.

He roughly pushes me against a tree once more, although this time there's no knife against my neck.

His face is scrunched up with anger, still enraged from me murdering one of his pack members. Welcome to my world, arseh*le. Your fellow pack member just murdered Dylan as well, so the feeling's freaking mutual.

"Give me one good reason why I should let you live." Not a question, a demand.

"You've kept me alive for this long, so there must be some reason," I point out. It was true; he had many chances to kill me, so why hadn't he done it?

The Alpha smirks for a second, but then points a finger in my face accusingly. "The Alpha King said to bring any shifting females with us. God knows why, but he said it was important," he informed me, "but he won't know if I 'accidentally' killed one."

I try as hard as I can to keep my face blank; I will not give him the satisfaction of my fear. "Go ahead." I shrug my shoulders. "Do it."

I don't generally seem to have a way with words, but the werewolf in front of me doesn't know how to react.

17

Someone tugs on the shoulder of the Alpha, our eye contact breaking in a blink. The other boy is younger than him, but he still looks like he holds an important role within the pack.

"Chase, lay off." He nodded towards me. "She's coming with us. King's orders, you know that."

The Alpha—Chase—turns back to glare at me, his jaw clenching one more time before he loosens his grip on my body. "You're going to wish that I killed you."

CHAPTER TWO
King

"I'm headed straight for the castle, they wanna make me their Queen."

- Castle, Halsey

A thousand eyes pierce my skin as I walk by. Being around so many people makes my body tingle, and I feel as if my chest has been opened up, revealing my cold heart. I wasn't good around people, especially those who were not classed as my race.

A hand shoves my back, forcing me up the steps towards the majestic palace. We're currently standing in the main courtyard of the King's kingdom, surrounded by walls that makes me feel like I'm dwindling low on oxygen. The stone is a brutal change from soft mud, and the lack of greenery within the kingdom walls makes me nauseous.

"Move it, b*tch," one of the pack members orders me, and I comply. There was nowhere I could run, and human nature was forcing me to continue walking; no matter what, I didn't want to die. My parents had saved me for a reason, and I would live up to their names. Dylan had died to save me, as well.

The doors of the castle are a rich mahogany that squeak slightly on the hinges as they are forced open. Of all the places I had envisioned myself to be at this point in my life, I hadn't expected to be here.

The journey to the kingdom of Arla had been a long one through the night. The wind had battered my body, and my hands still felt as though they were frozen blocks of ice. That was Alaska for you; harsh and cold, just like me.

The inside of the castle is luxurious. Even better than the ones I have seen in my most vivid dreams. Red curtains are draped from the top of exquisite windows that scale ten metres into the air, set in cobblestone walls.

The air is freezing even though roaring flames from torches lick the darkness, the stench of soot uncanny. Before me is a set of stairs, red carpet laced with gold running along the rough stone. They head up into darkness, and I can't help but gulp.

I hear the guards murmur something to another werewolf who is standing at the door. Despite having extremely sensitive hearing, I am unable to pick up their conversation. I don't think I want to. God only knows if they're talking about whether to kill me or release me. It's most likely the latter.

The guard abruptly snaps me from my thoughts as he drags me after him, and we mount the stairs before I have time to complain. It doesn't seem right for me to be in a place of such beauty. I am a worthless, good-for-nothing rogue to them.

But what shocks me more is the werewolf waiting for me, and by his side, another well-groomed werewolf with clean hunting clothes and a cape that is coloured a deep emerald. It is a strange sight, but as soon as I lay my eyes on him, it's obvious who he is. The Alpha King.

His eyes are pale crystal with age, and his skin sags around his face like a rotting apple. His hair is still managing to cling to his head, but the grey pigment provides me with enough evidence to realise that his days were limited. Of all the werewolves I had met and witnessed in my life, I had never seen one so old.

They took me to talk to the Alpha King. Of all the sh*tty people, the Alpha King.

The guards continue to escort me towards the man who ruled over the packs. Somewhere between the stairs and the "great" man, my legs give way. This was the man who had given the order to kill my group of "rogues". This was the man who had innocent blood on his hands.

As the guard forces me to kneel, I can't bring myself to look him in the eye. All that I can think is murderer. I am a murderer, yes, but I had a reason to be. He, on the other hand, didn't have a good reason.

"Rise," the Alpha King orders, his voice gritty from age. I wonder how old he is. Sixty, maybe? I don't think that I've ever seen anyone as old in my life. Werewolves are lucky to survive until forty.

Slowly, I get to my feet, still afraid to make eye contact.

"This better be good, Chase. I had to miss a meeting about the rogue war for this . . . confrontation," the Alpha King growled.

I glance to my side to see Chase step forward. He clenches and unclenches his jaw nervously, seemingly scared of the sheer power of the man who stood before him. I almost laughed—the Alpha King was pathetic, and for Chase to be afraid of him just made the situation worse.

"She's a shifting female, sir," Chase informs the King. "We were culling the group of rogues as instructed, and she retaliated with her wolf."

The King begins to pace in front of me, arms placed stiffly by his sides. Each step reverberates off the empty chasm of marble walls, each turn making the blood in my veins begin to slow, my head beginning to feel light. I want to throw up, preferably all over the King's royal clothes.

"So you brought her to me as a candidate for the Alpha Trials?" I don't know what the Alpha Trials are, but the words send me spinning into a world of confusion. For a second, I feel as though I've been submerged in a bucket filled with ice.

The Alpha King's face scrunches with anger, and I expect him to shout at the top of his voice, roaring at Chase as to why he brought a weak, female rogue to see him.

But he doesn't. Instead, he does the opposite; he nods.

"She'll make a good competitor." Then he turns to me, but I refuse to meet his gaze. Those pale azure eyes would slice me apart like the North Wind if I did. "What is your name, rogue?"

As much as I don't want to reply, I can't stop the words from flowing out of my mouth. "Don't call me rogue," I growl. I keep staring at the ground, studying the deer hide of my snow boots.

The Alpha King walks up to me, and before I know it, his cold and rough fingers are on my chin. He automatically forces my head up, his eyes captivating mine.

"Look at me when you talk to me, " he orders me, his disgusting touch leaving my body. "Now, I'll ask again, what is your name?" The seconds tick away, and his rage grows. I know that it's not long until he explodes.

"Rogue," I reply. He wasn't my king. A king didn't kill those under his rule.

"Your name." The Alpha King persists.

"As you seem so hell-bent on calling me a stupid rogue, then that's it. My name is Rogue. It's not like you care anyway," I say defiantly. I'm not afraid to argue with the ruler. He was a blemish on our society. He had killed without reason. Never respect a soldier who kills for blood and power. Respect a warrior who kills for reason.

In the blink of an eye, Chase is on me with a knife to my neck. All I can picture is the battlefield around us, my body pushed up against the tree. He won't kill me. Not here.

"Tell the King what your name is or I swear to God, I will slit your throat," Chase commands me, the knife breaking the skin of my neck.

"You won't kill me," I pant out.

22

"Tell me your goddamn name!" he shouts, and finally, I give in. I am not one to give up, but I have had enough struggle for one day.

"Alaska. My name is Alaska," I say while pushing Chase away, wiping my neck with one of my sleeves. It comes away soaked with crimson. Chase stumbles across the room, unable to stay upright from my strength, and I have to stifle a laugh. Arseh*le. Serves him right to threaten me.

To me, the term "Alpha" meant nothing. You are either born with the strength of an Alpha due to genetics or you aren't. Strength doesn't make you a good leader, nor does it allow you to act more privileged than everyone else.

The King draws a shaky breath before continuing, "Well, Alaska, I am getting old, and I do not have long left. Nor do I have an heir to take my place when I die." The King begins to pace again, running a shaky hand through his flaking scalp. "Therefore, I have created the Alpha Trials to find the next Alpha King or Queen to take my place. Only Alpha males and shifting females are able to compete, and this is what makes you compatible to enter, if you chose to.

"The challenges will consist of fighting within an arena, against another werewolf. Some fights will be with weapons, others without. With you being a rogue, if you are defeated, the winner will likely kill you.

"You can accept my offer and become part of the Alpha Trials, or you will be executed tomorrow at dusk. It's your call." The Alpha King finally stops walking and sits back down on his throne, the huge metal piece of furniture appearing to swallow the shrinking man whole. "But the only way you will come out alive is if you win, Alaska. Do we have a deal?"

He's asking me if I want to die tomorrow or die in a competition. Whether, after all these years, I would give myself up to be quietly beheaded. Just like that, I would be gone from the world. No one would remember me. I would be a cloud of dust in the memories of others; an unwanted part of their minds.

Alaska Morgan was a fragment of glass from a smashed mirror that could never be mended. She was something that was never meant to exist in this world.

No one had such a haunted past as I did, and yet I am still here. I still battled through so my parents's actions won't be in vain. And for what? To let some measly sword slice through my neck?

I don't think so.

I'm Alaska Morgan, and I'm a rogue. There is no shame to my name—no shame to the fact that I'm a rogue. I am Alaska, and no matter how much they torment me and scar my skin, they will never damage the real me inside.

The Alpha Trials sounds daunting, but it's nothing a rogue can't handle. We had sat through blizzards in shaking tents, whilst they had played cards in the warmth of a vast castle.

I have battled far too hard to surrender now.

Because life is for the living, not for the dead. And I'm not dead. Not yet.

I raise my chin higher and stand as straight as I can. I want them to see that I'm not just any old rogue that just happens to be able to shift. I am stronger than they all anticipated.

"Yes, I do," I say, my voice as strong as the tides of the sea.

If I die, I die, but at least I would go down fighting. That's another thing that the Alpha King didn't know about rogues; we never gave up. Never.

CHAPTER THREE
Competitors
"And I know that somewhere inside that cold, lifeless exterior,
there's an actual human soul."

- Stiles Stilinski, Teen Wolf

Chase has disappeared. As I glance around, he is nowhere to be seen. I don't know why I even care, but I do. He's an Alpha male, so that must mean that he's also a competitor. Maybe he went to catch up with all of the other tributes.

The thought of fighting him again makes my body writhe with a strange sensation. I can't tell whether it's rage or excitement, except this time, I know that I will beat him. I will not allow myself to die at his hands.

I have since been directed away from the castle and down flights of stairs to the cold dungeons beneath the grand building. Icy water slides along the walls, an eerie dripping noise reverberating throughout the chasm.

"This way," the guard orders me as he opens the door to a cell, except this is no ordinary cell. The ceiling scales metres in the air, the cobblestone walls lit by single flame torches at random interval. Above my head, an ancient chandelier hangs from the rock, cobwebs coating the non-existent candle and wiry metal frame. The air is pungent with decay and the odour of wolf pelt, stinging my nose like pollen in spring.

But the main attraction of the room is the huge table in the middle. A variety of different meals are scattered on the oak surface, and other werewolves sit around it, voices filling the otherwise stagnant air. All except five werewolves are male, and there are at least forty in the room. I'm surprised that they can all fit in here.

As soon as the metal clanks open, everyone is silent. A thousand eyes peer at me from different angles, melting into my soul.

They must know who I am, otherwise they wouldn't be staring at me the way they are.

I straighten my clothes and pick up a plate from a side table. It's clear that these are the people I will be competing against, and looking at my competition, I stand little chance. As the Alpha King had warned, they are all Alphas, their muscles bulging and each trying to intimidate one another.

The guard has since left me to the wrath of the other competitors. It's not like I enjoyed having a guard, but at least he made me feel slightly safer than I do now.

But hey, I could make some friends. Or not, because making friends was not a speciality of mine. My sarcasm and harsh personality normally sent people scattering. I can laugh, don't get me wrong, but opening myself up to someone has always been a challenge. Trust issues have made my life hell since I was thrown into that river five years ago.

I glance at the table and the men staring at me as if I was some goddess. I am pleased to see that the other end of the antique counter is deserted.

"Welcome to the party, rogue!" one shouts, causing the rest to chuckle. I feel my rage begin to grow into a tight ball of fury as I walk past them, but I won't release it. Not yet. I will save that for when we are all competing.

They continue to peer after me as I saunter to the other end of the narrow room.

26

"Quit staring," I utter confidently as I feel their gazes begin to drop. "It's rude."

I take a seat and help myself to a portion of chicken from a dish in front of me. It's strange having everything here in front of me. As a rogue, I had relied on hunting to keep myself alive. After taking my food, I look up again and see Chase at the head of the table. So that's where he disappeared to. His head is leant forward onto his fist, a single elbow propped up on the table in a powerful pose. His eyes infiltrate my own, and I feel as though he's trying to burn a hole in my skin.

Abruptly, plates clatter as two people come to sit opposite to me, diverting my gaze from the mysterious Alpha who had previously held a knife to my neck.

One is male, and the other is (thankfully) female. The man looks around nineteen, with a mop of brown hair and beautiful mocha eyes that I could gaze into all day. Not that I would, but they look more as though they belonged on a woman rather than a full-grown man. His face isn't as stern as Chase's; they were softer making, making the boy who sat before me look genuinely kind.

The girl has much sharper features, but she is beautiful as well as striking. Her eyes are a penetrating shade of azure, constantly shifting from one object to the next. Her hair is slightly ruffled but the otherwise straight brunette hair didn't have any flaws. A row of braids runs along either side of her head, woven with red string. Perhaps a distinct symbol of her pack. She is what I had always imagined a shifting female would look like.

The male looks in the direction I had just been staring in and sees Chase's glum expression as he starts to pick at his food.

"Looks like it's his time of the month again." The boy jerks his head towards Chase, flashing a smile my way. The girl lets out a snort. After a few seconds, he politely holds out this hand. "I'm Josh." He gestures to the she-wolf beside him. "This is Azra. You must be the rogue."

I don't know what to make of him calling me "rogue". He seems like a nice guy, and he is actually trying to cooperate with me, proving that he doesn't care whether I am a rogue or not.

I take Josh's hand. His grip is strong and firm. He will not be easy to beat, although he looks it. Can I trust him, though? Trust is a foreign concept to me, but having a so called "friend" could help me understand it.

"Alaska," I say, leaving out my surname, because who the hell wanted to know my surname anyway?

Josh greedily picks up a chicken drumstick and rips off a chunk of the charred flesh. "You missed the opening ceremony," Josh says after swallowing. "Don't worry, though. It was just a bunch of crappy fireworks and a parade around the whole city, and then we got blessed by the Alpha King. Nothing much." Josh shrugs his shoulders. I try to figure out whether he's joking or not, but his face remains serious and I feel my cheeks redden in response.

Azra rolls her eyes as she nudges her piece of chicken breast with her fork. "Don't mind him. He's just being an arseh*le as usual." She looks up at me, confidence clear within her cerulean irises. "Nice to meet you, Alaska."

I nod at her, not because I don't want to talk to her, but because I don't know what to say. Having been separated from pack life for so long, this is all new to me. And to be frankly honest, I hate it.

"Sorry about coming in like that," Josh apologises after another bite of meat. "You just looked lonely."

I open my mouth to respond but Azra beats me to it. "God, Josh. Leave her alone."

"I didn't do anything!" Josh gapes at his friend. I wonder whether they were siblings, although the resemblance is almost non-existent.

"You talked."

"Since when was talking a crime?"

"Since you opened that big fat mouth of yours."

"Now that is low," Josh retorts, leaving his food to fold his arms across his chest.

"I'd get used to it, if I were you," Azra concludes with a roll of her perfect, pristine eyes. Then her sapphire orbs snap to me once more. "Sorry. I've lived with him for ten years. You get annoyed after a while."

I guess that means they aren't siblings. They were childhood friends, just like I had been with some of the children at my old pack. I barely remembered their names to this day. After all, I wanted to forget as much as I could about the Shadow Claw pack. The memories would trigger nightmares if I didn't bury my ancient grudges.

"It's okay." I chuckle quietly. I am not a confident person. That much is obvious.

"So, what's it like, you know, being a rogue and all?" Josh asks me. It feels as though my whole body has been picked up by an invisible force and hurled outside my comfort zone by a million miles. Did this guy understand how to be sensitive? Because he wasn't pushing the right buttons.

I glare at him. "There's no difference to a normal pack wolf."

Josh looks puzzled, the smile on his face diminishing somewhat. "Really? Because I've been told lots of stories where rogues are bloodthirsty creatures."

"Do I look like a bloodthirsty creature?" I say in a monotone. The words slip from my mouth before I realise how bitter I am being to this boy. He plucked up the courage to come and talk to me, so why am I trying to turn him away?

"No." Josh glances at me, realising that it's an uncomfortable subject. "I was just curious. I've never met a rogue before."

"Not many people have," I state, "but trust me, you're lucky you haven't. You wouldn't want to meet a real rogue."

29

"A 'real rogue'?"

"The nightmare rogues. The ones that will tear you limb from limb and smile while doing it," I explain. Josh is just curious, as I would be, although he could have asked me in a more sensitive way. "I fled from my pack because they found out I could shift. The only reason I'm a rogue is because I don't belong in a pack registered under the Alpha King."

Josh nods his head as he understands my situation. "That makes more sense."

Azra once again rolls her eyes. "Just let her eat, Josh. If you were trying to flirt with her, then . . . let's just say it didn't go well." The girl continues to send me a smile, making me feel suddenly warm in the cold dungeon area.

Josh's cheeks heat up slightly, the pastel skin turning a light cherry. Even if he is good looking, the thought of a boy trying to even get near me makes my stomach churn. Love is something I don't understand. My understanding died the day my parents did.

Perhaps love does exist, but not for me. I am a nobody going head on against the world, and the sad thing is that I don't even care if I lose. Okay, maybe that's a lie. I don't want to die, but there are times when we no longer have a choice.

The two people across from me don't talk and allow me to eat my food, but I can barely taste it. Fear is gushing its way through my system as I suddenly realise how unlikely it is that I'm going to get out of this situation alive. It's not only the fear of my imminent death, but also the fear of how I will be killed. I don't want to die a slow and miserable death.

When I finish my meal, I look back up the table to see someone I had hoped never to lay eyes on again. My heart begins to hammer in my chest, the steady thumping being the only thing keeping me sane.

Because before me sits the face of a demon. The crystal blemish in his eye is still visible, and his face is as unusual as I remember it. Age has not faired him well.

Titus. The one who discovered my secret and played a part in killing my parents. And since he's here, that can only mean one thing: he's the Alpha of the Shadow Claw pack. My pack.

The bastard.

My throat is dry, burning for even a drop of water. I can't speak; it feels as though my vocal chords have been shredded. My limbs seem to have a mind of their own. They get up and walk over to the beast. Seconds click by, a clock whirring in my head, gears clicking into place, adrenaline being released into my bloodstream.

Azra and Josh don't move. I can see from their confused expressions that they are unclear what my motives are.

Titus doesn't realise that I'm standing there. He continues talking to the other alpha beside him, oblivious to my presence. I doubt he even remembers me; the girl who could shift. I still don't see why it is considered a crime.

So I do what anyone in my position would do to get his attention; I tap on his shoulder, his head turning in my direction, and then punch him in the face.

Titus propels himself from the bench so that he is standing, his hands clenched in both shock and retaliation. "Hey! What the hell was that f—" Titus gazes at me, realising who I am. "Alaska? You're supposed to be dead," he growls, his wolf beginning to rise to the surface.

"It's nice to see you too, Titus." I smile at him. Then I punch him in the face for a second time.

Titus's hand doesn't fly to his face as it would for a normal werewolf in pain. Instead, he allows the trickle of blood to run down his chin, as if it's a trophy of strength.

"You b*tch!" he curses, swinging his own fist my way. A few seconds ago he was reluctant to fight, but it's obvious to him that I'm not going to back down.

Ducking under his punch, I snarl at the twenty-five-year-old wolf. "Well done. I am, technically, a female dog."

31

Titus doesn't like my remark. He isn't ugly in general, but the distorted look on his face makes him appear as attractive as a shrivelled grape. He charges forward, his head meeting my stomach.

Normally, the blow would not hurt, but with my previous bruises from the fight yesterday, small pin pricks of pain flare across my body.

His huge figure almost knocks me to the floor, but I use the advantage of his exposed stomach to punch him as hard as I possibly can. My strategy works, and the monster releases me from his grip.

Instead, he turns to punching me. It happens so quickly that his fist connects with my face, right below my eye socket. That will leave a nice mauve bruise.

I begin my attack, ramming my fists into any part of his body I can make contact with. The only fuel that keeps me going was the rage within my heart. I was supposed to be alpha. No, my parents are supposed to be leading the Shadow Claw pack. The only reason they aren't is because of him.

I want to rip out his throat. To tear a hole in his heart that is so large that he will have no way in hell of even gasping before plunging into the abyss of death. I want avenge my parents.

But before I can take my vengeance out on the beast in front of me deserves, a pair of hands hold me back. They are strong and easily keep hold of my spindly limbs.

Josh pulls me away from the fight, my breath ragged from the struggle. I look like the rogue I am, but I don't care. Let them see it. Let them see the beast Titus had created.

I'm thankful that Josh pulled me away before it was too late. God only knows what damage I could have done to Titus, and the Alpha Trials haven't even started yet. I don't even consider the fact that I might've been the one crippled at the end of the spar.

Josh takes me back to the bench, but not before leaning in and whispering something in my ear, "Save it for the arena."

I can feel the handsome boy smile. His words strike deep into my flesh, because in that fleeting moment, I realise that Josh thought exactly like me. Now that's how you make me like someone.

CHAPTER FOUR
Caged

"You didn't see that coming?"

- Pietro Maximoff, The Avengers: Age of Ultron

There's always a time in your life when you feel completely and utterly caged. When you feel as though you're snared in the centre of a giant maze with no exit and no way to escape. When you have nowhere else to go, because everything and everyone wants to kill you.

That's how I feel right now. For me, the Alpha Trials only has two outcomes: death or becoming the Alpha Queen if—and that's a big if—I win.

But I don't want to win. I don't want to be the Alpha Queen. I am a rogue, and always will be. Maybe if I win I can resign straight away, but something tells me the kingdom won't let me do that. They choose the strongest leader to fight a war, and if it's me, then so be it.

And the other option—death? For some reason, I don't want to die. Here I was, cornered in the place where I thought I would never end up in my wildest nightmares, and I was still alive. I had lived to see daylight.

I don't know why I want to live but it's in our nature I guess. We are survivors, and no matter how hard we fall, we will always pick ourselves back up again.

"What're you thinking about, Alaska?" Josh asks as he gives me a sly grin. "You were giving me the dreamy eyes for a second, there."

I fold my arms across my chest but feel a small smile edge its way onto my face. Last night, Josh, Azra and I had chosen a sleeping quarters to share for the tournament. They had gotten to know me, and I had actually made friends.

I ignore his question. Last night, he pointed out I had a habit of doing that. Screw habits, this is my personality, and I'm not going to change it now for some boy, even if he is cute. "Call me Ali."

"Oh, so it's 'Ali' now? I thought you liked the nickname 'Rogue'." He raises his eyebrows.

"It's easier to say," I point out, because it was true.

"Technically it isn't," Josh challenges with a quirk of his brow.

"Stop flirting, lovebirds." Azra scowls from the corner. The room we all stand in is a part of the arena, brick walls surrounding us like a stagnant catacomb. The air is still and cold, the light shining through the tiny windows circling us. The room is filled with all the other competitors, waiting to get a glimpse of who they are fighting against. "Pay attention."

In front of us is a nail, hammered into the wall so that it sticks out at a ninety-degree-angle. It's strange to think that we are all relying on this one nail, but it's where the battle schedule is to be hung.

A sturdy guard with a greying beard and shoulder length hair steps forward, a huge board clutched within his mighty grip. For some reason, the strange sensation of fear sweeps over me in a fleeting wave. He is huge, and other competitors here are equally so. If I'm put up against any of them, I know that I will die.

Josh squeezes my shoulder in anticipation, and I roll my eyes. I don't need reassurance, and physical contact feels weird.

35

He's being nice, I know that, but I'm not used to it. I am a hundred thousand miles outside my comfort zone.

I hear Josh take in a sharp breath and I turn back to see his flared nostrils. "What're you so worried about? It's just some names on a crappy board."

"Yeah, but those crappy names could knock me out of the competition." Josh sighs as the guard begins hanging up the board, heads popping up as people try to get a glance of their opposition.

It's strange to think that tomorrow, only half of us will be standing here. Tomorrow, half of us will be dead or gone. We aren't supposed to kill, but there is no rule saying we can't. And if I lose, I will definitely die.

"Why are you so dependent on this, Josh?" I ask bitterly. Everyone is acting strange about this whole prospect. "What is so important about these trials?"

Josh turns a puzzled face my way, as if I don't belong on this planet. "Are you kidding me, Alaska?"

"Ali," I remind him firmly.

"Fine, Ali," he retorts, rolling his eyes slowly. "This competition decides who is the next Alpha King or Queen. This is the first time in three centuries they've held such an event. To win is a huge, huge honour."

"Wow," I say sourly, perhaps more than I had anticipated. "Who filled your head with all that crap?"

Josh shakes his head. I wonder if he regrets choosing to be my friend. "It isn't crap. If it was, you wouldn't be here. You would've decided to be beheaded if it was pointless. We're all here for a reason, and I'm here to make my pack proud." Someone coughs next to me, and a small smirk edges its way back onto Josh's face. "That's why we're here," Josh concludes, draping an arm around Azra's shoulder.

I nod. I can understand where he's coming from. Pack wolves are very proud creatures, and winning the Alpha Trials gives the pack wolves more pride and recognition than they could ever ask for.

"I understand why you're doing it," I defend myself, eyes diverted to the huge board in front me, "but I can't afford to think like that. Tomorrow, I could be dead."

A hand clasps onto my shoulder and I am spun around to meet Josh. "Don't say that," he growls, teeth bared in a protective manner. "You will be here tomorrow. You won't die."

"They'll kill me if I lose."

"You won't die," he insists. "We chose to friends with you because you looked fearsome. You had that look on your face, showing that even if the world collapsed beneath your feet at that very moment, you would clasp on to anything to gain life. You're not a loser, Alaska. You're a survivor."

I stare at him. Am I really that readable? It feels as though someone has simply opened me up and read me like a book, the font being size two hundred. I feel completely and utterly bare, as if I'm not wearing any clothes.

"This just got really deep," I comment.

Josh rolls his eyes, but I can see a smile form on his face. "Shut up and pay attention to the board," he replies with a wink, leaving me hanging from a thin line, waiting for him to continue.

I turn back around, the gloomy darkness making it near impossible to read the names on the wooden board. The light is orange, casting a strange shadow over the handwriting.

I flick over each name, until I find mine. It looks as though it's been written by a five-year-old.

Then I see the line joining me to my opponent. William.

William. Of all names, William. There's nothing wrong with it, it's just . . . old. And boring. It makes me think of an ancient werewolf king who I had learnt about in my old pack.

I swivel on my heel to face my new friends. They both look unfazed. Azra's jaw clenches as she continues to stare at the name paired with her own.

"Good? Bad?" I ask, nodding towards Josh. The brief and meaningful conversation we were having a minute ago seems to have spontaneously combusted into thin air.

Josh looks uncomfortable as he shifts on the balls of his feet. He looks as though he doesn't belong in his own skin. Scrap that, it looks as though he wants to shed his skin and grow another one.

"In the middle." Josh scans the room as other wolves saunter around, barely talking to one another or looking anyone else in the eye. Josh points to a slender wolf. "His name's Jasper. Extremely skinny, but extremely fast. You?"

I shrug my shoulders. "No clue. Is William good or bad?"

"Crap," Azra curses as she listens in to our conversation.

I twist my head so that I can gaze her in the eye. "What?"

Azra nods her head towards a werewolf who stands a few heads taller than me. His face is lined with greasy tresses, and it's easy to deduce that he's at least thirty.

Not only that, he is a giant. His arms are guarded by chunks of muscle and his size is utterly staggering. His clothes barely fit his bulging thighs, and the snarl plastered on his face seems to be stuck there by super glue.

His tanned skin is slathered with dried mud, as though he hasn't washed in weeks. Thinking about it, that would explain the sickening smell of decay emanating from his direction.

"That is William," Azra says, and I gulp.

I give Josh a side glance. "On second thought, you might lose. You know, just a one in a million chance of winning," Josh states.

The news hit me like a wrecking ball. My opponent is the size of Mount Everest and looks like a Viking brought forward in time by a time machine. My changes of winning went from one to zero in the bat of an eye.

"Good to know you have faith in me," I mutter and begin to stagger out of the dim room, the darkness snaking around me as

I follow the cobblestone footpath. "This was a stupid idea. I need to get out of here."

I had already tried to find an exit while the others were asleep, but each exit was guarded by at least two werewolves who weighed double what I did. Even when I managed to find the courtyard, I was effortlessly escorted back to the sleeping area. Surely there is one way to escape, no matter how vast the castle is or how extensive the amount of guards are?

Azra grips on to my shoulder, stopping my actions. "Ali, there's no way out. Security has tripled due to the Alpha Trials. You can try, but they'll kill you in the process, and we're not going to let that happen."

"Remind me again when you two became so protective over me?"

"When we decided to make friends with a rogue," Azra replies. Okay, that hurt a tiny bit. I was a rogue, but it wasn't like I was a completely different species.

"Josh and Jasper, into the ring!" the same guard who put the wooden board up shouts, the bold voice reverberating off the walls of the stone chasm.

I glance at Josh as he nervously gulps. He wipes his sweaty palms on his shirt, but his forehead has already become beaded with the substance due to nerves.

Azra gives her best friend a hug before I can say anything. "Good luck," she says into his chest, her voice somehow managing not to crack in the process. She doesn't sound like her best friend is about to be put through the most traumatic event of his life. "You can do it. Aim for the throat. Use whatever weapon they give you."

Azra and Josh exchange smiles as I stand around, like an awkward third-wheeler at the back of the group.

Finally, I make eye contact with Josh. The moment I look into his mocha irises, I know that he can do this. He's an alpha, and he will prove that today.

I blush and smile at the boy without meaning to. "Good luck, Josh."

And with that, Josh disappears out of sight and into the unknown.

"Come on." Azra tugs at my arm, pulling me to the pathway lining the arena. Here we are, below the stands, but there is a gap of about half a metre that enables the competitors watch their competition fight.

Josh and his opponent—Jasper—stand opposite one another as the crowd roars above us like beasts, devouring the moment to preserve it until the end of time.

The guard—or rather the 'enforcer'—steps forward and bellows, "Fight one, round one of the Alpha Trials. The match will last until one of you is unable to continue. The winner will move on to the next round and the loser will be sent home." The guard pauses, raising an arm in the air. "Good luck," he mutters as his arm comes down, and the fight begins.

The spar blurs before me. One moment, Josh is being knocked in the face, and the next Jasper is held in a head lock. The crowd above me continues to yell, scream, bellow at the top of their lungs as if there is no tomorrow.

Finally, after the haze, I manage to pick out Josh standing above Jasper, delivering a monumental kick to the other boy's skull. The battle over. Josh has won.

Azra lets out a sigh of relief beside me, and I send a small smile her way, thankful that he's okay.

"Alaska and William, into the ring!" the same guard shouts, my bones turning to ice, becoming so fragile that they will surely shatter.

Everyone turns my way, and I stand as still as a statue. I'm afraid that if I move in the slightest, the world will come crashing down. Now I understand why deers freeze when they're caught in headlights; it's as if every cell in my body is screaming, "Please don't see me. Please don't see me."

40

But of course they can, their cold stares snaking through the general tranquillity of my brain.

Azra pushes me from behind, edging me forwards. "Good luck," she whispers, but her tone is shallow because she knows the outcome. We all do. "Don't stress it out. Just use your anger and you'll kick his arse."

The participants around me part like the Red Sea for Moses, eyes glaring and eyebrows raised.. They whisper as I slowly go past them, the murmur of my name, the faint buzz of a chuckle. They think that I can't win, but maybe, just maybe, I will live to see these disgusting, blank walls once again.

I see Chase somewhere in the crowd. He doesn't make eye contact with me, but I can feel his eyes piercing the back of my skull, as if he was trying to open it with the power of his mind. I shudder. I don't know why I am so bothered about him so much as looking at me, but it's unnerving. The fact that I even care about what he's thinking when he looks at me is not okay.

I reach the entrance of the arena, the sunlight only a few steps ahead. Dust motes prance through the air as Josh walks past me. Once again, all he needs to do is bow his head, meaning the same thing yet again; good luck. But it also means something else; goodbye.

Next comes Jasper, dragged out by two guards, his feet scraping carelessly along the gritty floor. His head lulls from side to side, evidence that he is still conscious.

Beside me, the alien noise of clicking knuckles alerts me to another presence. Hands large enough to cover my head continue the snapping noise. I shake off the feeling as the huge man saunters and takes his position next to me.

The guard is next, leading us into the arena. I try to force my legs not to move, but they don't obey. They seem to have a mind of their own as they try to protect their owner from a painful punishment for not even walking into the ring.

Sunlight blinds me as I gaze around, seeing the huge arena surrounding me. Hundreds of faces peer at me, all cheering for the other werewolf standing beside me. Beneath my feet, the sand threatens to infiltrate my boots, the arena so wide and circular that it will be hard to corner my opponent.

And before my eyes, in his royal robes and looking out of place within the citizens of the city, stands His Highness. He looks at me, raises his chin, and diverts his gaze. It's oka, prick, I don't want to look at your shrivelled face either.

"Fight two, round one of the Alpha Trials. The match will last until one of you is unable to continue." The guard hands each of us small silver daggers, which I gratefully take. At least I know how to use it. Years of practice in the rogue pack and hunting in order to survive has served me well. "The rules are the same as earlier. Good luck," he states, but I feel his head turn towards William. Of course he doesn't want me to do well, let alone the rest of the population.

The guard brings down his arm and then sprints out of the ring, the yelling of the crowd dying like his fading footfalls.

William smirks at me. I thought that someone over the age of thirty wouldn't do something of that nature at this age.

"I'm going to make your death nice and slow, so that they can have their show." William bares his teeth, his yellow canines exposed to the sun. "Have fun dying, rogue."

I snarl at him. "It's Alaska," I say my name, but he doesn't so much as bat an eyelash.

An earsplitting shriek rips through my opponent's throat as he slices with his knife, bringing it down in an arc. I spin out of the way just in time. If I had been a millisecond later, the blade would have made contact with my skin.

I spiral around to growl at him, bending my knees and holding the knife out in front of me, my battle position telling him that I'm ready, although mentally I feel as though I will never be ready. Not for a competition like this.

"You're swift, I'll give you that." William sneers as he swipes with his blade once again, but his actions seem jerky and uncomfortable; he is not accustomed to such a weapon. "But you're not escaping death this time, rogue."

When will they realise that calling me rogue makes them look pathetic? I'm not even a true rogue. If I showed them one of those, they wouldn't survive to see another day. I had only encountered one once when it crossed our territory when I was still part of a pack. The beast was killed before my eyes, and it was one of the earliest murders I remember witnessing. It was one of the many events that had shaped my past, and continued to weld together the loose strands of my future.

The true rogues had killed her.

I will never forget the blood in the snow around her tiny body, seeping into the soil to generate new life.

I fail at avoiding William's next attack, backing away too slowly as the male knocks me over onto the ground. My back hits the hard floor beneath me, accompanied by "oohs" and "ahhs" from the audience. One person even yells, "Slit her rogue scum neck!"

I shiver at the remarks, but I'm quickly back on my feet, breathing rapidly to try and gain some oxygen, when I realise my vulnerable position. Above me is my opponent, fists clenched so tight, it seems as though the bones are breaking through his pale skin.

A fist meets my stomach, and I immediately double over in pain, flimsily treading backwards as I begin to splutter up blood, spraying William with the liquid. Somehow, he doesn't seem fazed by it, but I can't let him see how much his strength had hurt me, so I grit my teeth and bite my lips until it draws blood.

Abruptly, a hand wraps itself around my neck, the freezing knife pressed against my windpipe, almost crushing the air from my lungs.

For a second, I'm too shocked to move; any movement I create, I feel as though he'll slice my neck open, and that would be it.

Maybe it's not so bad to die, here in the sand, by the hand of a monstrous guy. Maybe I would let myself think like that, but my animal instinct takes over, and my elbow connects with the man's stomach.

He doesn't flinch much. Not even a flicker of pain crosses his face as I spiral out of his arms, knife at hand.

However, he seems dazed. I quickly kick his arm, knocking the knife from his grip, sending it flying metres behind him. Going against every single moral my father taught me about having a fair fight, I keep my own weapon clasped firmly within my grip. William is three times stronger by default, so I need this advantage to win.

William retaliates, punching me in the side of my head, my reaction speed too slow to stop him. If I had been a normal human being, I would have been knocked out without a doubt. The fact that we were werewolves gave us superiority to the creature that composed half of our DNA, especially because of our faster healing rate.

I block his next attack by shielding my face with my hands, but the protection doesn't last long. My midsection lies exposed, so he just punches me once more in the gut instead.

I try to keep a stoic expression, but by now I feel as though I'm deteriorating into pieces.

"Go on Alaska!" someone calls from the stands, the voice distinctly Azra's. "You can do it!"

"Yeah! Go Alaska!" a stranger screams out from the viewers, not caring about my rogue background. Nobody else joined his pointless cheers, but the words spark hope within me—and one spark is enough to light a fire.

My heart thrums, my muscles ache, my body is ablaze. And I thrust all of my power into one blow, time slowing down as my fist makes contact with the monster's head. I slash with my knife, but William momentarily knocks my arm away so that all I inflict is a shallow cut across his left cheek.

The blow created by my hands is harder than I think. William's arms pinwheels backwards as he struggles for balance, which he unfortunately gains.

Yet again, his clenched hands appear as his feet land wider apart, giving him a more secure base.

"So the rogue can fight." The wolf snickers at me, somehow finding time to do so.

"Why are you acting so surprised?" I retort with a shrug of my shoulders.

William opens his mouth to reply, the beginning of a word forming in his voice box. He never finishes that word. I punch him in the throat instead.

William produces a horrible gurgling noise, but his arms still manage to shoot up and reach for my neck. I defect his arms away, but he punches me again before I can protect myself fully. My hands fumble for my knife, slick with sweat, but after years of practice with a similar weapon, I'm able to regain control and thrust it deep into the man's abdomen without a second thought. But in a swift motion, William pushes me away, allowing me time to gather my strength as the knife is left lodged in his body.

The blaze inside me roars into an inferno, the blood gushing through my ears, blocking out any sound from the crowd. All that exists is me, this battlefield, and my opponent. Nothing else. We are floating in the middle of existence, tipping precariously on the seesaw of life and death. If William gets another chance, I will lose my balance, fall, and die.

There are only a few steps that I needed to do, and one million ways it could go wrong. And there was only one way it could go right.

I step forward so quickly, William has no time to react to my actions before I deliver another skull rattling punch to his head.

It's hard to reach his ginormous height, but I myself am not too small and a little jump gives me the elevation I need.

My opponent sways for a nanosecond, but I use all my might in that tiny space of time to kick William's legs out from under him. His bulk of muscle topples to the ground at lightning speed, his head bouncing up as it rebounds off the floor.

He's not unconscious, but it gives me enough time to act.

I wrench the knife from my opponent's chest, the pulse of my heart racing through my fingers as adrenaline poisons my bloodstream. Yet William reads my actions as I raise the blade above my head and hits my arm away, knocking the knife ten meters to my left.

I'm up on my feet before I can comprehend my actions, snatching up the weapon as though it's about to deteriorate from the lack of use.

I can throw a knife, but I can also miss. It isn't my favoured weapon, and if I miss this opportunity, that one way of doing my plan correctly will combust. I will die if this doesn't go right. I'm caged and swallowed up by the arena with nowhere to run—nowhere to hide.

William is already on his feet, his eyes squinting as he raises his his head up. His hand brushes off the sand from his face, and then goes to run over the tender lump where his head made contact with the arena's sandy ground.

He spots me, his mouth wide open and his nose bleeding so profusely that it's already dripping down onto his shirt. Will people miss him if I decide to kill him right here, right now? His pack will be left unprotected, but it's me or him. He is as cold hearted as the rest of them.

A snarl forms on his face, and it remains there. His limbs begin to move, sprinting towards me and closing the distance between us with each passing second.

I take a deep breath, focus on the one way, and let the knife fly.

William's life ends with a gurgle.
And the crowd stares at me in silence.

CHAPTER FIVE
Nightmare

"Forever does not make loss forgettable, only bearable."
- Cassandra Clare, City of Heavenly Fire

"Four more fights to go." Josh sighs as we disperse from the long day of battles. Azra had been victorious over her opponent, and all of us have moved on to the next round.

I raise my eyebrow. "Four?"

"If you get to the finals, that is," Josh points out, and I nod. I want to get to the finals so that I can have a chance at surviving the tournament, but I don't want to become queen.

However, there is another option. If I am put up against Azra or Josh and lose, then they will let me live. That's the only other way that I can escape this torture alive, and we all know it.

I turn to look at Azra. It's obvious when I gaze into her crystalline azure irises that she's uncomfortable with the prospect of me dying, almost as uncomfortable as I am. I can read her eyes—today, they look like a tropical storm, with white horses cresting bright blue waves.

Josh places his hand on the small of my back, steering me towards the dining room as we head for dinner. The contact is strange on my body, but I ignore it as he pushes me towards the noisy chatter of the other competitors.

The cobblestone hallways all look identical; grey, bleak, and composed like a stack of precariously balanced rocks. I don't have

48

the foggiest clue where I'm going, and I'm glad to have someone like Josh to escort me.

We round yet another corner, an open flame torch eating at the darkness. At least I recognise this part of the ancient and crumbling hallway; it leads to the dining hall.

All of a sudden, I begin to feel nauseous, as if my stomach has suddenly been churned a million times in one second. Bile rises in my throat as my footfalls become weak, and I no longer feel as though I can support myself. My sudden reaction doesn't have an explanation, I just feel as though I want to curl into a ball and shrink so small that I disappear off the face of the earth.

I don't want to go into a room full of people who want to kill me. Since I had slaughtered William in cold blood, I know that they would all be furious. Each and every one of them will want to rip the flesh from my bones.

Josh notices my discomfort and supports me with his other hand. I wonder if he thinks I'm going weak at the knees because of his touch. "Ali, are you okay?"

I shake my head. "They're going to kill me," I whisper, suddenly frozen in place like a statue. I had killed someone today, yet here I am, standing outside like a dog with its tail pressed firmly between its legs. God, I am so messed up.

Josh squats as I sink to my knees, becoming eye level with me. His eyes are still beautiful, perhaps more beautiful than my own.

"No, Alaska, no they won't." He gives me a hand up so I'm back on my feet. "Everyone in there hated William, trust me."

I shake my head in disbelief. "Well, at least he wasn't a rogue," I hiss between my teeth, not anticipating how harsh my words sound. I feel my legs confidently drag me towards the dreaded dining room. I'm petrified at the thought of going in there but, somehow, I don't feel daunted as I get closer to my destination.

"Alaska!" Josh shouts from behind me, followed by the echoing of heavy footsteps. "I'm being serious."

I roll my eyes, not hesitating to falter. I'm not used to being social, and Josh feeding me lies is not helping. He's a good guy with the right intentions, but nobody has lied to me without consequences. I want to trust him, but I've only known him for two days. It takes much longer than that to build up my trust.

I march into the dining room, and all eyes turn towards me as I stand there, my hands flying to my sides and foot freezing in mid-air as I decide to not continue forwards.

Yet again, I am surrounded by a storm of angry eyes, scowling at me as if I am the devil. I can tell just by looking at someone that they want to kill me, their eyes filled with the complex drive of bloodlust.

Time pauses as my eyes flick over to Chase. In that one second, he nods, and the whole room bursts into cheers.

My heart skips a beat. What the hell is going on? As I look back at the eyes I thought wanted to murder me a second ago, all I see now if joy, as if a mountain has been lifted off the shoulders of every werewolf within the confines of this room.

I swivel on my heel and Josh smiles at me. So, he was telling me the truth. Maybe I should believe someone once in a while.

His face bears a grin so wide, it's as if he's trying to mimic the Cheshire Cat. Then he raises an eyebrow and places an arm around my shoulders.

"I told you," he murmurs. "They all hated him."

My eyebrows crease as we grab a place and take a seat where we sat yesterday, the bench still empty as if where we had previously sat was slathered with poison.

"That was awesome!" someone calls from the room, but there are so many voices that it's hard to tell what exact direction it comes from.

"Nice one, Alaska!"

50

"Who knew the rogue had guts?" another yells.

"Who knew the rogue could fight?"

"William is freaking dead!"

I take my food as quickly as I can, instinctively wanting to get out of this room as soon as possible. As everyone notices my discomfort, they all settle down and get back to their conversations.

"Tell me about him," I suddenly say, the words leaving my lips before I can process them in my mind.

Azra looks up from her steak, a quizzical look looking right at me. "Who?"

"William," I state firmly. If everyone else is going to make a huge deal about his death, then I might as well know what the fuss is about.

Azra sighs as she puts down her knife and fork, placing her hands together on the table. "William was an alpha who used fear to rule over his pack. If one person ever stepped out of line, he would kill them before they had a chance to explain themselves." Her azure pupils captivate mine as she continues, "He killed his own daughter when he found out she could shift. He was a monster, and you killed him."

I can't believe my ears. It feels as though a secret has been whispered to me so quietly that I can barely hear it. "He killed his own daughter? That's . . ." I glance up at the ceiling as I try to find the right word. "Sick."

Someone brave enough to sit next to me clatters their plate on the table, greedily taking a ginormous cut of stake from the dish.

"It's more than sick," the stranger pointed out, using his knife to signal to me. "It's psychotic."

I glare at Chase as he takes a mouthful of meat, chewing quickly as he strives to speak more to me. I take notice of the light stubble lining his jaw and the sharpness of his perfect jawline. Whether I wanted to admit it or not, he was handsome. In a brutally beautiful way.

I tense as his arm brushes up against mine and he tucks into his food like nothing's wrong. But something is very wrong—he tried to kill me twice, and he doesn't want to see me when I snap.

"I'm sorry, but who invited you to our conversation?" Azra enquires, a look of pure bitterness plagued over her face.

Chase grins through a mouthfull of food. "I did."

"Well, you're not welcome." Azra shrugs her shoulders, crossing her arms as she distracts herself from her food.

Chase gives her a sympathetic smile. "Well, I'm afraid that you can't tell me what to do."

I turn my head and glare at the older werewolf. He's certainly not a likeable person, and cocky to say the least. He had held a knife to my neck and threatened to kill me yesterday, and yet here he is trying to talk to me as if he actually cares? Who does this guy think he is?

"Piss off, Chase," I growl at him and then spot an empty spot in the corner of the dim room. Using my free hand, I point to the oak table with a single chair drawn up next to it. "No one wanted you here, so go do us a favour and disappear."

Chase is stunned by my words, and tilts his head my way. "That's no way to speak, Princess."

"So I'm a princess now?" I laugh in disbelief. Is he seriously trying to flirt with me? "I thought that I—and I quote—'have no place in this world.' You know, being a 'blood thirsty beast' and all."

He glowers at me, his gorgeous eyes turning sour. "I'm sorry?"

"It's called karma, arseh*le," I state and get up from the table. I've suddenly lost my appetite. "I'm not hungry," I conclude, storming out of the room and leaving my friends behind.

"Great, now look what you've done." I hear Josh accuse Chase as the two pack wolves run after me.

52

I don't turn back. An invisible hand propels me forward as I navigate myself through the maze, trying to locate my shared sleeping quarters.

This competition is a lot to handle already, and I didn't need Chase's attention to make it worse. I had already fought one battle, and I feel completely and utterly drained, like a battery that's running on the last of its energy. This was a terrible idea. Why don't I just let them kill me? If it hadn't been for my basic instinct to survive driving me forward, I would've died a long time ago.

I fling open the door of my room and jump on the nearest bed, the soft white material of the mattress welcoming me into its arms. At least there's food and a proper place to sleep here. Out in the wild, you had to be used to surviving on the bear minimum of resources; in here, everything is laid out for you like an all-you-can-eat buffet.

I curl my body into a ball as I feel the bed dip. Glancing up, I see Josh. He reaches down to stroke my hair. His fingers tease the strands, lightly tucking the loose locks behind my ear.

"Sorry, Josh. There's just a lot to take in at the moment." I sigh as I sit up on the comfy bed. Azra is nowhere in sight, perhaps purposely giving us some space. "The Alpha Trials, I mean. I may be a rogue, but I'm not strong enough," I spill my insecurities. I'm not strategic. I win down to pure luck and hope that my will to survive outweighs my opponent's.

"Alaska, trust me, you're strong enough. You always have been, you just can't see it," Josh tells me, but I push away his hand as he begins to stroke my hair again. It's beginning to get a little strange.

I turn to face him, his eyes enveloping me in their beauty. I don't know how long I stare at them for, but as the seconds tick by, I feel as though I fall further and further into their fathomless depths.

"Don't lie. I'm tired of people lying to me."

Josh's eyes betray the fact that he is hurt. A twinge in the deep mocha makes me realise that my words actually have an effect on him, but—as usual—by the time I realise, it's too late.

"I don't lie, Ali. I'll repeat it so you can believe me. You *are* strong enough, you just can't see it."

"I—" I begin, but Josh holds up his hand for quiet.

"The strength you're looking for"—he taps his breastbone, signalling to his heart—"is in here. It always has been, and always will be."

I smile at him, not because his face is gorgeous, but because he's right. "When did you become such an inspirational speaker?"

Josh shows me his wolfy grin. "I was born one."

"Yeah, yeah. Keep telling yourself that." I chuckle with a wink, my sorrow dissipating.

At that, I roll my eyes and lie back down on the bed. After the events of today, my body feels as though it's slowly wasting away, my organs shutting down as my body becomes too drowsy to function. Even my battle with Chase wasn't as exhausting as this.

"I'll see you in the morning," Josh whispers as he pats my shoulder, the bed rising once more as he retracts his body weight.

His footfalls are so light, I don't know he's gone until he blows out the torch, leaving me in complete darkness. The only sound I could hear are the scratchings of a mouse, the vulnerable creature skittering across the floor in the hallway. It's comforting to be alone for once.

And just like that, completely and utterly alone, I fall into a deep slumber.

☽

My muzzle sniffs the air as I tentatively glance into the shadows, afraid that someone will appear from under the cloak of night. It's a full moon, and the only light being shone is the silvery stained moonlight streaming through the curtain of trees as I quickly dart through the foliage.

Each time one of my paws hit the cool and wet grass, I feel a strange sensation run up my spine. I'm a shifting she-wolf. I could shift.

Well, sh*t.

Being the only shifting she-wolf in the pack was dangerous, and it was a secret I would not be able to keep for long. When you've been stuck in a group of fifty people for all twelve years of your life, who know each other like the backs of their hands, word spreads fast. I just have to keep my discovery low key, otherwise I will soon find a wildfire brewing on my hands.

I shiver as my bones begin to crackle and snap, a howl of excruciating pain leaving my muzzle as I fall to the ground. This is my first shift and the aching is unbearable. Everything is unbearable. Why does my life have to be so complicated?

After a few seconds, I feel my claws disappear to form five slender fingers on each hand and within seconds the pain ebbs away. I am left exposed to the elements, with only the thin shifting garments my father was able to smuggle to me sticking loosely to my sweating skin.

I nervously glance around, afraid if someone has seen me. If they discover my secret now, it will be the end. They will kill me because they are scared. Why? Because being a shifting female is apparently a threat.

In this area, the grass is bright emerald in the day but a gloomy midnight in the dark. Whereas others think that this clearing is beautiful and mystical, it's not hard to see past the limited beauty and see the true horror that's disguised by poison ivy. The clearing borders the pack's tents, the first shelter only being twenty metres away.

"You really thought that you could keep your little secret from us?" a voice snarls from the ghastly shadows. The owner of the voice isn't much better in appearance as he slinks from his hiding place at the edge of the clearing.

I feel the blood in my veins turn to ice, and soon I'm unable to move at all, my body stuck in the same shocked position for what seems to be hours.

"I-I'm sorry?" I ask, gulping as the twenty-year-old wolf saunters towards me, fists clenched tightly.

Titus snarls at me. "You heard what I said." He raises his lips, exposing his pointed canines embedded within his crimson gums. "When were you going to tell us that you could shift?"

I ignore his question. How did he know? I wasn't able to sense him at all when I was in my wolf form, so how did he suddenly appear out of nowhere?

"I can't shift," I state defiantly. I'm not going to let this arseh*le spread the secret that I can shift.

"Liar," he spits out. He stalks up to my frail body, his face so close to mine that I can see the saliva dripping from the corners of his lips like a bulldog. "I saw you shift." He leans back, folding his arms across his chest and laughing. "Just you wait 'til I tell them."

Being twelve years old, I feel completely and utterly exposed as the huge werewolf towers over me, his muscles easily showing through the thin material of his shifting clothes. Just like all of the other males, he has shifted tonight, but the pack must've gotten back before I arrived.

"You wouldn't dare," I hiss, but my words tremble as my body itself shakes with fright.

"You'd be surprised, b*tch." His harsh tone causes me to flinch, and as I take in his strong demeanour and physical appearance, I feel rage begin to boil within my chest, threatening to explode into a furious attack that will ultimately result in my demise.

Come on, Alaska. You can take him. You're fast; he's not.

I try to tell myself that it's okay—it's okay. But it's not. I will never escape this infinite circle of fear.

Instinct takes over as my legs propel me forwards so quickly that my actions are a blur. I muster all my strength into a single punch, but Titus grabs my fist and squeezes until he hears the disgusting crack of bones.

I can't help it. I scream.

Through the tears and the pain, I scream at the top of my lungs, releasing all the pain, all the anger, all the fear stored within every cell of my body.

And through the pain, I slide my eyes shut and fall to the ground, my hand throbbing as if it has been crushed by a wrecking ball. I grit my teeth, and let out one more yell before the consciousness subsides and I slide back into the confines of darkness.

☽

I'm still screaming when I awake, eyes wet with tears although the droplets have not formed. The memory still wracks my brain like a cannon and I effortlessly wipe my eyes using the bed sheet before anyone can see.

I wipe my sweaty palms on the duvet as I take deep breaths, trying to sooth my aching throat. Why did I have to dream about that? Titus is the one person who had single handily ruined my life. Why would I want to remember what he did?

"Alaska," Josh calls softly from behind me, causing me to jump back into the bed once more. "What happened?"

I run a hand through my hair, trying to get a hold of the situation. "It was nothing," I say quietly, although the look he gives me tells me that he knows I'm lying.

"You were screaming, Ali. I think the whole castle heard you," he responds. I don't want to think about how I look right now, because the sight would be a horrendous brown-haired girl with huge ebony eye bags.

I shake my head, panting loudly as I try to regain my breath. Out of the corner of my eye, I see Azra roll over and place a pillow over her head, trying to block out our conversation. "It was a nightmare."

"About who?"

"God, you are so persistent. It doesn't matter, okay?" I scowl, but I don't have enough energy to follow it up with a snarky comment.

Josh nods, accepting my state. "Well, tell me if you need anything." He slowly peels himself from my double bed, and heads back to his own.

But as soon as he leaves, my body begins to shiver with dread and anxiety. When Josh is here sitting with me, his presence makes me feel safe. For some reason, I need him. No, I crave him to stop the panic streaking through my blood vessels.

Just before Josh makes himself comfortable in his bed, I call out for him, my own voice surprising me as it slices through the silence, "Josh, wait."

He turns and studies me, my wolf senses picking out his handsome face in the dark room. Even now, it's easy to see that he has removed his shirt, and he stands with his muscular torso exposed.

"Yes?" he murmurs softly.

"Can you stay with me? Please?" I plead. Every brain cell was yelling at me not to let this stranger into my bed, but he soothes me. I need him to stop the nightmares.

Josh nods once with a smile. "Sure."

He crosses over to my bed and takes the other side, stroking my hair once more as I settle down to get the rest I need to make it through the rest of the competition.

"Thank you."

As he rolls over to the other side of the bed to give me space, I feel my eyes droop and my body relax. My sweating ceases, and I am able to sleep before the nightmares parade my vision once more.

After that, the nightmares never threaten to surface again.

CHAPTER SIX
Ruptured

"She wasn't looking for a knight. She was looking for a sword."

- Atticus

The next two battles rushed past me like rapid waterfalls. I had swiftly beaten both of my opponents, who were luckily smaller and more fragile than the monster that was William. I had not killed them either. It was wrong, and I did not want the other werewolves to portray me more as a murderer than I already was.

But the truth is that I am a killer, no matter what I want them to think of me. It's like I have a giant arrow over my head, signalling the horrific deaths I have caused over the past few days because everyone is staring at me intently and quizzically when I walk past them. None of them smile, with the exception of Josh and Azra.

And sad thing is I want to kill Titus. He destroyed my life, slaughtered my parents, and tainted me. The mental consequences I never thought possible were something I thought I could withstand. Now, I realise taking a life haunts you forever. I will never be okay with it, and I have to live with my terrible decisions for the rest of my life, carrying them on my shoulders like a crushing rock. If I lose my balance, I will fall.

I scan the stands circling me, spotting the glaring azure eyes I'm so used to. There, in the swarm of onlookers, stands my friend with a black eye and bruising around her neck.

Yesterday, Chase had beaten Azra in no more than two minutes. He had strangled her until she went unconscious but luckily released his grip before her life disappeared altogether.

Despite her anger after waking up, Azra didn't let her defeat weigh down on her. She accepted the fact that she had lost to the strongest opponent left in the competition.

As the wind howls past my face, pushing the loose strands of my brunette hair behind me, I look across the vast expanse of the arena and towards my opponent. Whereas I had hoped to come up against Josh or Azra once during the competition, luck has not been on my side. It's as if the three of us were repelling opposites.

With the ancient sword nestled in my grip, the warm metal touching my skin, I squint my eyes at my opponent. Of all people, they had to pair me with Titus, the deliverer of all my pain. The one person who single handedly ruined my life by uttering a few words. The one who killed my parents.

With all the suffering and resentment boiling in my veins, one thing is clear: one of us has to die. And it won't be me.

Apart from Azra being quickly eliminated out of the Alpha Trials, Josh had managed to succeed and win his previous two battles to face Chase in the semi-finals. I hope with all my soul that he wins, because going up against Chase will break me. I had fought him once already, and even that one time was too much for my body to handle.

I blink away my trance, the battlefield drowning in a dull and hazy yellow, regaining my attention. The distance between me and my opponent felt like it was kilometres, both of us at different ends of the universe. He is down in hell while I'm on the ground, determined to slay my demons one by one, starting with Titus.

"You afraid, rogue?" Titus snarls, the harsh whisper blowing across the hundreds of thousands of yards until it reaches my ears.

Everyone seriously has to stop calling me rogue. I have told them my name, and I don't appreciate being associated with something so bloodthirsty. I am a rogue, but I'm not a true rogue. I thought that I had made that clear already.

I raise my chin, sword clenched so tightly in my grip that I'm afraid that I'm going to leave an imprint of my hand. "No," I say to my opposition defiantly, feet apart as I try to prove to him that I'm strong. Didn't the defeat of William shown that?

I'm a little bit scared that I won't win, but my vengeance is bone deep and I'm sure that the raw emotions buried inside me won't let me die by the hands of this devil.

"Fight one, round four of the Alpha Trials. The match will last until one of you is unable to continue," the guard states in a bored tone before bringing down his arm, marking the beginning of the fight.

I gulp as Titus grins at me, clearly confident that he was going to win the fight. Could anyone get any cockier? The answer is yes. It's Chase.

The beginning of the fight is fast paced as Titus makes the first move, sprinting towards me at full sprint, the metres disappearing to centimetres until he is right in front of me. His giant shadow consumes my body as he brings down his sword in a mighty swing.

I meet his weapon with my own, the metallic clang the only sound rebounding off the walls of the arena. The crowd is silent. I block out the crowd and the ground beneath my feet, only concentrating on my opponent in front of me. All that exists in this world are the swords in our grasps and our bodies as we float through infinity.

No one can touch us. We exist on the tipping point. If I let my sword slip even a millimetre, then we will crash and fall out of the tranquil empty space we have created and I will lose.

"I will tear you limb from limb and make your death slow and painful, you disgusting rogue," Titus growls. I feel my arms begin to ache as I continue to hold down his sword.

I raise my nose as I hear a hiss form on my lips. "I'm no true rogue. You know that more than anyone."

I use my strength to push the man away, and Titus finally releases the grip on his sword and staggers back a few metres, the arena falling back into position and the gritty sand still below my footwear.

I glance around as we take a breather, my muscles aching from the few seconds of battle. God, how did allow myself to become so weak?

"You thought that shifting she-wolves were bad," I point out as I desperately think of something to say. "But here I am, in line to possibly become the next ruler of this kingdom. She-wolves were never bad. You just wanted to pack for yourself."

Titus points his finger at me, his face scrunched with fury. "Don't you dare test me, rogue. I will just make it more painful for you."

"I'm not testing you," I mutter impatiently, my muscles finally feeling ready to battle once more. "I'm speaking the truth." Titus raises an eyebrow in fake confusion. "You knew you could never win against my father, so what better way to become alpha than spread my secret and pretend that it was a curse? You knew that it was a gift, and you knew it would earn you the pack.

"You are a coward, Titus. And you will die as one today," I finish, my palms beginning to become sweaty around the handle of my blade.

Titus laughs at my comments. "Are you done now?" he asks, clearly unimpressed, but I know that it's just a cover up. He knows I'm telling the truth.

I shrug my shoulders. "I could go on all day, but I've got a fight to win," I spit through gritted teeth and tear at the tall male, plunging my sword straight into his stomach. The sword manages to slice through flesh for a mere second before Titus punches me in the skull, causing me to back away from my advance.

Titus glares at the incision in his stomach. He places his left hand over the wound which comes away stained in deep scarlet. Yet his balance is still stead and his face never once shows any signs of pain. Sadly, the wound will be healed in a matter of minutes.

"You really thought that that would kill me?" I can hear a laugh behind his sullen tone.

"No," I say blandly, my teeth still clenched. I know he's the strongest opponent I will face, but it the idea of killing wasn't as impossible as I thought. Werewolves were always hard to kill, anyway. With their much faster rate of healing, Titus's wound will vanish during the battle.

We don't need to speak anymore, and for that, I am relieved. The bitter conversation we have exchanged is enough to show one another the hatred writhing through our bodies, like coiling snakes ready to pounce.

Titus is the first to spring. Yet again, he swings his sword with all his might, and I only barely have enough time to bring my own blade above my head to protect my neck.

My opponent's sword is deflected, but he quickly attempts to batter me again with another swipe of the silver blade. Sunlight gleams off the shiny surface, blinding me for a second, and I squint as I tighten my grip around my blade.

It's not enough. I feel the blade ripped from my fingers as Titus bashes it away, exerting his sheer power over my tiny frame and leaving me exposed to his wrath.

With nothing to protect myself, I instinctively curl my empty fingers into fists. I feel completely and utterly exposed, as if I'm no longer protected by my own skin. But for some reason, I also feel comforted.

As I scrutinise the male in front of me, he no longer seems as daunting as before. He looks like the coward he actually is, hiding away behind his sword as though the silver blade was his lifeline.

Titus puts all of his force into his next swing. From the momentum of his swipe, he is forced to spin around when I dodge the easily telegraphed attack. I take the clear opportunity to leap on his back. I thrash my legs and punch him in the head, but his hand swiftly clasps around my forearm before I can continue my attack.

Like a feral hurricane, he flings me on the ground, causing me to groan as the impact rattles through my shoulder. I let out a short, sharp breath as the pain begins to consume my body, but I know that my shoulder blade is not broken; it would hurt even more if it was.

I shield my eyes from the blinding sun but it offers little protection from the rays until the huge and bulky shadow of Titus swallows me, the shadow of his sword to my right.

Titus raises his lips, canines elongated into a grotesque smile. "Have fun dying, rogue."

"Fun isn't usually the thing I associate with death," I spit at the older man as me places both hands on the sword, raising it above my head. He stands with the sword aimed at my chest, ready to go in for the killing blow.

I gulp as I lay still, petrified by fear. My eyes are wide open, only able to observe the events as they play out before me. At least, that's what I want him to think.

In the blink of an eye, the sword plummets towards the ground, aimed straight my breastbone. Like a lightning bolt my instinct to live shoots through me and I manage to roll out of the way at the last millisecond, just before the sword makes a loud thump as it hits the bare sand.

A smirk lands on my face. He didn't see that coming. I am much faster than he had anticipated.

A roar of rage rips from Titus's vocal chords as he notices that my deceased body is not on the end of his sword. I can imagine what his face looks like but I don't look because I have better ways to use my time.

This time, my legs obey me. I kick Titus between the legs from beneath him. I watch as his hands flail in front of him, dropping the sword in the process.

Caged by his toppled body, the blade lies under the man as he blinks away the fury in his eyes. I can sense that he's close to shifting, but I command my body to stay calm. Panicking will cause me to make rash decisions, which will lead to my demise.

Narrowing my eyes, I realise that I can't retrieve his sword, unless . . .

As Titus staggers to a crouching position on all fours, I kick him so hard that he lands on his side, the sword no longer protected by his body. Blood sprays from his mouth, his nose crunching out of place. As quick as a cheetah, I sweep up his sword and turn to get my own.

I see the fallen battle blade metres away, but my attempt to spring away was halted. Titus's hand reaches out to grip my ankle desperately as he realises my plan. If I take away his weapon, then I would have a much greater chance of winning this battle. No matter how fast I am, I am no match for his strength and combat skills.

Almost tripping, I manage to kick the man in the face with my other leg. Titus lets go and I stumble the few yards towards my previous weapon, greedily gathering it up in my hands.

Staying alert, I stare up at the crowd, turning a fraction of a degree to face the beautiful eyes of Azra. I don't mean to, but something about the roar of the crowd entices me in. I ignore the fact that her lips are pressed into a thin line and concentrate on my hearing as an exasperated growl slices the air behind me. Even though it's only been one second, I can feel each microsecond ticking away. Titus will be on his feet in a couple of seconds, if he isn't already.

The hairs on the back of my neck prickle as my werewolf instincts take over. My heart suddenly begins to beat quickly, as though it's trying to break out of my ribcage. Each beat sends a jolt of adrenaline through my body and, finally, I pluck up the courage to turn around.

Before me stands a huge werewolf, its brown and scarred muzzle almost at the same height as my head. He is just as powerful as I remember. He's still the monster who killed my mother with one swipe of his claws.

Nothing in the rules said that we can't shift into our wolf forms, and Titus clearly using this to his advantage.

Stay calm, Alaska. Stay calm.

But I can't. Fighting a fully-grown werewolf and surviving is almost impossible, especially for a weaker she-wolf like me. Unless I shift, there is no chance I will win this battle.

It takes every ounce of will in my body to not shift. I have the swords and they are more useful than claws to me. I can win this fight without shifting, and I'll prove that. After all, I have trained with swords for my entire life. Finally getting to use them is like unleashing an atomic bomb.

The wolf growls lowly at me, as if it has something lodged in its throat. I study the huge blemish that runs across the nose of the animal, making the black skin appear to have a ruby undertone. He has been through hundreds of battles, and he has the scars to show for it. But so do I.

The ground beneath my feet falls away once more, leaving me and Titus alone, floating between eternity and death. Only one attack will determine who will fall . . . and who will rise.

"Bring it on, you coward!" I scream, beginning to twist my body, ready to get enough power in the blade so that it can kill my arch-enemy in a single hit.

The wolf doesn't need to be told to attack as he begins to rush towards me, his paws moving at such infinite speed, it seemed they no longer touched the ground. I watch as the muscles contract and relax, the boulder of muscle barrelling towards me at such a fast rate that I can't think.

My mind is a jumble of thoughts, all racing around at the speed of light. It's impossible to make out what's going on as numerous theoretical actions whizz through my head. My whole body screams at me, telling me not to die.

I blink and shake my head furiously, shattering my thought processes. The solution to my problems is simple: throw the sword and kill Titus. Then the pain will be over and I can have my revenge.

The world sets into place, and with a battle cry, I launch my sword through the air. I watch as it revolves through the air, each turn causing me to skip yet another beat of my heart.

And as the wolf rears up, jaws open wide, ready to take a bite out of my flesh, the sword meets its underbelly. The jaws automatically grit as the creature lets out an animalistic whine, death consuming Titus in a matter of seconds.

I stand over him, the other blade gripped firmly in my hand as I raise it above my head. Sunlight gleams on the handle, reflecting the glare onto Titus's matted fur like a beacon. With one swift movement, I bring down the weapon, straight through what I presume to be his heart. The action takes a mere second.

The werewolf writhes before transforming back to its human form, the pair of swords still burrowed deep into my enemy's flesh. It's obvious that there's no way he could heal his wounds now.

Blood sprays from the man's mouth as his body spasms, and it takes all the will in the world to stop me from spitting on his body. He might be a murderer, but I'm not disrespectful to the dead. Too many innocent—and tainted—people have died before my eyes to allow myself to fall in the trap of not respecting their lives as I should. But I will not respect Titus's life; I will forget it.

The man stops wriggling helplessly on the ground. His deep, bottomless eyes capture my own and, for a moment, I see the puppy he once was. His true soul that had been draped by the power hungry monster for numerous years.

I drop the other sword, the metal poisoning my grip. I watch helplessly as the man's body begins to go rigid and still, his breath leaving him like a gentle gust of wind.

I have won. I'm going to be in the final, against either Josh or Chase.

I can become queen.

I think I'm going to throw up.

I never wanted to be queen, but at the moment it looks like that's my only way out of the Alpha Trials. If Josh loses to Chase, then maybe I will have to win, just to survive.

Or maybe dying is better than becoming queen . . .

A sudden wave of nausea overcomes me as I begin to stumble out of the arena, hand placed over my mouth. Not only have I just killed Titus, I have become more of a murderer. When I killed William, it was because he would have killed me in turn. This time, it was because I wanted it—I wanted Titus's death..

But something else is wrong. My sharp werewolf instincts are going wild, as if the world has begun to crumble away beneath my feet.

I can't look at the people surrounding me, because one glance at the crowd roaring my name will tear a hole through my soul.

What have I gotten myself into? I don't want to be their queen. I'm socially awkward and I can't lead a pack, let alone a whole freaking kingdom.

I feel tears begin to burn my eyes but I force them down. A girl who has just defeated her greatest enemy shouldn't show any sign of tears.

"Alaska?" Josh calls out as I race out through the gate and back into the ebony safety of the hallways below the arena. Multiple guards stood where the other competitors used to chat and watch their competition intensely.

I have come all this way, and for what? Nothing. To avoid death.

Apparently, I'm that desperate to live.

I shake my head as I hurl myself onto the ground, my back aligning with the icy stones of the hallway. I bring my legs into my chest, and sit there as Josh and Chase disappear to decide who I will fight against in the finals.

Maybe I can run away, I tell myself, trying to comfort my thoughts despite having already tried it. Why are you so afraid of death anyway, Alaska? Your parents have gone through it, so surely you can too.

I know that the voice in my head is right. Why should I be afraid of something so inevitable and unavoidable such as death? The answer: human nature. My brain and my body will not allow me to go down without a fight.

One of the guards groans as he hauls Titus's corpse into the catacombs, the weapon I planted in his chest still firmly held in position. The guard then drops the body, right in my line of sight, and I almost feel as though he's doing it on purpose. Bile rises in my throat but I push it down. Being sick right now was not an option.

"You should watch the fight," the older guard recommends, his bushy grey eyebrows shadowing part of his eyes. "See who you'll be up against."

I don't bother to argue with the authoritative werewolf. Maybe if I get to look at how both Josh and Chase fight, I will have an idea of what I was truly up against. Maybe I can even use their own tactics against them.

Swallowing the tight ball of vehemence stuck in my throat, I clamber to my feet and peek out of the metre thin slot at the two male werewolves.

I'm expecting the fight to be long and hard, but one minute in, I can see that Josh is already tired. Neither have been given weapons for the round, and Chase continuously batters and dodges Josh's punches as he continues to persist in knocking his opponent out. Josh is a worthy opponent, but in his last match against a much larger wolf, he's sustained multiple injuries.

His arm still has the slim white scar from where his opponent's sword cut him five days ago, from his previous battle. He hadn't regained his full strength since despite days of recovery, and it shows. He is a good fighter, but even I know that he was lucky to make it this far. And by looking at the defeated snarl on his face, I think he knows it too.

Josh throws another punch towards Chase's head, but Chase easily ducks the sloppy and uncoordinated attack. That's when I realise Chase's battle strategy, he's wearing Josh out.

"Josh!" I call out, trying to alert him to Chase's tactic, but the roar of the crowd is too loud for him to even contemplate hearing. He's going to lose if Chase keeps up his tiring tactic.

The events play out in front of me as I am helpless to stop it. One minute, Josh throws all his might into one more punch, but Chase swiftly grabs his arms and twists it behind his back.

Through the yells of encouragement and dismay from above, I am able to hear Josh as he whimpers and moans from the pain. The noise sounds like an atomic blast, each groan causing my heart to thump faster. I begin to worry that Chase will seal the deal by killing him.

And when I think that it's almost over and that Chase has decided to kill the Alpha before him, Chase kicks Josh so ferociously in the head. I watch as spit flies from my friend's mouth before his head touches the ground.

I let out a scream, hands covering my mouth as my lips part. That looked painful, and I'm far too protective over Josh to let Chase get away with kicking way harder than necessary.

Josh has been defeated. Chase has won. And that only means one thing; I have to win so that I won't die. I have to become queen.

And cell by cell, my body begins to shut down. I don't want to be queen. Correction. I won't be queen.

I am Alaska Morgan, and I am a rogue. Not royalty.

The piercing cry of a horn diverts my thoughts and immediately, I glance into the perplexed faces lining the stands of the arena. Some of the onlookers look petrified, whereas others are tugging their weapons. Something is wrong, just as I suspected, and it isn't the fact that Josh has been knocked out cold.

Guards rush past me, bashing my shoulder with little care as they hurry off to their unknown duties. I hiss at the agonising pain spiralling through the limb as each one passes. Each has a sword welded in their grip, their eyes stony and emotions non-existent.

"Hey!" I call after them. "What the hell is going on?"

I only hear a muffled reply, "War."

My heart begins to thump even faster than it had done during my spar with Titus.

War? With who? Is this why the Alpha King wants a successor so desperately? Because they have been at war this whole time?

Crap. That's why they killed our rogue pack. That's why they hate rogues in the first place. Because the only explanation I can come up with for this war is that it's the rogues; the real ones who don't hesitate before decapitating a child's head from their body—like they had done to one of my pack mates.

Just the memory makes my whole body shiver.

I quickly turn my gaze back to the arena and see that all hell has broken loose. The King stands from his chair, waving his arms to try and calm his people, but his power has been lost. He can't do anything to settle the chaos of the crowd.

As I look closer, I see a werewolf with tattered clothes and a cut along his forehead. His beard is so intricately tangled that it looks as though he has a bird's nest perched on his chin. But what gives him away is his bold and steady movements, his heavy footsteps lumbering his body towards the King.

Panic takes a hold of my body, and upon seeing the demon, I scoop up the sword from Titus's chest. Maybe it isn't so bad that the guard placed his corpse here in the first place.

Clutching the blade with all my might, I handle the sword with ease, sprinting out into the piercing sunlight. Blinking rapidly, I pick out my target as he readies to throw his own weapon; a knife which is covered in some form of excruciating poison.

In a split second, I pause. Am I really going to save the King's life? Especially after he ordered the demise of my rogue pack? Or am I going to kill the real rogue, the true threat to everyone in here?

The King or the rogue? The King or the rogue?

My mind is suddenly made up as the rogue bolts forwards, and in a whirlwind, I spin my body around, and hurtle the trustworthy blade towards its target.

Standing frozen with fear, I watch as people duck out of the way of the sword in the nick of time. Many curse at me, glaring in my direction, but fall silent when they hear the thunk of metal on bone.

The body falls down the steps as the creature's heart stops almost immediately, finally finding its grave on the lowest ranking of seats.

Even though I'm unaware of it, this rogue is the first I would kill, and it will certainly not be the last.

CHAPTER SEVEN
Empty

"When are you going to get it through your head? We're in this together!"

- Hermione Granger, Harry Potter and the Philosopher's Stone

Josh huffs as he limps behind me, an arm draped around my shoulder as we rush through the crowd to try and get to safety. An elbow shoves me to the side, causing me to hiss but I ignore the pain. I want to get as far away from the rogues as I possibly can. I have seen what they can do, and I do not want my fate to be sealed by such a beast.

Josh's strides were wobbly as he staggers along, his head constantly lulling as he grows dizzy. He woke up two minutes ago but we were forced to run to safety due to the havoc.

"Alaska!" someone calls over the chaos—a voice I do not recognise.

I don't stop. Azra and Josh are safely with me and I have no need to be distracted. This is war, and I don't want to be killed when I'm so close to escaping the violence.

The same person pulls on my shoulder with a hard tug, forcing me to face them. I come face to face with the steely cobalt eyes and sharp jaw line I dread to fight tomorrow. His hair's ruffled from the fight and he has a fresh cut running along his cheek, dripping thick crimson blood.

"Alaska!" Chase shouts in my face so that he can be heard above the racket. "The King has asked to see us. We need to go now!"

I glance around at the werewolves pushing and barging past us through the corridor, some descending into the chambers below the castle, some sprinting up to the turrets, to wherever they think will be safe.

Halting, I shake my head. It takes one look at Josh to make rage fizz through my veins. Does he really think that I will simply follow him after what he did to me and my pack? After what he did to my friend?

And so, I slap Chase hard across the cheek with the cut, leaving my hand stinging with pins and needles. I hope it hurts him more than it hurts me.

"Don't you dare come near Josh again, arseh*le," I growl and feel my legs picking up the pace as I continue my ascent towards the entrance of the castle. Through the noise and shouting, it will be easy to slip out unnoticed. Then Chase can have the title he rightfully deserves.

Chase persists and grabs my upper arm, holding me firmly in place.

I try to jerk my arm away but he's too strong. "Get off me, you dick!" I shout but he doesn't comply.

Chase doesn't comprehend my words as he opens his mouth to say something. This better be good, otherwise he'll find yet another hand mark across his other cheek. "It's a competition, Alaska. I did what I had to do, like what you had to do to Titus."

I clench my teeth together, ready to argue in defence, but I realise after a second that he's right. I had to kill Titus to win, and he had to hurt Josh to get into the finals. He wants to be king, and I want to survive. But I won't give him the satisfaction of my forgiveness.

I growl, "Just stay away from us."

"Alask—"

"Piss off, Chase!" I hiss, hoping that he'll finally give up, but his grip stays firm. It's going to be much harder defeating him than I had first planned.

"Please, Alaska. The King needs to see us now," Chase continues. Is he ever going to give up? Will he ever accept that I need my own space? No, of course he won't. Because he's Chase, the king of arrogance and cockiness. Well, at least he was a king of something.

"God, don't you understand the meaning of go away?" I roll my eyes, and with one final attempt, I am able to wretch my arm out of his iron clamp.

I saunter off, and Chase stays frozen in the same spot, as if his feet were stuck to the floor with superglue. He watches me carefully, with Josh and Azra beside me. At some point in the previous minute, Azra has taken Josh from my shoulder and propped him up on hers instead.

"You need to come with me, Alaska!" Chase bellows at the top of his voice, the sound effortlessly reverberating off the stone walls as I begin to see the dim light ahead of me.

I keep looking forward, but show him my middle finger as I continue climbing. A group of guards barge past us towards the exit, trying to get to the walls that caged the valley so that they can hold off the rogue attack.

Why are the rogues attacking now of all times? They've had years to attack whenever they pleased, and here they are, trying to break in so that they can take over the kingdom.

I, of all people, know that they can succeed, but the walls are so strong and the fighting force within the city is too great for any rogue to break through for some time. The only way that they can succeed is to kill the king and wait it out. If they block our connections with the packs populating the forest surrounding Arla, then we'll be screwed and everyone will slowly starve to death.

I am metres from the entrance before someone steers me off to the right, pulling me so ferociously up a flight of stairs that I am unable to resist until we're ten steps up.

"Get. Off. Me!" I demand in a clear voice as Chase pushes me up the stairwell, the pathway much darker than the main exit of the castle. "When will you realise that you can give up? No one's going to label you as weak if you do."

Chase shakes his head as he stands behind me, blocking the path down the stairs. "I was ordered by the guards to take you to the King. And don't think that I don't know about your attempt to escape."

I open my mouth, ready for a hasty retort but nothing springs to mind. "I-I wasn't . . ." I stutter but almost face palm afterwards. With the way I'm behaving, anyone could've known what my plan was.

Chase doesn't say another word as he signals for me to keep climbing, and I obey. Tomorrow, I will have the chance to take out all of my stored up anger on him in the ring—if there is a tomorrow.

"Did the guard say what the King wanted to see us for?" I pant as we reach the top of the staircase, greeted by a wider corridor. Paintings hang on the wall, the faces of previous rulers glaring at me in their painted forms. On the ground lies an exquisite rug laced with gold in an ancient symbolic language which I cannot understand. This is the type of luxury a werewolf dreams of but can never get.

It's clear that we have arrived on the top floor of that castle, where the King and his family live. I can't believe how easy it was to get inside, but maybe the guards who are usually here have been called up to defend the castle from the rogues.

Chase shakes his head once more as he leads the way through the castle, as if he knows the place like the back of his hand. "No," he replies in a gruff voice as he parades beside me.

Thankfully, he doesn't make another attempt to grab my arm. "But I have a good idea."

I am about to reply when I almost run into the sturdy chest of a guard. He holds his sword by his side, his huge body blocking the doorway which we were supposed to enter. So this is where some of the guards have disappeared to—to protect the King. Of freaking course.

"Let them enter," a gruff voice orders the guards and they move aside, revealing the King with his grey beard and ancient, saggy skin. I never want to be as old and immobile as him. I would feel useless and a burden to others. Maybe there's a reason why werewolves die so young.

I stumble forwards into the large room; the same area where I had agreed to take part in the Alpha Trials. Looking back on my decision, I feel the walls press closer and closer to me, wondering when they will come so close that I'll eventually be crushed. The oxygen disappears from my lungs, and I feel as though I am suffocating. This is the place I signed myself up for imminent death, but also the slim chance of freedom.

I remember the naïve girl who had walked into this room without knowing what she was going to face over the next few days. Since then, I have killed two more werewolves and stained my name with even more blood. The girl who was dragged up those stairs no longer exists. She is a ghost who haunts this room. She died the moment I agreed to participate in the Alpha Trials.

Chase kneels the moment he is a few metres away from the King, but I come to stand next to him. Last time, I had knelt but over these past two weeks, I have learnt to never give up, and I'm certainly not going to give into the King now.

The ancient man glowers at me when I do not go on my knees but I ignore his piercing gaze. I will not give in to someone who had ordered the murder of innocent lives, including Dylan's.

When Chase realises that I'm not going to kneel, he stands up and places his hands behind him, trying to be respectful to the

King. The Alpha raises his head in respect whereas I stay in my standing position, making no effort to make myself look in any way presentable.

I wonder where Azra and Josh are. I had been forcefully pulled away from them before I had the chance to say goodbye, but wherever they are, I hope that they are safe.

"You asked to see us, sir?" Chase addresses the elderly man. I make no attempt to talk.

The King nods and begins to walk from his throne to the level ground, pacing slowly in front of us. "I wanted to congratulate you two on getting to the finals," the King begins and pauses his strides. "Whoever wins tomorrow, I would like to say congratulations. I know that either one of you will make a great ruler.

"But the rogues are attacking because they know I am weak and that the Alpha Trials are taking place. The reason they are attempting to invade us now is because they do not want Arla to gain a king or queen. They can easily overthrow the kingdom when I am dead." The Jing pauses. "They have come here to kill you two and myself."

I feel the blood in my veins slow and turn to ice. I already have the possibility of dying tomorrow. I don't need another threat that brings me any closer to death.

"We will hold off the rogues for as long as possible, but the victor tomorrow will be crowned. I will resign as soon as the winner has been made clear," the King concludes. "We have a war to fight, and Arla needs the strongest leader it can possibly get. But until tomorrow, you must rest. We will try our best to keep you safe. My guards will escort you to my safehold until the battle commences tomorrow."

I roll my eyes. Nowhere is safe, especially if the rogues manage to make their way into the city. I don't know how big their army is, but judging by the panic of the inhabitants, it must be verging on huge.

"You can't just keep us locked up in the castle," I retort, stepping forward, although I have no intention to. "We're better use out there on the battlefield than here."

The King nods solemnly. "I know, but I can' t ensure your safety out there. This kingdom needs a ruler, and I'm not going to let you two run around with the risk of getting killed."

I roll my eyes and cross my arms as I stand here, glaring at the grey eyes of the King. Although he might appear weak and fragile with age, his eyes are as hard as titanium; impenetrable.

"Guards!" the King calls, waving a finger to those behind him, except they never come.

"Crap," I murmur as the king swivels on his heel, instantly getting the sword from his from his belt. The archway is just out of eyesight, but as we all round the curb together, we see that the guards standing at the archway have disappeared, streaks of bright scarlet blood in the place where the armoured soldiers once stood. "They're here," I say.

The two guards who stopped us from entering the room in the first place rush up behind us, placing their bodies before the King as some sort of barricade.

"Sir, the attack was a distraction," one of the bulky werewolves informs him. "A second group entered the kingdom using one of the underground passages."

I watch as the King swallows, not in fear but in defeat. As his protectors tighten their stance, he turns towards me and presents the handle of his sword. "Take it, Alaska. You need to protect yourself."

I raise an eyebrow. I have chosen a side, and right now, it's looking like I had made the correct decision. "Don't you need it?"

For once, the corners of the old man's mouth twitch up. "I'm a dead man, anyway."

I stand in silence as I take the cold handle, the brittle metal feeling alien in my touch. It's a beautiful sword with a thin and razor sharp blade that's easy to manoeuvre.

Abruptly, an arrow impales the first guard and then the remaining one as a bow appears around the corner where the rogues supposedly are. The two protectors fall, leaving the King exposed once more. It only takes me a second to realise that we will be lucky to get out of this attack alive.

The King withdraws another sword, his chest rising and falling slowly as he prevents himself from hyperventilating.

Chase throws a knife towards the rogue with the bow as he exposes more of himself, the knife finding the young rogue's skull. The corpse falls to the ground in slow motion, the boy's lifeless fingers dropping the weapon as he falls.

The rogue's tactic surprised me. Usually, they charge head first into battle as if each and every single one of them has a death wish, but this is a structured attack. Maybe they aren't as feral as I thought.

But then my thoughts are shattered as the windows smash, causing me to flail backwards in surprise. The rogue with the bow and arrow was yet another distraction.

As soon as I've balanced myself, the rogues are already sprinting towards us, faces scratched, bruised, and covered with dirt. Each and every single one of them has a strange wild aspect within their eyes, turning them a deep yellow.

I jump in front of the King as a rogue swings his axe towards me. I duck as the metal causes the marble beneath my feet to crack and retaliate with slice from my sword.

The metal effortlessly cuts through bone, the rogue's hand carrying the axe detaching from the his body. The rogue squeals in pain, but I stab my sword straight through his heart before he has a second to compose himself.

Another rogue is on my case before the other falls to the ground. This one looks even younger than me, with perfect skin and a mop of greasy blonde hair. His eyes are only slightly yellow, but they still hold that feral aspect I have grown used to seeing.

The young boy swings his sword, and I slide along the marble floor to avoid getting sliced in half. While sliding, I begin to hyperventilate as I realise how close I have come to death. Again. I would roll my eyes at myself if I could. Sometimes, I wish that I could be fearless, but everyone is afraid of something. I just happen to be afraid of having a long and painful death.

I stand up the moment I am out of the rogue's reach, steadying myself before leaping towards the boy, sword gliding through his body before he can turn around. Rogues may be reckless, but it doesn't mean that they're good fighters.

There are only three rogues left. Chase is fighting one whereas the other two are advancing to the King. One bolts towards the old man, but he is surprisingly quick to slash it down before it can commit regicide.

The other rogue, however, is different to any other rogue I have seen. His hair is blonde—almost white—and his irises are so dark it appears as though they are melting into the pupil. His face is sharp like Chase's, but his eyes were more slanted, and his nose has a ridge in it from where it has been previously broken. His skin is so white, he blends in with the snow that carpets the trees outside.

But that isn't the only peculiar thing about this one "true rogue." His face bares no scratches, and he walks silently and calmly towards his prey instead of charging just like every other beast in the room. Just gazing at his slender body and precise movements makes me realise that he's important.

The white-haired rogue slowly paces towards the King, a long and thin sword clutched tightly in his grip. The feral werewolf flourishes the blade once, the blade cutting the air in front of the King's face as they begin to get into their fighting stances.

I feel a growl echo from my vocal chords. I don't particularly care whether the King lives or dies, but I did choose a side and I'm going to fight for it until my very last breath, just as I had done to avenge Dylan's death.

The young rogue looks no older than twenty-five. He slowly rolls up his sleeves as if he has all the time in the world. His moves are smooth even as the battle rages around him, with Chase continuing to slash his knife at the huge rogue before him.

With no intentions, a battle cry follows the growl from my throat, my legs automatically moving forwards as they charge towards the mysterious rogue, every cell in my body buzzing as if wildfire was spreading through my limbs.

I can't begin to describe my hatred for the mindless beast who haunts children's nightmares, but whatever that rage is, it's forcing my body to move, forcing air to rapidly fill my lungs, and forcing me to face the rogue before me.

I lash out with my long sword, not quite anticipating its reach. The silver does not meet the pale skin of the boy with platinum hair, and I withdraw my sword as soon as I realise my attack has failed.

On the plus side, I have distracted the rogue from the King. On the down side, I am the boy's next target.

His head snaps in my direction in the blink of an eye and his feet immediately begin to pace towards me. The boy's pale lips pick up into a smile when he realises who I am.

"You must be the rogue," he snarls, his voice soft, almost like a whisper. If anyone is the opposite of Chase, then this boy is. "How does it feel to betray your own race?"

Betray my own race? I was never a rogue. Not a real rogue. Not one like him. He's completely and utterly crazy.

I don't reply for a few seconds, time elongating as I gaze into his eyes. At such close proximity I'm able to tell that his eyes are a very, very dark brown, his pupil camouflaged by the iris.

Instead of forming words, my arms thrust forward, sending my blade straight into the man's stomach. Except it never reaches the guarded skin. Instead, dark-eyed rogue moves his own sword in the way and pushes my own back to be, causing me to stumble back.

"Did you really think that it would be that easy, b*tch?" he spits out to me, a smirk still on his face. He loos like a very attractive devil.

I wish I could nod in response, but he does not give me time. As swift as lightning, I feel the brittle handle of his sword whacking against my head, my skull immediately bursting into flames of agony.

My legs give way as I feel the inferno roar on my scalp, devouring my thoughts. I feel my lips open to scream, but I can't follow through on it and my brain won't let me think.

Sh*t, that hurts. A lot.

I try to focus on the scene in front of me, but my vision is blurry. My mind spins as though it's a never ending roller coaster. I have been lucky not to be knocked out altogether, but maybe falling unconscious would have been better than this torment.

I wait for a few seconds, blinking away the moisture in my eyes. Second by second, the haze begins to clear and the fogginess inside my brain ebbs away.

Soon, I have a clear picture of two pairs of feet; the rogue and the King. They constantly move around, one pair much clumsier than the other.

Finally, my head is almost clear and I'm able to look up to see the glint of a sword. I can't process the actions properly, but all that I see is the splatter of blood as a body crashes to the ground, a sword stuck in the back of the corpse.

I stagger to my feet, head shaking in disbelief and fear. My hands clench into empty fists as I realise that my sword had fallen from my grip.

No. This cannot be happening.

The King's dead eyes stare up at me, his ghost joining my own to haunt these corridors until the end of eternity.

On my feet, I feel my body begin to sway as the dizziness kicks in once more, but not nearly as powerful as it had been a minute ago. The fog clears enough for me to see Chase fight the rogue expertly, forcing him out of the window.

The rogue glances at me once more, smirking like an evil villain before disappearing over the window sill. I wish that would be the last time I ever see him.

Abruptly, my head throbs once more and, with the pain of failing to defend the King, I feel my legs fall beneath me, causing my body to hurtle towards the ground. I didn't care about the King in the slightest, but his death left the kingdom vulnerable. We were going to have to face the rogues without an experienced leader, and the thought makes me shiver.

"Alaska," Chase says as he rushes back to me and catches my useless body before the fall can cause any damage. Despite being in my opponent's hold, I feel safe in his strong arms, as if nothing can touch me. "Are you okay?"

I shake my head; of course I'm not okay. The king is dead, and the city is leaderless. They need me or Chase to lead, and I wasn't ready. I don't want to win, but I don't want to die. What the hell am I supposed to do?

I don't know, but I don't care anymore. Fate has taken me down this path for a reason, and I was going to follow it.

And for this tiny moment in time, I feel as though my soul detaches itself from my body and I fade away, leaving the shell of my skin behind. I feel empty—I feel as though the world will be better off if I didn't exist.

CHAPTER EIGHT
Sacrifice
"A moment of pain is worth a lifetime of glory."

- Unknown

My heart is thumping inside my chest, as if it's a volcano about to explode. I can feel the lava burning its way through my soul, creating a scorching hole where my heart should be. My stomach is blazing with an inferno of butterflies, and my lungs feel as though they're breathing in fire every time I take a breath. Every movement hurts, and no matter how many times I tell myself *"It's okay, Alaska, it's okay"* reality comes crashing down on me.

I nervously gulp, but even that feels painful as my throat refuses to swallow. I have never felt like this before. Perhaps because this time, I know that this is the end. There's nowhere to run; nowhere to hide. This is it.

I tremble as I stand and wait below the arena. Last night had shaken me much more than it should've. Every time I blink, an image of the King tumbling to the ground flashes before me, and it stings. Why I am reacting in such a way, I don't know. Maybe it reminds me of my parents's deaths.

Even though the the King died, the guards and the kingdom's army were able to hold the rogues long enough for us to get to the arena. The rogue attack has slowly ebbed away, leaving a few rebels in the vicinity of the kingdom, but it's still enough to threaten the city. Whatever the beasts were planning, they're holding it off for the time being, as if they are allowing us to choose a new ruler.

God, how have I even gotten this far? What did he have planned for me?

"Choose your weapon," a gritty voice commands me. It takes me a few seconds to realise that the sound has echoed from behind me, produced by a larger, more rounded guard who looks out of shape compared to the others.

I glance at the selection before me. Both Chase and I are staring at a weapons cabinet laid neatly with newer and shinier weapons. Some tiny part of my mind wonders whether they are specially made, cleaned, and sharpened for the battle ahead of us.

My hands graze over the sword I was been given last night. I still have it because some part of me never wants to let go. I had been given it as a gift, and although I despise the deceased king, I can't help but like him, too. He had shown me respect, which was more than I deserved.

I pat the sword at my side and turn so sharply on my heel that I almost lose my balance. I quickly skitter my feet into a safer position, bringing my hands firmly by my side. My aim was to try and not make a fool out of myself, yet here I am, undermining that goal. Damn you, nerves.

"I'm ready," I state, unsheathing the beautiful sword from its scabbard. It's clear to see that this sword had been crafted for royalty—and who knows, I might be the next Alpha Queen.

But the truth is that today, I have to make a decision; Alpha Queen or death? Lead a kingdom and numerous packs, or choose the easy option out of this hell hole? It's my choice, and it's one that I cannot make. Not yet.

Perhaps I will never have to make it.

Chase follows my lead and takes a sword from the rack, choosing the same weapon as mine. Perhaps to make the fight fairer or maybe it's because it's his preferred weapon.

Chase curtly nods at our escort before the wide man nods himself. Despite his larger shape, he moves surprisingly quick; I find it hard to keep up with him as we parade through the deserted catacombs below the arena. With no competition left, the place is so quiet; you would be able to hear a pin drop from the other side of the corridor.

Our footsteps are the only noise we hear as we continue to stalk the hallways like ghosts; one of us will soon be, anyway. They'll be left to haunt these forsaken walls forever, confined within the kingdom as if it was an impenetrable fortress.

Finally, we reach the dreaded entrance to the arena, the metal gate drawn up to allow us to pass. Sunlight hits my face almost immediately, and the arena is so quiet, it's like no one is watching.

Except they are. Most of the kingdom stare at me so closely that it feels like they are trying to pry apart my body, cell by cell. Many of them scowl; they don't want a rogue to win. Others, like Josh and Azra, simply nod to wish me luck.

I am weak. I have bad technique. This isn't going to end well.

The wind clumsily flings loose hair in my face, partly obscuring the view of my death bed. I had rushed to make two messy French braids this morning, but for now, that is the least of my worries..

Chase and I stare at each other as the warrior wolf raises his arm, mouth opening to bellow the rules to the rest of the werewolves in the arena. I glance up to the box where the King once sat in all his pride and glory, seeing it empty of life.

"Welcome, citizens of Arla, to the finals of the Alpha Trials!" the guard announces, but barely anyone claps. They all wear morbid faces, as if they have been claimed by death. And that's when I see it; killing the ruler is like directly killing the kingdom itself. With no one to follow, the citizens are just lost spirits.

The few that do cheer quickly grow silent as the armoured wolf continues. "Unlike the other rounds, this fight will have a different rule. Today, only one will emerge victorious," the guard states, causing the butterflies in my stomach to rapidly reproduce like a plague of locusts. "Today, the fight will be to the death! If one wishes to surrender and offer mercy to the other, only then will they be allowed to live."

Since when has that been a rule? Why has nobody told me? I know that Chase will most likely kill me anyway, but there's still that flutter of hope left in my heart that he will let me live if he is to win. Now it looks like I only have one choice.

"Good luck," the male finishes and backs away, lowering his arm to signal the beginning of the match, but it's as if a nuclear bomb has been dropped. I can see everyone perched nervously on the edges of their seats, anticipation riding on top of all the spectators' shoulders.

Chase stands before me in a sleeveless top, revealing his bulky muscles. He is all an alpha was expected to be; strong, handsome, and daunting. Even when I look into his eyes, I see the true look of power. He is the king they deserve, but what will win? The want for power or the need to survive?

"Are you ready?" Chase asks as he gives his sword a whirl out of boredom. He's a strange opponent. One who's confident that he will win. The only problem is that I have seen him fight, and I know his tactics. He will try to wear me down like I'm a battery, but I will try and do the same with him too.

I shrug my shoulders. I have to stay strong, even if every single part of my body is shaking. I remember the last time we fought, and his immense power had effortlessly crushed me. I will not let that happen again.

I grit my teeth, taking a long and slow breath, preparing myself for the battle ahead. I nod at the Alpha before me. "As ready as I'll ever be."

Chase considers my answer and appears to be happy with it. His face even has a hint of a smirk on it. His handsome eyes glint menacingly at me as he flicks his wrist once more, creating a perfect arc with his metal blade.

We continue to stare at each other, the sand from the arena gently settling into my boots due to the light breeze. The sky above us is grey and dull, just like the previous night had been when I was forced to stay in a room with guards outside my door for the duration. Their plodding patrols alone had kept me up all night, and God only knows what my eye bags look like now.

After a few moments, Chase raises his eyebrow. He clearly expects me to attack first, but even I am not that stupid. It's one of the first rules of battle and has been plugged into my system since birth.

"Are we going to fight or not?" I ask out of boredom.

Chase clenches his jaw when he realises that I want him to attack first. He bows his head slowly. "Yes."

His actions are a blur as he spins his blade towards me while his own body pivots in a circle, creating a distant whistling noise before his sword meets my own. I grit my teeth as the blades ring together, but we both quickly retreat.

This is unlike the battle with Titus. He held his blade against mine, trying to overpower what little strength I had. Chase is using a different tactic against me, so I will have to change mine too.

The young werewolf before me goes straight for my stomach, jabbing the sword towards my flesh. I arc my back into a curve to avoid the blade ripping through my skin and quickly batter his sword away with my own.

Now it's my turn. If I'm going to win this, then I want the fight to be a quick one. I don't have time to become exhausted and finally give up because I have no energy left within me. I don't want this battle to become even harder than it already is.

I slash with my sword precisely, but Chase just ducks or counteracts my attack with his own steady strike every time. After a few attempts to try and wound him, I realise that it's pointless to keep slashing with my blade. He will keep avoiding the attempts, and soon I will tire, leaving the crown as his.

Males are faster, stronger, and better in combat than females. Sexist biology.

With one final try, I clench my teeth and put all the strength I can muster in my muscles behind one blow of my sword. I think about Dylan, who had been taken from this world before it was his time. He deserved so much better than to bleed out in the middle of the bleak white snow-stained landscape.

My mind suddenly flashes, and it feels as though I am standing on the same cursed ground I had been perched on the night my parents were slaughtered. I can see my mother's face but it's blurry. All I can make out are her brown eyes; exactly the same as my own. I feel her hand push against my flesh as the arrow buries itself into her heart, shoving me into the gushing river behind us.

The water swirls around me like a mystical veil, wrapping me tightly in its glacial grip. I gasp, and feel the water filling my throat.

And then I'm drowning. Again and again and again.

The gush of the water seems to wake me up. I feel a chill run down my spine as my eyes automatically focus back on reality. I have only been absorbed in my thoughts for a millisecond but it feels like it's been decades.

In that final attempt, I place all my anger and hatred into one strike so powerful, I hope that his sword goes flying in the opposite direction. But it doesn't. As the blades meet once again, he matches my potency with his own.

We hold our positions, and I feel a bead of sweat slowly run down my face as my feet begin to slip backwards, my muscles too exhausted to react. I'm not strong enough to conquer Chase, but I have the brains to outsmart him.

I grit my teeth so tightly I think that they're going to shatter into a thousand shards. I don't want this to be over, but even now I know that this is the end.

Chase suddenly jabs his sword forwards and manages to put a cut on my cheek. Taken by shock, I stagger back as I feel a sting coming from where the handle had made contact. My hand flies to my enflamed wound and it comes away sticky with the ruby resin of blood—something I had grown used to seeing over these past two weeks.

I feel my anger grow so strong that it takes control of my body, forcing my conscience out of the driver's seat to take the reins. My infuriated body hurls another swing of my sword at Chase and given how riled up I became, I am able to batter his weapon away from his hand.

I growl as Chase widens his eyes in shock. He, just like many others, had underestimated me. Maybe I have even underestimated myself.

My wolf nears the surface as my instincts become more animalistic and my senses sharpen. I refuse to let my body shift, and it silently obeys through the blinding rage. I can't see anything; my vision is blurred with red. After stuffing my emotions into the deepest, most fathomable depths of my soul, they have finally surfaced in one final push to keep me alive.

I swipe with my sword across Chase's mid-section, but he's just fast enough to dodge out of the way before I can get close to ripping his flesh. I try and strike him again, but he ducks under my blade and swiftly springs on his heel to grab my wrist as I bring it backwards.

Using his toned body and bottomless strength, Chase naturally flings me over his shoulder as if I weigh no more than a sheet of paper.

92

I feel my body make contact with the ground, my bones vibrating like an electrified wire in an alternating magnetic field.

Completely and utterly winded, I stagger clumsily to my feet, my mouth open like a fish out of water. I've felt like this many times throughout my previous fights, but none have left me feeling like this.

I have lost my sword in the process, and as Chase allows me to teeter to a standing position, I see that it's too far away for me to retrieve. I will have to fight my way to it, and that includes going through Chase.

Chase's sword is close to my own, and I know that all I have to do is get to them before he does and then this crappy contest will be over.

I feel a drop of blood slowly trickle from my nose and shakily wipe it away. All the while, Chase stares at me as if I have come from a different planet. Is he surprised that I'm not giving up? Because if he thinks that I am, then he had clearly been bashed in the head too hard as a baby.

I lurch forwards, swinging my fist and hoping that it connects with his jaw. I feel the air rush out of the way of my charging hand as it whistles forwards.

Chase's hand reaches up to block my punch and the other manages to hit me in the stomach. I feel myself reel backwards to try and get away from his next punch, but it lands directly in my stomach once more.

A gurgle emerges from my throat as I cough up blood, spraying it on his face. Dazed, Chase blinks for a second, and I take this opportunity to tackle him to the floor, pinning his hands to his sides with my legs.

He looks up at me with his huge and mysterious eyes. Even now, in the midst of the torment of battle, I can see the strange gold flecks that reminded me of my mother's hair. But as I look further into his metallic gaze, I can spot something else hidden deep within the iris.

Fear.

It's too well concealed to know whether it's genuine, but the look on his face is enough to give away the idea that Chase's defeat is not a mirage.

Chase's chest rises as he tries and pushes me from his body, but I use all my strength and will to keep him contained. I'm not the heaviest werewolf but with my extra muscle mass, I might weigh more than I thought.

As I gaze at Chase, a flood of memories swell in my brain, threatening to make it explode. All I can picture is the sword slicing straight through Dylan's figure and his body going still as he was flung to the ground like a worthless rag. Chase didn't kill Dylan, but he had been there. He was the alpha who lead the massacre on my friends and adopted family. I will never forgive him for that.

A bubble furiously rises in my chest like an eruption of magma and I feel my limbs consumed once again by rage, which I cannot control. As I force Chase to lay still on the ground, I am powerless as my fists ram into his face, punch after punch.

I don't know how long I'm there for, but by the time I'm done, my fists are raw and blistered. At some point, tears have formed in my eye. My vision is a haze of water, trapped in Chase's cryptic stare.

He's still conscious but only barely. As I deliver my final punch after realising that I have done enough damage, his head lulls to the side like a baby in his sleep.

Confident that he is practically unconscious, I withdraw myself from my victim. You would have thought that I would feel something like guilt or sympathy, but all that's left of my heart is a black hole. My heart was stolen when my parents died, and that abyss only grew when Dylan was slain before my very eyes.

My steps are fragile as I move to pick up the two fallen blades, collecting one in each hand. They feel like poison in my grip, and can feel that it's slowly corroding my flesh away from my bone.

I was never raised to be a murderer but . . . here I am. The events of my life have rounded the edges of my personality and sharpened me. I am the finished product, and I'm not proud of it. I'm a monster. I kill. Maybe I should be labelled as a rogue.

But more importantly, I don't deserve to live. Chase does.

I can feel the eyes of the audience trailing my every move, observing what I'm going to do next. I almost laugh. Isn't it obvious? This is a fight to the death, and with Chase barely conscious on the ground, he's an easy target.

My opponent has since woken up. Dazed, so now his movements are laboured and slow. He gradually gets up on his knees, but I use most of my remaining strength to push him back so that he is kneeling before me.

His eyes are startled as I place both swords in the shape of a cross at his throat. All I have to do was move my arms to decapitate the handsome young man before me.

Chase looks as though he has a tear in his eye, but his sturdy face shows no sign of weakness. Even in death, he was a warrior, as any other werewolf should be.

Chase shrugs his shoulders, despite the swords resting on them. "What are you waiting for?" His expression is solemn, pleading me to get the job over and done with. "Just get it over with."

I can't kill him.

Even if he had been at the scene where Dylan died, he still hadn't killed my ex-best friend. He has also tried to kill me, but he didn't. There's nothing he has done to make him deserve such a horrific—yet heroic—death.

I look away, biting my lip nervously. Tears threaten to pour from my eyes, my body overwhelmed with a foreign emotion I can't quite figure out. What has this man done to me?

I can't kill him.

I look back at Chase, his face still as bold as it had previously been. "Take care of them, Alaska." He nods to the

95

people surrounding us. "They deserve a strong leader, and you are that leader."

I inhale sharply because the words flowing from his mouth are lies. I'm not strong enough to lead a whole city. It will break me from the inside. I love being free; keeping me cooped up in a castle will deteriorate me.

I shake my head, stepping back slowly as I withdraw the swords from Chase's neck. I chuck one to the side and then one in front of Chase so that he can access it more easily.

Chase gives me a shocked look but I ignore it. He wants to be king, and this is his opportunity.

"I'm not," I state quietly. I feel my legs give way and fall to my knees. I can't rule, and if I kill Chase and lead the kingdom, it will be like signing the death certificates of everyone in the city. I have come all this way to escape my demise, but I will never be able to escape fate. I have run from it long enough. Now, it is time to turn and face my demons.

Kneeling before Chase, he stands up and gathers the sword the King gave me, shaking his head slightly to try and rid his dizziness. I look up at him with huge, wide eyes, hoping that he will get this over with quickly.

"Alaska!" a familiar voice desperately calls out from the spectator area but I ignore the frantic shout. I hope that Josh will be able to accept my sacrifice. If he only knew what I had witnessed in my life; maybe then he will understand.

Chase places the sword across my neck. He knows that he hasn't won the crown rightfully, but he's still acting like the cocky bastard he is. I have sacrificed myself to let him live, and every part of my brain still believes that he will kill me. It's the rules, but I hope that he might spare my life. He has done it before, and maybe—just maybe—he will do it again.

"Give me one reason why I should let you live." Chase's face is blank as he speaks.

What kind of question is that? Is he actually thinking about letting me live? I'm a rogue; any other competitor with any sense would've plunged the sword through my heart moments ago.

I feel my lip tremble as the sword pushes closer to my windpipe.

I blink rapidly. "That's the problem. I can't."

Chase sighs as he weighs up his options. The blade presses ever closer to my windpipe, threatening to slice the skin. Less air reaches my lungs, and my body takes quicker breaths as I begin to hyperventilate; both from fear and oxygen deprivation.

Chase glances around the stadium and the silent faces. Every single member of the crowd is on their feet, anxiously watching to see who will be crowned king or queen. The man then snaps his gaze back to me, the powerless girl knelt before him.

We stay there for what seems like centuries, but within one blink, he turns away and chucks his sword to the other side of the arena. He pants heavily with anger, his body moving up and down with every breath. It's clear to see how hard it is for him to let me live.

I kneel there, shocked. Amidst the sand and the concrete, I sit on my legs, completely and utterly stunned, as if I have witnessed the death of my mother all over again.

He turns back to me, fuming, his eyes infiltrated by a beautiful silver tint. "I have one condition if I let you live," he spits furiously, unleashing his inner beast from within. He doesn't want to let me live, but I know deep down that the crowd will hate him if he kills me. They won't accept his leadership if he doesn't show mercy to the true winner who gave up her place because she knew she wasn't fit to rule.

"Name it."

Chase lets out a tiny growl as he slowly loses control to his wolf. "That you, Alaska Morgan, will be my second in command."

CHAPTER NINE
War

"For every king that died, they would crown another."

- Daniel In The Den, Bastille

If there's one piece of advice I would give about coronations, it's that you shouldn't go to one. They're as boring as a piece of pristine, blank white paper. And the fact that Chase smirked at me for most of the ceremony does not add to the effect. About ten minutes into the service, I had already began regretting my decision to spare him.

The only upside of the whole ceremony is the traditional party held afterwards. Whenever a new king or queen is crowned, all of the alphas are invited to a special after party to, well, get plastered.

"What're you thinking about?" Josh asks as he comes to stand beside me on the balcony. He looks handsome in his human-style suit and tie, the navy fabric making his youthful eyes seem brighter.

I, on the other hand, stayed in my fighting gear, with the addition of a cape draped over my shoulder to signify my position as the King's second in command. The red velvet material compliments my bland pigmented tresses. My sword is still firmly sheathed in my belt, despite the formal event. I'm not going to dress in a fancy dress for a party I don't even want to attend.

I don't even hesitate to tell him the truth. After the whole Alpha Trials ordeal, I feel as though I've known Josh for my whole life. "How much of a dick Chase is," I reply in my usual, blunt tone. It's no wonder why I don't have more friends. Josh snorts before I continue, "What? He was smirking at me throughout the whole coronation."

Josh shakes his head, taking a sip of beer from his cup. Unlike other werewolves who drank champagne at the royal event, Josh has opted for beer. "Anyone would've smirked."

"Are you actually standing up for Chase?" I question in disbelief, a note of laughter carried in my voice.

Josh rolls his eyes slowly as he places his hands on the balcony, clasping his fingers together. He arches his back, leaning down as his gaze drifts over the celebrating city. The courtyard below is bustling with werewolves, torches painting the pitch black curtain of the sky in scarlet. Happy cheers reverberate from the chasm, creating a peaceful and safe atmosphere as I wonder what awaits us outside the city walls in the morning.

What are the rogues planning? Are they going to try and kill Chase now that he's king? He might be an arseh*le, but he doesn't deserve to get savagely destroyed by a mindless beast. Nobody does, unless they are Titus.

"Alaska, he is our king," Josh says with a sigh, a white cloud of exasperated water vapour appearing before him.

"So what? Does that mean that he's suddenly a better person?" I enquire as I stand up straighter and cross my arms defiantly over my chest. Josh shoots me a disapproving look.

The teenager shakes his head. "No, but he's our king."

"I heard you the first time, and I'm aware of that. I didn't sit through a two-hour service for nothing," I state, the bitter and cold air seeping into my veins. I'm glad that I didn't wear a dress. I would've frozen to death.

Josh shakes his head as he lets out a small chuckle. To be honest, he's probably regretting the decision he made to befriend me. I'm hoping it's just me, though. Without his or Azra's support, God only knew where I would be at this chapter in my life.

Josh leans back from the balcony, the warmth of his presence slowly fading like the sun dipping behind the mountains at dusk. "They just brought out dessert. You coming?"

Dessert? Food that isn't meat or salmon, which I have been living off in the wild? After a life of savoury dishes and rough meals, I think eating sweet food won't settle in my stomach too well. I have to admit, though, I have a soft spot for cake.

I wave a hand at Josh. "I'm good."

"Suit yourself." He sighs, fiddling with the cufflinks on his suit. I hear the faint grumble of Josh's stomach before he begins to saunter away from the marble ledge, leaving me isolated from everyone else in a ten-meter radius.

Finally alone, I am able to pull in a deep breath, filling my lungs to the point where I think that they're going to explode. Then exhale, returning to my steady breathing pattern.

I tilt my head towards the sky. It's clouded over, the overcast water vapour parading above my head, mocking my existence. But after a few seconds, I notice a tiny hole in the dense cloud, the bright luminescence shining through the gap like a lifeline.

I wonder whether my parents are up there, among of the stars. Of course, the truth is nobody knows whether heaven exists or not, but a small part of my shadowed soul hopes that they can see me now. That, as they gaze down from the inky canvas, they are proud of me and what I have been able to achieve.

Probably not, given the amount of blood on my hands, but I still hope that they watch over me. Then, at least, I wouldn't truly be alone.

Wrapped tightly in my thoughts like a sticky cobweb, I shake my head to try and clear my mind. They aren't coming back. Nobody from my past life is. Dylan, my parents—even Titus—are all gone, lost within the void of death.

100

In fact, I have been so caught up in my thoughts, I didn't notice the steady breathing behind me. Each inhaled breath causes a whistling noise as the male stands behind me. I can't see his face, but I have a good idea who it is.

"Isn't it a bit cold to be daydreaming?"

I spin on my heel to come face to face with Chase. His face is so close to mine that I am forced to let out a distressed squeal. Anger builds in my throat. Why is he here? What the hell does he want with me?

"No," I reply bluntly, turning back to the view below me so I don't have to look at his face, handsome as it was. The only person I want to have a conversation with is Josh, and he's currently stuffing himself with cheesecake or some other sweet delicacy. Or even Azra but she's inside the castle, avoiding the cold.

Chase comes to stand beside me, our upper arms touching for a second. I don't feel anything except for the soft fabric of my jacket over my skin, but his presence is too close for my comfort.

Chase waits for a few minutes, studying the same pinpricks of light I have been gazing at. Then he opens his mouth to speak, his deep voice compelling me to listen. "Would you care for a dance?" he asks.

I whip my head around in confusion, confronting the King once more. "Are you being serious?" I chastise, my eyebrows scrunching together to form delicate folds of skin above my brown eyes.

Chase bows his head slowly. Thankfully, he is no longer wearing his crown. "Yes," he replies, adopting the same position Josh had earlier, stretching his forearms out on the sturdy wall of the balcony.

"Well, in that case, no."

"I thought that you'd say no." Chase sighs as he stands back up, straightening his back. I hear the sharp, echoing click as his spine snaps into a more preferred position.

I shake my head, eyebrows furrowed, still uncertain. "Then why did you ask in the first place?" I ponder. Furious with myself, I divert my sight so that it is looking into the open doors before me, leading into a luxurious room covered in a ruby carpet encrusted with gold.

"It was worth a try," Chase says in a breathy voice, his hand brushing my upper arm to gain my attention. His attempt to make me stare into his hazel eyes is successful. I slap his arm away from my limb, but stop when I see the snarl forming on his face. If there is one thing I don't want to do, it's piss off Chase.

"I guess you want to know why I'm here."

I shrug. "Not really."

"Well, since you're my second in command, you will have to do as I say," he orders, but the hint of his infamous ghost smile and twitch of his lips signals to me that he's joking. I hope he is, because there's no chance in living hell that I'm going to dance with him. I can't walk in a straight line most of the time, let alone dance elegantly like everyone else can. It was as if they had all completed multiple lessons before attending the occasion. Since when did werewolves dance?

"If you order me to do anything I don't agree to, then I'll kick you in the balls," I warn, raising an eyebrow. His ghost smile is still there, haunting his handsome features, as if he thinks I am joking. Trust me, I'm not.

Chase chuckles at my remark. "You don't mean that."

"Oh, I'm being serious," I reply sternly. At some point in the previous minute, I have crossed my arms over my chest. Thin strands of hair batter my face as the wind torments them in the winter's ruthless hold. "I can demonstrate if you'd like."

Chase flashes a shining grin. "You know what, I'm fine," he utters clearly before continuing. "So, about this second in command position. It's important that you follow my orders. I am your king, and you are the second most important werewolf in the whole city. You will be an inspirational figure for the rest of the city to look up to."

I cringe at his words. Whereas some crave the celebrity status, I prefer an isolated lifestyle surrounded by those I can trust. I'm not inspirational, someone to look up to, or, quite frankly, a leader.

"Tomorrow, I want you to train with everyone else and get ready for the war ahead of us. The rogues have not started their attack yet, but they will soon. When they do, I need you to lead the charge on the battlefield." He glances at me with stern eyes made of steel. He looks indestructible.

I hold up my hand to stop him. "Wait, I'm supposed to be training? Shouldn't I be the one teaching?"

"You use your anger to fight, but your technique isn't perfected," Chase summarises my abilities in a sentence.

I let out a shocked breath. "But I beat you in combat. I won the Alpha Trials. If anyone needs to train, then it's you."

Chase releases yet another shaky breath. It's clear he's not used to arguing or being told what to do. "The only reason you won is because your rage and fear was stronger than my strategy. Whatever's happened in your life, it drives you to make it through to the next day."" Chase pauses, noticing my unease. My stomach begins to churn as I feel the rest of my body float away into the pit of regret. I do not want to think about my past life twice in one night. "You need to learn to fight properly."

"But—"" I open my mouth in protest but Chase rudely cuts off my words with his overpowering voice.

"I'll see you tomorrow in the courtyard, eight o'clock sharp," he growls, sauntering away back to his party.

☽

I rub my shoulders vigorously as I stand outside in the courtyard, shivering in my thin fighting jacket. Since last night, the light wind has picked up to a gale, a paranormal whistling noise echoing throughout the kingdom as the wind's hands make their way through the tiniest cracks in the castle walls.

The sky above my head is stormy, grey clouds pregnant with rain water ready to give birth and spray us with the clean liquid contained within them.

It's one of those days where the moon is still visible during daylight. As I peer up grey canvas in the sky, the crescent moon shining like a tiny thread of light within the obscurity. In a week, the moon will almost be full, ready to continue its eternal cycle.

I clutch a bow in my hand. After the briefing from Chase, I have chosen to practice with my least competent weapon, which happens to be a bow and arrow. Chase has told us to work on our weaknesses, and I'm following his orders, perhaps the only time I ever will in my life.

I stretch the string back so that my cool, smooth fingers rest against my face. The feeling is strange, sending shivers down my spine, the alien sensation on my cheek diminishing when I send the arrow flying.

Arrows lay strewn around the cloth target; only one was able to puncture the hanging fabric. I'm pretty useless without a sword. I can't get to grips with the elasticity of the bow string nor can I point the arrow in the correct direction.

"Breath in," someone beside me murmurs. I am surprised to see Azra hold a bow confidently.

"What?" I question, lowering my bow.

Azra rolls her eyes as she takes an arrow from the stand beside her, loads her bow, and aims at the target. The arrow slices straight through the middle.

It's my turn to roll my eyes. "Chase told us to work on our weaknesses."

"And I decided to help you instead."" She shrugs, placing the bow over her agile body before parading over to me with some sort of ancient and paranormal elegance. "If Chase thinks that I'm going to start following his orders, then he's wrong. He beat up Josh. He's lucky his head is still on his shoulders."

I nod slowly, biting my lip as I raise my bow once more and load an arrow into the delicate weapon. This bow was crafted from wood—most likely oak—with intricate carvings chipped into the material and polished to create a glossy finish. It's stunning.

"Now take a deep breath in," Azra instructs. I know that she's good with the weapon, but part of me doesn't want to listen. I hate following orders.

"Azra, I really don—""

"Do you want to be able to shoot this thing or what?" she cuts me off and, out of the corner of my eye, I see her arms fold across her chest.

I grit my teeth. "Yes."

"Fine. Then you'll do as I say," Azra states simply, rising on her heels for a moment before dropping back down to her usual height. Her small body is soon behind me so that she can see where I'm aiming the arrow.

I haven't realised quite how small she is until now. Her figure is much more petite, her height a few inches shorter than my own. But even so, her tiny size makes me respect her more. With less body weight to throw around in hand-to-hand combat, she is at a clear disadvantage, especially up against males, but her battle strategies are carefully formulated, giving her the upper edge in combat.

"Relax," the teenager gives her second instruction after I have taken my deep breath, filling my lungs with rich oxygen. "Now, aim the arrow slightly higher than where you want it to go."

I raise the weapon in my grasp so that the shaft of the arrow is just above the central point of the wooden stump that's covered in the brown material of old and unwanted clothes. "That's it," Azra confirms, agreeing that my hand is in the correct place. "Stay calm, and loose."

I inhale once more, another round of voluptuous air filling my lungs to the brim. Then, with all my hidden calmness, I loosen my grip on the bowstring and watch the arrow glide through the air. The wooden arrow strikes the wooden target in the bottom left hand side, but still on target, nonetheless.

I see Azra beam at me from the corner of my eye. Her whole face lights up, crinkles forming at the sides of her eyes. She looks beautiful in this moment; calm and happy, something I rarely see. She's already stunning as it is, but with her elated smile and straight teeth, her beauty becomes boundless, like a fresh cobweb after a morning frost.

And after a second, her smile drops, her laughter lines disappearing and face turning ghastly pale. For a moment, I think that she's staring directly at me but then I notice her eyes focus in on something behind me. I am just about close enough to see the glassy reflection in her eyes. I can see the shape of a horse carrying a rider through the gates, which have clanked open without either of us noticing.

I curiously glance over my shoulder and immediately regret doing so. A charcoal pigmented horse neighs mercilessly as its dark eyes give it a demonic appearance. The creature adorns a white sock on its back right foot but, apart from the slight change in colour, the beast appears before us like a monster.

But it isn't the only monster present. Saddled on the back of the stoic horse sits a rogue, his thick deer-hide coat wrapped around him like coiling serpents ready to use their venom.

Chase storms forward in a whirlwind from behind us as he stops teaching a ten-year-old how to use an axe. His face is slack of expression, but I can see he's red with anger.

Despite the rampant rogue entering the city walls and the fuming Chase, my mind drifts to Josh. Where is he? He had wandered off during training, opting for a different regiment, and since then I haven't caught a glimpse of his striking brown hair.

As if to answer my thoughts, Josh rushes over, panting heavily as he wipes the sweat from his forehead with the back of his hand. He must've been doing physical training, most likely hand-to-hand combat.

After his defeat against Chase, he has never been the same. Part of him had died when his head hit the arena floor. It's as if someone has taken away a chunk of his soul, followed by the majority of his self-esteem.

He rarely smiles. He never takes compliments. Something has crushed his spirits, and I can feel my heart deteriorating just looking at him. It pains me to see someone in such a vulnerable and lifeless state without being able to help them.

The ache is almost unbearable. It tears at my heart strings; it savagely pulls apart my soul. And there is nothing I can do to ease the pain.

Josh opens his mouth in a belated gasp, as if he's about to form words, but his lips then press together and his expression turns rigid.

Last night had been the first time since the Alpha Trials Josh had acted like his old self, and something tells me that I will never be able to see that cheeky, dessert-loving side of my friend again.

My attention focuses in on Chase and his fighting gear. Gone is the red velvet cape and gold crown which laid on his short hair. Now in his sturdy clothes made for battle, including a belt stockpiled with an assortment of daggers and a long recently-forged sword, he looks poised to kill.

"What is the meaning of this?" he bellows at the top of his voice, mere metres from the rogue.

The rogue stays on the saddle of his horse. His hair is a thick, woven mess of murky vines, flying into his face as he opens his mouth to speak. For a rogue, he doesn't look too savage, but his face is still covered in a fair amount of healed white scars.

"Hunter, leader of the rogues, has officially declared war on Arla and King Chase of the Northern region," the werewolf speaks calmly, his voice carrying over the gathered crowd due to the gale. "There is no debate against this war. Whether you choose to ignore this announcement or accept our declaration, you will perish."

"Well, isn't this cheery?" Azra whispers so quietly, I am only just able to pick it up among the howling wind and mutters of other Arla residents.

I snort at her comment but, given the situation I find myself in, I quickly stop and furrow my eyebrows. "I thought that we were already at war?"

Azra shakes her head. "A war can only begin when it is declared by one of the sides. Chase didn't want to declare war immediately because he wanted to train for as long as possible until the rogues declared it first," she says in a hushed tone, constantly flicking her eyes around her to check that no one else can hear her words.

I nod. "Makes sense." But only partially. Any normal werewolf who had recently been introduced into such a community would think that we were at war the moment they attacked the city or when the brutes killed the previous king.

As I continue to study the male rogue, I notice that his body is very stocky, particularly his broad shoulders, reminding me of Titus's excessively large form.

My brain switches like an automatic rifle, and before I am unable to hit the kill switch, the rage kicks in like a roaring wildfire.

There's one outstanding reason why I hate the real rogues more than anything else on the face of this planet. The reason I have a passionate distaste for them is because of my old best friend, Cordia, back at Shadow Claw pack.

One day, when we were taking a trip to the Scarlet Bone pack to gather much needed supplies, Cordia had run off, chasing an artic wolf—a rare sight which was seen as a blessing. When we had caught up with the young girl, her body was mauled to shreds and her limbs strewn on the bloody snow. Her mutilated corpse hung like a puppet without strings. A note had been pinned to her crimson chest with a long and gruesome dagger.

The yellow piece of paper had read, "Never cross our territory again" in messy scrawl. There had been no question that it was the rogues. Only rogues could have performed such an ominous and heart-stirring slaughter on a child; only they had the capacity to be that heartless.

Butterflies erupt violently in my stomach as though it has been tainted with poison. I feel my body cramp and then abruptly wake up. The whole world flashes before my eyes like a crystal ball. I see the rogue in his corrupted saddle, his face bland yet seemingly holding a smirk that could chase any sane werewolf to hell.

I think of Cordia. I think of the previous king. And then I think of Titus, and no matter how much I try to close my eyes and deflect them from the rogue, all I can see when I stare into the real rogue's face is the man who ruined my life.

My hands feel numb as they fumble with whatever is unfortunate to lie in them. I don't realise that I've loaded an arrow into my bow until I take a deep, flustering breath, remembering what Azra taught me moments ago.

I hear a whizz as I release the bow string. For a second, everything blurs, and all I can see is the minimalistic figure of the rogue. All I can hear is the—for once—steady and rhythmic hammer of my heart. Thump, thump. Thump, thump.

Thump. This time, the noise isn't my heart.

My gaze focuses once more, the haze clearing in a blink. The rogue's body slackens, his faint smirk drops, and his huge figure falls to the ground, landing on the arrow stuck in his abdomen.

The rogue doesn't die immediately. He spits up blood onto the muddy floor and rolls over, taking his weight off the arrow. His tummy fluctuates like waves on the sea, moving up and down as he helplessly gasps for air. The relentless horse, missing its rider, neighs in dismay and begins to gallop off in the direction it came, leaving the expiring rogue to die without his animal companion.

I should be sorry but I'm not. Cordia is dead because of his kind, and we are stuck in this position because of them too. I wouldn't even be here if the kingdom 'didn't need a ruler so desperately.

Every single person in the courtyard stares at me in shocked silence, but only Azra is the one to comment on my rebellious stunt.

"Nice shot," she murmurs, even though my aim was sloppy and landed the blow a long ways away from the heart, where I was aiming.

Chase takes the opportunity to climb up onto one of the steps, his presence overwhelming us as he stands taller than anyone else in the crowd. "Prepare the guards. Twelve groups will be sent to protect and escort each outsider pack back to the castle. Half will be put into groups. The other half will stay here to protect us," his voice booms, resonating eerily across the courtyard-turned-battlefield. The people listen to their king intently. "We leave tonight."

Chase steps down, his expression as hard and unfathomable as a great white shark. Cobalt eyes focus on mine as he marches straight towards me.

Before I can jerk my arm from his reach, he grabs it and pulls me away from Azra and Josh so that they are unable to hear our conversation. He takes two seconds to blink before speaking in his predictable outraged tone. "What the hell was that for?"

I blink furiously. He of all people should know why I did what I had to do. It was just one less rogue to kill on the battlefield. He knows about my "anger issues'" and had so graciously explained last night about my fighting strategy.

I shrug my shoulders. "To let them know that we're at war."

CHAPTER TEN
Chaos

"Don't do anything stupid until I get back."
- Bucky Barnes, Captain America

I clench and unclench my jaw slowly as I walk purposefully through the snow, my feet sinking into the white flecks as I wade towards our destination. We are only five minutes away from the pack after a two-hour trek and my limbs felt like they are submerged underwater. The exhaustion means that I could no longer feel them.

If anyone tells you that werewolves don't get tired, they're wrong. We might have greater stamina than humans and other lifeforms, but we are not machines. We get tired, as any wolf would tell you after a long and laborious hunt.

We haven't shifted into our wolf forms either. The thin clothes that we wear that stays on when we shift is too thin to keep the cold out when we will supposedly arrive at our destination. We would not be able to carry the load of weapons strapped in our belts, either.

Tousling my thick brunette strands of hair over my shoulder, I glance to my right to see sturdy warrior werewolves flanking me and leading the parade. There are about fifteen of us, but what distresses me the most is that they are all male. All tower above my petite frame—apart from the heavily-loaded round male lumbering at the back—and their faces are lined with battle scars and stubble, some of which have grown out into beards.

The other problem is that Azra and Josh are not with me. They have both returned to their pack to escort them to safety, leaving me with the ruthless Chase who ordered me to escort the Scarlet Bone pack. I can understand why he wants me to lead this escort: The Scarlet Bone pack is the centre of trade and communication between werewolves and the human world, but it is also the closest to rogue territory. For all we know, the pack could be lying in ruins when we arrive.

I whip my head to my left, lightly shaking my head before my cheeks can become too crimson to look anywhere but straight ahead. God, I'm the most socially awkward person ever. Not that it matters anymore. This is about winning a war we are almost certain to lose, although Chase doesn't want to admit it. It's evident that it is near impossible to beat the unstoppable power of the wild rogues, especially when they have waited and built up their army over numerous tedious years.

A jet of water vapour pours into the air from my mouth, creating a small cloud before my glazed eyes. The world around me reflects the same icy pigment as my breath in the still night air, an incorruptible and unblemished blanket of snow laid perfectly on the fauna surrounding us. It's hard to think how easily the beauty will be destroyed by our laboured footsteps, but then that's what werewolves do; we destroy things.

We kill each other instead of uniting. We turn beautiful landscapes into battlefields. But more importantly, we torment each other. It's rare to find true friendship in this world, and even when you think you have found your one true mate, even they can turn their backs on you.

I let out a strenuous breath as I arduously make my way over a small hill, obscuring the view beyond. As soon as I reach the peak, I have to blink rapidly to ensure myself that I'm not hallucinating. Before me is one of the most beautiful sights I have ever seen. Sometimes, I'm glad that I 'didn't die just because I am able to experience irreplaceable spectacles such as this one.

Tinged with the eternal pink of dawn, a small cluster of brown wooden huts stand bravely in the middle of the valley below us. Clusters of werewolves move around happily in the dazzling torchlight, only revealing part of the village like a veil of mist. I see the glint of an auburn tinted face speaking to a group of other pack members, the early-risers sauntering around in a orange-dyed daze.

It's beautiful to see such harmony. Tears even threaten to fill my eyes as I spot three children in the limited light chasing one another, huge grins plastered on each of their faces.

And here I am about to shatter this tranquillity. They don't know that we're at war but they will soon. The Scarlet Bone pack has lived a peaceful life with connections to the human world, particularly trading weapons made with sturdy metal from the humans. Now, that peaceful lifestyle will be gone forever.

My feet move swiftly down the slope, gliding over the snow soaked ground like an infernal cloud. For once, I feel weightless as I allow a smile to creep onto my face.

All too soon, we reach the bottom of the slope, the forest breaking into bare terrain. All that stoops before us is the flat ground of the valley stretching for a mile across, and God only knows how far the river stretches until it reaches the sea.

Taking a deep breath through my nose, we step out into the unforgiving and bleak landscape, exposing ourselves to the pack before us. That is the good thing about the location of this pack; you can always see your enemies coming.

After five minutes of dragging my feet through the heavy snow, we finally reach the pack where another large werewolf greets us. I don't know why all warriors are so large, but it must have something to do with how much they train.

The guard werewolf gives me a cold, hard stare as his eyes burrow into my own. I can hear his brain click and whirr as he tries to figure out whether I am friend or foe. Finally, his lips move, forming words. "What do you want?"

I straighten myself, taking all emotion away from my face. Being second in command, I have to look tough. Look weak, and I will easily be overthrown.

"We're here to talk to your alpha," I mimic the words Chase told me to say when I arrived. I'm glad that I even remember them in the first place.

The man quizzically glances at each of the soldiers behind me in turn. His deep blue eyes obliterate the air between the warriors and him, terminating most of the doubt. Yet it's clear that he doesn't recognise any of the werewolves before him, and I have since removed my commander attire for the prolonged journey.

"What about them?" he questions, jerking his head in an unfashionable manner to the men behind me.

"Alpha King Chase sent us.'" I sigh. I knew that this wasn't going to go to plan, but hopefully I can get out of this situation without a fight by using my crap words. "Trust me, you'll understand when we tell you our situation but we cannot wait. We must see your alpha now."

The guard rolls his eyes, placing his spear behind his back. I didn't notice the weapon until the movement but it's nothing important, unless he decides to send it straight through my heart. "Fine. Follow me, and if you dare touch anything, you will be terminated."

"Lovely," one of the warriors from behind me murmurs, but I pretend that I didn't hear him. He's probably one of the two immature sixteen-year-olds sent with us to gain experience.

The bulging man before us saunters through the dark light, his shoulders swinging rhythmically with each step. From a metre away, it's easy to tell that he effortlessly reaches six feet, with wide shoulders and a body made for combat. It's no wonder why he's the protector of this pack. I hope for their sake that they have more warriors like him.

I almost walk into the man's rock-hard back as he stops and speaks through a thin layer of fabric obscuring the inside of a brown tent from the outside world. It's one of the few tents in the mix of huts and cabins, but it's by far the largest and the most luxurious, with recently replenished deer-hide.

"Alpha Alexsandra, there are some werewolves sent by the new Alpha King to see you," the man speaks just audibly through the material.

My ears cringe at the distinct and thunderous noise of fabric moving on fabric and then pick up the light but tough female voice through the tent. "Let them in."

The man slowly lifts up the thin cloth entrance of the shelter and I duck under cautiously, wondering what awaits me on the other side. The other werewolves attempt to follow me but I hold up my arm. "Keep an eye out while I talk to the Alpha," I instruct them. "I won't be long."

I hear the cloth settle behind me as I finally enter the room. It's nowhere near how I expected it to be. On the ground is a thick and luxurious carpet like the one in the castle, however this one is much more worn underfoot. Wooden furniture is laid neatly in the large space with a bed in the right hand corner and a chest of drawers, a table, and a chair in the other. It's clear that this is a permanent home, unlike the temporary living-quarters I have been used to with my rogue pack.

But the most startling yet beautiful thing in the room is the Alpha herself. I immediately take in her deep, perfectly tanned skin, but then my eyes fall on her hair. It's ruffled and messy, sticking out at irregular angles, yet the style seems to frame the woman's face perfectly. Tied into her tresses is a single feather hanging on her shoulder, guarded by the mass of hair falling just past her collarbone. Her eyes are large, brown, and not nearly as sharp or striking as my own. Her lips are pale and seem to melt into her skin, giving her yet another edge of mystical beauty.

116

Despite her stunning features, the woman only appears to be in her early twenties, perhaps late teens. It's strange to think that she is in control of the most important pack under the protection of Arla at such a young age. Moreover, the fact that she's female is refreshing. We live in a sexist society, and for a woman to be at the top proves that females are just as strong as men.

Her face, on the other hand, tells a different story. There's no sign of emotion. Her eyes are set like unbreakable diamonds. Just one glance from her makes it blatantly obvious that she's not one to be messed with.

"I presume that you are here to tell us that we're at war with the rogues and that we must leave with you immediately to go to Arla," the woman states as she stands firmly with her hands loosely hanging by her sides, her right hand resting carelessly on the weapon in her belt.

I am astonished by her words but try to hide the shock from my face. "Yes," I reply in the same tone of voice she had used herself.

The woman nods and looks at me with the same blank expression, as if she has never seen a she-wolf like myself before. Judging by the look in her eyes, I can tell that she's deciding whether I'm a threat or not. If she knew the version of me that existed two weeks ago, then my blood would already be sprayed on the canvas surrounding us.

I stretch out my arm as a sign of respect. This is one woman I do not want mess with. "I'm Alaska."

The woman nods, grabbing my wrist in a werewolf handshake. "My name is Alexsandra, but call me Alex."

After a few seconds, her grip relaxes and I allow myself to take a shaky breath as I slowly withdraw my arm. "You're right, the rogues declared war. We've been ordered to bring you back to Arla to protect you."

Alex paces around her tent, her delicate hands fluttering over the wooden backboard of her bed and then resting on the arm of the sofa placed permanently in the middle of the exquisite room.

Alex bows her head, her brunette locks moving perpendicular to the floor. "Yes, we know of their nature. We've spent most of our lives fighting them." Her voice still sounds bored, as if she's sitting through Chase's coronation for the second time.

I grit my teeth. Is she not going to sense the blatant hint that we need to leave? "We need to go, Alex. Now."

Alex shrugs her shoulders, as if she doesn't care what happens to her pack. What kind of alpha thinks like that? "Then you go. You as the second in sommand should know that we will never abandon our pack grounds for something as petty as a rogue war."

My eyebrows scrunch together before I can delay my action. "So you're willing for everyone in your pack to die? Are you insane?"

"No," Alex says as she pouts her lips. "We won't leave. This is our home, Alaska. You must understand that. If anyone needs to leave, it's you. As soon as they know you're here, they'll attack."

I bound over to her and look her straight in the eye. Despite my medium height, I'm still a few inches taller than her, allowing me to exert my dominance with more success. "I don't doubt that you can handle yourself. I'm sure you could kill me in less than a second if you decided to do so. But the rogues out there are nothing like you have experienced before. They will kill you; they will burn this place to the ground."

Alex raises an eyebrow.

I sigh and hang my head down and into my hand, trying to calm myself down. I then lift my head to look back at her, anger boiling through my veins like fire had met gasoline. "I've seen what they can do. They don't care who you are, how old you are, or how

118

important you are. They just kill.'"' I raise my voice, my face becoming a fascinating artwork of rage.

If I looked in the mirror at this moment in time, I wouldn't be able to recognise my own face. I inhale a few times, using a hand to scrape the hair out of my face before continuing. "They killed the previous king. When I came here years ago, they slaughtered my best friend all because she crossed their territory. She was only eight. Please tell me that you don't want the same fate for your pack."

Alex doesn't seem to comprehend my words, as if her ears are plugged into a different frequency. "They won't suffer that fate," she states, but not before a flicker of worry on her face casts doubt on her words. She raises her head, tentatively sniffing the air. She suddenly recoils, as if she has smelt poison. "Those bastards," she growls, finally dropping her serious face. "They're here. They must've waited for you to arrive."

I gulp. "Then we need to go. All of us."

The Alpha gazes at me as if I'm a toddler. Her jaded eyes and slack face give me the sense that she thinks I'm stupid. As if I'm drowning but haven't noticed.

"They could've attacked at any moment before you arrived, but they waited,'"' she says in realisation out of nowhere. Alex walks patiently over to wardrobe, opening it up to reveal an array of clothes on the left and a pile of weapons on the right. She carefully selects a sword from the rack, followed by a bow and a quiver of handmade arrows. "They must want a hostage to negotiate. After all, you're the second in command," she replies as she straps the sword to her belt. She smiles when she looks satisfied with her preparation. "You're the second most important person in the city."

I shiver. "It's not like I want to be."

Alex's eyebrows remain raised. "Well, whatever you think, you are the second in command to the King. They want you, and we will not give you to them."

I don't know how to respond, so I usher a quick, "Thank you.".

The corners of Alex's pale lips twitch up, but not enough to form a smile. The small gesture is more a sign of gratitude than friendliness. "Let's go."

The abrupt tearing of fabric causes us both to turn rapidly to face the door. The features that meet us are welcome, and I almost allow myself to sigh when I notice the Arla warriors standing at the entrance with the male from the Scarlet Bone pack who had escorted us.

"Alaska, the rogues are here," one desperately says, and as I glance at our small group, I see the fear infiltrating the huge werewolves's eyes. It's strange to see such strong men out of place due to a few rogues. "We need to get everyone and get out of here."

"I know," I utter and run out the tent.

To my left, someone screams. The sight before me is rejected by my eyes, the picture blurring with tears of sorrow and resentment.

No. No, this can't be happening, I tell myself, and pinch my arm to try and wake me up from the nightmare. We can't be too late.

Before me, the world is on fire. Tents burn as huge, ugly, and mutated werewolves lumber around with torches, setting anything in their sight alight. Another girl screams to my left, a piercing wail which is cut off so suddenly I don't have to guess what happened to her. War rages around us, and I spot one of Arla's own warriors fight off a rogue as he nears our group.

He's one of the younger members. His chubbier cheeks and less polished physique makes him appear only fifteen, but I know that he's actually sixteen. He doesn't stand a chance against the might of a rogue. Before the proper battle has even begun, I know how it's going to end.

"Get out of here! Go!" the boy yells as the rogue flips him over. I watch in horror as a sword is impaled into his stomach. He dies within seconds, a feeble fist flopping from the sword plunged into his stomach onto the gritty mud.

A strange noise echoes from my vocal chords. I can't tell what it's meant to signal at first, but the abnormal puff of air at the end makes it sound as though I'm distressed. In truth, I'm not only distressed; I'm horrified.

My eyes uncontrollably begin to water. He was too young. Maybe he was only a year younger than myself, but he did not deserve a death like that. No one did.

Alexsandra appears from the tent behind us and swiftly flings a knife at the murderer before us. The blade spears the rogue's skull and his distorted body falls on top of the teenager's.

"What are you still doing here?" Alex shouts as she speed walks towards our group, grabs me by the shoulders, and spins me around so that I'm facing a clear path out of the camp and back to the white flossed forest. "You need to go! I don't want them destroying our camp because you're here."

I feel bitterness building up in my chest, like fear intensifying into a nightmare. How ironic. I came here to save her pack from the rogues, but now I'm the sole reason that her camp is being set ablaze.

I force the nightmare away and wake myself up from the gruesome phantasm. "We're not leaving without you! We came to protect and save your pack, not leave it to get slaughtered."

Alex grabs me by my shirt, pulling my face towards hers. We're so close that I can feel her rhythmic breathing on my face. "We will not die. We are stronger than you think."

"I don't doubt that, but look around you. Do you really want your pack to be burnt to death? And even if you drive them off, you'll have nowhere left to live!" Alex looks at me with startled eyes and very quickly flicks them back to the battlefield. If she intends for me not to notice, then she has failed.

121

I of all people know that she wants to remain strong, and appear it too, but there are some situations where you run out of solid bricks to build up your walls. Mine were smashed down years ago, and I haven't bothered to pick the smashed up pieces since, but it is clear that Alex is not someone who will ever give up on stacking the fragments.

One of the warriors by my side suddenly jerks forward with his sword, driving through the chest of a rogue. The world slows before my eyes, the rapid tick tock of the clock slowing. I watch as the second hand jumps, the action taking seconds to complete. Finally, I am allowed to think, but my head is in such a mess, I can't tell the difference between cold and boiling hot.

"We don't have time for this," I mutter. My words appear to burn Alex and snap her back to reality. Her eyes harden and she clicks her jaw. "Look around us. We're losing. We need to go."

Alex stares at me with her steely gaze, her eye colour reflecting my own. Then, her brain clicks and the gears begin to whirr profusely. "Fine," she whispers, as if she is choking on her own words. She turns to the warrior from her pack. "Round up everyone on the east side. Me, Alaska, and half of the Arla warriors will round up the west."

"This way." Alex nods her head into the thick, black, and uninviting smoke. She grabs my arm and hauls me along through the well-trodden pathways between the dwellings.

A woman stumbles in front of us, coughing severely into her hand. I grab her arm, propping her up with my shoulder and aiding her to the other side of the dense and suffocating smog.

"Harper," the woman croaks, her throat dry from the smoke. I feel my eyes begin to tear up as the substance infiltrates my eyes.

"Shh," I say but the woman rips and tears at my hold like a rabid animal. She doesn't look old—no older than forty—but her face gives her an ancient visage, with multiple lines creasing her brow from stress. She's most likely a mother and Harper is her child.

The woman stares at me with big, pleading eyes. "Please, my mate . . . my child. They were in our tent . . ."

Alex comes to my aid, retrieving the woman from me. "Iris, stay calm. I'm sure Harper's okay. She's a clever girl. She knows what to do in situations like these. You have to come with us."

"No, no!" The woman—Iris—thrashes in Alex's arms, but the Alpha keeps a firm hold on her pack member. "Harper!"

Alex ignores the rant of the crying woman and turns to face me. Her hand points so quickly behind me, I don't notice her fingers moving until they're right in front of my face. "Alaska, behind you."

My body stills with some strange fear. I dare to turn around. The rogues are at least ten metres away but I know that it's too late to run; they have seen me. My feet are glued to the spot and won't obey my command to move; it's as if I'm paralysed.

A strange wave of confidence rushes over me like a tsunami, flushing all of my doubt away. I won the Alpha Trials. I have beaten Chase. Hopefully my anger can defeat these opponents as well.

The first one runs at me blindly, his bald head aimed towards my abdomen in an attempt to head-butt me. I hold my nerves as he charges, my cheeks flushing red from the effort of not moving my body. Finally, at the last second, I sidestep and swipe my sword across the man's body. He collapses in defeat. I stab him again in the back just to make sure that he is truly dead.

The second one is over me before I can react. His thick arms wrap around my fragile body and chucks it at the nearest dwelling as if I'm as light as air. My body hits the hard wood with a loud thud, sending thundering shockwaves soaring through my body, shaking my vision like the tremors of an earthquake.

I raise a hand tentatively in front of my face and blink as the fingers distort into branches. My eyes sting with water from the smoke. Luckily, I have hit a building which has not been set alight—yet.

I try to get on my feet but my legs crumble beneath me, leaving me crawling on the ground, my limbs still failing to find enough courage to stand. My vision unexpectedly blurs into a puddle of madness and soon I am unable to distinguish between the fire and the rage filling my vision.

Something gruesome and wet hits my face and a kick lands in my stomach. I rush to place a hand on the target zone of the blow, ache spreading through my body. "Pathetic," my opponent murmurs, but I am unable to locate him or the direction of his voice. All I can hear is a deep ringing in my ears and his voice haunting my mind. "You'll pay for what you've donez, traitor."

Traitor? I'm the traitor? I was never a true rogue in the first place. And how the hell does he even know who I am?

I grit my teeth and feel a sharp pain in my eyes, signalling that they have changed colour. "What did you call me?"

The rogue growls. I still can't make out where he is but at least he hasn't kicked me for a second time. "You heard me," he says before pausing for a second, "traitor."

"It's Ali, b*tch."

You just messed with the wrong girl, arseh*le. I leap to my feet as quickly as I can. The movement is not perfect and I stumble forwards due to the momentum of the thrust provided by my muscles, but I manage to stay upright.

I take a knife from my belt and blink away the haze in my eyes. It still looks as through I am gazing through a plastic screen that has condensed water droplets formed on the smooth surface, and the plastic is tinted scarlet.

The rogue is standing in front of me before I can properly snap out of my dizziness. He's how you expect the usual rogue to look; broad-shouldered, with multiple scars and fresh cuts, and a

124

huge body which looks capable of anything. Oh, and let's not forget the shoulder length tangled mess of hair and beard.

I notice his exposed frame and almost smile to myself. Rogues may be good fighters but they sure as hell can be stupid.

I lash out with my knife and he raises his arm to block my blow. I swing my arm back as he attempts to block another attack, leaving his abdomen completely unprotected.

"I'm not a traitor. I wasn't even a proper rogue," I hiss through my teeth as I release the knife from my grip and drop it to my other hand that's near his stomach. "I'm packless, dickhead."

The rogue staggers backwards as I bring the knife to his abdomen. His face contorts into a look of shock as his body slackens, blood pooling from his mouth in a crimson waterfall.

I stand there, panting as I retrieve my fallen sword from the ground. But as soon as I open my lips, I am forced to shut them as the smoke takes all the moisture away from my mouth. Coughing, I lean over and sway towards pathway where Alex and the Arla warriors had been standing.

All that is left are the ghosts of their existence. The heavy and thick smoke has swallowed them whole. And in their place, stands a girl. The third rogue.

If I were in a cartoon, my eyes would be standing on stalks, elongated metres from my head. But this is not a cartoon, so I stare instead.

Never in my life have I seen a female rogue. I don't want to sound sexist but from what I have been taught about rogues, they never let females fight because they are deemed "too weak" to do so. My arse, they are too weak. I won the Alpha Trials, and I am nowhere near the strongest female I know.

Not only is she a girl, but she is beautiful as well. Her hair is light brown in colour that flows in waves down to her ribs, and her face is adorned with large azure eyes. Unlike Azra's sharp and gorgeous features, this girl has a much sweeter look, with a softer

125

nose and long, angelic eye lashes. The only thing not angelic about her face is the smirk plastered on it.

She smiles at me sympathetically, somehow frowning at the same time. Even though she is pretty, the facial expression creates an ominous shadow over her face and dehumanises her features.

"What?" she enquires at my shocked expression. "You weren't expecting a girl?"

I shake my head. "Rogues don't let girls fight."

The girl's smile grows, splitting her face into two equal halves. "Well, that's the perks of being Hunter's sister, although he doesn't let his mate anywhere near battle. Shame, really. She's good with a crossbow." The girl then rolls her eyes, taking a machete from her belt. "Whoops, I probably told you too much, but I guess that doesn't matter. You'll be dead in a minute."

"You can say what you want b*tch, but I'm not dying today," I growl, the burning sensation in my pupils telling me that my irises are still a metallic pigment; that I'm on the brink of transforming. I'm angry at her words, but I'm also startled that Hunter—whom I remember being the leader of the rogues—has a mate, or even a sister.

The girl twitches her lips. "We'll see about that."

A battle cry cries out from her mouth as her face becomes a mask of anger and bloodlust. She licks her lips as she pushes herself into the air, machete in tow. Luckily, I'm at an advantage with my longer weapon but she appears to be much more nimble and agile than I first anticipated.

The girl brings down her weapon in an arc, and I swerve to the side, feeling the rush of parting air next to my arm where I had stood seconds ago. The brunette lets out a shriek of frustration and turns around, her chest heaving with frustration. I guess that she's the same age as me, but with her creased face and features, she looks like the oldest werewolf I have seen in my entire life.

Swiftly, before I have time to react, the girl swings her sword and manages to cut a deep gash across my arm. I grit my teeth, a whistling breath rattling through the hollow bones as I force myself not to cry out in pain.

So this was her game, attack when I'm least expecting it.

"What?" She looks at me with fake concern. "You weren't expecting that?"

She expects a reply, so I don't give her one. I swipe my sword precisely across her body, but her own machete meets mine before I can cause any real damage. I push my sword forwards into her body using all the might I can muster from my arms, but she manages to keep the blade away from her body. My cut feels like it's been incinerated by a flamethrower, but I don't give up.

"Hunter asked for me to deliver you alive as a hostage, but I don't think he'll mind if I 'accidentally' slip my machete into your heart," she sneers, our faces so close that our noses are only millimetres apart. Fire swirls around us in a tornado, yet I do not focus on the smoke suffocating my lungs or the heat burning my skin.

Her sneer sends a shiver plummeting down my spine but I ignore it and latch my blade onto hers using the handle. Using all of my stored strength, I clench my teeth together and tear the blade from the girl's grip.

The machete flies over my shoulder and into the fire engulfing a dwelling behind us. There's no way she is going to get her weapon back. I finally have the upper hand.

"Clever," she says and, as quick as a lightning bolt, punches me on the jaw. I blink, my mouth open in shock. How did she move so fast? "But I'm only just getting started!"

This girl is getting on my nerves. She has one of those unlikeable and annoying personalities which you can't avoid, nor is she a nice person. I don't picture myself as the nicest person in the world but at least I don't go around telling everyone that I'll kill them the moment I meet them.

This girl is also cocky and arrogant. She's what you expect the most stuck up person in the pack to be like; a b*tch.

127

She throws another quick punch at my face. I am able to curve my back but not in time. Her fist connects with my face and I feel the crunch of my nose being displaced. I whine at the sudden wave of pain, but I am quick to slash with my blade. It finally connects with her leg.

The metal slices deep into her muscle, and—by some miracle—manages to miss any major arteries.

"You b*tch!" the she-rogue whines as her left leg collapses to the ground, leaving her standing on one leg. Her face is no longer contorted with excitement but with pain instead. The face that she wears doesn't look like something that belongs among her features.

I sigh. "I can say the same to you."

"He'll kill you if you kill me," she warns as she hobbles backwards. Her good leg loses balance and she topples over onto the mud scattered with dilapidated grey pigment of ash. "I swear to God, he will kill you."

I frown at her. "Unlucky for you, I don't believe in a God."

Her azure eyes widen with realisation before she releases an animalistic cry which churns through the inferno surrounding us. "Go on then. Get it over with. Kill me."

I gulp.

"No," I state calmly, the smoke flying into my mouth and ridding it of moisture. "I'll leave that to the flames," I finish and bring the hilt of my sword down against her temple. She falls before I can complete my action. "Burn in hell, b*tch."

I feel like a rock has been lifted off my chest, just for a boulder to take its place. I don't want to be like this person; a killer.

I wish I wasn't a freaking second in command. I wish that I was still back at my "rogue" camp and that Chase had never lead the attack to wipe us out. I wish that none of this had happened. Then maybe, just maybe, I would be normal. Well, as normal as a werewolf could get. But this is war, and getting blood on my hands is inevitable.

Your fight is not over yet, Alaska, I remind myself. As I gaze around at the plumes of soot and red-hot flames, I realise that I am trapped in a maze of fire and that there is no way to escape. No matter where I look, each path is blocked and any exit is showered in crimson.

"Dad!" I hear the voice in the distance, but it's close enough to reach. "Someone, help! Please! Help!"

I sprint towards the desperate voice, choking on the air which has turned acidic. My legs move too quickly for my body and I almost stumble as I run blindly into the flames.

"Hello?" I shout back over the cracking of the hungry pyre.

"Help!" the voice comes from a clearing and I spot a log cabin ten metres from where I stand that is heavily burning. My heart speeds up with exhilaration and thumps continuously as I make my way towards the wooden handle. "Someone, please help me!"

I curse when I see that the door is already on fire. Taking a deep breath, kick down the door and burst into the room in a shower of sparks and embers. The interior is beautiful. The seats are made of wooden tree trunks, cut horizontally to show the rings captured within the bark. A bed lines the right side of the small cabin and a large diamond-shaped rug lays across the wood grain. That is one half of the room. The other half of the room is a cloud of light.

In the middle of the room is a girl reaching out into the flames. She screams as she reaches into the yellow glare but quickly withdraws her arm as the flames lick her skin and leave the limb a melted mess.

"Dad!" the girl cries. I can't see her face but her posture is small and her curly hair is neatly done into a ponytail. She only looks about nine years old from the back, and her childish clothes and lack of weapons give me the impression that my guess is near accurate.

I rush over to her and scoop her up in my arms. Her body jolts with surprise but her limbs soon relax in my arms.

"Shh," I whisper gently in her ear. "It's okay. You're going to be okay. We just need to get out of here."

The girl turns towards me and all I can see is an evaporating stream of tears. "My dad was sleeping and-and he's still in there," she whines and begins to thrash against my arms. She points to the flames with her boiled arm.

Instead of running towards the fire as the girl wishes, I run away from it. I pick up my courage to try and run through the burning doorway. I cover my hair with one hand and the girl with my other and surge through the door.

I land the other side unscathed, but it's only the first obstacle of many I have to face. The inferno around us has since grown, the tents collapsing into heaps of ashes and white-hot remains. I see the outline of a skeleton in one tent and the burning body of another beside it.

And finally, after days of battling the torment, I can no longer take it. We could have saved these people. Instead, we let them burn.

Only now do I realise the truth; we aren't werewolves fighting for the right cause. Or people trying to do the best for others. We are only doing what we have to in order to survive. We are only saving our own skins. And we are all monsters for being so selfish.

And for what? For territory. That's what the rogues wanted. Power and territory.

"We need to go," the girl in my arms cries, snapping me back to reality.

I look at her and her darker, unblemished skin. "Are you Harper?"

The girl nods, and I show her my best smile. She raises the corners of her mouth as a response, but no words form on her lips.

"Okay, Harper, I want you to hold on to me as tightly as you can," I say as calmly as I can be, even though my organs are gradually shutting down and all my bodily functions are giving up on me. "Can you do that?"

Harper nods once again, never breaking eye contact. Her eyes hold the strange sensation of fear disguised by courage but her body shows no signs of that fear. I don't want to think about what's going through her mind. She just watched her father get burnt alive.

"Good," I state as she tightens her arms around my neck, almost strangling me. And with that, I begin to run into the skyscrapers of light, searching for the safety of the snow, although I know that wherever I go, I will never be safe. None of us will.

CHAPTER ELEVEN
Scars

"Everyone has a breaking point. If you push far enough, you'll find it."
- Unknown

Dull cobblestone walls close around me before I can blink. The journey has been short, and I was lucky enough to emerge from the fire unscathed apart from a few minor scratches. Harper, on the other hand, has suffered a severe burn down her whole right arm. Although werewolves see scars as marks of bravery, Harper would see her burn as a blemish that makes her unattractive and unpleasant to look at. Any nine-year-old shouldn't be made to feel like that at such a young age.

As I continue to confidently stumble forwards, I feel empty, like I'm just wearing my skin but there's nothing inside of me. I can't hear my heart or feel the constant churning of my starving stomach. I feel like a balloon ready to burst. I feel as though my head is about to explode.

The Alpha Trials wasn't enough to break me on its own, but the burning of the Scarlet Bone pack has finally triggered the raw emotions concealed within me.

"Alaska." Alex shakes my arm but I ignore it focus my gaze ahead, piercing through the barricades before me. I have to find Josh and tell Chase the news. We're going to take those b*tches down and I don't care how. No one leaves me this vulnerable and gets away with it.

132

"Alaska, please, I need to talk to you," Alex pleads from behind me but my legs mechanically carry me deeper into the castle. I still refuse to turn around and decide to wave my hand instead. "Not right now, okay? I'm sorry, I just need to talk to Chase," I say, my voice letting on that I am on the brink of tears. And for once in my life, it's true. The salty water droplets have gathered up in my eyes, threatening to spill at any moment in the near future.

I climb the steps that lead up to the throne room. The guards let me through without giving a second glance at my crumbling shape. I don't want them to see me like this—or anyone else, for that matter—but it doesn't look like I have a choice. I need to see Josh so that he can cheer me up with his crappy sense of humour. Although I hate to say it, I need to talk to Chase as well.

I finally reach the throne room, which—to my surprise—is full of other werewolves with a distinctive scents. Looking at the pattern of stern, blank faces and muscular physiques, there is no question as to who these people are. The Alphas.

Azra is the first to spot me through the crowd. I know that she's not an alpha, but she's there for Josh. After the Alpha Trials, she has earnt respect from many of the other werewolves within this very room, so no one will question her presence either.

Azra runs up to me and stops before she can hug me. She studies my face like it's the most fascinating painting she's ever seen, her gaze burrowing deeper into my soul. I hope that what she sees isn't the cracked remnants of the person who once existed.

"Alaska." She sighs but then notices the glint of water studding my eyes like jewels. "Are you okay?"

I shake my head and, for the first time in my life, push her away. "I'm fine. I-I need to talk to Josh," I whisper. I can feel her body tense from the pure isolation radiating off of me but I don't have time to feel bad. Azra is an incredible person, but she's not the werewolf that I want to talk to at this moment in time.

"I'm here," a voice speaks solemnly from behind me. He must've seen me brush Azra away. I know that he's more protective over Azra than anyone else.

Congratulations, Alaska, you just pissed off your only friend.

I turn so slowly it feels like I'm moving through water, the dense and pressurizing liquid forcing my body to take hours just to turn. An exasperated sigh escapes my mouth as I battle the currents, the water filling my eyes and drowning them with tears.

I don't realise that I'm crying until my legs start running out of the room and into a separate corridor that leads to the king's chambers. I don't want to be here but there's nowhere else to flee, and whatever part of my mind has taken over, it's one that forced me to come here.

A hand catches the back of my jacket, pausing my legs in midstride. My mind is still whirring like the constantly flaring sun but my legs have given up.

"Alaska?" he speaks gently. This time, I turn so quickly I almost slip on the polished wooden floors below us—the velvet carpets did not line this corridor.

I jump into Josh's arms before he has a chance to step away from me. I grip my arms behind his back, squeezing so tightly that he lets out a laborious breath, as though I'm breaking every bone in his body. My legs dangle weakly on the floor and I bury my head in the side of his neck. Surprisingly, my head fits perfectly into the crook of his neck, like we're two puzzle pieces fitting together.

I can't see Josh's face, but I can imagine what it looks like; his deep mocha eyes wide in astonishment and his eyes watering. He has always had a soft spot when someone else is crying and he, just like everyone else, has never seen me cry before.

We have been in this position before, and he had told me to draw strength from my heart to keep my blood pumping endlessly around my body. For a time, I've done that. I looked into the fathomless depths of my soul to find my thoughts scattered.

134

Now, there is no heart left for me to turn to. After the horrifying two weeks I have endured here, it has broken me. Soon, I won't be able to repair myself.

"I can't do it, Josh," I sob into his shoulder as his arms begin to loosen around my body. "I-I can't. I saw a whole village burned to the ground. I saw people being burnt alive. I saw a child lose her father."

You'd have thought that being a werewolf would've prepared me better for life. Being exposed to death daily, killing someone isn't far from the werewolf norm. Most have blood on their hands. But it still doesn't sit well with me. I have morals my father taught me, and not upholding them feels like a slap in the face.

Josh rubs a soothing hand down my back but then thrusts me away from him so abruptly that my back hits the wall behind me, creating a loud, echoing thud on the rock. His eyes holds sympathy but he blinks, and any sign of sympathy dies with it. His face hardens, his jaw suddenly appearing sharper and his eyes more angular, like slits. He looks slightly monstrous with his dark pigmented eyes and shadowed face in the limited light, but I know that he did not intend to appear like this. He intends to snap me out of my daze and mould my heart back into its correct shape.

He strides towards me, and I back against the wall in response. "Alaska, wake up. This is not you," he lectures me as he snaps his fingers in front of my face. His words are quick and harsh, rattling through my brittle bones. "The Alaska I know is stronger than this. She won the Alpha Trials. She beat Chase, and came out the other side stronger than ever. She killed a rogue messenger without batting an eye. The Alaska I know is a warrior, and I know that she's still in there."

I gulp, liquid from my nose running into my mouth, mixed with salty tears. "You don't understand, Josh." My tears begin to fall more rapidly, as if five years of not crying has finally caught up with me. "I'm broken."

Josh steps even closer, so close that he is able to grab my hands and hold them in his own. His thumbs draw soothing circles on my scarred skin, but it barely lightens my mood. "No," he speaks very gently, pushing a strand of hair away from my face after releasing one of my hands. It then goes to cup my cheek, running his thumb over the skin. "You're not broken. Ali, just because you cry doesn't make you weak. In fact, even the strongest warriors cry. Tears are a measurement of your bravery. And your scars, each of them tell a story of how you survived. Of how you were stronger than your opponent. It's okay to cry if you allow it to be okay. There's nothing wrong with showing a little emotion. It's the part that makes us human."

I wipe away the tears from my eyes, the emotions finally ebbing away. Josh is right, I'm still here. I just need to resurface and look at the world with a different perspective. Then, against all odds, I laugh. "Thanks for the lecture, Josh."

"Alaska Morgan, you are the strongest person I have ever known." His words cause me to smile inwardly, although I doubt my face projects the emotion the way it should. "If anyone can get through this, it's you. I know you didn't ask for any of this, but you're doing amazing." And with his final words, he leans in and places his lips on my own.

Startled by his sudden action, I push him away, his eyes wide in shock. What, so he thinks that he can just kiss me and get away with it? No way, arseh*le.

Maybe I do have feelings for him, but with my messed up past, I constantly find it difficult to differ between friendship and love. But right now, I do not like him. Not like that.

"Ali—" Josh begins but I cut him off by slapping him hard in the face. I turn so sternly that I almost slip once more but manage to gain my balance in the fear that I will embarrass myself even more if I fall.

"And she's back . . ." I hear Josh murmur from behind me. I can sense that he's smiling from the light tone of his voice.

Did he just kiss me to snap me out of my daze? Did he steal my first kiss just to sort out my problems, which I had finally figured out how to solve? He's still my best friend but what he did just put a wedge between us which will be hard to move. I feel my chest expand with each angry breath. Fuming from the events that happened, I race out of the corridor, leaving Josh behind to think about he's done. Well, at least I know how he feels. I also know that he will leave my room so that I can sort out my own feelings for him. It will take time, and he knows that.

I am a warrior. Warriors do not cry. I repeat to myself as I race back out of the narrow walls and back into the huge room where the alphas are crowding around a large table in the centre of the cavern. There are twelve alphas in total, including Chase himself, and two females. I spot Alex on the other side of the huge oak slab, waving her arms as she effortlessly explains something to the other members surrounding it.

"Alaska," Chase's voice cuts precisely through the air like a dagger. Feeling a growl rip from my vocal chords unwillingly, I indignantly seal my lips shut as quickly as I can before I can embarrass myself further. "Come join us," Chase says and I see him gesture to the table as I look in his direction. In my absence, his jawline grew a light stubble, and his face already looks tired, with haunting eyebags and sharper features.

I nod and walk over to the wooden piece of furniture, sitting next to Chase before he continues talking about what do with the rogues. Only when I'm right in front of the bench do I realise what is on it.

Maps from the human world are strewn over the surface, concealing the wooden grain. There are a dozen or so blue highlighted areas in different parts of the Alaskan forest, labelling each pack. Towards the North a huge crimson blotch, as if someone had accidentally spilt an ink bottle onto the paper. "Rogues" is written on the red blot in black block letters, causing me to gulp. The red area is twice the size of the blue area surrounding the kingdom of Arla.

I hold up my hand in front of Chase, pausing his words which I haven't even bothered to listen to. There's one piece of information he needs to know before we are to attack; one piece of data which could mean the difference between winning and losing. The difference between life and death.

Chase rolls his eyes, agitated by my hand held in front of his face. "What is it?" he growls at me, but I raise my index finger to shush him and I use my other index finger to study the map in more detail. The rogue territory is surrounded by mountains, near where my own group of "rogues" had lived.

I wonder where they all are now. Are they safe? Or have the rogues killed them all for trespassing? I shiver when I realise I might never see them again.

"Hunter, the leader of the rogues, has a mate," I state and, for some reason, Chase appears to have a blank face. His features drop any sign of human intelligence and emotion. "He has a mate," I repeat in an attempt to make more sense to Chase.

Why is he acting so confused? The advantage is obvious. Chase doesn't have a mate, but Hunter does.

In a blink, the Chase I know is back with his steely gaze and jawline sharp enough to cut through bone. His face snaps to my own, his blue eyes locking on the soft cocoa of my irises. His face lights up as he parts his lips in an attempt to smile and for the first time ever I see a "happy" Chase.

Long gone are the prominent eye bags; long gone are the tense fingers and slumped shoulders; long gone are the wrinkles of anxiety across his forehead. Instead, his features are replaced by calmness, and in those few seconds he looks like he's about to hug everyone standing in a ten metre radius. I hope he doesn't because I'd be the first person he would hug, which is a terrifying thought.

Chase's smile widens as he opens his mouth to speak, exposing his perfectly lined teeth. "Tomorrow, we train," he announces. Although his face suggests that he's slightly ecstatic, his voice does not hint any sign of emotion. He's like a carnival with an array of bright, luminous lights but with no sound or cheery music.

"On Wednesday, a group of fifteen werewolves led by Alaska will enter the rogue territory and attempt to kidnap Hunter's mate," Chase gave out his orders triumphantly, like he has won a participation medal as he points to a location on the blue and red blotted map. The small area his finger finally comes to rest on is a tiny black square on the edge of the rogue territory.

I blink. I'm leading it? This is news to me.

"Alaska, you will take the group through here. It's an old human mine that was shut down years ago, but there's another entrance in the centre of the rogue territory." He gulps, and only then do I get a sense of the danger he is putting us in.

I think about the coldness and how soggy the walls of the pitch black mine. I have been frequently told about how dangerous mines are by other werewolves during my upbringing. A shiver runs down my spine, like an icy water droplet running down a window pane in the clutches of winter.

"If you navigate the tunnels correctly, you'll end up a mile away from the main rogue camps."

Alex impatiently taps her fingers on the other side of the table, my heightened hearing able to pick up the rhythmic thudding with each pat against the material. "May I ask how you know all of this?" she enquires, a frown ridden across her face.

Chase nods. "An insider."

Alex does not look pleased with his answer, as if she's expecting more information, but she does not press him for further details. She withdraws her hand from the table, her fingers no longer melodically tapping the wood.

"Two days, Alaska. That's all you have to train," Chase says to me. "If you're okay to do this, that is."

All heads collectively turn in my direction, numerous pairs of eyes in varying shades of colours gazing at me thoughtfully.

Some of the alphas stare at me like I'm a weak, seventeen-year-old girl. Others, such as Alex, look at me with respect, their heads held high and hands clasped in front of them.

I can't help but smirk faintly. Despite my partial fear of the dark and the thought of the suffocating mine on top of trying to kidnap Hunter's mate who is probably the most protected person in the whole rogue territory, I don't want to appear weak. I'm a warrior. Warriors do not cry.

"Count me in."

CHAPTER TWELVE
Storm

"I run from wolves tearing into me without teeth."

- Wolves Without Teeth, Of Monsters And Men

A cool breeze gathers in the courtyard, blowing across the cobblestone and whipping my delicate brunette tresses into my face, momentarily blinding me. The courtyard is lined with werewolves, each huddled in their own unique jacket to avoid the winter chill.

Chase stands in front of us, his red cloak hanging precariously off his shoulders and his arms pressed firmly to his sides. To everyone else, his face appears blank and expressionless, but I know that the sullen look in his eyes signals that he's worried. He's worried that the plan will fail.

"Good luck," the King speaks to me and the other fourteen werewolves standing close behind me. I can't see their faces but I can imagine them: strong in the dawn of the task that will either result in death or success. Even from ten metres away, I can spot the strange gold flecks glittering solemnly in Chase's eyes. They are like minuscule drops of forbidden sunshine, trapped eternally in his gaze. Today they particularly stand out, and as I stand patiently, I count four of them in one eye and six in the other. It's strange, but I have nothing better to do, and it distracts me from the dangerous task ahead of us.

I bow my head at him. "Thank you," I utter quickly as a reply. Normally, I would've rolled my eyes and told him that I didn't need it, even though I know I did, but that isn't a good idea in front of a crowd of his people.

I gaze back into his wondrous eyes and see something I have rarely spotted within the depths of his irises; worry. No, not worry—he's scared.

Scared that I won't come back or scared that his plan will fail? Whatever the answer is, it drains all remaining hope out of my body like a tumbling rockslide, cascading to the ground in a hopeless pile. If Chase is scared that something will go wrong, then he's almost ninety-nine percent sure that it will fail.

I tilt my head behind me, spotting the rest of my group bowing their heads to our king in respect. In all honesty, Chase isn't a bad king at all. He's a strong leader who does what is in the best interest of his people, and no one has challenged his rule yet, which I take as a good sign.

With one final glance at the crumbling city walls and the plain grey tiles below me, I take a deep breath to diminish my fear. The oxygen runs through my veins like a tsunami, making my cells buzz with a faint electrostatic feeling. Each footfall sends a jolt of electricity running up my limbs, spiralling into my bloodstream and settling as faint hope.

"Alaska!" Chase blurts out suddenly. I whip my head around, wondering why he called my name.

I raise an eyebrow, unsure of what he is going to say next. "Yes?"

Chase's lip quivers, as if he is shivering. "Please be careful," he mutters. For once, I think that he is genuinely worrying about me.

I show him a faint smirk. "When am I not?" And with my last remark hanging in the air like the severed chord attaching a puppet to its puppeteer, I saunter out of the castle walls and into the beyond.

The group follows behind me in pursuit as we trudge through the light dusting of snow. It wisps around my ankles like weightless feathers parted from the creature they originally belonged to.

Vibrant emeralds and dilapidated greens lie hidden beneath the veil of snow, the white powder suffocating the branches of the trees as they sag towards the frostbitten ground. The world is cloaked in beautiful white. This is the one thing I love about winter.

The harsh crunching of snow being compressed alerts me to the presence of a running werewolf. I sigh as the footsteps finally stop when they're beside me. Using my peripheral vision, I am able to pick out the dark eyes and messy brown hair that I have grown accustomed to in the past few weeks.

"Josh?" I question, my eyebrows furrowing.

Josh waves in a childlike manner. "Yes, that's my name."

I roll my eyes at him, watching as he smiles at me. "What the hell are you doing here?" I snap, my words perhaps a bit too harsh. "I told you to stay with Azra."

Josh shakes his head as his hand carefully checks for the knife in his belt. "You really thought that I'd sit there and wait for you to return with the thought of you getting killed?" Josh raises a bushy eyebrow at me questioningly but it only causes me to roll my eyes once more.

"Yes," I state through gritted teeth. Ever since we had kissed, our conversations have been more or less normal, but as soon as the topic comes up, we both go quiet. It's a strange thinking that my best friend has kissed me. and I'm still pissed off by that.

"You clearly don't know me then." Josh exhales loudly. He stops and I stop as well, coming face to face with him. I swiftly cross my arms over my chest, narrowing my eyes at him. Josh takes a step forwards, resting his hands on my shoulders as if I'm a child, but I don't shrug them off.

143

"Alaska, when you first came into the dining room during the Alpha Trials, I made myself a promise to protect you. I don't know why—we hadn't even talked—but I knew that you were different," he speaks clearly, and I watch as his mouth bravely forms each word, his lips twitching for each syllable.

My eyes are still narrowed at him but I drop my arms clumsily to my sides. "I don't want you getting hurt, Josh," I begin. "Go back now, before it's too late," I finish and ball my hands into tight fists as my legs voluntarily jog after the group of werewolves who walked past our argument without even waiting for their so-called "leader."

Yet again, the snow crunches under his feet as he regains his place by my side. "I'm not going anywhere," Josh says, his tanned face focusing on the challenge ahead of him.

Before us stands a great mountain with snowy peaks and the odd sliver of rock underlining the area where an avalanche has happened. It's the same mountain which stood next to the Scarlet Bone pack—the place where we are supposed to be going, and the one place I never want to return to.

Harsh sunlight cascades around the trees like a falling curtain, and I can't help but notice the way the delicate snow reflects the piercing light. I take in a deep breath, filling my lungs with clean air, the scent of pine needles and animal hide pinching my nose. Without realising it, I become absorbed in the beautiful world around me. The towering trees; the deserted landscape stretching out before us like an ancient glacier; the ice forever shifting on an endless journey towards the pull of gravity.

In fact, I have been so absorbed in my surroundings that I don't notice the darkness pouring out of the forest like a massive wave produced by the ocean after a hurricane. Long and stretched out shadows are slowly being etched across the scene as the final glimmers of sunlight fade, the limbs of trees elongating into ruthless teeth and claws. Many people think that the forest is alive

144

and buzzing during the day but it's actually during the night when the habitat chirps with a strange, ominous life.

A cool object is slowly pressed into my hand and I tentatively look down to see Josh's slim yet muscular hands push a metal bar into my own. I rub the patterned surface with my thumb, finding a small bump on the metal. I click it and almost jump out of my skin as the path before me is illuminated by the bright rays of torch light.

"What the hell?" I question, still in shock at the object in my grasp. "Where did we get torches from?"

Josh scrunches his nose as if he's a child. In that moment, I want to sprint up to him and give him the largest hug I can muster, but I don't. There's still an awkward air settling between us. "It's from Alex. Someone from her pack had them in their rucksack when they fled from the pack grounds. She figured we would need them in the tunnel."

Normal Alaska would've said something snarky along the lines of "If I was running for my life, I would definitely think 'oh let's get some torches while we're at it.' " But this isn't normal Alaska. Nor is it normal Josh.

Whatever the kiss has done to us, it has diminished our friendship slightly, but it's still my last shining beacon of hope. I have no one else except Azra but they came as a pair. If I lose Josh, I will lose Azra too. Then I will truly have no one—unless you want to call Chase a friend which quite frankly, I do not.

Instead, the strange Alaska mutters, "She was right."

Josh tilts his head towards me, turning on his own torch. I don't know how long the batteries would last for, but I hope that they will at least keep the torches lit for the duration we are in the mines.

"We're here," a gruff voice states. I blink to clear my vision as a looming cave comes into sight as we finally reach the top of the hill we are climbing up, our eyes cast down into the valley below. The night has descended fully, leaving the snow suffocated world in

145

a diminished view. The opening to the mine is an outline of splintering wood, with a pitch black hole leading into the unknown.

"You know the route, right?" the same man asks and I slowly nod my head.

"We take the second left then the first right, and we should arrive by then. The mine is rarely used, so there isn't that many paths to take," I say matter-of-factly. Josh raises an eyebrow. "Chase made me memorise it," I answer to his strange look.

Josh sighs, flaring his nostrils in the process. He doesn't mutter another word as he begins to descend. With a light flutter of my eyelashes, I follow after the group. Even though I'm supposed to be the leader, it doesn't feel like it, and I'm glad for that.

I don't think twice about my slight fear of the dark as we are plunged into the endless tunnel. There are only three torches in the group, which cast yellow rays of light across the dank mine. The walls are slick with water that roll down the jagged walls in tainted droplets, appearing green against the faded rock.

The walls seems to press on me as we continue walking, every breath sending an icy flood of water into my lungs. I rub my arms to try and warm myself up but it doesn't work. Instead, I bite my lip to divert my thoughts from the dropping temperatures.

The cave walls continue to narrow, causing my breathing to quicken with a slight jolt and feel as though all the oxygen in my lungs has been used up. How long will it be before I don't have enough air to stay standing?

Time blurs into a whirlpool of amber light and slimy rock, and each new point in the cave looks exactly the same as the previous points had done. The world is a hurricane of stone and granite, my head pounding as I try to figure out where we are and whether we have gone the correct way.

Finally, just when the torment was about to get to me, I walk into someone's back and nervously look up to see that I had walked into the sturdy back of one of the warrior werewolves accompanying me on this mission. He turns back, his harsh gaze

146

meeting my own before his eyes flick back to the entrance ahead of us.

I sigh in relief, spotting the faint glimmer of crimson torches burning in the night. The others quietly turn off their torches and I am soon to follow, placing the metal object in the belt around my waist where the rest of my weapons are.

"Is this it?" I ask, only to receive blank stares. I was the person who was supposed to lead them in the first place and I hadn't even accomplished that.

A smooth hand shakes my arm, the skin tingling under the man's touch. "Alaska, are you okay?"

I gulp. No, I'm not okay, but only because my fear of the dark and small spaces has gotten the better of me. I throw Josh a smile to try and persuade him that everything's alright, "Yeah, why wouldn't I be?"

"You're hyperventilating," he points out and that's when I realise how quickly my chest is rising and falling, as if possessed by a mutant who can run at the speed of light.

"Oh," I mutter and immediately try to slow my breathing rate. I succeed after a minute and watch curiously as everyone else turns their attention to me. I flick my hair over my shoulder and confidently place my hands on my hips. I might be the only girl here, but I'm stronger than they all realise—at least, I hope I am. "Is everyone ready? This has got to be quick. Hunter's mate will be in the main dwelling, which I'm hoping is easy to spot. Try to blend in with the rogues when we enter their camp. You know what they act like," I instruct, still gaining some clueless stares. I roll my eyes. Wasn't I clear enough? "Just follow my lead."

I don't give them time to think over my words and swiftly wind my hand around the grip of my sword, drawing it from its sheathe with satisfying ring of metal on metal reverberating in my eardrums.

The snow crunches under my boots once more as I lead the group out of the cave, glancing from side to side to check that the coast is clear. When I notice that there are no rogues that threaten expose us, I stride forwards into the forest before us. A path has already been carved into the fauna by years of trampling. My hand begins to sweat around my sword as we get closer and closer to the rogue dwellings.

What if this goes wrong? What if the whole plan fails? Then what? Will we all be killed or held as hostages? How will we be able to weaken the rogues if we don't have hold of their leader's mate? Because having Hunter's mate gave us a huge advantage, especially if Hunter is willing to do anything to get his mate back.

Josh wanders beside me, biting his lip as he refuses to speak. It's the quietest I've ever seen him, and the first time I don't really want to talk to him. Of course, we have to be silent for the mission but even he will defy the rules and whisper a joke about the beard or random body part of one of the rogues. This Josh is different, and I hate it. I wish that we could take the kiss back. It isn't my fault, but I wish that it had never happened—at least, not until I'm sure that I like him back.

Five minutes tick by in silence. Then another five. Time whirrs on like a fan, but finally the light from torches begin to brighten, lining the outside of an enormous clearing filled with tents.

All of the dwellings are identical, with white fabric in a taut triangle shape and numerous wooden poles inside the tents holding up the secure fabric. They are all arranged in rows, stretching out into the night until we can't see the edge. But in the middle of the tents is a more rigid structure; a castle, in fact. The stone doesn't have turret emplacements, just a large building with high arching windows and an abundance of light shining through the gaps. A flag violently flaps in the torrent of wind. The flag is a plain scarlet; the colour of blood.

The only problem is that the place was silent. As the wind picks up, throwing the flag into an even greater frenzy, all that I can hear is the whistle of the air as it effortlessly passes through the campsite.

"Something's wrong," I state in awe. Where are they? Are we walking into a trap? "It shouldn't be this quiet."

"Maybe they're all asleep," Josh suggests, but I roughly shake my head at his idea. Rogues don't follow rules and they would certainly not have gone to bed this early into the night. Their guard should've doubled after the declaration of war, but there were none in sight.

I bite the side of my cheek, the metallic taste of blood spilling onto my tongue. It's something I only do when the pit of my stomach tells me that something is wrong.

"No, they're not," I utter quickly, getting all of the thoughts out of my head as rapidly as I can. I glance at every face in turn, taking in the range of facial featuresranging from a broken nose to a face half covered with unhealable burns. "What if this is a trap? What if they know?"

Josh's forehead creases with distress. "But how would they know?"

I sigh. "I don't know, but we're here now. We can do this. Stay silent," I whisper.

The fourteen other werewolves—and Josh—around me all nod in unison. "I'm not going back without a prize," one mutters, gaining whispered cheers from the other members of the group.

"I'm sure it's not a trap. How could they know?" another utters—Jason, I think his name is.

"Draw your swords. If this is a trap, we're not going down without a fight," I say, raising the volume of my voice slightly and the others reply to my comment with stoic expressions.

Without further ado, we hastily make our way out of the tree line that has concealed us within the blanket of shadows and out into the open clearing. The wind has died down, but it still whistles through the site like a haunting ghost.

149

As we hastily make our way towards the centre of the rogue's territory, the scene becomes more and more ominous. A fire still flickers with everlasting life, a bowl lying face down on the floor beside the flames. Our group takes another ten steps forward, continuously getting close and closer to our goal. The closer we got, the more my hope grows.

Continuing to stride forward, I spot a stand of swords that have toppled to the ground, the blades lying scattered in the frostbitten mud. That's a disconcerting sign that maybe this isn't a trap after all. The wind could've knock over the weapons, and if the rogues are planning an attack, they would've taken all of the swords to maximise their chance of winning. But that's my hope speaking; my gut feeling is telling me otherwise.

I shake my head and walk onwards towards our goal. I hate how the camp is silent, and by this point, I'm almost certain that it's a trap but there's no point turning back now. Not when we're so close to succeeding. We've come way too far to go away empty-handed. I don't care if I die trying to save the countless lives of others.

We finally reach the castle, the doors looming over us and appearing as two huge planks of wood blocking our entrance. The windows are too high up to enter, so we will have to find a way through the doors without anyone hearing us.

Underneath my feet is solid cobblestone weathered down to smooth tiles due to overuse. The courtyard stretches out before us, yet another sword stand sitting proudly in a corner of the castle.

"What now?" one of my teammates whispers. I hold up a hand to shush them.

I open my mouth, the gears in my head clicking noisily as I try to figure out how to respond. "I don't know," I reply "Maybe there's anoth—"

"Ah. Alaska. What a pleasant surprise." A masculine voice slices across the terrain like a blade made of diamond. A shiver

150

instinctively runs down my neck and along my spine, the cold freezing blood vessels.

Before me, the hands on the clock imprinted in my eyes slow, each hand taking a thousand years to finally tick to the next second. I turn on my heel, so silently and cautiously it feels as though I am chest height in mud. When I finally face him, I can't help but gulp.

I know his face. I know his permafrost black eyes and platinum faded hair colour. I know the soft yet bold appearance of his face. I know his elegant manoeuvres; the way he moves across the courtyard as if he's floating.

He was the mysterious rogue I had seen when the previous king had been murdered. He was Hunter, the leader of the rogues. He had been the one to deliver the killing blow to the King, and he would've killed me too if Chase and the guards hadn't fought him off.

A group of rogues triple the size of our own surrounds us, securing us in place.

"You seem surprised to see me," Hunter states as his hand flutters over to the rogue next to him, who stands with his arms outstretched with a long weapon in his grasp. Hunter gracefully takes the blade, studying the silver—almost white—metal of the sword before flicking his wrists and swirling it around him confidently. He then smirks at me, my face covered in a mixed expression of hatred and awe. "Oh, come now Alaska, did you really think it would be that easy? You knew you were walking into a trap." The man steps forwards but I stand my ground, refusing to show any sign of fear. The man only appears to be a year older than myself but his presence is ancient and daunting. "So, why did you still come, I wonder?"

My mouth hangs open in shock, and it takes me a few minutes to answer. "I—" I stutter. I have never been this scared in my life; never. "How do you know my name?"

Hunter snorts, his nose thinning at the action. "You're not the only side to have insiders," he answers, nodding to one of the werewolves beside me. My heart skips a beat as Jason steps out of our group and wanders over to stand beside Hunter. He curves around to face us, his features blank with a faint glimmer of pain and betrayal; the face of a traitor.

"How could you?" I spit at him, trying to calm down my temper but it's already too late. I lash out at him but Josh holds me back with a sympathetic smile. "How could you, you arseh*le? You know what they do. They kill and they don't even care. They—" I begin, but no words come out. I thrash my shoulders out of Josh's hold and push my hair out of my face. I grit my teeth and say, "I'm going to kill you."

Gone is the sympathetic Alaska who hates the killer inside her; gone is the Alaska who doesn't want to be a murderer. Jason is a rogue, and like the rest of them, he is ruthless. He deserves to die for putting so many lives at stake.

Hunter twitches his lips. "It's okay. I've got you covered," he responds and, without a moment's thought, he buries the sword deep within Jason's chest. The man dies in an instant, his eyes glassing over as they reflect the stars above him. Noticing my shocked face, Hunter smirks. "He was no use to either of us."

"What do you want, arseh*le?" I yell.

The boy with the platinum hair shakes his head, tutting in the process. "My dear Alaska, I think we both know what I'm after."

Bile rises up my throat, and I am forced to gulp once again to keep the searing liquid down. "If you want me, you can have me. Just leave them alone."

Hunter shoots me a sympathetic look. "If only I could." He takes yet another step forward, his tar black walking boots contrastiong the pale white snow. His hand lightly feels for something in his belt and before I can bolt and stop him, a knife is plunged into the heart of a werewolf behind me. "I mean, what would be the fun in that?"

I throw Josh behind me, a growl ripping through my vocal chords like the howl of an ancient creature that only exists in twisted fairy tales. My legs burn with adrenaline, my whole body engulfed by a raging inferno which I have grown accustomed to ever since the beginning of the Alpha Trials.

I flick my hands, my claws appearing in an instant, and charge towards Hunter as quickly as I can. All the while, the man smiles at me as if I'm about to hug him rather than thrust my sword deep within his gut.

I place both hands on the handle to secure my hold, thrusting the weapon with all the power I can produce from my muscles.

Hunter casually smiles at me as I near him, his arms drifting upwards for some reason I cannot figure out until it is too late.

When I am just metres away, the man's figure blurs and, in a second, I feel the sword being wrenched from my grip. The action is so sudden that I almost stumble over into the ring of rogues that surround our group.

Now equipped with my sword, Hunter moves at a speed unknown to werewolves towards Josh. My pulse throbs nervously in my neck and I painfully swallow the lump stuck in my throat.

No. Not Josh, please. I speak silent words which wrack my skull. Whatever happens, I don't want my best friend to get hurt. I swipe with my claws, but Hunter is too fast and blurs out of the way. No werewolf can move like that. It's-it's impossible.

In less than a second, Hunter triumphantly stands behind Josh with my sword placed against his neck.

Through my anger and rage, I blurt out the first thoughts that enters my head. "If you dare hurt him, I'll kill you," I hiss, my voice carried over the courtyard by the abrupt gusts of wind.

"Alaska, we both know that I could kill you in two seconds. You can't beat me. You can't win this war." Hunter's face becomes stern, the eerie blood-red light of the torches mapping the contours of his sharp and precise face in a deep scarlet reflection.

I ruffle my shirt, finding my belt hidden beneath the thick material. My hand skims the trusted handle of one of my few knives and I scramble to hold it threateningly in front of me.

"You're wrong," I say desperately, a chill running through my bones and tingling all the way down to my feet. Why? Because I know he's right. The chances of us winning this war are low. Hunter has waited for the prime moment to attack and he has chosen it well. "We will win this war. Don't underestimate us."

My comments only make Hunter laugh even more menacingly, the strange sound from his vocal chords burning a hole in my soul.

He presses the sword harder against Josh's windpipe, making my heart jump into my throat. "Just one slash," Hunter whispers, his chastising having ceased. "Just one slash and he'd be dead," the man continues. The edge of the blade nicks the corner of Josh's neck.

I can't bear it any longer. Josh can't die because of me. He can't die when I have the ability to save him.

"Stop it!" I scream at the top of my lungs.

The blade cuts further. The red smile grows wider.

My head explodes with emotional pain, and the words tumble from my mouth before I can stop them. "Please, just leave him alone!" I screech, my throat hurting from my raised voice. My knife clatters to the ground and I raise my hands to surrender. "I-I'll do anything you want, just please don't hurt him."

Tears threaten to spill from my eyes, stinging in my hazy view. Hunter continues to draw the sword across Josh's neck like the devil himself. Hunter tilts to head to the side. "That's sweet," he mutters and brings the blade downwards, drawing more blood from my best friend's neck.

I exhale profusely when I realise that the sword hasn't done much damage. Josh's wound will heal within minutes and only the side of his neck has been sliced.

Hunter steps back, smiling as if he's proud of his work. I want to tear his face off and slit his own throat, just to let him know what raw fear feels like, but I can't. If I try to act against him now, he will kill Josh, and the emptiness and guilt will crush me like a boulder.

Josh places a hand on his neck, the fingers becoming slick with his own blood. Hunter takes a step away from his prey, and I dash forward to confirm that he's okay.

I push away his hand to get a peek at the cut and notice that it is much shallower than I anticipated. I feel Josh's eyes burn into my skin as he reaches up and takes my hand in his own. The blood is wet against my skin but I don't care.

"I'm alright," Josh confirms, swallowing a knot stuck in his oesophagus. He bows his head slowly, his lustrous eyes glaring into my own with the same intensity. His eyes tell a different story from his bold voice—he looks scared. "I'm alright," he repeats, as if I didn't heard him the first time.

A flicker of platinum hair catches my attention. I divert my gaze back to Hunter, who is still wearing a triumphant smirk on his face. His hands flutter like a silent storm by his sides, ready to unleash a deadly blow of thunder and lightning when necessary. The left side of his lip twitches up, the skin above it pinching into wrinkles. They look peculiar against his flawless white skin.

Hunter snaps his long fingers together to draw our attention. "Follow me," he orders, and I have no choice but to obey.

155

CHAPTER THIRTEEN
Cold

"It's unbelievable how deeply you can affect someone and never know."

- Susane Colasanti

Slick, translucent water drips down the walls of the grotty cave as I push my back up against the wet surface. The room—which can be described better as a cave or prison cell—is dark, with a pair of torches lighting up each side of the cramped space. The walls are all rugged, with unique rock patterns digging into my back.

The light in the cave is limited, the glare of the torches on the walls turning my vision a dilapidated ruby. My body shivers, reminding me of the time when Dylan was slain before my eyes.

I inhale, taking a deep breath of the limited oxygen. The frigid air pushes its way into my lungs, stinging as I glance around the cell. The other members of my group each sit at random spots within the grey enclosure. Two of the men in the back corner are mumbling and one of the younger members of the team is huddled in a tight slit in the rock, his arms awkwardly bent over his legs as he speaks under his own whispering breath.

"I'm sorry," a voice blurts into the echoing chasm, causing everyone to stop what they were doing and swivel intently to gaze at the boy beside me. I myself shift my head so that I can see the cocoa of his eyes.

Today his eyes are stormy, tormented. There is a flare of rage blocking the resilient personality of the man I thought I knew so well, depriving me from knowing what he is actually feeling. Normally, I can delve deep into his irises and tell whether he is calm or enraged, but today is different, as if he has purposely shut himself off from me and the rest of the world.

I blink rapidly. "Sorry about what?"

Josh intakes a huge swell of air, before exhaling with a rusty wheeze. "About kissing you." For a moment, his shields are down, and all I see is a vulnerable boy sitting before me. "I-I shouldn't have done that, and I'm sorry."

My eyebrows involuntarily crease. "Josh, there's no need to apologise," I mutter under my breath, anxiously watching as the other men in the same cell pretend to be otherwise occupied rather than listening to our conversation. "I'm the one who should apologise. I just . . ." I pause, unsure of what to say next. It isn't my fault that Josh had kissed me, but I pushed him away because I've been unable to decipher what my mixture of emotions are. "I just don't understand my emotions. I don't feel like . . . that."

Josh hunches his shoulders. " Which is why I'm sorry. I shouldn't have done that to you."

"It's okay," I squeeze his arm for reassurance, and watch as his face winces. I must be stronger than I thought. He looks vulnerable, with crinkles lining the edges of his eye sockets. I quickly shudder away as I realise I'm causing him pain.

"It's . . ." Not your fault? Even if I want to believe it, it was his fault. He had been the one to kiss me, not the other way around. "Can we not talk about it? You're my friend, Josh, and I don't want anyone to ruin that."

Josh's mouth edges upwards and, for a moment, I am relaxed; thinking that we will be okay. But we're not going to be okay. We haven't eaten for the better part of ten hours, and Hunter will slowly kill us off one by one when he realises that Chase doesn't care about us—when he realises we don't have any information because Chase doesn't confide with any of us. To be honest, I would rather die than have a whole city collapse to the ground.

A ferocious growling sound tears into the cell, my eyes landing on Josh as he stares in alarm at his stomach. I open my mouth to speak but the voice produced is not my own.

"Hungry?" Hunter asks in a menacing tone through the bars of the cell. His face appears even paler in the abundance of torch light, the hues staining his ebony irises crimson; the colour of blood.

No one moves, as if even the batter of an eyelash will cause the abrupt demise of everyone enclosed in the cramped space. Everyone except me. My legs shake as I stand up, tired from underuse. I use the damp rock to help myself up as I stretch my legs. Hunter studies me intently, his eyes burning with intent evil.

"Yes," I hiss as a response. "That's generally what happens when you don't eat for half a day."

The male werewolf makes a tutting noise, the sound echoing through the chasm. "You should really be more polite to your hosts," he states.

I narrow my eyes into slits. "Hosts? You killed one of us! Do you really expect us to be polite to you arseholes?"

Hunter lets out a smug chuckle. "Not really, but it would be appreciated." The man smirks, then begins to laugh once more as my mouth hangs open in shock. When—not if—I get out of this cell, I'm going to kill him. Scrap that—I'm going to punch him in the balls and then kill him. "Anyway, it's too bad that you're hungry. Prisoners tend not to get food."

I roll my eyes at his remark but I'm not expecting food either way. However, it does piss me off that Hunter is playing mind games.

"Now, Alaska, I require your company," Hunter states with glee in his eye.

I edge closer towards the bars, wrapping my hands firmly around the iron until my knuckles protrude from my hands, turning the skin a cadaverous white. "I'm not going anywhere with you," my bitter voice spits.

"Well, Alaska, either you come with me or all of your friends die. Your choice." His face is sharp and alert like an eagle whilst on the hunt for prey.

"I hate you."

"I know." He chuckles, using a bony finger to wave forward one of the rogues at his side. The werewolf hastily opens the cell, and I retreat from the bars, still glaring at Hunter.

The rogue grunts, urging me to come forward. I do as he asks. He produces a rope, and I hold out my still-white hands for him to tie up. The rope encloses tightly around my limbs like vines, suffocating my fingers as they drop in front of me when the knot is completed. Not that it really matters whether my hands are tied or not. I will escape this hell hole.

A feral gold flashes in the eyes of the rogue soldier as he roughly grapples my right arm, hurtling me forwards so that I stand beside Hunter. I cringe at the loud bang as the cell closes behind me, leaving me sealed off from everyone I know and leaving me with Hunter.

"Is this really necessary?" I enquire, holding up my arms and the delicate rope work surrounding my wrists like a halo of thorns.

Hunter barely glances at me. "Not really, but we don't want you escaping."

I sigh and feel my muscles bulge in my arms. I pump all of my fury and channel my hate, instantaneously pulling my hands apart and snapping the rope. I glower at the material as it falls to the dark floor. "Well that lasted long." I exhale.

"No matter. You're not going anywhere, and I'm sure you're also aware of that," he reminds me with a derelict tone. His movements are a lot more twitchy and prolonged than I remember,

159

as if he can sense that something is wrong. His muscles are tense despite his generally calm posture, and there's a bead of sweat rolling down his forehead.

As the leader of the rogues, he must know there will be repercussions for kidnapping a whole group of werewolves from the other side of the battlefield but he has never seemed disorientated by that simple fact. If there is one thing I have learnt about Hunter, it's that he is never afraid. Never. He always has a smirk on his face, whether he's losing a battle or trudging over the bodies of fallen comrades. That's how I know that he is a rogue at heart. Even if he doesn't display the typically large and muscular frame or the same mindset as the true rogues.

I feel my heart collapse in tragedy. "I know," I reply, because no matter how hard I try to escape, Hunter will be on me in less than a millisecond.

We reach a flight of stairs, and Hunter elegantly leads our small parade up the rough steps. The building is ancient, with cobwebs hanging in every nook and cranny, every pocket of darkness, and every spare patch of rock that isn't shrouded by torch light.

Finally, we reach the top of the steep stairwell and enter a hallway. Without another word, we slip into the first doorway, opening up into the main chambers until we finally grind to a halt.

The room is spacious, with a bed at the end of the long room and a set of two human-made sofas to my right. A stretched navy carpet drapes the floor, running across the length of the blistered cobblestone. Tapestries hang on the wall, camouflaged by a husky shield of cobwebs, concealing part of the stories woven into the material. I spot the flash of a rusty sword and glance at a helmet on a human head. This castle had been a human settlement centuries ago and it turns out that the rogues have done little to clean up the place since arriving.

Hunter waves a hand to usher the two rogues behind me away. As soon as the door slams shut behind them, he gracefully takes a seat on one of the grey sofas, patting the seat beside him.

"Water?" The platinum-haired boy offers. He flexes his precise fingers towards a glass of water that has already been poured.

Shaking my head, I saunter over and sit on the couch opposite him, trying my hardest to not make eye contact.

"What do you want with me?" I narrow my eyes and fold my arms across my chest, sitting with my back straight and ready to leap into action if I deemed it necessary. "It's all good that you've kidnapped us and all, but why don't you just kill us? Chase doesn't care; he never will."

"Ah, but he does." Hunter smirks, rising from the chair as he takes a second glass of water from the table. He swings the translucent glass between his thumb and index finger, the colourless liquid never spilling out from his motions. "You should see the way he looks at you."

"Chase doesn't care," I repeat, my voice turning into a growl. My brain clicks like a spark, and I wonder whether I can take him on in my wolf form. Probably not, since I can't even beat him in my human form.

Hunter still wears his usual smirk, as though he has been born with it and it's permanently plastered on his face. "I know you don't believe me, but he does. And I'm counting on it." He shifts himself back down onto the seat and leans towards me, his lips pale and his eyes glazed with lunacy. "How long do you think it'll take until he comes to rescue you? First, he needs to realise that you're missing. Then, he has to hold a meeting and discuss unimportant plans that will nonetheless be shattered. And finally, he will come and rescue you because he doesn't want you to get hurt. You may think I'm a psychopath, but trust me, I know more than you think."

My eyes rake up and down his body, my face snarling with disgust. "You're right, you are a psychopath."

161

Instead of Hunter's smile diminishing, it grows. "It's nice to have that confirmed." He takes a sip of the water and then slams the glass down so hard on the table it smashes.

A tinkling noise echoes through the air, slicing apart the relaxed conversation. Hunter's face distorts to a stormy hardness, his eyes firm and his limbs rigid. "Chase will come, and when he does, I will kill him. You will lose this war, I can guarantee it."

"We're stronger than you think," I hiss. "We can defeat you."

"There is no defeating me!" he yells, spit flying from his mouth as though he's a rabid animal. Blue veins throb in his head, his neck straining as he edges even closer. "You can't defeat me. You will never defeat me."

Silence follows his outburst, and all I can pick up is the rhythmic breathing and a rusty creaking as Hunter sits back in his chair. He pants rapidly, his chest rising and falling with fury, and his fists clenched. I never thought I would see him like this; furious and wild beyond recovery.

The creaking noise ceases. Hunter glares at me. A clock chimes, and a voice rebounds momentarily around the room. "We'll see about that," the voice states as a blade whistles through the air, driving into Hunter's chest before even he can acknowledge the movement.

I swiftly climb to my feet and turn around to see Chase and Azra standing in the doorway, Chase's golden flecks reflecting the daylight streaming in from the windows. He smiles at me but not before chucking a sword in my direction which I am easily able to pluck from the air.

I twirl the weapon with my hand, admiring how light it was and how effortlessly I could manoeuvre it.

"I told you . . ." Hunter chuckles from the sofas, having made no effort to move. A plume of blackened blood has stained his clothes a dark pigment and his lips are surrounded by a splattering of blood. He's definitely, one hundred percent, a lunatic.

162

I don't question the weird hue of his blood—I don't have time to think about it. "I told you he cared," he repeats, taking me completely off guard as he thrusts the knife from his shoulder and lunges towards Chase.

"Chase!" I scream in terror, afraid that our king will be slain and then we will have no leader, but he is already prepared for an attack.

Hunter might be fast, and Chase might not reach his speed, but he's good enough to react to the attack. That's all he needs.

The King lashes out with his sword, causing Hunter to arch his back to avoid the blow. Chase doesn't hesitate to kick the rogue as he attempts to regain his balance. His frail figure lands on the floor in front of me.

I waste no time and swing my sword at his supporting arm as he tries to steady himself and stand up. The iron cuts through the skin cleanly, causing yet another rush of darkened blood to cascade down Hunter's arm and on to his hand before meeting the floor.

Instead of giving up, the bloodied man persists and attempts to use his other arm to help him stand up. I watch as the cut I recently inflicted already begins to seal up, healing at a faster rate than a werewolf should. There is definitely something different about him—something in his blood that makes him different.

Thud. My foot meets his hard stomach. The rogue rolls on the floor and lands with his arms pressed against the chilling ground. He spits a concoction of blood and saliva before standing up. Hunter shakes, his skin wax-like and his face a mask of enmity.

He's fast, but with wounds that severe he's about as fast as a normal werewolf.

Hunter's eyes shift to the knife lying a few metres away and scrabbles to reach it. He reaches out to grab the handle but I sprint up to the blade and defiantly kick it. Hunter grunts, jumping to his feet and wiping the sleeve of his shirt against his lips to try and rid his mouth of the dried liquid surrounding it.

The rogue starts moving towards me with his bare hands, but another dagger embeds itself into his collarbone, knocking him backwards. I have no time to say thank you to either Azra or Chase as I place both hands on my sword, sending it straight through Hunter's chest. The blade enters with ease, and the man on the other end of the weapon's eyes pop out in shock and pain. I twist the blade, letting go as Hunter tries to pull out the sword with cries of pain. As the seconds blur on, he flops on to the floor, dead, his bloody fingers twitching with demise.

I let the man slide to the floor, his corpse spilling blackened blood across the floor. I listen intently for a heartbeat, but nothing alerts me that the monster is still alive. Hunter's black eyes gaze up at the sky, forever stuck in place.

I feel as though my heart has frozen and become cold. Since when have I become so cold blooded? Granted, he deserved to die, but surely I should feel some form of sympathy? He has a family, just like I had. Perhaps they will mourn him when they realise he's no longer with them, perhaps not. My money is on the latter.

"Ali, we need to get out of here," Azra's voice snaps me back to reality, and I blink away the fog in my eyes, only to see Chase's face metres away from mine. I scrunch my eyebrows and flinch away, retrieving my sword from Hunter's limp body.

"I'll lead the way," I say, walking confidently past Chase and Azra who part to let me through. Chase doesn't even give me a second glance as I saunter straight past him and avoid his gaze. Why is he even here? He's the king. If the king dies, then the people will have no one strong enough or willing to lead them.

Despite not wanting to make my way back down to the cells, I mount the stairs and begin to descend without uttering a single word.

"What did he do to you?" Chase questions from behind me, worry lining his voice.

I shrug my shoulders. "Nothing, but he killed Jason. Turns out, he was on their side the whole time."

"Bastard." Chase's footsteps quicken as he catches up to me. "He didn't hurt you or anything?"

"No."

I spot Chase lower his head in my peripheral vision. There's no denying that he is handsome, with his mesmerizing eyes and sharp jawline but he's still an arseh*le. Yet, in the past I have always been attracted to the cockier wolves. It appears that I have a type.

"Hey!" voices shout as we reach the bottom of the staircase, faced by two rogue soldier with their swords clenched in their grasps.

I roll my eyes as the two rogues savagely surge forwards. One drops his sword in the rush and doesn't hesitate to pick it up as he continues to charge forwards, his fingers sticky with blood from an open cut on his wrist, inflicted at an earlier date.

His hands grapple towards me like a scarlet hook, outstretched like the curling tide, coiling from the strength of the ocean and abruptly releasing its deadly onslaught. His face mimics the same feral visage I had seen in Hunter's eyes the moment before he died—the look of a rogue.

My fingers feel nimble as I slash with my sword, slicing through one of the rogue's hands before it can touch me. The male barely whimpers in pain, as if he no longer feels anything except bloodlust and adrenaline. It's one of the many reasons they are practically unstoppable.

A blood-crested fist meets my face, my teeth grinding as my jaw is forced to the side. Ache blossoms in my jaw, and I hear a gritty click as I force it back into place. A shaky hand reaches up to wipe the blood and sweat off my face, only to come away in a torrent of ruby liquid—my nose is bleeding.

My face turns into a visor of animosity, my buried wolf instincts triggered from within. I grit my rattled teeth, feeling the sharp scrape of chipped bone with my tongue. Blood fills my mouth, the metallic taste blurring my senses as I clumsily swing my weapon in an ungraceful arc, meeting the rogue's shoulder.

I only manage to scrape the werewolf's skin, a light gash appearing on his shoulder between his torn clothes. The response I receive is a growl like no other I have heard before. I'm used to the animalistic whine from other werewolves, but this rogue sounds as though he's shredding his own vocal chords. On purpose.

My heart aches at the noise, contracting with some unknown fear and pain I have never experienced before in my life. What have any of these werewolves done in the first place to be this feral? To be a rogue? Some have been born into the world as a bloodthirsty beast against their will, and others have been forced to join some kind of cult. Some are naturally sick in the head, but none deserve this fate. Not one that is forced upon them.

My body feels numb as I step forward with the sword, finding the rogue's breastplate and hammering through the bone. There is no crunch, just the gurgle of foaming from my opponent's mouth before he sails through the ice-laced air and hitting the ground with a heavy thud.

I clench my muscles as I withdraw the slick sword, sprinting down the rest of the corridor with both Azra and Chase in pursuit, the other rogue having been slain. To my surprise, only the two of them have come to rescue us. Unless Chase has other men that are holding off the rogues elsewhere.

Blood rushes in my eardrums, each footfall rebounding into my ears like the boom of thunder during the apex of a storm. The blood in my veins begins to churn. My whole body feeling as though it's on fire and I am the source.

"Where are the keys?" Azra asks quickly in concern as we near the cell, and I ignore her, running blindly to save the other werewolves trapped in the cell. For all I know, they could be dead. You never know what the rogues will do.

I watch as Josh's partially obstructed head comes into view, his eyes widening at the sight before him, particularly Azra. Instead of slowing down, I clench my jaw so tightly that my teeth feel weak enough to shatter. Blood fills my mouth once more as I accidently bite down on my tongue too hard, the laceration numbed by the adrenaline in me.

My palms ram into the bars, gripping them before I take a huge breath of fresh air and rip the door open. My actions surprise me; I really am stronger than I thought.

"Josh!" Azra sighs as she rushes into the cell without hesitation, flinging herself into the arms of her best friend. Josh's hands waver for a second before firmly enclosing around Azra, tears forming in his eyes.

A pain erupts in my hand and I divert my gaze to see a cut across the skin from my successful attempt to force open the cell. Crimson residue seeps onto my hand from the slice, the skin surrounding the cut already beginning to seal up.

"Why didn't you do that sooner?" Chase's deep voice questions with a hint of amusement. I step away from the cell and surprisingly close to the Alpha King himself. Close enough so that I can glance into his eyes. Just like Josh, I can barely read him. He has the same gold flecks swimming in the sea of deep cobalt of his irises, highlighting how bright the varying pigments are. They are beautiful—perhaps too beautiful for such a man. Yet, there's something dangerous about the look on his face. Something that makes me feel . . . different.

I smile at him but it only lasts for a second. "There were guards," I answer curtly.

Chase nods. "I see." His hand reaches out, touching my forearm lightly, but the speculation in his mind doesn't falter. "Are you sure you're okay?" This time his question is much more enforced, as if he's expecting an honest answer.

I taste metal in my mouth. "I told you I was fine, Chase." I exhale with frustration. Why does he even care? Or rather, why is he pretending to care? "Why did you come back for me? You're putting your whole kingdom at risk."

A strange look appears on his face, as if fear has swallowed his courage. "I—" he stutters, his arm tightening its hold on my forearm, pastel rings forming around his fingers. "I couldn't bear the thought of you getting hurt."

"Then don't."

Chase smirks while quirking his eyebrow. His smirk is much more welcoming and genuine that Hunter's. "Don't what?"

"Don't bear it for me. I can bear it myself," I say defiantly as the others walk past us, Azra and Josh trailing at the back, with tears in Josh's glassy eyes.

Chase nods. "If you say so," he responds, his gaze dropping down to my lips for a millisecond before he glances back to my face, as if nothing happened. Maybe it's my imagination. Or maybe he does care.

Something sparks in my heart. Something that makes me feel sickly nervous yet buzz with adrenaline. Something that only Chase makes me feel.

CHAPTER FOURTEEN
Desire

"I loved you recklessly from the moment I knew you. I never cared about the consequences. I told myself you wanted me too, and so I tried but you never did. I wanted you more than I wanted to be good. I wanted you more than I wanted anything, ever. "

- Cassandra Clare, City of Heavenly Fire

Fighting without my sword feels strange. I miss the lightweight feel of the blade and the complete precision I'm able to gain by using it. But, just like many other things—including my hope—I have been forced to leave it behind at the rogue camp.

Instead, I am using a heftier sword with less grace, which I am finding harder to manoeuvre. Every time I slash with the weapon, my limbs feel heavy, as if I'm submerged under a tonne of water. Even my sight seems blurry, making it hard to distinguish between reality and fiction.

Frustrated, I lash out one more time at Josh, only for him to effortlessly parry my attack away.

"This is pointless," I say exhaustedly. "We all know how to use a bloody sword."

Josh laughs in amusement. "Tell that to Chase."

I quickly tuck the loose strands of my hair behind my ears, gazing around the crowded courtyard in an attempt to get a glimpse of the King. "Perhaps I will," I murmur as a response. "And it's not like all these people are going to have to fight." I point my head towards Harper, who is training with Alex ten metres away from us. Her black hair looks like they were swept by the wind and her eyes are glazed over with depression. It's not how a nine-year-old should ever look. It pains me to see her that way.

Josh beams at me, illuminating his cheeks with a healthy glow. The downcast features and looming eye bags I have grown used to back in the rogue territory have since disappeared, leaving his skin a healthy pastel pigment.

"They won't, but it's just a precaution. Rogues are notorious for attacking when we least expect it," Josh explains, and I nod in understanding.

"I would know," I reply, my teeth clenching together furiously. Images of the previous king falling on the cobblestone with empty eyes shivers into my mind and I flinch. Blood stains my view as I throw down my sword and trudge away from Josh.

I need a better sword if I'm going to be on the front line of this war.

"Hey, Ali!" Josh calls frantically from behind me, his tone filled with concern. I don't look back. "Where're you going?"

My fingers tingle with an unknown energy as I walk through the swarm of people, stepping to the left to dodge the path of a blade and ducking to avoid a clumsy punch. The place is alive with anger and the stench of sweat, but it has a good atmosphere. It's the atmosphere created by a group of people who will never give up.

"Chase," I address the King, who turns around with his sword, swinging it towards the base of my neck, and resting it there. I feel a sharp nip as the metal threatens to break the skin, but the smile on Chase's face is the only reassurance that he's not going to kill me.

"Really mature," I murmur with a roll of my eyes.

Chase takes away his sword without hesitation, a fleeting look locked into his cobalt eyes. "What can I say?" He smirks, washing out the grin until it vanishes completely. He's panting from a hard day of training, hairline slick with sweat. "Anyway, what do you want, Ali?"

"A new sword," I request bluntly. His expression remains unchanged, his handsome smirk still on, the corners of his lips not even twitching for a second to speak. "And to talk," I add, which he reacts. To talk about why the hell every time I look at you, I get butterflies despite hating you.

A shaky hand wavers up to his head, running through the fine dirty-gold hair on his scalp. A heavy stubble is scattered on his jaw, underlying the amount of time he has been busy by his duties. "As a matter of fact, I need to talk to you as well," he replies with a steely silence. He drops the sword carelessly to the mud, thick liquid splashing up on to his human-made joggers. Not the best choice of clothing to train in.

I raise an eyebrow. "Does this involve Hunter? Because I'd rather not think about that arseh*le right now."

The male before me shakes his head in a quick motion, his short hair barely moving. "No. It's about . . . something else. About . . . the war."

His hesitation startles me, but I think nothing of it and bow my head slightly to continue to conversation. "Good. And they have to train using weapons other than swords. If we want to win, everyone needs to be able to use whatever weapon they can get their hands on." The words flood from my mouth like a torrent. "Not everyone's going to fight. I get the preparation, but surely the guards are more important to train. They're the ones protecting us."

"I know." Chase sighs through his nostrils, elongating his nose for a second. Sunlight catches the rims of his eyelashes, sparkling them up into an immense illuminated blonde shade. "But you must understand that these people have been training their whole lives."

Chase moves impatiently ahead of me. I catch up to him, matching my quick pace to his long strides.

"Then why are they even training in the first place?" I ask, a mortified expression smothering my face. "We should be preparing for war! Hell, we should protecting the city by sending out patrols."

Chase grits his teeth as he shoves his palms against the doors of the castle. The dark wood gives way immediately, swinging into the stone wall harshly, shards of rock cascading onto the floor. "We are. But these people have never fought rogues before. They haven't trained enough. They're not ready—mentally ready, and that's what I'm trying to prepare them for."

My mouth is still pursed in confusion, but I allow the words to slowly sink into my skull, infiltrating my mind until I can separate them out and make sense of his speech.

"You're preparing them mentally? For all the loss, destruction, and death we will face?" I enquire. In the blink of an eye, my body moves in front of him, halting his tracks. "Chase, you don't understand. No one—and I mean no one—can ever be prepared for that kind of loss." I of all people know that.

Chase barges past my shoulder, knocking the breath from my lungs. It's only now I realise how strong he truly is. Yes, he's almost killed me—twice, might I add—but even then I had been too enraged and caught up with my hatred to admire the power coursing through his nerves. He is the definition of power.

"I know," he murmurs as he saunters ahead, clumsily marching up the stairs to the throne room. I'm unsure why we're in the castle in the first place, but I continue to follow, determined to have a proper conversation with him about the war. He chose me as his second in command for a reason, and I'm sure as hell not going to let him down now.

Only when we reach the throne room, the circular table in the centre an unrecognisable mess of map and pen markings, does he stop. I take into account his tousled and windswept strands of gold lining his scalp and the dramatic flare of stress in his eyes. His face is toned scarlet, but whether that's from our excursion or

172

something completely different, I do not know. He stinks of fresh snowfall and sweat, but it makes my heart skip a beat rather than shrivel my nose in disgust.

Chase pauses for a second, intently studying the map with a concentrated and penetrating focus. His eyes scour over the feeble piece of paper, his hands beginning to twitch—no, tremble—uncontrollably. I want to reach an out take his hands to stop them from quivering; to tell him that everything will be okay.

But I don't. My hands stay firmly plastered by my side, as if stuck there by an invisible force. Even when Chase surges forwards with a howling battle cry towards the table, they do not move.

Chase slashes with a dagger at the paper, creating a ginormous tear through the material. With another swipe, the paper is torn horizontally, separating the mountains from the forest and the forest from the battlefield. It's as if he's sketching the scars on his soul; each tear representing a broken and irreparable heart string.

My eyes glower in horror as he continues wrecking the one vital source of information we have. Why is Chase behaving so strangely? Why is he acting like an arrogant toddler having a tantrum? Maybe he isn't as strong as I once thought.

"Chase," I call out to him quietly. As the thud of the table being upturned reverberates through my eardrums, I have no choice but to raise my voice. "Chase!" I shout at the top of my lungs, finally grabbing his attention.

His eyes are glowing yellow, a rabid colour as he shifts his head to glance at me. His chest rises and falls rapidly like waves, heaving as he attempts to calm his temper. His hands are now clenched fists by his side, no longer quivering with the static electricity of rage, the dagger having fallen from his tight grasp onto the floor.

He steps forward, his eyes waning a pale gold, reflecting in the sun as it streams through one of the arched windows. But then

I suddenly realise it's not his eyes that are reflecting the light—it's tears.

Holy sh*t.

"Chase?" I mutter quietly, still and unmoving like a statue. "Are you okay?"

Blood streaks from the King's palms as he extracts his claws digging into the flesh to try and make him forget the pain I cannot see. "We're—" he begins, but his voice is too weak to continue the sentence. I don't know how to feel. Shocked? Confused? "We're never going to win. We can't. I can't lead these people. I'm a crap king and everyone will suffer for it."

I take another wary step closer, close enough for me to reach out and take his hands. I uncurl his bloody fingertips, clasping them in my own filthy hands as I stare at the light stubble dotting his jawline—he's taller than I had anticipated. I clench hard on his swollen palms, trying to reassure him that everything will be fine, even when we all know that the kingdom will fall and us with it.

"Don't you dare say that, Chase," I reply as strongly as I can, but his crumbling heart is causing mine to shatter with it. "You know you're a good king, and we are going to win this war. I promise you. This is what they want to happen. You're strong. Don't let them get to you."

Chase shakes his head, a frown forming across his handsome features. "Don't make promises you can't keep," he murmurs, the yellow in his eyes having completely disappeared. Something flickers behind the metallic flecks of his irises, sparking something deep within my soul. The sensation grows as he pulls closer to me, shifting his hands so that he's gripping my own rather than the other way around. My skin ignites where he touches it.

"I'm not, Chase," I say but his precise and powerful presence causes my voice to come out as a hushed whisper. "I'm no—"

I'm interrupted as his lips press onto mine.

His action takes me by surprise and, for a moment, I'm too shocked to move. Too stunned to shift even an inch.

I don't know what to feel. My mind is endlessly spinning in a torrent of emotions, drowning out my thoughts as my eyesight begins to fade. I can see him and only him; nothing else exists. We are the world, and everything else is a non-existent, empty vacuum.

"Why is he kissing me?" and "Do I like Chase?" are two out of the thousands of thoughts hurtling through my brain.

It's not until I realise that I'm kissing him back that I can answer my questions.

His hands reach around the small of my back, hungrily pulling me closer as I reach up my bloody fingertips to run a hand through his hair. They're softer than I expected.

Chase's hand abruptly reaches up to my face, cupping the scarred flesh delicately. Lightning ignites and sparks fly where his skin meets mine, the infinite boundary a surging wildfire of flame and inferno. My body is tingling and alive, as if a thousand live wires have been strapped on to every single nerve in my figure.

Chase is the spark, and now I feel like I'm burning alive with lust and impulse.

And the way I'm feeling can only mean one thing: I like Chase. I'm attracted to him too much for my own good. This feeling—the feeling that causes butterflies to flutter in my stomach—is something that's been welling up for weeks. It's something I can't ignore.

The truth hits me like a truck, knocking the air from my lungs until I feel like I'm suffocating on my own breath. There's a reason I haven't been able to figure out my feelings; it's because I had already figured them out, without even realising it. I have never liked Josh that way because I liked Chase of all people instead.

But the truth confuses me. Chase had held a knife at my neck and threatened to kill me. He had almost killed me—twice. He hates my guts, my attitude; everything about me. So why do I have these feelings? After all we have been through, Chase is the one person I would never expect to end up liking. Never.

Despite the war raging within my brain, I feel my hands pull him closer, gripping his face with both of my palms. I can't help but feel . . .

Alive. And let's face it, I haven't felt that way in a long time.

His rough lips move against mine with a burning passion, and although the whole scene seems to take up a decade, the action lasts three seconds before we're forced to pull away by a voice.

"Ali?" the distinct voice calls up the stairs and the person enters the room before Chase and I have the time to fully pull away. "I just wanted to ask if yo—" Josh begins, but his sentence automatically fades as he notices the close proximity of mine and Chase's bodies.

Josh's face flares up with a hidden pain. He tries his best to conceal the effects of his shattering heart but it's no use. Tears already stain his wet eyes, giving him the appearance of someone who knows much more than their years.

For the first time in my life, I feel the faint twinge as a chord inside me snaps. I have broken him, possibly beyond repair.

How could I do this to him? How could I do this to my best friend?

"Josh—" I say, my voice inaudible and poison to my own ears. My legs rapidly move towards him, but he turns the corner with haste.

I sprint to the doorway but it's no use; he's already disappeared into oblivion.

CHAPTER FIFTEEN
Azra

"In the end, all she was, was cracked glass waiting to be shattered."

- Unknown

When someone irrationally knocks on my door, thumping with as much force as they can put, I almost jump out of my skin. Despite the battles I have been through and the wars I have witnessed, I still can't help myself as my heart skips a beat, reminding me that I'm human. Well, half human.

"Who is it?" I call from the empty room, my voice effortlessly rebounding off the cobblestone walls.

Chase made sure that I got my own room when the Alpha Trials concluded, and although I had argued against it—mostly because I want to be closer to Josh, not Chase—it now feels like my home.

Home. Something I have not had in a long, long time.

No one replies, the eerie silence stirring my thoughts like a deadly concoction. The hollow sense in my skull does nothing to numb my thoughts, but someone is definitely at the door. Someone who doesn't want me to know who they are.

It takes me ten seconds to put on a jumper and grab my sword, carefully stalking towards the door like a predator would with its prey. Still mentally exhilarated from the sudden thump on the door, my hand tightens around the blade; so tightly that I feel every contraction and relaxation of my blood vessels.

I reach out to open the door. What I expected to see was a heart broken Josh or worse, a reincarnated version of Hunter. But neither of them are at the door.

Instead, a bright and stormy pair of azure eyes glare at me, filled with hatred.

The figure moves so quickly I have no time to react to her. One moment, I'm standing in front of the door and the next, my back collides with the solid wall, the door slamming shut before I can call out for help.

Every inch of air is expelled from my lungs. I open my mouth in slight agony, winded. The rough stone against my back feels cold, sending a shiver down my spine and escaping into the floor through my toes, a tingling sensation rushing across my skin.

Is she one of them? This whole time, had she been a rogue in disguise?

I shake my head, not because it isn't true—because I don't want to believe it.

"Azra!" I shout at her as she pins me to the wall, both of her hands grasped firmly on my upper arms as her eyes howl with rage. Her grip is so tight, I feel pins and needles ignite on my limbs.

Azra bares her teeth, but it's not the snarl of an animal; it's something much more than that.

"How dare you do that to Josh?" she shouts, her tone rattling through my skeleton like the chime of a weathered bell. Her words take me by surprise, and I loosen the hold on my weapon.

I raise my eyebrows, letting the sword fall from my grasp before shoving her away from me. It doesn't take much power, but she looks as though she could tear the world apart like a feral tornado afterwards. So this wasn't an attack, this was personal.

"What?" I manage to squeeze out, still winded from the impact of the wall. A bubble of guilt rises in my chest.

Azra's eyes narrow to slits. "You know what," she hisses. She sees my questioning look, the dark slots that resemble her eyes being hidden even further. "What? Do you want me to spell it out to you?"

"N—" I begin, but she butts in like a bulldozer.

"Josh likes you Alaska—or did—and now his heart is broken. Thanks to you," Azra says as if she's got poison lining her mouth and needs to spit it out. "And for Chase? What the hell! That dick-brain deserves no one! He pinned you to a tree, Ali! Held a knife to your neck and almost killed you. Twice! You could've been more sensitive to Josh! His feelings are messed up thanks to you. He came into my room and sat in silence for three hours!"

I open my mouth, but the sound that comes out is a sound that I have never made before.

"I know," I whisper, but the words do nothing to calm Azra's temper. I have always known she has a quick temper, but I have never experienced anything like this.

"Then what the hell? Josh is the best guy you're ever going to get—in fact, he's too good for you—but you throw him away like a piece of trash," she finishes. Although her words sting, I know better than anyone that they're true. "I don't even know why we became friends with you."

My heart feels as though someone has reached into my chest and squeezed it until it can no longer beat. I can't breathe. My mouth is aflame, unable to form words, and my brain sparks into an inferno of rage. Every single nerve in my body tingles with anticipation, yet all I can do is stare. My eyes won't even allow me to blink.

I want to shout at her, to rip out a handful of her hair, or tell her that they're the ones who made friends with me, but I can't move. I'm frozen in place like a statue, my expression never shifting from my startled features. Every single part of my anatomy won't respond. It's like I'm a ghost, forever seeing but never being able to touch reality.

179

A lump rises in my throat, my oesophagus choking on my own words. I have already lost my family. I don't want to lose my friends, too.

"I—" I attempt to say something, but all that comes out of my mouth is a hushed breath. "I didn't mean to." This time my voice is much more pronounced. "I never wanted to hurt anyone ever, yet that's the only thing I seem to be doing. And I know Josh likes me. I know that he deserves someone better. But I didn't know what it was like to feel about someone in that way. I do now." I pause, finding the right words to say, whilst Azra folds her arms defiantly over her chest like she's protecting herself and pushing me away in the process. "I love Josh, but as a friend. I love you, as a friend. And I like Chase—I don't know why, but I do. Whenever I'm with him, I feel like I'm something. I feel like I belong. I feel alive."

Azra blinks, but what I think is anger is really the reflection of tears. The amount I have witnessed over the past week has been immeasurable, and the last thing I want is to see someone else break down.

The girl shudders away as if she's seen me for the first time, her eyes running down my face like a brutal current. Her lips twitch for a millisecond, but she never blinks, as if the world will collapse if she even dares to close her eyes. She shrinks away from me, trying to hide in her own skin.

I rub my neck nervously, pushing myself from the wall. I want to reach out and grab her wrist. Just . . . something to make her feel better. But with her downcast eyes and face of agony, I can only stand there powerless. Again.

"I promised him," Azra whispers, although her voice sounds more like a gurgle. "I promised him that I would protect him. I mean, after all he's done for me, it's the least I could do for him."

My eyebrows fold in confusion. I understand that Azra and Josh have been friends for an extremely long time, but Azra's

180

words make me think that their connection goes even further than their bond. What happened to bring them so close together? Is it something to do with her hate of rogues? Because every time she ever hears the word rogue, her nose scrunches in disgust? But then again, why did she agree to become friends with me?

I shake my head. "I don't understand."

Azra laughs, holding one of her elbows delicately with her other hand. It's something I've never seen her do before, but then again, I've never seen her like this. Even her posture is slouched. Her fingers appear to repel her own touch as they flutter away from her elbow. I reach out a hand and place it on her shoulder. I rub my thumb against the skin, trying to comfort her the only way I know how.

"No," she murmurs. "Of course you wouldn't." The toothy grin she gives puts me at unease. There's something almost demonic about the facial expression. "You know I hate rogues, right? I hated the thought of being friends with you at first, but Josh talked me into it; to calm my hatred. But you know what? It didn't help; nothing would. Not after what happened."

Every single breath of air once stored in my body seems to have vanished. I know that she hates rogues, but I have never seen the blood-curdling rage that consumes her heart every time she sees one. Only now do I realise how hard it is for her to cope with me being her friend—and the one who broke Josh's heart.

But finally, everything makes sense. Her tough gaze; her bitter words when I do anything out of place.

"I—" I choke out. "I'm sorry," I apologise, even though whatever happened to her is not my fault. And no matter how many times I repeat that fact in my head like a mantra, I can't shake the feeling that she hates me for it. She hates me because of what I am, and she can't help it.

Azra buries her head in her hands, obscuring her face from my view. Is she crying? She never cries. In fact, she has barely ever shown any remorse at all, let alone allow anyone to see her in plain mental agony.

I'm surprised she hasn't yelled at me stay away from her and Josh, but I think that's because she knows I won't leave. I've left too many people to be tormented by their own minds, and Azra will not be another tomy tally.

"It's not your fault," she whispers. My body shrinks away with surprise. "I'm sorry. I shouldn't have said that. I know that people can't choose who they like. It-It happens. That's life."

My mouth opens in apparent shock, and my muscles won't respond to close it. Azra has never really been the forgiving type either, and whether she's being gentle for my sake or I'm seeing a completely different side to her, I don't know. It's strange to think that after just four weeks of knowing her, she still appears like a stranger. I know nothing about her.

Azra wipes the single tear that rolls down her face. It cuts a channel in her skin, the dark trail stark against her normal skin tone. In that moment, she looks much older than her years, as if a single tear can age someone a century.

"Believe it or not, there was a time when Josh and I weren't in each other's lives," she murmurs, a smile etching itself on to her face like a faint drawing. I'm afraid that even the slightest expel of my breath will cause it to drop, so I stay silent as she continues. "I mean, he was in my pack, but I never talked to him. You probably know, but an alpha's daughter isn't meant to talk to be associated with an omega."

My lips purse in astonishment. Although Azra has always been fierce, and I thought I had known her, I have never been able to see past the shield of armour she has put up to protect her heart. And now here she is, fully exposed, every single last scale of her tattered armour exploding into a fathom of grey and black. She had been an Alpha's daughter—which I don't know whether to be shocked or saddened by—and now she is nothing, at least to herself. If only she could see that she is everything to Josh.

182

Azra draws in a sharp breath. I hear the oxygen whistle through her bronchi.

"The first time I saw him, he couldn't even lift a sword." Azra's faint lips are drawn into the glimmer of a smile at the memory but it's quickly chased away into the dark chasm of regret. "I showed him how to use the weapon but my father saw us. He forbade me from seeing Josh, but we had become friends, even in such a short space of time. Soon, we snuck out to see each other. Just to talk. He was the only person the same age as me in the pack so, naturally, we got along. My father never noticed, and, well, this isn't really that important," Azra mumbles. "He's the only friend I've ever had. Until you, Alaska."

My eyes glaze over with a strange sensation, as if my body feels her stare prickle at my skin. A bead of sweat implodes on my forehead, but I decide to blame it on the temperature of the room: it's winter, but that doesn't matter. Not anymore.

I nod at her to go forward.

"Everything was going well. My parents had no clue about me and Josh's friendship, and the pack was happy," Azra sighs. My body unconsciously tenses with anticipation. "That was until they"—the girl shudders—"arrived. There were only about ten of them, covered in blood and dirt, and they claimed that the rest of their pack had been killed by rogues.

"So, like any other pack would do, we took them in and helped heal their wounds." I watch Azra's throat swallow, perhaps in fear. "Then, one day, a platinum-haired rogue took it in his stride to challenge my father's authority. They were bitter, cruel, and harsh. I remember sitting inside my tent as the two began to fight, covering my ears as their shouts and growls grew louder.

"It was only a matter of time before they started fighting to the death, but one went silent before they had been able to declare Deathmatch . . ." Azra's words trail off into an echo and her face goes slack, as if her soul has abruptly left her body. She looks

183

empty, just like I had the moment my parents were killed right in front of my eyes.

Her next words sting. "When I went outside, he was dead," she whispers, refusing to blink. It's as if I can see the fire that she saw that day blaze in her eyes, reflecting like a time machine. "H-He was dead, and there was nothing I could do to save him."

A shaky hand reaches down to the corner of my bed as Azra guides herself towards the wooden posts. Her legs visibly shake as she stumbles backwards.

Brunette bangs fall in front of Azra's face, obscuring her azure eyes. In that moment, I'm unsure of what I should do. I have never had a friend who has opened up to me like this before, and it feels wrong. I'm the last person you should come to in a moment of crisis.

The warrior's voice startles me when she speaks up, echoing against the stone walls in a will of woe.

"He took over. His fellow pack mates were given positions of authority, and my mother and I were thrown into the dirt by our own pack. We had nowhere to sleep, so we huddled in the communal sleeping shelter with nothing but the clothes on our backs. They controlled everything: the amount of food we ate; who hunted; who mated with who; who lived; who died."

I'm almost tempted to speak but I can't. My body won't respond to the signals I'm sending to my brain, and for that, I am grateful. I feel like my words will slice open the heavy air, causing it to belch invisible blood.

"I was lucky that I was not sentenced to death, but then came the day that my mother was. She had stepped out of line simply by mentioning my father's name." Azra's lips grow into a thin line, like the angular edge of a knife. "They dragged her out into the centre of the pack lands. They made everyone watch, including me. I tried to save her, but I was still young and weak. Fourteen, to be precise." Panic bubbles up in the girl's voice. Her hands waver as they lift to her face, clawing at her eyes so that she doesn't cry. " I couldn't . . . I didn't.

"After that, I felt distant. I distanced myself from Josh and everyone I knew. I mean, when you've lost both of your parents within months of each other, there's nothing else you can do." She grits her teeth menacingly as she removes her hands from above her eyes, clutching the bed sheets like she's trying to claw the life out of them.

"Josh finally gave up on trying to talk to me and we grew apart. Momentarily, our friendship was weak. I only saw him when we ate and when we had shared duties. Even then, we barely talked. I had faded, and he had decided to give me the space I needed. I guess that was a good thing, because I was tempted to tear apart everyone who even dared to talk to me.

"Then the shift came. I was fifteen, and it was a complete shock to me and the rest of my pack. They tried to hide my secret, but the Alpha found out soon enough." Azra exhaled furiously, taking a lock of hair and slowly weaving a plait through the fine strands. "The Alpha saw me as a threat, and he gave me a choice: either I be his son's mate or I get executed. I chose the latter.

"They dragged me to the exact spot where my mother had stood. At that point, I didn't care whether I lived or died. I just wanted to get away from this horrific world." The warrior's hands clench with even more tension and regret than they previously had, as if they were trying to squeeze the life out of my bed. "But Josh had other ideas. He would never let me die, and so he challenged the Alpha to a Deathmatch.

"Everyone knew he couldn't win. He was an omega going up against an alpha who had previously won against our own alpha. No one believed he could win." Azra's hands relax their hold, supposedly flinching before springing back to their relaxed shape. The skin has gone white where her nails meet the skin. "But he did. He used his anger to fight, just like you did in the Alpha Trials. He had trained for hours in his spare time to take on the Alpha. He made winning look easy.

"With his weapon and rage, he banished the rogue wolves from the pack lands; including the Alpha's son, Hunter," Azra spits the name like there's bile rising in her mouth. We both visibly shudder at the name, my chest suddenly burning with a strange sensation I can't even fathom.

It all makes sense. The hatred; the pain. The strange underlying meaning in her eye every time we look at each other. Everything.

"They killed my parents, Ali. And they're never coming back," Azra whispers, threatening to burst into tears once more, but I give her a defiant gaze to stop her actions. She has to be strong, if not for me or Josh, then for them. "I'm going to get revenge, I assure you."

I bow my head. "I know you will."

Azra nods in response, standing from the bed frame and rising like a resurrected ghost. Her face is no longer a white canvas, and all signs of tears have seemingly vanished within the blink of an eye.

She swiftly moves her hand, her delicate fingers flickering over the hilt of her sword before drawing the weapon. As she draws the blade, the sound of metal on metal reverberates soothingly throughout my chamber. Sunlight reflects from the newly sharpened weapon, glaring into my eyes before Azra lowers her arm, resting it at her side.

No longer does the broken and orphan girl exist. Instead, in front of me stands the strongest warrior I've ever known. And she will not fall. Not now, not ever.

I can feel the vengefulness smothering the air; so thick, it's almost suffocating.

My exhale breaks the silence and the bird song. "It's a shame we didn't kidnap Hunter's mate," I murmur. "Then you could've gotten your revenge."

The smile Azra gives me is a strange, twisted one. "Actually," she utters. "We did."

CHAPTER SIXTEEN
Feelings
"It's hard to have a heart when you've stopped so many others."
- Unknown

There are two things I hate more than anything else in this world. Number one: water. Almost drowning in a torrent of water the night my parents were killed has never helped my fear and sometimes even a small trickling stream is too much for me to handle. The second is small spaces; I can't stand them. No matter how much you try to mentally prepare yourself for being squeezed into the tiniest space you can fit, you can never truly overcome the suffocating sensation.

That's how I feel right now.

As my hand traces the gritty and grimy wall, I feel like all the air has been squeezed from my lungs. The corridors below the castle are so narrow that they can only fit one person through. If you bump into another werewolf, and one has to press themselves tightly against the wall to avoid collision.

It's almost a relief when I reach the end of the seemingly endless pathway, but it isn't over yet. The room that it opens up into is the exact same shade of dilapidated grey and the darkness lurks inside like an uninvited guest.

As I follow Alex into the stronghold, the first thing I notice is that it's not empty. Gathered within this dark room are five figures—or, as of now, seven. It's hard to make out who the five mysterious people are but one I notice immediately. With his long attire and strong face, it's not hard to make out the man I kissed only days ago.

We've spoken a lot since, talking about our past. Chase's father died two years ago when he took over the position of alpha at the age of eighteen. Now, twenty-two-years-old, he has been through countless battles and controlled a pack with seventy-two members before competing in the Alpha Trials. He has a sister who went to explore the human world two years ago and never came back. He hates that his eyes are so blue they almost appear grey and despises the smell of fresh rain.

The other shadows are much harder to decipher between. Two stand beside a vulnerable small figure, who is held between the two. I can instantly tell that she's female due to her miniature frame and long garments. The other men I presume are guards, although I don't press any questions. I know who the girl is and what her mate has done.

Is she the same as him? A bloodthirsty rogue looking for vengeance, or a harmless she-wolf who was forced into mating with Hunter like Azra almost was? So many questions. Too many unanswered.

Chase is the first to spot us as we enter the chamber. I expect to see a smile or some form of comfort lining his features, but instead I receive a sneer. "I told you not to bring her here!" he exclaims, stepping into a more brilliant concentration of candlelight.

Alex crosses her arms. "She had a right to know."

"And you don't have the right to disobey my orders," Chase retorts, shrivelling up his nose in disgust. I've never seen him like this before: power hungry. If I said that his sudden mood swing doesn't scare me, then I'd be lying. Perhaps kissing him was a mistake. "Get her out of here!" he commands. No one dares to move an inch.

I fold my arms over my chest. "I'm right here, you know," I spit through gritted teeth. I clench them so tightly, I feel like they

189

might shatter under the pressure. "And I'm not going anywhere. Either you explain to me why you didn't tell me about this or I'll punch you and ruin that pretty face of yours."

Chase scoffs at my remark. His foot edges forward, the toe of a worn leather boot peeking out beneath his long trousers but it freezes in mid-air when I shoot him dagger-like gaze. "You really want to know?"

"I wouldn't have asked if I didn't," I retort with a roll of my eyes. He has no right to withdraw such information from me, his second in command.

Chase bites is lower lip unconsciously, the scarlet skin becoming a dilapidated beige from the pressure. "Fine," he grumbles. His nose scrunches. "I knew that you wouldn't agree and that you would interfere, so I didn't tell you."

"You're right," I growl, resting my hands firmly by my sides. I scrunch them into fists, trying to keep my claws from bursting through my fingertips. "I don't agree. Not with torture." I have morals.

I step forward hesitantly, submerged within the darkness of the cell. My eyes alter to the abrupt shift in light, the girl's face now becoming a full colour painting compared to the faint outline she was just moments ago.

Her face is strangely soft for such a woman. Being Hunter's mate, I had expected her to have a scarred face and sharp, strong features that makes her look like she can crack a rock with her own bare fists. Instead, her nose is dainty and small on her round face. Her high cheekbones create a unique beauty to her appearance, and the shadows elongate across her face like fingers. Bright hazel eyes flash at me from below dark eyelashes, almost luminous in the near absence of light. Her hair is dark—almost black—and the contrast to Hunter's snowflake pigmented strands is enough to make my skin crawl. They are literal opposites.

I remember the time my parents taught me how to use a sword. I was seven and could barely fit my hand around the blade.

190

Back then, my father had had a beard and his face did not have the scar that ran from the corner of his mouth to his right eyebrow. He had looked young and unscathed by the building threat of rogues as they resurfaced.

Back then, I had been incompetent and scared by the sheer power of the weapon. It took me years to finally get used to the movement and weight of the blade when I swung it, but even now, it would feel alien to me occasionally. The mysterious girl is clearly not me but she appears as though she feels the same way I do; as if she doesn't belong in her own skin.

Scarlet drips from the girl's nose like a fountain, a splatter of shadowed stain appearing on her dirty shirt like the ink of an exploded fountain pen. Her arms are similar, with blue bruises labelling her as a victim to the torture done in this hell hole. Now I know why I've never been down here before. It's haunted by the screams of those left to die and rot here over the centuries.

Suddenly, the room seems smaller. My lungs no longer have the ability to breathe in oxygen. What are they doing to her? This is wrong. No matter how many lives are at stake.

And I know that I have killed rogues without even thinking twice. I left Hunter's sister to get devoured by flames. I allowed my parents to sacrifice themselves for a monster.

I don't care what Chase says—if this girl is innocent, then she doesn't deserve this fate.

I cannot move. I cannot speak. Even my mouth refuses to form the simplest of words.

"What are you doing to her?" Alex notes my sudden impotence and steps forwards to stand beside me. She doesn't make physical contact to comfort me like Josh would. Strangely, I miss his warm touch.

Chase growls, shifting his body so that his back is partially facing the pair of us. Despite his attempt to block us out, he cannot ignore us forever. Even though he's supposed to be the King of Arla, he can't face us. He can't face me.

191

"What are you doing to her?" I repeat loudly, Alex shuddering beside me from the volume of my voice.

Chase's figure wavers like a flag caught in a storm. Even I can see the edges fraying as the wind catches the fabric like a vice. He still can't turn to face me properly, so he doesn't. He places his thumbs in the waistband of his trousers, biting his bottom lip once more. This time, the pressure of his sharp teeth is too much for the soft skin covering his lips.

I blink rapidly to clear the water smearing my eyes. "Are you going to say something?" I stagger forwards and walk in front of the King so that he is facing me. I kissed him two days ago; that feels like a millennia now. "Chase, we can't torture her. What if she was forced to be Hunter's mate?"

Chase reaches out a hand, clutching the side of my face. I knock it off with my shoulder. "She knows about Hunter's plans. If we're going to win, this is what we have to do," Chase replies but his voice is soft. He doesn't sound like half the king he needs to be. "You know I'm right, Ali. We know nothing about this girl, and I'd rather risk one life than thousands."

I gulp. My hands are back into clenched balls. "What do you know?" I question, knowing that he's right. But I still can't accept what he's done.

"That Hunter plans to launch an attack on Arla in two days." Chase sighs with a shaky voice.

"Impossible," Alex interrupts. "We have ten patrols. We'll see them coming long before they have a chance to attack."

I uncurl my fingers. "That's the problem. It's not impossible, just difficult."

"Alaska's right," Chase agrees almost immediately, almost too quickly for my liking. "That's why I must do what I have to do to keep our people safe." Chase notes my glower, but my hand slides back to my side. I didn't even notice that it was resting on the cold hilt of my sword, the engraved and swirling pattern imprinted on my palm like permanent ink. Chase faces the guards holding the prisoner, her head sunk towards the floor in defeat. "Again."

I almost cringe when one of the werewolves yanks the girl's hair, forcing her head to stare at the empty ceiling. The ribs of her oesophagus line her throat like scars.

"What will Hunter do when he arrives?" Chase spits, trudging towards the prisoner with an eerie stillness. The girl pinches her lips into a tight white line, the corners of her eyes threatening to spill tears into the dirt below her bare feet. "Fine, let's start at the beginning. What is your name?"

Her hair is yanked even harder, although I know that this is not the worst that she has faced in the previous days. I have no doubt that she hasn't been fed since her arrival. Even through her tattered dress—or what could pass as a rag—I can see the faint impression of her ribs. I know that Chase isn't torturing her for my sake. I may have a fire in my heart but, having been a prisoner previously, I cannot help but feel empathy for the girl.

"Zara," Hunter's mate whispers. If I wasn't a werewolf, I would not have been able to hear her.

I raise my eyebrows in surprise. Even Chase appears astonished that she answers.

"And he will kill you," the girl continues without permission to speak. She speaks with a thick accent which I cannot quite place. "He will come after me, and he will kill every last one of you."

Is she crazy? Doesn't she know that Hunter's dead? Well, let's play along with her delusions. From what Chase asked of her earlier, he's doing the same.

It's my turn to bite my lip. "Aren't you a cheery person," I mutter. My legs move forwards until I stand before her. My fingers still trace the indent in my skin where I held the handle of my sword, the strange pattern an intruder on my flesh. "Look, what they've done to you is wrong," I begin, holding up my hand before Chase can intervene. "I know that, but this is war, and I hope for our sake you'll never see Hunter again. But these men aren't going to stop hurting you until you tell us what he's planning. They will let you live if you just tell them what he wants."

Zara sneers, her pointed teeth beginning to pierce the corners of her mouth as they elongate. Although female wolves cannot necessarily always shift like I can, many can partially shift. Claws can grow from their fingertips and their teeth can mold itself into canines.

I expect Zara to begin to cry or kick out with her slim legs. Instead, the prisoner sneers. Her teeth are irregular, with one crossed in front of the other like crossbones.

Then she spits in my face. I stagger back in astonishment, wiping the sticky saliva off my cheek with my sleeve in disgust. She is just as feral and rogue as Hunter.

Zara laughs. It's a strange chuckle, not dissimilar to her mates' own disturbing cackle. "You really think after torturing me that I'd tell you the truth, Pretty Princess?"

I can't help myself as my hand flies to my dagger, immediately pressing the metal against the base of her throat. "What did you call me?"

"Get that knife away from my throat, Princess," Zara dangerously utters.

The joints in my hand click as I fasten my grip on my weapon. "I'm not a princess."

"Oh, really?" Zara continues as rage begins to boil furiously in my veins. "We all know you're screwing the King. Don't even try to hide it. See, you're blushing."

"I'm not sleeping with anyone, let alone him!" I shout, the skin at my fingertips beginning to throb with agony as my claws break through the delicate beige layers.

Zara sniggers, not even afraid of the knife at the base of her throat. One movement of my hand and she could be dead. Sadly, she's more useful being a hostage than rotting in a shallow grave.

194

"You think I hate Hunter, but he's my mate," Zara continues, her nose wrinkling up as if she detests the sight before her. "He didn't force anything on me. We're in love. Maybe you should try it some time, Princess."

Scarlet flashes in my sight as I press the blade into the skin of her neck, earning a gasp of pain. "I don't want to hurt you, Za—" Before I can finish the girl's name, the castle trembles. Dirt and tiny shards of rock rain down on us in a landslide, minimising my vision to a grey fog. My hands slip off the girl's neck to cover my own head. My heart jumps to my throat.

What is happening?

A voice through the cloak of nothingness could be heard. "I told you he would come."

"Tell us what's going on right or we'll kill you," Chase yells through the ricochet of rubble.

My chest expands and contracts with every laboured breath, my body shutting down with a form of fear I've never experienced before. I fall to my knees, trembling. I can't remove my hands from the top of my head, petrified that the roof will collapse on all of us, entombing us in this forsaken place.

Someone's hand finds mine, a rough thumb running over the surface of my palm with ease, like it's done it a thousand times before. Chase.

I hear Zara laugh over the muffled silence, another tremor shaking the room once again. Through the haze, I spot four silhouettes, one running out of the cave, and Zara's petite figure flanked by the guards.

"You're all going to die!" Zara yells as they haul her away. "Just you wait, King Chase."

I shake my head as Chase half pulls, half drags me through the corridor beyond. The pebbles and dirt have somewhat stopped raining from above like hellfire, but my body is still shivering like a leaf caught in a hurricane. I move my hands above my head to protect it from any falling debris.

195

"She's crazy," I mutter, the words coming out as an exasperated and rugged breath. I doubt Chase could hear me but I don't care.

This is it. This is the war Hunter wants. And during war, there's no time for fear.

CHAPTER SEVENTEEN
Panic
"The good suffer, the evil flourish, and all that is mortal passes away."
- *Cassandra Clare*

The light above us is blotched. One second, the glare of a crystal white ray strikes my eyes in a sudden, unique agony, and the next, it is blocked by a shard of debris as the walls around us cave in. The ground shudders with every stone, every pebble, and every boulder that hits the floor with a boom that mimics thunder.

Chase's hand is still firmly plastered to my own. His hold is tight, refusing to let go, and I won't let him. I can't find it in myself to pull away from his safety and his touch. My hand feels as though it has been encased in lightning, a storm where there is no calm to halt the ceaseless bolts. My body feels alive, emanating from his touch and through my bone marrow like liquid silver.

My breaths are too rapid to regulate and my heart races so quickly that I can no longer tell apart the beats. I hate small spaces, and the fact that these passageways are narrowing even further doesn't help my fear.

"This way," Chase shouts above the ear-splitting rumble as the ground shakes once more. His voice merges with the vibrations but my ears know his voice like they know my own.

He jerks me around the corner, up a flight of stairs, and into the light. The sun's rays are a shock as I enter the castle from the underground. There are no guards standing in attention outside the entrance. The sight sends a jolt through me. The city must be in serious jeopardy if the guards have left their posts.

"What the hell is happening?" I pant, leaning down on to my knees in an attempt to catch my breath. The relief of not being crushed by a collapsing tunnel gives me a spark of hope but Chase is quick to put it out.

Chase gazes into my eyes with a sturdy stare, as though his irises are made of marble. "The rogues; that's what's happening," Chase growls, tearing his sword from its sheath with such ferocity that he rips the leather pouch from his abdomen, as if it's nothing but parchment paper. "Stay behind me."

"No sh*t," I pant.

Chase is angry: I can see rage writhe within every cell of his body, as if he's on a different frequency compared to everyone else. His figure blurs, distorting for a second, but I know it's just my vision.

Bile rises dangerously in my throat, threatening to choke me. Closing my eyes in disgust, I swallow it down with great difficulty. My body feels like it's made of helium, every limb weightless and vulnerable. Maybe my fear of confined spaces is even worse than I originally thought.

"No," I say slowly but my words come out as a choke. I grab his hand, sliding my fingers between his like a puzzle being fit together. Except this isn't any puzzle; there are one million pieces and the shape is contorted by emotions and memories that force other pieces out of place.

We aren't the perfect match, and that's why we fit together so well. Nothing's perfect; nothing ever will be. We have our rough edges, and so does the world. No matter how much they are sanded down to shape, they will always remain rugged at heart.

I grit my teeth, pulling myself towards Chase to steady my swaying figure. The scene before us is a brutal one but it's nothing I haven't seen before.

An abundance of coal black smoke suffocates half of the castletown, settlements up in a roar of gold flames as they tease the sky and torment those who try to escape to refuge. There are too many people to count and they're all running towards the east as if it's a beacon. I can see why; rogues are scattered around the city like beautiful stars in the night sky. Except these rogues are not beautiful in the slightest. In fact, they're the opposite, but that's not the only thing that causes my heart to skip a beat involuntarily.

The wall has collapsed. It no longer exists. Shards of stone slide down a heap of rubble like a landslide, marking where the barricade once stood strong.

Tears streak my eyes and I let them out. I never wanted to become Alpha Queen, let alone second in command, because of this very reason. A rogue war, like the other hundred noted in history, had been bound to happen as soon as the Alpha Trials had been announced. A kingless kingdom; what better time to attack?

My legs give way. My eyesight is blurry. Everything is distorted. My hand slips from Chase's like a stone falling into water.

I'm back to where it all began. "Innocent" people being attacked and slaughtered mercilessly by monsters. This is the world, and no matter how much I want to change it, I can't. Something inside me tells me I don't want it to change, anyway.

But I'm back on my feet before I can clear my head. Instead of reaching for Chase's hand this time, I reach for my sword. At the moment, it's the only constant in my life. Despite its dull blade and heftier weight than the weapon the previous king gave me, it's still mine. I haven't been able to call something mine in years.

"Alaska?" Chase questions as my legs wobble. I use the wall to steady myself, the stone biting into my palms like a vicious predator.

I feel my eyes shift colour, the darkness of the castle room becoming as vivid as luminous paint. Even though I cannot see my face, I know exactly what it looks like; feral, the gold of my irises adding a certain rationality to my appearance. I only look like this when I'm forced into a corner with nowhere to run.

"They're winning." I say in realisation and horror. My knuckles click as I clasp the hilt of my sword even tighter than previously. "She's right. We'll lose."

Something touches my face but my skin has turned numb. I can't tell what it is but as soon as Chase's face appears in front of mine, hovering like a ghost, it's clear that his hands are grasping my face tenderly. I lean into one of his hands, although I don't feel his thumb wipe away one of my tears.

I blink, the world turning into a chasm of black. When I open my eyes, Chase's lips are on mine. Unlike my skin, my lips feel every sensation of Chase's kiss, as though I'm subconsciously mapping them. My head feels light, both from the realisation that we are losing the war and the sparks igniting my veins into a whirl of embers and ashes. I have never felt so alive yet so doomed.

The kiss is short but as soon as he pulls away, I feel alive. My eyes flicker back to their original, dull brown with fire in my bones, electricity in my veins, and thunder in my heart. It's strange what a person can do to someone just by a simple kiss.

Chase begins to pull away but my hands clasp behind his neck, keeping his face only centimetres away from my own. His warm breath fans against my skin. The hairs on the back of my neck rise but not from fear; from a feeling rising in my bones that echoes through me like a storm.

I bow my head forward, resting it on his forehead. Chase sighs, his hands slipping down to my waist. I'm still panting with exhilaration, my breaths sharp and uncontrolled.

"We're not going to lose," Chase whispers. Wind scatters my hair that has escaped my French braids across my face. A loose strand of my hair tickle my cheeks like feathers. "And even if we do, it won't be over. It'll never be over."

I swallow the lump stuck in my throat, breaking away from the close proximity. We are needed on the battlefield.

"I know it won't," I state blandly and shake my head. Feelings have to come later. "We need to go. We're not going to save them by staying locked up in the castle."

Chase nods, leading the way down the stairs. Despite my residency in the castle, I still have no idea where I am. Every stone corridor and rough staircase appears the same as the one before it. Hallways merge into one, a straight line of wall stretching out for eternity before me. At the beginning, nothing. At the end, darkness. The only way to distinguish the different passageways are the intervals of the windows and bright, unique tapestries clutching on to the wall.

☽

My feet hit earth in less than two minutes. It feels foreign beneath my shoes, as if I've never been outside before. The emerald of the evergreen trees guarding the kingdom feel out of place in the abundance of scarlet light as it devours the battlefield. White snow glares at me with greedy eyes, the contrast between the red hot flames and the sterile, cold substance making my eyes ache irritably.

The rogues are everywhere and none of the Arla werewolves are in sight.

In spite of our argument, I scour the landscape for Josh but he's nowhere to be seen. Nor is Azra, with her piercing azure eyes that can make even the most innocent person feel corrupted.

"Where's Zara?" I enquire, raising my voice above the howling voices and battle cries. Earlier, this city was peaceful, with the underlying murmur of voices and songbirds singing the only sound stirring the silence.

Chase's face is lined with ridges of anger. Instead of one blade, he has opted for two. I recognise them as the two swords the previous king kept by his side and stowed away in his weapon cabinet. The metal is engraved with a strange pattern, the silver reflecting the ominous leaves of curling ivy as they run up the blade, spiralling around a moon positioned just above the hilt. The leaves appear to be suffocating the iron.

"Gone," Chase murmurs, his eyes downcast towards the ground. "The guards should've gotten her out of the city by now."

"Alex?" I say desperately. "The others?"

"They'll be safe," Chase reassures me with the hint of a smile.

I drop my sword, flicking my claws out as the first rogue notices us. He lunges towards us, his long hair catching fire from a burning residence beside him. The knots become a halo of orange as he lashes out with a simple dagger but I duck before he can inflict any damage.

My claws swipe across his throat in an arc, tearing open a gaping hole in the man's flesh. He coughs up blood, gasping for breath as he begins to tremble from the blood filling his lungs. The body falls to the floor, burning silently as it lays to rest in the dirt.

The rogue's death catches the attention of more bloodthirsty beasts. They all scowl at the pair of us, eyes red with bloodlust and anguish. Coming out of this situation alive will be like surviving a tsunami.

"Come on!" I yell, a red blotch appearing in my vision like a permanent blemish. I don't have the time to wipe away the blood trickling into my eyes. It must've sprayed onto my face when I ripped out the rogue's throat.

I feel feral; a wild animal trapped in the vortex of a tornado. But then again, haven't I always been this creature below the mask? Below the armour? Stripped down to nothing, I'm wolf and human. Beast and reason. Monster and anger.

I have been called a rogue for a reason. I kill my own kind blindly. But doesn't that make all werewolves rogues?

Maybe there are no rogues and werewolves, just like there are no good guys and bad guys. There's never black and white; just different shades of grey distorting the world into a translucent veil of lies and torment.

Chase is the first to spring into action. His sure-footed strides keep him out of the path of hungry flames as he surges forward like a panther. His target looks much more powerful than the King himself, but with a clean swipe of his swords, the rogue's head rolls across the mud, the straw-like hair catching aflame.

A hand grapples my shoulder, its claws ripping through my shirt and sinking into my flesh. Ivory cuts into me bone deep, blood gushing out of my shoulder at an uncontrollable rate. The pain is like nothing I've ever felt before.

I howl in agony before I can stop myself. My father taught me to never show any weakness during battle. The fact that I've abandoned my father's lesson hurts more than the wound on my shoulder. I'm sure that if he saw me now, he would be horrified at what I've become. Or maybe he would be proud that I'm fighting on the right side.

Or maybe he doesn't care, or can't because he's dead.

I elbow the rogue in the stomach—or what I think is the stomach. My elbow makes contact with flesh, a tingling reverberation spiralling up the limb and through my body like an uncoiling spring.

I hear a grunt, and that's enough to make me believe that my attack has successfully put him out of action for me to focus on another target.

I pick her out easily. The female seems mismatched, a blotch on an imperfect establishment. It's peculiar to see a female rogue in this environment, her long hair braided just like mine, except twice the length and much darker than my own.

Just like me, she bears no weapons; just claws and teeth as she half-transforms. I mirror her actions, claws raking at my sides, the ivory clicking together familiarly as I clench and unclench the thin fingers in anticipation. Shivers run up my spine as my skin begins to prickle with a sensation that now feels like second nature.

An ear-splitting crack rings out into the battlefield as my bones shift. I grit my teeth to try and contain my cry of agony within my mouth but end up biting my tongue instead. As my teeth sharpen, blood spills into my mouth until it tingles on my taste buds, uninvited.

The rogue growls in response, opening her mouth to show her curiously long canines, unable to shift further than her semi-wolf state.

I have always found it unfair and unusual as to why not all females are able to shift completely like the males could. The werewolf society has always been sexist—much to my disgust—but the reason for the rare female shifters is beyond me.

Perhaps it's something to do with genetics, something that was far beyond my comprehension. Like colour blindness. Males can be colour blind, whereas women have a smaller chance of manifesting it. Perhaps it's the same principle with the shifting gene. After all, I've heard of rare cases where males cannot shift.

The girl is older than me by at least five years and the scars on her skin are enough to indicate her experiences in battle. She holds her head high in competition, the lines in her neck standing stark, as if they were metal spikes on barbed wire. She looks like an alpha, but it is clear that she no longer resembles the pack member she once was. Her eyes droop from sleepless nights, dark bags looming below the pits of her eye sockets. Rogues don't let girls into battle, so this one must be special. Or the rogues must be desperate to win.

A hiss can be heard from her lips. I expected a growl or a howl from the woman, but it is clear that she is distinctly different.

I bound forwards, rising above the ashes and through the smoke like a jet. My brown pelt ruffles in the wind as I glance down at my paws, making sure that I miss the flames littering the mud. Snow hits the bare flesh of my paws, shocking me into an adrenaline fuelled silence.

My jaw opens, ready to strike the girl down. She punches me out of the way, her power knocking me down to the ground.

I'm back on all fours faster than I knew I could move. I swipe with my claws, the terrifyingly long talons tearing into the woman's leg with ease. I hear the scrape of bone and feel it against my lengthened nails.

The rogue falls onto one leg, and, as much as it pains me to take another life, I finish her off before she can take her last breath.

My shoulder has already begun to heal, but another rogue attacks my hindleg before I turn around. This time, the rogue has transformed into a wolf, his black fur submerged into the darkness surrounding us. The light is fading rapidly, but with my heightened senses, it is easy to distinguish the yellow of his glowing irises and white scars running across his face in a spiderweb pattern.

I leap forwards to try and bite the werewolf as both of his sets of claws leave deep gashes on my legs. The effort is quickly overruled by the rogue as he grabs my muzzle with his teeth. I yelp with pain, the animalistic whine sounding more pathetic than any other sound I have ever made.

I'm not a good fighter in my wolf form. In fact, I'm far from it. I have spent so long using a sword to battle my wars for me, I'm now unable to battle them myself.

My body clatters to the ground, my bones grinding against each other harshly at the impact. My head thuds with a numb sensation but it's gone as soon as I blink. I can no longer feel the throbbing in my shoulder. Instead, everywhere hurts; even my eyes as they glare at the rogues before me.

I try to get up but another wolf knocks me down. I pant and kick with all four of my legs but whatever I hit seems as solid as a wall, refusing to budge. I can't escape. Is this finally the end of my torment?

I peer at the rogue above me. A scar runs across his chin, white against the black cloud of smoke. There is no grey in sight. It makes the wolf seem unrealistic but I know as a fact that it is very real, and that this very real wolf is about to rip my throat out.

He will relish my death. The snarl adorned on his jaw is enough to tell me that.

I snap at the rogue but he presses me back into the mud with ease. All of my escape attempts are fruitless.

Abruptly, the snarl falls off the rogue's face before he can take my life joyously. Blood spurts from his mouth, dripping onto my face in hot, sticky droplets. I wrinkle my nose in disgust, the wolf's body falling on top of me before I can move out of its way.

The weight knocks the air from my lungs, as if a one hundred-kilogram weight has been rested on my chest. I open my mouth to suck in a breath but I can't. My lungs have been compressed so much that I cannot inhale.

My hands frantically scramble to free me from the cage of death. With all my might, I push the corpse off my body. To my horror, my grey shifting clothes are smothered with blood, the abdomen and shoulder area ripped to nothing but shreds.

Finally, air floods into my lungs so rapidly it's like I'm flying. Without realising it, I begin to hyperventilate, my legs wobbling as I feebly wrench myself up off the floor.

My eyesight is hazy, and as I finally manage to stand on my own two feet, I see that the battlefield is clear. For now.

Chase stands in the centre of a clearing, his whole body heaving as he breathes heavily. Corpses lie at his feet, mutilated and sliced in half. To him, this is his life. He has been raised to be a ruthless alpha ever since he was born, and being the king doesn't diminish that responsibility from him at all.

"Ali!" I turn my head in the opposite direction.

A black silhouette appears in the haze of my eyesight. I have to blink rapidly to make sure that I'm not dreaming. That the boy is real. But of course he is real. Holding his stomach with a line of crimson staining his garments and clothes, Josh appears from the ashes, dust in his hair and a golden blaze rising behind him like wings.

A smile catches my face. I haven't seen or even spoken to Josh for days.

But Josh isn't smiling. As he comes more into focus, I can see the lines of worry on his face marking the skin like contour lines on a map.

"Ali!" he screams in desperation, sprinting towards me, but my mind's too slow. I can feel the seconds wind down, one trillion times faster than normal.

I catch a glimpse of white-silver, pitch-black eyes . . . and the gold hilt of a sword.

And that's when the blade rips straight through my body.

CHAPTER EIGHTEEN
Battle

"But if I'm it, the last of my kind, the last page of human history, like hell I'm going to let the story end this way. I may be the last one, but I am the one still standing. I am the one turning to face the faceless hunter in the woods on an abandoned highway. I am the one not running, but facing. Because if I am the last one, then I am humanity. And if this is humanity's last war, then I am the battlefield."
- Cassie Sullivan, The Fifth Wave

Everything is numb. My limbs, my joints, my skin; it's all weightless. My eyes blink. The world doesn't exist. Only the ground, myself, and the sword are at play in this field of nightmares.

An inferno rages from the right side of my abdomen. I glance down in horror to see that the blade has gone straight through body like it's nothing more than snow. A crimson circle of blood bellows from the wound freely, the sword being the origin, the diameter of the distorted shape ever growing.

My claws break through my fingertips, drawing part of the agony away from my battle wound. The grey ivory breaks through the surface of my pale skin, a roar escaping my mouth in pain. My breathing is so shallow, I feel as though it's stopped altogether.

I can no long feel anything in my legs, but they refuse to topple down as the sword sits in my body. I can already feel the skin around it begin to heal restlessly, but there is only so long until it's too late for the sword to be pulled out—too late to save me.

An animalist scream tears across the burning battleground, my watering eyes trailing to find Josh but he halts as the weapon is turned. I cough up blood, spraying tiny beads onthe waterlogged earth. Even against the brown of the dirt and dust, the red stands out stark like a flag. A flag of surrender? I'm not so sure.

"I'll give it to you, Alaska," a familiar voice says in an amused tone. Every cell in my body wants to rip out his heart and watch the light fade from his eyes. Yet again, people have died because of this platinum-haired devil, and I am unable to save them. "You're proving hard to kill."

I refuse to believe that he's here. He's supposed to be dead. I watched the life drain from his eyes.

The boy pulls out the sword with a mighty tug. I hear my healing flesh protest against the metal as it is withdrawn, the relief short as the agony takes over.

I keel over, clutching my stomach. My knees hit the wet floor, the icy water seemingly freezing the marrow in my bones. I cough blood once more, flecks of it on my hands like blemishes. My wound is already beginning to heal, but I will have an ugly scar to prove that the gaping hole in my abdomen once existed.

I clench my hands into fists, the skin still wet with red residue. How is Hunter not dead?

"H-How? Do you ever die?" I retort, clumsily rising to my feet. My hands grasp at my belt, coming away with nothing more than my hunting knife. My sword lies somewhere in the rubble and dirt, a relic to be found in the smouldering ruins of the city. I've only seen destruction like this twice in my life. Alex's pack, and now this. It's enough to make a person hide the good half of their soul for the rest of their unforgiving life.

Hunter raises his invisible eyebrows. His hair is so white, they appear decayed and non-existent against his faded skin tone.

"I hardly think that a knife is going to help you." The male shakes his head, flicking his wrist and sword in succession. He makes the weapon appear weightless, just like the way he walks as though he's floating on a grounded cloud. The platinum-haired werewolf raises a hand to something behind me.

I turn around in bewilderment. Josh is supporting Chase as he stands, clutching his side all the while. A hole is torn in his garments, claw marks raked down his side, creating valleys like a ploughed field. My heart jumps to my throat in fear, even though I tell myself that he's okay. Chase is okay.

A hand abruptly grips my waist, pulling me into Hunter's hard chest. Though the leader of the rogues looks like he can snap me in half with a jolt of my arm, he holds on to me strongly like a stone statue. I don't need to feel the cold against my throat to know that Hunter has placed his sword there. It presses against my windpipe, threatening to slip further and plant a hole at the base of my neck. The recently sharpened blade breaks my skin, and I bite my lip to try and keep myself from yelping in pain. I don't succeed.

I widen my brown eyes without meaning to, immediately feeling weak, as though Hunter has already won. I want to cry out to Josh or Chase to save me, to do something as I stand powerless at the rogue's will, but it's useless. All I can do is watch the blade rise and fall on my neck with each laboured breath. The oxygen whistles through my teeth.

"Come any closer and I slit her pretty neck," Hunter speaks slowly and with satisfaction. I don't need to turn around to know that he's sneering. It's a look I've grown accustomed to during the few times I've had the "privilege" of meeting him. Josh and Chase seem frozen in place. "Good," Hunter continues.

Chase's hands are already clenched, his blade dropping from his hand in surrender. Two rogues lie at his feet, both not moving. We are monsters.

"Just tell us what you want," Josh says, licking his lips. His face is plastered with ash and blood. I can't even begin to fathom

210

where he was before the horror occurred. And where is Azra? Is she safe? After everything Hunter and his rogues have done to her, I won't let them touch her. "Please, just don't hurt her."

I glare at Chase. His lips move but words do not form. Surely he has something to say? I could die today. My blood has already stained the snow, and more could follow. Why was he acting so calm about everything? In all fairness, I hate being objectified. They don't need to beg for me to be kept alive; that was my job and mine alone. Since when had both grown so protective over one stupid werewolf girl who has the ability to shift?

My hands pry at Hunter's thin yet muscular arms. They refuse to budge even an inch. The pale pigment of his dilapidated skin is disturbingly white against my tanned complexion. At least the cool tone reflects the ice in his non-existent heart.

Hunter laughs—a long, almost mechanical, laugh used by villains in superhero films. "I want my mate," the man replies. He presses his sword so tightly against my neck that my air supply is cut off. I desperately clasp at his arms, but that results in him knocking my deep wound intentionally. I whimper in response.

Josh's eyes are stern. "We can do th—"

Hunter removes an arm for a mere second, holding up a single finger. "I'm not finished," he continues. Oh, he's enjoying this. The arseh*le. It's as if people dying turns him on. "I want you to surrender."

My hands stop fumbling for a second, as if they've hit pause. I see the blank gaze distort Chase's face and immediately know what he's going to do.

"Chase!" I yell. "Don't. Please don't. I'm not worth it, for God's sake."

But Chase does what he normally does in similar situations—he chucks the dagger from his belt and raises his hands. The blade sticks out the soft mud blade first, scarring the battlefield.

211

Hunter loosens his grip around my throat, the edge of the blade pressing sharply into my chest with each inhale. "Chase," I half shout, half scream, my teeth gritted like white bone vices. If only I could tear out Hunter's throat with them. "No. I'm not worth it."

Hunter's chest rises and fall abruptly, his clothes rubbing against the fabric of my own. I decided to wear a thick, human-made winter coat earlier to keep out the cold, but with the garment shredded from my shift, I'm shivering despite the fire and anguish raging inside me.

"It's a strange thing, love," Hunter says softly, almost like a whisper in my ear. "The way it can heal a person." He pauses, lowering the sword completely. Chase's eyes stray from my own, transfixing on something behind me. They don't blink, the golden-cobalt eyes concentrated by the dusk light. "And tear them apart."

A firm hand pushes at my back, separating me from Hunter. But I know what's going to happen next. I've seen enough fights to know exactly what he's planned.

My hand scampers for my final dagger, the other clutching the wound as a new kind of agony soars through my veins like an adrenaline rush of poison.

I swirl my hand around just in time for it to stop Hunter's sword from entering my body once more. The two metal objects collide with a reverberating clang. I use all of my remaining strength to push the leader of the rogues much longer weapon away from my body.

Exhausted, I fall to my knees. The watery mud soaks through my leggings, trickling on my skin like an icy bucket of water.

"Ali!" Josh shouts as my vision is shrouded by Hunter's shadow. I can't see Josh nor Chase but the thundering sound of footsteps sparks hope in me. "Don't you dare touch her!"

The sword is under my chin before I know it. I look up through the dark slits of my eyelashes, like monsters stirring my vision, to see the blotched image of Hunter smiling menacingly in a grin that splits his uniquely angular face in two. He pushes the sword upwards, forcing me to look away from the ground and into the horizon.

He's going to kill me. I have to do something, I tell myself, yet my muscles are slack. I hate this—feeling completely and utterly useless.

My eyes gloss over with water but I bite my tongue to stop the tears from forming. Crying will come later. Survival has to come first. It always does.

I scream as my bare palms make contact with the blade, my hands receiving an extremely sharp cut. The blood appears in a morbidly black colour as it drips through the cracks of my scars embroidered on my skin. It's beautiful, in a way.

Strength rages through my arms as I push the sword away, palms bloody, panting in exhaustion.

Hunter stumbles to the side, giving me enough time to get on my feet—or rather, for Chase to haul me to my feet. My winter boots sink pathetically into the mud like it's quicksand.

"We need to go!" he shouts in my face, half-dragging me behind him.

Despite the situation, I still have time to roll my eyes. "You think I don't know that?" I yell back, resting a hand on my stomach as we begin to run back towards the castle with Josh in tow.

"You can't run from this, Chase," a surprisingly loud growl echoes behind us. I hear the immediate crackle of bones snapping like twigs, alerting me to the fact that the monster has become an even greater heinous beast.

Chase puts his head down, narrowing his eyes as he picks me up in a millisecond, lifting me over a pile of burnt bones. I taste the bile rising in my throat.

"Don't listen to him," I whisper as I grip on to his wrist. Josh surges in front of us, immediately heading straight through the oak doors of the castle and leaving them open for us to follow through. Chase shoves me in as gently as he can through the barricades, slamming the wooden doors behind us swiftly and placing the huge bolt across the equally huge door. The stone walls have never felt so cold. If we're lucky, we can lose Hunter in the castle. He doesn't know the corridors like Chase does.

"I wasn't," he replies quietly.

Chase halts. The gold flecks of his eyes are much more prominent as he gazes at me. The slither of a smile appears on his face as the weak rays of light hits his handsome face through the fine window. I can't read the expression. It's something I've never been good at. His soft hand reaches up to cup my cheek and I lean into it.

"I almost lost you," he whispers, the other hand winding around my waist. He tries desperately to avoid my wound but his attempt is fruitless. He pulls me closer into his chest. I can smell his relaxing scent of pine trees and fresh dirt drift into my nostrils.

It reminds me of summer, and the time when my father took me out to go and practice with my new sword which he had won in a bet against the previous alpha. "I-I almost lost you," he repeats, bowing his head towards the ground.

I furrow my brow as I watch a tear roll down his cheek. I wipe away his tear gently before placing a soft kiss on his lips. Sparks fly, and although everything about our feelings towards each other doesn't make sense, I can't deny that I know that Chase is right. He is right for me. I can't imagine anyone else making me feel the same way in the future. I love the mystery behind him, and our physical chemistry is unlike anything I have experienced before.

"You do still know that I'm here, right?" Josh says awkwardly, completely and utterly ruining the moment.

He waves at me as I break away from the embrace, wiping my own face with the burnt sleeve of my top. It must've caught on fire while I was attacked by the rogues but with my pain, I hadn't even noted its existence. Just like the way I ignored Josh. "I mean, there's nothing else happening, right? Just a freaking psychopath

214

coming to kill all of us, probably in the most grotesque way you can probably think of. Oh, and did I forget to mention the fact that the rest of the city is probably still being slaughtered by mindless rogues?" Josh speaks so quickly, his words become a mush of syllables. He takes a deep breath and shrugs. "You know, nothing much. It's not like we're going to die or anything."

"Sorry," I speak for the both of us. Chase bites his lip, giving me a guilty smile as I squeeze his hand, forgetting the blood plastered on it. "I'm still here, Chase. I'm okay. And Josh is right; we need to go. Is there another way out of here?"

Chase nods sternly, releasing my hand from his comforting grip. My hand immediately feels empty without his, as if part of my soul had been snatched away from right under my nose.

"Follow me," he orders and we oblige quickly.

The castle is oddly silent as we wind through passageways. Where I expected to be battle cries and Arla citizens begging for their lives, there is nothing but empty air. It's not like everyone dropped what they were doing and ran—it's like they never existed in the first place.

Finally, we reach a door that overlooks the drop into the natural mote that protects the left side of the city. It's no wonder why the other werewolves have automatically run for this side of the fortress. The wide torrent of murky water separating the kingdom from land is extremely hard to cross, something a rogue will never try to attempt.

I gulp as I eye the grey water, the the occasional shimmer of white from faint waves rising like horses from the deep, rearing out wildly with their hooves. The drop itself is at least ten metres— survivable, but dangerous. It only takes one glance at Chase to know what he's thinking.

A vision of nightmares abruptly engulfs my vision like a bare flame. I feel water flood into my throat, literally pry open my lips and soak into my body as I grip at my oesophagus.

My vision blinks back out to a sterile white, the world cold and frigid in comparison. My hands lower from my throat as the black patches swell away into nothingness.

"Chase," I begin, my fingertips softly running down his bare arm through the claw marks of his shredded t-shirt. I see the hint of a six pack through the grungy material and look away as my cheeks flash red. "I can't do this."

I gulp, gazing down at the chasm once more. More bile rises in my throat, and this time, I can't keep it down; I empty the contents of my stomach into the roiling water, leaning over the cobblestone banister. It's the only thing separating me from reality and my dreaded nightmares. "There must be another way out."

"There isn't." Chase clasps one of my hands as Josh stands back awkwardly, chewing his thumbnail. "What's wrong?" he asks. The intensity of his gaze forces me to drop my gaze to the grey flooring.

A peculiar smile takes over my features. I'm unsure if I'd even be able to read it if I was looking at my mirror reflection. "I just really hate water," I confess.

"What a pity," a voice echoes as the doors to the balcony open eerily, the sound of the rushing water cut from my ears. A dark boot peers through the gap, like vicious oil escaping from a tank. Next comes the shining, luminescent reflection of his sword. Finally, his discoloured hair. "I guess I'll just have to kill all of you."

Instead of Chase pushing me behind him, I do the opposite. It's me he tried to kill earlier. Now it's me he will have to kill first.

"You do realise that there is a concept called 'giving up,'" I snarl, bearing my teeth as they elongate. The pointed ends of my canines prick my bottom lip like two fine needles. "Maybe you should try it sometime."

Hunter draws his dark clothing out of the way of his belt so that he can sheath his weapon. "As much as I admire your stubbornness, Alaska . . .," He wipes off a blotch of blood—my blood—from his sword. "I do not admire your sarcasm."

"No one asked for your opinion, arseh*le."

The wolf sniggers. "They didn't need to."

Hunter steps forwards, his sword sliding against its sheath like a death bell. We all collectively step back to keep the distance between us relatively the same. My back hits the solid rock behind us, making the man before us sneer further. Unless we jump—which is practically a death sentence—he will possibly slaughter all of us. He definitely has the capacity to do so.

"We surrendered," I hiss, desperate not to jump into the water. "Now leave us alone."

Another step forward. "But where's my mate?" Hunter enquires, his dark eyes lingering like much-despised pests. He waves a hand around the stale air, uninterested. "I don't see her, and if I remember correctly, those were the terms to keep you alive."

He presses forward, and I savour each beat of my heart, fearing that it might be my last. There is no reasoning with Hunter. He either gets what he wants or you die.

Chase's fingers tickle my palm as he leans in. I can feel his lips move gently against my ear, his voice so quiet it sounds like the whisper of winter. "Do you trust me?"

Do I trust him? Good question, because I honestly still don't know the answer.

"Oh, come on, Chase," Hunter murmurs. "Don't be a coward. Be the king everyone else so blindly looks to for guidance, whom everyone will commend for bravely dying in battle."

Chase's hand flinches away from my own, coiling into fists. "I'm not a coward."

Hunter drifts his hand in front of us, inviting him to fight. "Then show me," the rogue taunts, flashing teeth as white as his skin and hair.

Chase begins to step forward but I put a hand out to stop him. I shift my head so that my eyes can take in his mesmerising complexion. He nods, as though he can read my thoughts.

"I do," I say. "I trust you with my life, Chase."

And with that, he takes my hand, grabs me around the waist tightly, and pulls me over the edge. I blink away the fear as my stomach fills with an infestation of butterflies. I blink and, before I know it, I'm falling straight into oblivion.

CHAPTER NINETEEN
Mate

"I've been taught that love is beautiful and kind, but it isn't like that at all. It is beautiful, but it's a terrible beauty, a ruthless one, and you fall - you fall, and the thing is - the thing is you want to. You don't care what's coming, you just want who your heart beats for."

- Elizabeth Scott

As soon as my eyes blink open, dissolving the seemingly impenetrable darkness of sleep, I roll on to my side, sputtering water out. I squirm in agony as the liquid flows freely through my lungs, choking my throat like a vice. I close my eyes, pitch blackness taking over once more. I can't help but think of the first time this had happened to me five years ago, except that time, I was alone.

Not again. Oh God. Not again, not again, not again.

I begin to panic.

My chest heaves suddenly, rising as another mouthful of water is heaved onto the floor like a waterfall. It then stops for a second. I open my eyes, right before I cough again and again to rid the water from my body.

Only when I'm certain that my lungs are no longer swimming in water, I hastily sit up, only for a hand to abruptly rest on my back to help support me. My eyesight is blurry beyond imagination, and the only thing I can actually see is a skin-coloured shape, with a dark splash of brown at the top of what I presume to be his head.

"Alaska?" the male asks, my hearing distorted. But I would recognise that tone anywhere; Chase.

I blink rapidly to clear the haze, although it doesn't do much to help. This time I can make out his features. The sharp edge of his jawline; the gold flecks suspended in his cobalt eyes, as if hanging by invisible threads; his strong features that looks as though they are carved from stone.

He's beautiful, I think to myself. And he's mine. I realise with a jolt. Alaska, the girl who has not known love for five years, has finally found what she's been missing.

A grin splits Chase's face as soon as I am fully able to focus. It's something I rarely see him do, and his straight teeth are yet another thing I commit to memory.

"Hey," he whispers, pulling me into his hard chest in one swift movement. He's crouched next to me as I lay in an area of soft grass, the sound of rushing water overpowering my other senses. The abundant emerald grass tickles my legs through the thin fabric of my plain black leggings. His hand cups my face, his thumb running against my cheek once more. It's hot against my stone-cold skin.

I smile tentatively at him. "Hey," I whisper as a response, leaning into his hand. Despite my water-logged clothes and soaked hair, he makes my skin tingle like a thousand fireworks exploding.

He withdraws his hand and I suddenly shiver. I remember crashing into the water and swimming to the surface to taste the fragile air, only to get dragged down by the monstrous currents.

I remember the water filling my lungs like air would fill a balloon until it exploded into a spray of plastic confetti. I remember the dark water, consuming my body—suffocating me—like writhing tentacles. It was just like the night my parents had sacrificed themselves for me.

I reminisce the fall, right before the water. The way Josh had gazed at us with a sudden awe—and realisation that he had to follow us or risk death. I can't remember what he chose. I had broken the surface of the water at that point.

Josh, I think back to him. My best friend. The one person who has been there for me over the course of these few weeks.

Abruptly, my legs shift from under me, holding strong like the iron frame of a building. I expect them to crumble, to land me back on the soft ground, but for the first time they don't.

Chase rises with me, a discombobulated look showing through the cracked features of his face. My hand slides around his arm, gripping tightly as my heart begins to beat at an uncontrollable rate.

What if Josh is dead? I don't think I'll be able to live with myself if he is.

Chase tries to pry my hand off, grunting slightly in the attempt. As a response, I strengthen my grip, so tight that the skin around his forearm has turned aluminium white.

"Josh," I say out loud, the name sliding off my tongue as though it's been embedded in my memory since birth. I gaze around, but there's no sign of him. In fact, there's no sign of life around us; just ancient trees as their branches creak in the zephyr like unused joints when they are abruptly moved. Water runs into my eyes from my hair—whether it's genuine water or my tears, I cannot decipher. "Josh," I repeat. "Where is he? Is he okay?"

Finally able to break my fisted hand from his limb, Chase holds it. He shakes me to snap me out of my daze but it does absolutely nothing to ruin my trance. "Ali," he says in a voice that sounds like he's warning me. "He's okay. I saw him jump after I resurfaced."

I snap my eyes from the faded ground to his eyes, the gold so prominent in the dawn light. My heart thunders against my chest like a feral storm. It feels as though it's under so much strain that it

221

will eventually burst, the heart strings tearing and the cardiac muscle no longer usable.

Chase soothingly circles my wrists with his fingers, resting just above my soaring pulse. I try to focus on the steady beat of his own heart, but my ears are deafened by my own heartbeat. I need to stop being so paranoid. I need to see Josh.

"You promise?" I mutter, my voice hushed. My vocal chords are tender from the water; they scrape against each other like sandpaper each time I talk. I grit my teeth to help the pain subside, but it does little to ease the aching.

Chase nods. "I promise," he replies. He leans forwards slowly, as if in slow motion, before capturing my lips with his own. It's as if he's asking for my permission before he completes the task. The kiss is wet but it feels warm as it deepens. "I haven't seen him since, but he's okay."

I pull away. The ground is carpeted in patches of snow. The trees glint silver, icicles formed on the dead branches of a nearby oak. It refracts the streaming sunlight across the floor in a blaze of gold, like encapsulated fire. A river bank rolls down into the clutches of the feisty torrent of water, mud consuming the grass. Numerous footprints are implanted into the softened soil, the rugged indent of a shoe perfectly outlined and preserved like a fossil.

I have no idea where we are and no idea where we're going to go. So much for that plan.

"Where are we?" I ask tentatively, grabbing a handful of my waterlogged clothing. My hands fasten around the bottom of my shifting t-shirt, wringing out a handful of water that falls to the ground. Mud splashes on to my leggings, but they're already drenched in enough filthy water for me to even care. I wriggle my toes in my boots and hear them slosh around noisily. I cringe at the noise.

"Where are we going?" I ask almost immediately after the first question, barely giving Chase any time to answer.

Chase drops his hands from my wrists and takes a step back. He is weaponless, just like I am. He appears uncomfortable without anything in his belt. It's strange to see the numerous hunting knives and the pair of swords missing from their usual leather sheathes.

"We're south of Arla," he states, and my mouth opens wide in shock. South? A wolf's instinct is to always go north. "And we're going to a human building. One owned by a pack of isolated wolves. It's always been a place of sanctuary in times of need for pack wolves," he tells me, and I nod my head dubiously in understanding. Except I don't understand it. Nothing makes sense.

Surely, if we're going somewhere all pack wolves take refuge whenever something unscheduled happens in their lives, the rogues will know where we're headed? "The rogues don't come this far south. It's too close to the human world." He pauses. "You won't like it," Chase adds.

My eyebrows furrow. "Why won't I like it?" He can't immediately tell me I won't like something—he doesn't know me well enough.

Chase doesn't shrug like I expect him to. Instead, his body grows rigid like a corpse. "You just won't," he insists sullenly, keeping his head towards the ground. He turns his back on me, pulling his coat off his body and wrapping it around his waist.

I nod, frustrated that he hasn't said anything else. "Okay," I murmur, my legs moving confidently to stand beside him. "Let's go."

☽

The abandoned human hotel stands alone in the forest like a mountain; tall and stark, the roof smothered with a metre of freshly fallen snow. The walls appear to be washed by time, the white merging into the dilapidated surroundings like a chameleon.

223

The quadrilateral building is basic; rectangular windows are indented and equally spaced out from each other. I watch curiously as someone walks past one of the clear windows, perhaps going down a flight of stairs. Thankfully, the person is oblivious to note our existence.

However, the surrounding clearing of the hotel is completely the opposite. Tents are sprawled out in an uneven fashion like a fallen box of matches. A fire rages in the centre of the cluster of tents, the logs acting as benches whilst the unfortunate stand around doing nothing more than talk and appear agitated and constantly on edge. The ruby and tangerine pigments remind me of the inferno back within the walls of Arla. Of all the suffering these people should've never experienced.

If humans knew that werewolves existed, many would be jealous of our abilities. You have to be a real werewolf to realise what a hardship this life brings. Wild wolves rarely live beyond thirty, and we've always lived with the overhanging threat of rogues. Humans have it easy compared to us.

Lost in my train of thought, I stumble over a navy rucksack slung outside a permanent wooden hut. It must've been a separate, expensive room when the hotel was up and running years ago. I curse under my breath as I flail, finally managing to regain my disorientated balance.

My failure to walk normally draws the attention of some of the werewolves carrying out their daily chores. One carries a bucket of water, the transparent liquid splashing over her clothes as she stops abruptly to gaze at Chase. Another stops sharpening his axe, the air filled with silence.

"Chase," I whisper as we continue to walk forwards, towards the centre of the clearing. I pull my now dry shirt closer tomy body, beginning to shiver. I hate being the centre of attention, and with what feels like one thousand eyes, each peeling back layer after layer of my skin, I bite my tongue. The action draws blood, but the metallic taste is something I have recently grown used to. "You're right. I don't like this," I continue.

The man beside me takes my hand in his, entwining the fingers into an unbreakable bond. This time, it does something to calm my nerves, but standing next to the King who is presumed dead is not the best way to avoid attention.

As we continue trudging forwards—dragging our exhausted feet heavily in the snow—more and more werewolves turn our way. Some point, some whisper among themselves, others begin to follow us. I gulp as my nerves begin to consume me, but I refuse to give into the sickening feeling growing rapidly in my stomach.

"You'll be fine," he consoles me. "You'll see Josh and Azra soon."

My heart begins to thump rapidly at the mention of my best friends. Even though Chase had told me that Josh had jumped after us, his story doesn't seem to add up. Hunter is faster than any other werewolf I know, including Josh and Chase, and his swifter reaction time would surely stop Josh from jumping before he had the chance to. And Azra . . . I haven't seen her since this morning, when she had been sent off to patrol the perimeter of the city.

Sh*t.

The patrols were the first to be attacked by the rogues. What if she's dead and we don't even know?

I blink so harshly that my eyeballs begin to hurt. I can feel the salty sting of tears in the corner of my eyes but then shut them for a second, squeezing the tears away. I'm not going to cry in front of this many people.

A crowd has gathered, and we finally reach the fire pit, which is now dwindling down to glowing embers. Werewolves of all ages stand in front of us with a look of awe collectively drawn on their faces. What? Had they all automatically presumed that their king was dead, lying face down in the snow, a sword through his heart?

"Ali!" a voice calls above the racket. All conversations cease, as though they have been cut in half by a knife. I don't even have the chance to make out the face of the boy rushing towards me until I'm in his thin arms. The force from the imminent embrace knocks the air from my lungs, and I gasp as the werewolf begins to wrap his arms around my smaller frame even tighter.

My hands linger by my side for a second, unable to move. In fact, I can't speak. I'm so overwhelmed with relief that I can't even bring myself to look at his soft features. I no longer need to remind myself of his long eyelashes and pale lips.

"Josh?" I exhale quietly. My eyes are open wide. I don't want to think about what I look like at this moment in time. My hands move around him like clockwork, sliding gracefully out of Chase's grip without much resistance. I allow my fingers to clutch his shirt, almost desperately, just to remind myself that he's real—that he's alive.

"Oh my God," I whisper.

Josh rests his chin on the crook of my shoulder. "I was so worried," he murmurs. "When I came here and you hadn't arrived—" He pauses, and for quite a while. I can't bring myself to find the right words, so I don't. I just stand there, my arms engulfing him, my nose pressed up comfortably against his collarbone. "I thought something bad had happened to you, and I . . ." Yet again, he stutters. I can hear the tears lining his eyes. "I realised I couldn't live with myself if something did happen to you."

My hands subconsciously grip Josh's shirt tighter. He flinches from the movement, but I refuse to let go. I won't let him go ever again.

"I was worried about you, too," I admit, although it doesn't take a genius to figure that out. My voice falters, the sudden change in pitch obvious in the consuming silence. I hate the way everyone has stopped talking to stare at their second in command. "I was so scared that Hunter had killed you."

226

Josh laughs hastily, sucking in a breath. I don't know how to read his actions, so I just continue to stand there, refusing the let go.

"Alaska," he breathes out.

I raise my head to look at him. His face is shadowed as the sun shines on him at a peculiar angle. "Yes?" I question, the corners of my mouth quirking up into a faint smile.

Josh shakes his head, the dark hair on his head spiralling in the wind. They've grown longer in the past week, almost falling into his eyes.

"Thank you," he whispers.

I rest my cheek against his shoulder, listening to the rhythmic pulse of his heart. "For what?" I ask gently, pushing the hair from his eyes.

He presses me tighter against his chest. "Everything," he replies with a heave of his chest. "For changing my life, and for the better. I don't think I'd be able to stand Chase as king without your snarky remarks constantly undermining him."

Josh's heart rate is steady against my ear. "Josh," I say slowly, the words slowly pouring from my mouth without my consent. "I should be the one thanking you. I don't think I'd be alive without you."

The boy sighs, a smile etched onto his soft face. "You don't need to thank me." His cheek rests against my hair tentatively.

I love you, I want to tell him, but I refuse to speak. I love him like a brother. For sitting beside me on the day we met, despite the fact that I was deemed a rogue and you were an alpha. For supporting me throughout the Alpha Trials and seeing it through with me until the end. For smiling and laughing even when I'm a b*tch. For staying my best friend when I smashed your heart into one million unfixable shards. For being Josh, the boy who will selflessly sacrifice himself for the right cause.

"Alaska," a female voice calls from behind me. I pull away from Josh nonchalantly, squinting my eyes as I move out of his shadow.

The woman before me is someone I do not know very well, but have grown to admire over the past two weeks. Her hair is still sprawled around her face like wisps of smoke, framing her square face well. Two plaits along the left side of her head are entwined with the white of her feather, a typical hairstyle for a female in power.

I nod to her. "Alex." I'm unsure what to say, considering our circumstances. I'm just glad to see that she escaped unscathed.

Alex bows her head in response, her hands rested calmly by her sides. I rarely see her without her sword fastened in her iron grip. "It's good to see you," she states with a smile. Her tone remains neutral.

Suddenly, a figure sprints from the crowd, wrapping her arms around my waist for she cannot reach any higher. I stagger back in shock, a smooth fountain of black hair tumbling down the girl's back and hiding her face. But I know the child's stature like I know the back of my hand.

I give the figure a quick hug before bending my knees to glance down into Harper's deep irises. "Hey," I whisper. I shoot her a smile and she sends me a toothless grin in return. She looks more beautiful than usual with the mud and grime no longer caking her face. "You okay?"

Harper nods.

The girl then pries herself from my body but remains defiantly at my side. I take the opportunity to scour the growing crowd for Azra, but her piercing blue eyes are nowhere in sight. If she's safe, surely she'd be with Josh?

I nudge the boy standing next to me with a measured amount of strength. "Where's Azra?" I ask, not daring to glance his way just in case the look on his face breaks my heart.

Josh's face contorts into a smile in my peripheral vision, most likely to shield his demoralised feelings. "She's not with you?"

It's my turn to be confused. Why would she be with me?

"As much as these reunions are heart-warming, we have much more pressing matters at hand," a deep voice cuts through the noise.

Although the tone rings distinctively like a man's would, I am astonished when I spot a woman standing before Chase with her arms crossed. She's probably one of the oldest werewolves I've ever seen, but her light blue eyes resemble something from my past, as if I recognise her. The woman shoves her index finger behind her, obnoxiously ordering us to follow her into the building. She's short, but her strides are long as they carry her towards one of the oak, white framed, doors.

The ancient woman turns her head to gaze at me as I silently take a step forward. I give Chase a side glance, but he just follows the woman without question. "It's nice to finally meet you, Alaska," the she-wolf speaks loudly over her shoulder. Her voice is shrill; the commanding tone of an alpha or someone in a similar position. No one dares to speak as she walks through the crowd, people stepping aside to let her through. The crowd is unnervingly silent. "I've heard a lot about you."

I bite my lip. This is not how I had intended my day to go. "Well, most of it's probably bullsh*t," I tilt my head to the side. "But thanks. I don't know if I can say the same about you." I'm much happier staying with Josh, I want to add on, but I stop myself before I make yet another enemy.

The woman laughs—a quiet, strained noise. "I'm Logan," she says as we near the door. I briefly look behind me to check that Josh is following us and smile inwardly when I notice he is. "And I've been in charge of this outpost ever since it was abandoned," Logan continues. It's strange that her name is notably masculine, as is her articulation. "We take in any wolf who needs help, including outcast rogues."

229

I shiver at the mention of rogues.

Logan opens the door, her hand clasped so tightly around the metal handle that I can hear the shuddering vibrations of her clicking knuckles.

The action reveals the interior to the hotel. The corridor is painted a dull ivory, wooden doors placed at equal distances from one another as they line the walls. A rugged and repugnant navy-blue carpet smothers the floor, worn by many shoes down to a pale blue.

"I understand your hatred towards rogues," Logan states, making sure to glower at Chase after me. "And I understand that you do not want to wait around and talk about pointless matters. We are at war—a war that we need to win, and we all need to work together to do so."

The silver haired wolf's words are probably the most blunt, yet meaningful words I have heard in a very long time.

She leads us through a set of double doors, opening up into a room overlooking the fraying tents down below in the gardens. From here, it's easy to see the overgrown ivy climbing over rotting wood, writhing across the grass like an outstretched hand. The deep emerald-stained shrubs outlining the main garden were uneven, branches of different lengths poking out where they should not be. It's just as wild as the life I am currently living.

A desk is the centrepiece of the room. Papers lie sprawled on the surface, each sheet neatly arranged and the contents on the paper handwritten in the same font. The writing is extremely tidy but I can't read a word, even with my improved eyesight. A glass of water lies upturned on the desk, soaking numerous pieces of paper, the ink in huge blotches of blue and black. It looks like someone was in a hurry.

Logan elegantly walks over to the desk, past the numerous black filing cabinets lining the walls. It's clear that she's very much in touch with the human world. A sheathed dagger is the only out of place object in the scene, the dull metal reflecting the light into my eyes as I stagger uncomfortably into the room. Incoherent runes are embedded within the blade, swirling across the weapon like a cloak. *I recognise those symbols,* I tell myself.

Then it dawns on me. That's why Chase said I wouldn't like this place.

"I know you," I state firmly, gripping the edge of the varnished oak desk whilst Logan occupies herself by sitting down in the black leather chair opposite me. I run my fingers across the uneven grain of the wood, ignoring the splinter that chips away and sticks into my finger like a miniature knife. I can't find the courage to look at her, so I don't. My eyes never leave the intricacies of the skin on my hand. "I know you," I repeat. "You visited the rogue pack I was in when we were in need of supplies."

After all, I have seen that exact knife before. I remember it, although I do not remember Logan's face.

Logan nods distantly. "I visit all packs as often as I am needed."

"But you were there when it"—it being when Chase's pack had slaughtered my own—"happened," I murmur, my tone growing angrier by the second. "When it happened. You were there, and you did nothing to stop it." I'm crying now, but the light tears are enough to give me the courage to face the woman sat before me. Her eyes are icicle blue—piercing and perceptive like a hawk. "You let them slaughter good people; you knew that."

Logan raises her hands, partly in defence and partly to stop my rambling. "I had no power. If I did, I would've tried to do what you did and stop it," she replies calmly, tapping the tips of her ageing fingers rhythmically against the human piece of furniture. "So I led them here. It's the best I could do, and if I hadn't, they would've all died." She pauses, only to gaze me right in the eye. "I'm the only reason half of them lived to see another day. And you did not know me, Alaska Morgan, nor do you now. You have no right to blame me like that."

"To hell with whether I have the right to blame you or not," I shout. I know that she's right, but I need to be angry. I need to let out the building pressure coiling under my skin.

Logan lowers her hands. "I'm not arguing with you, Alaska. The rest of your rogue pack are here if you want to see them later. They wouldn't be, if it weren't for me."

I stop, blocking out the sound around me. The heavy breathing of the numerous werewolves in the room, the blood rushing through my ears, and the hammering of the steady wind—all gone.

She's right, in the same way that I'm wrong.

"Sorry," I apologise. I step away from the table, my back accidently pressing into Chase's firm chest. "I'm sorry. I shouldn't have said that."

The room falls into an awkward silence. There are eight wolves crammed into the four walls, including myself, Logan, Chase, Josh, and Alex. The others are all male, whom I recognise but cannot put names to their faces. Azra is nowhere in sight.

"Let's get back to the war," Chase orders firmly, as a king should. I've never heard him use such an authoritative tone of voice before. It startles me a lot more than I let on. "Hunter has the kingdom, and he knows our location. What's the plan?"

Logan crosses her legs. She smirks at Chase, as if she's proud of him. "For a king who was not even selected to rule, you do make a fine leader," she says clearly and without fault.

"If you forget the countless murdered werewolves that were supposedly under Chase's protection and the fact that the kingdom was hijacked by a psychopath, then yeah, he's a great leader. Truly, one of the best," Josh comments. I can't help but show the glimmer of a smile.

Chase clenches his jaw. I watch it pulse out of curiosity. "I was selected," he states, ignoring Josh completely.

Logan shakes her head distinctly. "No, you weren't," she retorts with a bitter edge to her otherwise calm vocalisation. "Alaska won the Alpha Trials. She should be queen, not you."

Chase begins to take a step forward but I latch on to his hand. My fingers slide into his.

"Chase is the rightful ruler," I state in his defence. He had almost killed me, but he had saved me twice. Doesn't that at least count for something? "He won. How does not matter. He is the king, and we must all respect that."

Logan nods, although not in agreement. From the look in her brisk eyes, I can tell that she's reading me like I'm an open book turned to the final page.

"Fine." She finally agrees but her words are bitter. "But you must know what you have to do to win back Arla, Chase. After all, there is no other way. Their army is twice as large as ours, and Hunter is much more willing to send his soldiers off to slaughter."

Chase nods solemnly. My eyebrows pinch together once again. "What is she talking about?"

The King's grip suddenly stiffens. His body language is strange—almost rigid, like a machine. His back is completely straight, appearing unnatural, and the metallic flecks adorning his typically bright eyes have lost colour.

"Chase . . ." I dig my nails into the skin of his hand. "What is it?" I enquire forcibly. "What do you have to do?"

For the first time, Chase's eyes are watery. The one word he mutters sends a shiver spiralling into the concealed depths of my heart like a bolt of electricity.

"Deathmatch," he murmurs.

Logan claps her hands together in a menacing manner. Only now can I see the shadows underlying her large eyes. They appear a constant on her weathered face.

"Exactly," she speaks with precision, like a bullet; straight to the point. The elder stands up from her chair, running a hand

233

along the wood as she trails towards the ruler. "But the question is, are you willing to do it?"

I see Chase gulp out of the corner of my eye.

Because everyone knows what deathmatch is, especially against an alpha much stronger than yourself; a death sentence. A fight to the death between an alpha and another wolf to gain control over the alpha's whole pack and land.

I want to tell him no, don't do it. But I can't, because if he doesn't, everyone else will die. I can't tell him that it's okay, either.

"Hunter is much faster than any werewolf I have ever known," Alex interjects. Her opening couldn't have come at a better time. "And stronger, too. Alaska already killed him, and he came back somehow. If we try again, we'll need to make sure that he's dead. We'll need to use a weapon that will kill him almost instantly."

I watch Logan's face with precision as it lights up with a notion of knowing. It's as if a light bulb has just switched on in her head. "I know what we must use." The woman pauses, leaving the eight of us waiting for her suggestion in suspense. "Wolf's Bane."

Chase acknowledges the suggestion. His hand is still tight around mine, although I can distinctly tell that my thumb running against his skin is doing nothing to calm him.

He exhales. "I'll do it."

I glance up at him, willing myself to allow me to scream at him not to do it. To stay, for me. To not be added to the extremely long list of people I have lost, possibly including Azra. God, I feel so selfish, but he makes me feel alive. Without him, I don't know how I'd be able to smile again.

Logan smiles. "Great," she mutters. She signals to one of the other alphas in the room. "Send riders to inform the rogues of the challenge." Her crinkled face somewhat resembles puff pastry. She turns to mine and Chase's direction. She rubs her hands together, her smile growing. "Let's get some food and prepare the others for tomorrow. Then I'll show you to your room."

234

☽

Only when the door clicks shut behind Logan do I finally breathe a sigh of relief. The air flows freely from my lungs, just like the choking water had earlier. It's as if a weight has been lifted from my chest. I hate being the centre of attention, and every second in front of Logan's perceptive gaze made me feel like I was being skinned alive. It's not a welcoming sensation.

"So, do we get to share a room?" Chase asks with a daring smirk, trying to cover up the fact that he just signed himself up for slaughter. I see right through his protective armour, peeling away the layers of skin to the scared boy hiding beneath. He looks like a child curled up in his own skin.

I scrunch my nose in fake disgust. "Looks like it." I can't keep the agonising pain of losing Chase out of my voice.

The room is right on the top floor of the hotel and has clearly been prepared for the arrival of a special guest. The flooring is made of exotic timber, cleanly sliced to show the unique wood grain in each plank. The room is open plan and much more exquisite than anything I could've ever imagined a human room would look like.

Red velvet curtains cling to the walls, hung beside high arched windows that opens up to a white balcony as it fades into the dark facade of night.

The area is spacious despite the large quantity of beautiful furniture. A double bed sits in the far right corner of the room, right beside the white framed doors. Grey sheets, almost resembling moonlight, are slathered across the bed like liquid silver.

Ebony drawers reside next to the luxurious four-poster bed. The shade of bone makes my skin crawl, so I quickly flicker my eyes to the next object to avoid bile rising in my throat.

235

A vase with withered flowers stands to attention on a mantelpiece above a built-in fire pit, a circle of black leather sofas surrounding the non-existent flames. They are the only thing that seems out of place in the vibrant room. Even the dim lights were welcoming. It means that I can convey my true emotions on my face without having to worry about Chase stealing a glance at them.

Logan had called it the Penthouse, although that word means absolutely nothing to me.

I run straight towards the bed, diving head first into the soft material without a second thought. The sheets are soft—the softest thing I have touched in my life. So, this was what it's like to be human. Expensive and reclusive rooms without having to watch your back every second of every day. It sounds like a peaceful life.

Chase's light chuckle echoes across the room as I sit up. I straighten my back and perch on the edge of the bed with wide eyes. The mattress dips below my slender body.

My eyes lazily drift to Chase, who has his back turned to me. His movements are rigid, and all evidence of the previously lighthearted conversation and his laugh have since vanished into thin air. He pulls off his coat in a staggered movement before turning to unlace his shoes and kick them off with agitation.

"Chase?" I call to him to break the immeasurable silence. He stops taking off his belt to gaze up at me, my face distressed. "I—" I begin but don't know how to finish the sentence.

The man before me raises a perfectly shaped eyebrow. In this light, his face is even more angular than it generally is. It's as if his features are carved by the Gods themselves.

"If you tell me not to go through with this, you can sleep on the couch," he jokes.

I fake a smile. My stomach is churning like an underwater current. My hands fidget as my mind races at one hundred miles per hour, unable to focus on anything but the overhanging threat of what is going to happen tomorrow.

"I need you," I tell him. "I don't know why, but I do. When I'm without you, it's like . . . it's like I can't breathe. I'm scared because I don't know why, and because I don't know what'll happen if I lose you."

Chase lets his belt fall to the floor with a metallic clatter, never breaking eye contact. "Alaska?"

I shake my head. "I don't understand love, or feelings, or anything for that matter," I say as my voice shakes. The tears have returned once more—it's easy in my current emotional state. "But I understand how I feel when I'm with you."

Chase takes a step forward, closing the distance. I rub my arms as goosebumps rise on the surface, tiny lumps on my skin like permanent marks.

"It's like I'm a live wire," I murmur. I don't care if I sound like a whiny b*tch; I don't care about anything except Chase. "Like, there's no spark until you're there with me.

"I know you were never meant to be good for me." I exhale, running my palms up my legs. "You tried to kill me; twice. You pushed me up against a tree with a knife at my neck and threatened to end my life then and there. You told me I'd wish that you'd killed me.

"But you saved me, too. You spared my life in the Alpha Trials, even though I was nothing more than a rogue to you at the time. You fought hard to protect me when others would not and Josh couldn't. Sh*t, you even resurrected me today after I drowned in that river." I have to pause to gulp. I feel the water splash in my mouth like a fountain of blood.

"And you know, I'm glad you didn't kill me," I state defiantly, rising from my seated position. My nails rake down my forearm. "They say there is no such thing as fate. That there are no destined mates, but you feel right."

Chase takes yet another step forward. His feet, clad in black socks, rise and fall in slow motion with each step. "Don't talk me out of this, Ali," he murmurs. "It won't work. I'm going to challenge Hunter tomorrow, no matter what."

I raise my hands in frustration. "You don't get it! I know you have to do this, and I wish you didn't have to! I know! I know everything you're going through because I've been through it myself, time and time again!" I yell, determined to show him how I truly feel. If he can't see, then maybe what I'm feeling is wrong. Maybe it isn't what I think it is. Maybe this weird connection we have with each other is temporary.

It's my turn to step forwards, minimising the distance further. I can feel his empowering presence from where he stands, as if his stretched shadow is looming over me like a giant.

"Don't you understand?" I lower my voice. Thankfully, this is the only room on this floor. Josh has been placed in a shared room on the floor below us, but I know he won't be able to sleep—Azra hasn't appeared.

"I—" I pause, then take a deep breath. "I like you," I whisper. "A lot more than I should, in case that wasn't obvious."

Chase remains silent. The frigid air is unsettling as it coils around us like a transparent serpent.

I blink away a tear and feel it roll down my cheek, cutting a channel into the reddening skin. I cast my eyes to the ground when the silence becomes too heavy—it's as I had suspected. He doesn't feel the same way I did about him.

"I like you, too."

His words slice apart the empty air as if it didn't even exist.

My heart begins to race so quickly in my chest, I'm terrified that it'll miss a beat, snap the heartstrings, and cease to function. I dart my eyes to his in a microsecond, not even daring to break the eye contact by blinking.

I study his face. The curve of his perfect lips. The lust encapsulated in his steely blue eyes.

"What?" I utter without comprehending what he said.

Chase gulps. I watch his Adam's apple bulge minutely as he does so. He raises a hand towards me. "I like you. I think I always have," he says. I reminisce to the time when we first met and he tried to take my life. How could he have cared about me when he threatened to take my life with one slip of his sword? He sees my perplexed look.

"I know I almost killed you, and I still regret the arseh*le I was. But I admired your courage and your strength. Even in the face of danger, you stood strong when the rest of the world fell around you."

The corners of my mouth twitch up into a toothless grin. I tuck my loose hair behind my ears, the agitating strands tickling the side of my face. "I still don't get it." I sigh, finally feeling free enough to open up to him about the truth. About why I'm unsure whether these feelings are as real for him as they are for me. "Guys like you, they don't fall for girls like me. You're one of the most handsome men I have ever met, and I'm, well, not even pretty."

When I met him, he didn't deserve me, but he's changed. The more I've gotten to know the Alpha, the more he's opened up and softened. He's not heartless around me like he is to others.

Chase takes another step, finally standing right in front of me with his perceptive gaze. He rests his index finger below my chin, tilting it up so he can see every single striking feature of my unusual face.

"You . . ." he whispers, leaning in. My heart jumps to my throat as a shaky breath leaves my mouth. "Are the most beautiful woman I have ever laid eyes on, Alaska. And I don't care about looks, anyway. You're an incredible person who will do anything to save the ones she loves."

I desperately want to turn away, to tell him that I'm not falling for his handsome face and that he should go and screw some other willing werewolf. But I don't. I can't look away from his stunning features. It's like my eyes are transfixed on the most

239

beautiful sunrise I have ever seen, twilight tangerine and salmon pink staining the sky like permanent dye.

His hand falls away from under my chin, my head automatically dropping. I quickly raise it again, my hair falling in front of my eyes without permission. I can still see Chase through them clearly. I can still see him reach out to tuck the strands behind my ears slowly, the soft skin of his fingers grazing against my burning cheeks. A trail of sparks runs down my spine like a firework chain. My feet are already tingling with pins and needles.

"I love everything about you," he whispers as he finishes tucking my hair away. But he doesn't move his hand; it hovers on my skin. "I love the way you don't understand feelings properly. I love the way you scrunch your nose whenever I make a sarcastic comment. I love the way you punched that dick before the Alpha Trials had even begun, right in the nose. I love the way you're proud when someone calls you a b*tch. I love the way you scrunch your hands into fists until they bleed when you feel uncomfortable, and I am too far away to hold your hand. I—"

"Please don't give me a Josh lecture," I interrupt him, the faint glimmer of a laugh shining through my words.

Chase smiles, showing his white teeth. They're the brightest thing in the room. "I like you, Alaska." He's radiating as he says it. "Feelings, relationships, love; they're a strange concept but it's real. And what's between you and me, it's real."

"Chas—" I begin, but I'm interrupted as his lips crash on to mine. They're soft as they move, and, for once, I'm not shocked by the action.

My hands stay firmly by my side for a second—twitching— not knowing what to do. I've only really done this a few times before and the action is foreign to me, like learning a completely new language.

But my hands abruptly take control. As one of his rests on my face and the other around the small of my back, I use mine to pull him closer. So close, in fact, that there is barely any space separating our bodies.

They clutch the back of his t-shirt, swiftly pulling it over his head to reveal his hard body beneath. I catch a glimpse of his ripped body but sharply turn my attention back to the kiss as his tongue slides into my mouth.

Sparks ignite up my arms and legs. Everywhere he touches, my body tingles with a longing sensation that I can no longer control. It devours me; makes me hungry—hungry for more.

I jump up and wrap my legs around his waist as it swipes away everything on the closest piece of furniture; an antique evergreen wood table. The shiny dark surface reflects the dim light in the room.

We break away from our kiss as Chase fumbles for my shirt, pulling it off my body. In that moment, I feel completely and utterly exposed. Of course, I'm wearing a bra, but I've never shown this much of my body to anyone before, let alone a male. Chase's scrutinising gaze makes my skin tingle.

"You're beautiful," he whispers, pulling me closer to him. His hands fall to my back, tightening around the skin carefully as it ignites into an inferno of lust.

His lips fall on my neck, planting kisses where he will mark me; if he marks me.

I bite my lip. Am I ready to go through with this? But then again, is anyone ever ready?

If I do this, I'm bound to Chase forever. But even in these short few weeks, I feel something telling me deep within my soul that we are meant to be. That I'm supposed to with him, whether it's for the rest of my life or the rest of his. That if he dies tomorrow, I will still feel him the way I feel about him today.

I bite my lip, dropping my hands to his chest. My slow movement draws his attention, eyes flickering back to my face. He appears worried, although the morphed pigment of his gold eyes tells me otherwise. He's ready.

Chase brings a hand back up to my face. "Are you okay?" he asks so calmly it makes the hair on my arms prickle from how much it's standing. How can he be so composed despite the fact that he could die tomorrow? That he could leave everyone behind without so much as batting an eyelash?

"I don't know," I state truthfully, my gaze falling to the floor. The oak stares back at me blandly. "Actually, you know what? I'm not okay. How can you be so calm about sentencing yourself to death? These people need you." Chase gazes at me solemnly. "I need you."

Chase's hand attempts to sooth my soaring anger but I brush it away. I can't lose one of the only people I have left, whom I loved. My mum and dad had died to protect me, as had Dylan. I'm not going to let him follow.

"I have to," Chase says with resignation, his voice wavering. "You know that. I have no choice."

I breathe in slowly. "I know. I just don't want to lose you," I reply.

My mate shakes his head. "You won't, I promise." He leans forwards, his forehead pressing on mine and resting there like an unspoken connection.

I nod, water running down my cheek. It's as if all the tears I haven't cried in the past five years have eventually caught up with me. I think I've cried more in these few weeks than my whole entire life.

"You'll win," I utter. I pull him closer to me. "I know you will."

Chase smirks but it's not daunting in the slightest. "Are you sure you still want to go through with this?" It takes me a second to figure out that he's talking about mating.

Am I ready?

But then, when am I ready for anything?

Time elongates into an endless string of countless numbers and long pauses. I nod my head in consent.

The corners of my mouth form a smile. "Yes," I say. "Yes, I am."

CHAPTER TWENTY
Deathmatch
"I know what I'm risking. My life for theirs."

- Bellamy Blake, The 100

"You don't have to do this," I muse. The air is still and bitter, as if it has been laced with poison, waiting for its chance to strangle me contently.

I glance warily at the man in front of me, remembering the blissful night before. The way his lips felt on mine; the way it felt when our skin touched. The sensation was so hot, it was like he was branding me.

My hand subconsciously reaches for the mark on my neck; two pin pricks of whitened skin, where the bite marks have healed over from last night. To any other species, they would be meaningless. A battle scar and nothing more. But to me, they mean the world. Literally. They show that Chase is mine, as much as I'm his. I have worn a shirt with a high neckline to make sure that it is covered up; I don't want people to privilege me just because I'm the king's mate. I'm still Alaska, the girl who has fought, cried, and kept her head down; the girl who is lost.

The morning has been eventful—more so than I hoped. All of the soldiers have been called up to fight, and in the scrabble of weapons, sweat, and armour, Chase had been lying by my side as we enjoyed our last moments together. It's strange how something you love with all your heart can be torn away by the simple uttering of words; the initiation of a Deathmatch and Chase's proposed sacrifice. I still can't believe what he's doing but I know that it's for a greater cause.

I can't tell myself that he'll die or that he'll be okay. Every time I glance at his perfectly chiselled face, I remind myself that it's okay. Chase is going to win and everything will be over—apart from the aftermath, which will subsequently lead to war.

"You know I have to," Chase states, his jaw taut as he strains his face to keep composure. Despite his best efforts, I can see the cracks through his delicate skin. He's falling apart. I can feel it too. It's like a leech has latched on to my heart, gradually eating away at the organ. It feels like a weight has been placed on my chest, and even with the mightiest of heaves, I can't lift it off. "That's why I was chosen as king."

I sigh as he reaches out to snake an arm around my waist. Before, it felt strange; like water and oil refusing to mix. Now, it feels as natural as counting from one to ten.

My ears pick up the unwelcome plodding of footsteps. I don't turn around to know that it's Alex approaching us. Logan made sure that the matter was handled with someone we know, otherwise I'd be tempted to rip the person's head off.

"It's time," the Alpha mutters. I can hear the sympathy in her tone, but I cannot bring myself to wrench my gaze away from Chase's fascinating eyes. The gold flecks have returned, brighter and more brilliant than ever before. They shine like the sun on a summer's day, full of life—which could soon be so devilishly snatched from him.

Chase pulls me closer, closing his eyes and snapping our eye contact in half.

"You're going to win," I reassure him, but even I do not believe the words.

My mate reaches forward, placing his lips on mine and lingering for a few seconds. The air is laced with frostbite, but I feel as though I'm sweltering. Sparks tingle through my lips as his soft lips move against mine.

I shiver when he pulls away. "No matter what happens," Chase begins, "promise me you'll protect the kingdom."

I almost glare at him in disbelief. I never wanted to take part in ruling the kingdom, and the only reason I'm second in command is because Chase had spared my life in the Alpha Trials. If he dies, then the role of leader will fall back on to me, and I'm nowhere near ready for that burden.

"I will," I reply, looking up at him through my dark lashes, my vision shuttered. "I promise."

Chase takes both my hands in his, giving them a hopeful squeeze. A nervous smile twitches on to my face without permission. I bite my lip to try and hide it, but Chase has already spotted the action. He can't bring himself to smile.

"I love you," he whispers, capturing my lips for what could be the last time.

I stifle a laugh.

"So you're about to go off and possibly die, yet you say the most cliché thing possible?" I say sarcastically. I don't want our possible last moments to be a chasm of depression and loss. I rifle a hand through his hair, the soft locks delicate to the touch.

"Sorry, did you want it to be more . . ." He pauses. "Romantic?"

I roll my eyes. "I'm not really one of those girls who's into roses and kittens. So, no," I reply as my face strains to smile. I can hear the irrational beating of his heart, the racing thumps so loud in my ears, it's the only thing I can hear.

A tear rolls down my cheek as I pull him into the tightest hug I can muster. I squeeze my eyes shut so tightly they ache, but the pain is worth it. Chase's hands wrap around me, balling in my coat as the breeze swirls around us with tormented pleasure.

"I'll see you soon," I whisper in his ear so minutely that only he would be able to hear it. I'm aware of the five hundred warriors positioned behind us in case we have to improvise in taking the city back as our own; one thousand eyes, scraping over our figures, our hold, our touch. This is the kind of attention I hate but Chase makes it all disappear into a cloud of fog.

We pull away. Somehow, the man before me has managed to keep his composure. His face appears as though it is made of iron; unmoving and expressionless. Exactly what he needs to be to win.

His hand is still fastened around mine. He holds it even tighter, the skin paler than my usual tanned complexion. I want to pull him back and kiss him one last time. I want to scream at him not to do it. I want to end Hunter in any and every way possible.

But I don't do anything. I don't tell him that I want him one last time or that I yearn for his touch. I just stand there as he walks away. His fingers brush against mine as his hand falls away, mine remaining outstretched. A shiver proceeds like a storm down my spine. I feel lost without his touch.

As Chase walks to his death, I watch in fear as he clenches his hands into impenetrable fists. The hands I was just holding. I can hear the snow crunch under his boots as I stand, looking at where fate has brought him as his seconds spiral away into the chasm of death. The wind pulls furiously at his hair, wrenching it over his head and possibly into his face. Not that he cares.

Because everyone knows the rules of Deathmatch. It has long been a tradition in the werewolf world, sought to relinquish alphas from their leadership position within a pack. It's a vicious contest that ends in one of the two competitor's death. It's also stated by law that one of the competitors has to be an alpha. It's well known that the matches occur just for power. Whoever wins gains influence over the loser's pack.

I glance up towards the army standing before us. The swarm of black figures is positioned in rows, each of them wearing a snarl of bloodlust on their damaged faces. With my enhanced eyesight, I can see the faces of those closest to me. If looks could kill, theirs will certainly render me deceased before I even get close. The blood staining their face is old, rusted brown clots lying on their skin like unspoken trophies.

And then there's Hunter, concealed in the circle already laid out for Deathmatch. The match is strange, and I have been informed of the rules on the half day journey by Josh.

He had told me that a black circle is placed on the ground to enclose the competitors. In the ring, the fight is even. Both the competitors are given the same weapon, which means that the wolf's bane sword will have to be used at a later opportunity should it present itself. If the two competitors are to break the circle, which requires strength, due to the strange enclosing power of the black powder used to contain the challengers, then the fight will become uneven and the battlefield will be as large as they need it to be. Josh has also informed me that it's practically impossible to break the circle and that it's better that way.

Hunter's hair is as white as the snow itself, blending into the hauntingly colourless horizon. Black eyes scour Chase as he strides towards Hunter, his army positioned on a gentle slope, rising above ours, gazing down on us as though we are nothing more than rodents that need to be dealt with.

As Chase gets closer, a grin splits across Hunter's face with glee. I want to rip it to shreds with my claws alone. Someone so screwed up should not exist.

And that's when I see the girl standing next to him, shrouded by the rogue leader's heavy armour. Her clothes are ripped in places, the left leg of her leggings sporting a hole larger than the size of my fist. A blood stain runs down her cheek from a healed cut, although she clearly has no way of washing it away. Her face is slathered with mud, merging into the crimson of her blood like paint. If it isn't for her perceptive azure eyes, I would've mistaken her for someone else.

My chest releases a choked sigh. Bile rises in my throat but I keep it down. The acid burns at the back of my mouth like poison.

I take a step back, knocking into Josh's arm inadvertently. He flinches away, as if my touch is burning him.

"Josh," I whisper, but something tells me that he already knows about Azra. Afterall, he's been awfully silent since we entered the huge clearing outside the crumbling walls of Arla. In fact, he hasn't even spoken a word. "I'm so sorry," I murmur.

What else am I supposed to say? At least she's alive? But that's not true, because death is better than being held within Hunter's clutches. It's better than ongoing torture.

My limbs are frozen in fear. Thankfully, we still have Hunter's mate in our grasp; the joker to play when Hunter holds the Ace of Spades in his grasp.

My eyes shift back to Chase, taking in every movement as my heart rate begins to go faster than it ever has before. Part of me can feel the nerves writhing through his body, subduing him as he keeps up his armour, blocking out emotions.

But even from here I can hear Hunter's laugh. The wind carries it across the large expanse of land as if he is speaking through a megaphone.

I crease my eyebrows anxiously. Why the hell is he laughing?

Hunter's chest rises and falls sadistically, both hands hovering lightly at his sides. "I thought that I was challenging the ruler of Arla," Hunter shouts, his eyes burning a scorching hole into my pupils. Why is he looking at me, of all people?

"What're you talking about?" Chase answers back. "I am the ruler. I am king."

Hunter's lips form a smirk. "But you're not the rightful ruler," he sneers, his eyes appearing darker than they had previously. "You lost the Alpha Trials."

Chase raises his head high. He knows that he has to appear strong in front of the kingdom, to give them hope. But having his position questioned will only result in those who have so blindly followed him questioning where their allegiance lies. They will question his right to the throne, and he will lose power.

"The only reason you are king is because the rightful ruler didn't want to be queen," Hunter continues. My hands clench into fists. "When your riders came to inform me of your challenge, Chase, they stated that the ruler wished to compete against me in Deathmatch for the throne of Arla. Therefore, I would like to face her," Hunter states boldly. His head bows towards me. "Alaska, if you may."

One thousand eyes turn curiously to give me a fleeting gaze. The rogues sneer, their bodies tense with the anticipation of an impending fight.

I feel like I'm being suffocated as the oxygen from my lungs expels itself. I can't breathe. How has it come to this? I don't want to face Hunter again after I have already killed him, but with every single pair of eyes in a one hundred metre radius on me, I have no choice but to compete. Again. To risk my life. Again.

Hopefully, this pain will be over soon, I tell myself. Maybe, just maybe, this time it's close to being over.

I step forward but Josh's hand restrains me. I shrug it off with ease, ignoring the hurt look scattered across his cute face. It's a tangle of emotions that I can't even begin to unravel.

"No, Alaska," Josh warns.

"I have to," I whisper. "Don't you sees that?" I continue to walk forwards, refusing to glance back to see his reaction in case it shatters my courage.

My legs carry me up the slope, past Chase and his grim face. He has turned a ghastly shade of white, not dissimilar to the pigment of Hunter's silver hair. His fingers wind together absently as he stares ahead of him, focusing on something that simply does not exist. I walk straight past him.

250

When I reach the circle, the black arc missing a metre to allow me to enter, I hesitantly step through. My hands reach for the blade strewn carelessly on the ground five metres from Hunter's leather clad feet. Thinking that he's so close makes my skin crawl as though maggots are wriggling over every square millimetre of my skin.

A rogue places a trail of black powder behind where I had entered, sealing us away from the others. I can feel the power emanating from the substance, pulsing like a beacon.

I gaze into Hunter's pits—others would call them eyes. "You've gotten what you want," I state as the foreign sword weighs down my grip. I tilt my head towards Azra. "Now let her go."

Hunter's face remains emotionless as the seconds tick by, before splitting into a toothy grin. It makes me happy when I see that his teeth are far from perfect. His front right tooth is at a slight angle and the left one has a huge chip where half a tooth should be.

"Okay," Hunter states solemnly, suddenly quirking up into a straighter posture—abruptly alert. "But in exchange for my mate."

I raise an eyebrow. Zara is well out of sight.

"I can sense my mate, Alaska." Hunter snarls like the vicious animal he is. His fingers flicker up to his palms before drooping in a strange rhythm. "I know that she's here."

I roll my eyes, crossing my arms over my chest. "Fine," I state bitterly, nodding to Chase.

It takes a minute for him to return to the army, pulling Zara out from behind the lines of warriors prepared rigorously for battle. I suck in a breath as a rogue approaches with Azra, knowing the betrayal that could ensue.

It doesn't. I let out a shaky sigh of relief as the exchange is swift, and Azra plunges into Josh's arms as he holds the back of her head as if he is holding a newborn child. He rests his smooth chin on her head, closing his eyes as a droplet of transparent water slips

251

into Azra's greasy hair. In that moment, I see how much she means to him. Without her, he would be hollow; incomplete.

Hunter is cruel, but nobody can be cruel enough to kill Azra if it means the death of his mate. Even so, he's a sadistic bastard.

Hunter captures my vision as he rolls up the sleeves of his battle gear. Unlike me, he came prepared. Despite the rules saying that the fight has to be fair, Hunter wears a silver chest plate, reflecting the dim sunrays into my eyes and momentarily blinding me. He also appears mentally prepared, whereas I'm nowhere near ready to fight after yesterday.

"Are you ready?" Hunter says, rubbing his palms together before retrieving a sword the exact same make as mine from his belt. Why does everyone always ask that? Isn't it obvious that the answer is no?

I nod, unsure of how this would start. I had heard of Deathmatch as a haunting story around campfires back when I was a mere child. I had never anticipated its actual existence. Now here I am, ready to die for some pathetic kingdom and to save the lives of everyone standing behind me.

The only way I can win is if I break the circle. I need the wolf's bane sword to ensure that Hunter doesn't mysteriously revive.

Hunter is the first to move. Instead of a war cry, which I had expected, he moves silently, as if his feet never truly touch the floor.

His sword swipes across my body before I can blink, and I arch my back as quickly as I can. Thankfully I'm saved from the sword's path, but the exhilaration doesn't last long.

Hunter prepares for another attack as I back away. I bite my tongue, stimulated by fear, the bitter taste of my own blood exploding into my mouth like a bomb.

Hunter's blade swings across my body once more, but this time, my sword is in the way to parry his attack. I push his weapon away as it edges closer, using most of remaining energy to do so. I'm exhausted after yesterday, but my newfound feelings for Chase means that I have to survive. Not for us; for him. It will tear him apart from the inside out if I die. It would've been the opposite all but two months ago.

I push him backwards, his feet skidding on the ice hidden deep underneath the powdery snow. My sword cuts clean across his body, but only to come into contact with the metal chestpiece as he ducks and rolls out of the way.

"I thought that this fight was supposed to be fair," I say angrily through gritted teeth.

Hunter lunges towards me, nicking my right leg before I retaliate. The cut is small and shallow; something I shouldn't be worried about.

"You should've come prepared then, Alaska," Hunter remarks. He steps closer boldly. "You know you can't kill me, so let's make this quick." Another step. I can feel his breath fanning against my face. He can easily take everything from me right here, right now. One quick movement and I could be decapitated.

I spit in his face. My sword finds his left leg, cutting cleanly through his muscles and down to the hollow bone beneath.

Hunter's face distorts into a mask of agony but within seconds it subsides. I look in horror as the skin around the wound already begins to heal.

He is no ordinary wolf. He should be dead.

Hunter notices my attention has drifted and he smiles. "Why don't you ask that question you've been burning to ask ever since we met, Alaska?"

I ignore his question, my heart beat so deafening I can barely hear his unimportant words anyway. I spin in a circle, using my momentum to bring my blade against his skin.

Instead, it meets iron. The clashing sound breaks me from my trance, reverberating through my ears like the worst case of tinnitus.

253

Hunter pushes my blade to my chest and continues walking forwards until my back hits something hard. I glance back, only to see nothing but the two armies stirring with the will to fight. To slaughter. An invisible wall.

Hunter's face is just inches form mine. I can't help but think of how Chase is reacting, but I push him from my mind.

"Why don't you ask it?" he roars in my face, a droplet of spit flying onto my cheek. I squirm under his weight as he presses his weapon dangerously close to my windpipe. The only thing stopping him from slitting my neck is the sword I'm holding across my chest as a lifeline.

I refuse to crack under the pressure. "Ask what?" I enquire as calmly as I can but my words are rushed. Furious, in fact.

My calm response just makes Hunter angrier. "About why I'm not dead. Why I'm so much better than any werewolf could ever be," he says.

I shake my head. "I don't give a sh*t," I utter before my voice turns into venom. "Go screw yourself."

And with that, I push him from my body, my sword directly aiming for his throat. He moves away quickly but it meets his face. All that I manage is a scratch across his cheek, which has already begun to heal within the second. His movements are a blur, and he's on the other side of the circle in a blink.

Hunter's eyes hold a wild fire as he glowers at me. His jawline pulses as he wipes away the blood from his face, as though bleeding is a foreign concept to him.

He staggers forward, precisely arcing his sword to meet my stomach. I don't have enough time to react as the blade makes brutal contact with my skin, tearing a hole deep within the layers of my hope.

Instead of a fire igniting in the wound, it grows cold. It doesn't hurt.

"My dad always wanted to be strong, but he couldn't be that," Hunter rants as I clutch my stomach to put pressure on the

254

cut. I lean over, retching up blood. "He wasn't, so he turned to making me as strong as possible."

I gaze up at him through my eyelashes. "I don't care," I state slowly, finding every ounce of strength within me to raise my sword, making another attempt for his head.

Hunter bats mine away as though it's nothing more than a butterfly. Then he reaches forward at lightning speed, drawing a line across my leg, cutting deep. I scream as the blade slowly makes contact, immediately falling to one leg, unable to hold myself up.

Hunter makes another advance but I effortlessly throw him off with a slice of my sword. Despite painful injuries, I don't give up that easily. I rise to my legs, but Hunter's sword lifts up my chin as soon as I'm back on both feet. But he kicks away my wounded leg so that I'm crouched before him.

"Of course you care," Hunter whispers in my ear. "Don't you want to be powerful? Don't you want to rule over Arla? I mean, surely that's why you chose to compete in the Alpha Trials rather than be executed?" he growls. I want to rip his tongue from his mouth, to stop his angry words fuelling my own blind rage. "You wanted the power, and now you have it. But you can have so much more. You could join me."

There's silence for a few moments.

"You're sick," I state unemotionally, "if you think that I'd even join you for one second."

Hunter processes my words. However, the blade resting at the crook of my throat doesn't slide further like I expect. Instead, his gaze is neutral, his pulsing jawline the only sliver of evidence of the infuriated Hunter I had seen beforehand.

"Shame," he murmurs, his free hand running across my face, pulling away my top to reveal my mark. I curse under my breath as he stares at it with beady eyes. He releases the material and it once again covers the two white pricks of skin. "I'll take joy in killing you."

His fingers linger on my skin. A building rage is focused in my chest. I hate him—I hate him so much. I don't care what impact killing him will have on me. He has turned the world into a brutal shade of corrupted evil. He has to die.

Before, during the Alpha Trials, I had used my rage to fight; now, I'm back to using it as my weapon. I know I can't rely on my anger, as much as I can't rely on any of my other emotions, but I need to feel that hunger for revenge. I need to watch my parents die time and time again, just to fuel the electricity in my veins.

I slap Hunter's hand from my face, wrapping my fingers around his freezing skin. He tries to pry my grip away, but I'm already on my feet, squeezing until I hear the satisfying snap of crushing bones rattle against one another.

My hand twists his wrist around as he howls out in excruciating pain. He grits his imperfect teeth.

I don't change my emotionless face. He's getting what he deserves.

"Like I said," I spit. "I don't give a sh*t."

Hunter gasps as I kick him in the groin, rendering him useless on the floor. Next, my blade finds his neck, resting there before flicking up in a swift movement.

But I'm not fast enough. Hunter places his palm on the end of the blade, breathing heavily as he rises to his feet. He still has hold of my sword.

My eyes are wide open in shock as I pull back my sword. I can hear Hunter's wet blood against the metal as it slides effortlessly through his hand.

But my shock doesn't last long. I shoot my hand straight forwards, my fingers becoming clammy as I begin to sweat with the fear of my impending death.

The sword doesn't make its mark where I wish it to. Instead, it clatters against Hunter's armour without so much as making a dent.

Hunter's hands, still slathered with his own black blood, indignantly takes hold of my sword, cutting deep wounds into his hand. The contrast between his pastel skin and his dark blood is disturbing. And with a bulge of his muscles, he tears my sword from my grip.

But I don't give up. My hands may be empty, but it gives me even more will, even more reason to fight.

My hands are already in tight balls, the knuckles cracking under the pressure. My first punch manages to make direct contact with Hunter's worthless face, his nose knocked out of place. I feel it shift under my skin with a sickening crunch.

My next punch is less successful. Hunter knocks it away with his forearm, his bad hand dangling limply as he slowly staggers towards me. In this moment, he appears as normal as he'll ever be; wounded and broken.

I punch again, but my third punch is sloppy. Hunter sees me let down my guard, my posture weakening, and wraps the long fingers of his good hand around my enclosed fist. His hands don't look like a warrior's; they're thin and emaciated, long fingers elongated unnaturally. They look like painter's fingers; delicate and not meant to harm.

Hunter twists my arm at an unnatural angle but I spin away from his grip before he can cause any real damage. I don't want a dislocated shoulder.

Hunter's hand finds my throat, cutting off my air supply. My legs reaches out to kick him, but it makes no impact on him.

Despite my lack of oxygen, my hands don't fumble for the ones choking me. Instead, they take Hunter's hand that's still healing before he can flinch away and crush it once more. He was stupid enough to put the hilt of his sword in his damaged hand. I would've sighed in relief as soon as he drops it, except I need to find enough air to breathe first. I kick him in the shin for good measure, which earns a hiss.

Hunter's face peels into a snarl. "Goodbye, Alaska," he whispers much too loudly than any whisper should be. It cuts apart his jagged breathing, our confined shapes, my lost hope. It's the last voice I will ever hear.

The invisible wall is once again at my back. Although it does not theoretically exist, I can feel an agonising pain rush through my skin as Hunter forces me against it even harder.

No matter how many times I try to punch Hunter anywhere, he always manages to block my attack. He's unnaturally fast, and I'm too slow to keep up.

My oxygen supply is now dwindling low as Hunter's hands remain on my throat. I attempt one more time to force them away, but he doesn't even budge an inch. Black holes have already begun to engulf my vision like an all consuming plague.

"Any last words?" Hunter jeers.

I raise my legs to kick, but every kick is a waste of energy: I'm getting nowhere.

The pain is too much for me. If I die right here, right now, like hell I'm going to let Hunter have the satisfaction of my pleas for mercy.

"Go to hell," I spit.

And that's when the wall behind me shatters.

CHAPTER TWENTY-ONE
Finale

"I have lived that life already. In the mud, in the shadows, in a cell, in a silk dress.

I will never submit again. I will never stop fighting."

- Mare Barrow, Red Queen

I'm up on my feet and standing before Hunter can even blink. Despite the surge of questions going through the raging tempo of my brain, I push them aside. I can figure out why the wall has broken later. I need to focus on killing the bastard first.

With my hand around my recently suppressed throat, I stagger away from Hunter as he swiftly rises from his feet. He appears unscathed but the rage boiling in his bottomless eyes tells a very different story. Something so deviously evil lies deep within the depths, twisting into tight coils; ready to be unleashed. I know what he is capable of. We all do, and that's why he needs to die.

"Chase!" I shout, my pace picking up as I begin to breathe laboriously. My head spins, not enough oxygen flowing into my lungs. I can already feel the skin of my neck bruising and aching without my consent. I bite my tongue to make the pain go away.

He knows what he needs to do, but it's too late. I stumble on my own feet, my exhausted and crippled body unable to keep up with the pace. I grunt as I fall forwards, but I turn so I can see Hunter as he sprints straight towards me.

259

I scramble to my feet, only just quick enough before he can rip my head from my body. He still doesn't have his sword but his clenched hands are enough to portray just how angry he is.

"Just you and me, Alaska!" Hunter shouts, merely five metres away from me. I wish it was further. I wish we were on opposite sides of the Earth. Maybe then I can feel comfortable in my own skin.

My empty hands feel abnormally light when it's not weighed down by a weapon. But there's a crushing weight on my chest that refuses to lift. Every time I breathe, it's fixated there, pressing against my ribcage and refusing to let me inhale.

I hear Chase's heavy panting from beside me. I feel my body spark with courage—and the need to touch him.

I grit my teeth. "Go to hell!" The words flow from my mouth like a torrent of black ink.

Hunter's face grows notably angrier—more so than it had been before—and I watch as red lines of rage stretch across his face, his lips elongated into a pale line. His high cheekbones make his face appear as sharp as razors; that is the face of a killer. It suits him and his white skin. Everything about him, I can't help but associate with death. Like the way a body turns the same shade as his skin when it's deprived of life.

Chase's dark cropped hair appears in my field of vision, and I nod to him as Hunter begins to let an agonising growl tear through his body. His teeth are bared, a crooked smile forming.

In one swift movement, my legs shift towards Chase as Hunter continues to run straight towards me. As soon as I get close enough to Chase, he flings the sword up in the air. Even from here, I can see the yellow-tinged blade slick with wolf's bane.

I grab the hilt swiftly, but I can't find the courage to turn around. The battle needs to be somewhere I have the advantage if I have any chance of survival. My brain flicks through the possible locations with each laboured footfall. The castle. I know it better than he ever will.

The two armies have exploded into action around us. I sidestep as a rogue tackles a pack wolf to the ground, clawing off his helmet and exposing his head with one swipe of his dirty claws. I can see the crimson splatter across the ivory like a permanent stain.

Blood has already coated the snow, those who barely got a chance to battle laying at disorienting angles, some with their eyes wide open, some with them closed. All I can hear is the overwhelming and collective clang of metal on metal, battle cries swapped for screams of agony. The stench of violence is sickening.

I don't even blink as I pass by Chase. I'm so fixated on the stone structure before me that I can barely think about anything except for regulating my exhilarated breathing.

A snarling rogue enters my vision as I leap over a pile of shattered rock, the shards pointing up towards the sky like daggers, but as soon as he sees Hunter, who I presume is right behind me, he steps out of my way, his face a concoction of delight at the thought of my demise.

"Alaska!" Hunter roars. He sounds further away, but I already know I cannot outrun the beast. He must be ten metres behind me at the most. The thought makes my muscles momentarily tense but I shake my head to ward off the stiffness. I have to be brave, even if my heart is freezing at the sheer coldness of Hunter's stony heart. "You can't run away from me!"

Oh, but I am, I hiss inside my mind. I don't need to make him any angrier than he already is.

Another pile of rock and I'm past the collapsed wall. I think of everything that had been enclosed in the tight circle of the city. I remember the tents, housing multiple packs who were staying to spectate the Alpha Trials. I remember the happy cry of children, running through the mud without caring how much of it got onto their clothes. And I remember being dragged through a crowd, everyone staring at me as I anticipated death.

I remember how this story began. Maybe this is how it ends. That was merely weeks ago, but it feels like eternity. The woman entering the walls now is not the same girl that entered the kingdom a month ago.

But I abruptly stop as a crowd of people join me in my bid towards the castle. Some are soldiers, too afraid to fight. Cowards. Others are children—those who aren't even meant to come with us today.

I spot a shock of black hair and tanned skin, and my heart stops. I can't feel it beat. Maybe that's because my body's turned numb all over. She looks tiny in comparison to the rubble, running past the statue that once sat as the centrepiece to a memorial fountain without even faltering—she has grown so used to destruction, it no longer seems out of place to her young eye.

Harper. And she's alone. I can't see Alex, Azra, nor her mother. They must've been separated.

No, I feel the words at the back of my throat, but they do not form.

Snow crunches behind me, and I curse under my breath. My grip around my new-found weapon has tightened, knowing that no matter what, I can never let it go. I almost recoil at the pungent smell of the wolf's bane, the viscous yellow liquid slathered across the blade just like the snow carpeting the ground. The scent explodes in my nose; a putrid smell of poison and death. I almost pinch my nose as I gag. Wolf's bane is poisonous to werewolves, and even the smallest cut with this blade can render me lifeless.

The hair on the back of my neck rises. I know Hunter is there, ready to make his killer move. I can't see his face, and for that, I am glad; I've had enough of it.

My eyes narrow and my muscles wind up and contract. The quicker this is over, the better.

My father taught me what to do when someone creeps up from behind. He had used me as the attacker, and I was scared out of my skin when he abruptly spun around, hands leaning out to enclose me in a tight hug. I can still hear his musical laugh echo in my ears. Even his death has not tainted that jovial sound that surfaced many times in my childhood.

So, I do exactly what my father did. My heel throbs as I push it down into the ground, keeping both of my hands stable around the iron. I don't raise my eyes, not even daring to glance into my opponent's pitiless stare.

The swipe never hits. In fact, Hunter's further away than I originally thought. He already has another sword in grasp but it doesn't seem like he'll use it.

I glare at him, loose strands of my hair falling into my eyes. What is he waiting for?

"Aren't you going to fight?" I yell, stepping towards him like a fire refusing to go out.

When I get close enough, my free hand balls into a fist. I can't stop my body as my curled fingers make a direct route towards his smirking face. I wait for it to collide with freezing flesh, but Hunter effortlessly dives to the side, the movement seamless and without any openings. It looks like he's floating on a cloud; untouchable and out of reach. How can something so sinister look so elegant?

At the same time, I slash with my sword, but Hunter steps backwards and out of the way in a split second.

My hand makes its way to his worthless face once more. He ducks this time, spiralling away until his thin posture is stood in attention behind me.

I whirl around, my hair catching in my face as it turns into a mask of anger and hatred. Again, I lunge forward, this time my fist connecting with the iron chest plate. I scrunch my nose up as pain coils through the fingers, but I distract myself by kicking with my right leg. It lands right on his shin, but the blow is not powerful enough to knock him off balance.

"I admire your efforts, Alaska," Hunter purrs. He takes a step back as I try to bash him once more with my curled fingers. I reach out again, so angry, so enraged by him and his actions that I am unable to stop myself from doing so. This time, he catches my hand, holding it securely in his paper-white fist. He looks me dead in the eye, the black irises all-consuming in the morning light. "But you're not going to win."

Finding whatever strength is left within me, I pull my hand away with a quick burst of energy, rendering me exhausted.

"Say what you want," I spit. It drips from my mouth, entwined with blood. "You'll never get away with this." Panting, I feebly wave an arm to the inner walls of the city. All signs of fleeing deserters and those not fit enough to fight are gone. Chase is nowhere in sight, undoubtedly caught up in the massacre outside the remnants of the cobblestone wall. "But if I die today, there will always be someone else who will step up and oppose you. No matter where you go, people will hunt you, and one day, you will die. If not by me, by some other infuriated person sick of the death you bring everywhere you go.

"You're no leader," I continue, taking a step back as my palms begin to sweat. I can feel the sword slowly sliding out of my grasp. "The only reason they follow you is because they were forced to become monsters by you and your dad. They follow you out of fear, not because of who you are," I shout. My voice reverberates off every single bit of shrapnel and every bit of chiselled rock; agonisingly breaking Hunter's soul. Bit by bit; cell by cell.

Because there is only one way I can beat him.

Hunter always appears to be in a mentally stable mood but he has created the delusion that he's superior and that everyone envies him. He thinks that he's the best leader the rogues have ever had and that he will lead them to victory. All I have to do is not crumble from his attacks and shatter the shield protecting his soul from the burning truth.

Hunter scrunches his hand tightly until his knuckles turn an even paler shade of white than the tone of his skin. "Shut up!"

264

Some sick part of me wants to smile, but I press on. "You destroy everything you touch," I say, lips pinching up to expose my elongating canines. "So I suggest you take off that crappy piece of metal protecting your heart and fight like a true leader."

Hunter glares at me, but after two seconds, he lowers his eyes as though he's ashamed of himself. The weapon slides from his grip, clattering to the snow-clad ground with no more than a silent thump. I raise my head as he pulls the armour off, revealing his plain navy-blue t-shirt underneath. A sweat stain runs across the centre of his chest, just above his pulsing heart.

The rogue's jaw pulses as he raises his head back to its original proud position. His leg shifts, taking a step forwards with a menacing presence. I can feel the darkness engulfing his body, reaching out towards me and wrapping around me like elongated tentacles.

"You have your fair fight." He smirks, all signs of anger having vanished. I almost bite my tongue—again—in frustration. There has to be a point where he breaks. Where he is so enraged, nothing can soothe his temper. I just have to keep pressing further. "But you're not going to win."

I bow my head to the side. "I'm sick and tired of you saying that," I say bitterly, swallowing nervously as I bring myself to place a footstep towards him.

I force myself to bury my fear deep inside my soul, next to where my love for any other human being used to be locked away. This time, I'm the one who's aggravated. It tingles through every cell of my skin, alive like warriors fighting an endless battle. "Yes, you're stronger than me. Yes, you're faster than me. Hell, you're better than me in every way, but you need to get this into your psychotic mind: even villains have downfalls," I muse. Hunter's already put his barriers back up, the true emotion behind his infinite eyes obscured. "And yours will be more than spectacular."

To my astonishment, Hunter doesn't laugh. Instead, a wolfish smirk grows on his lips like it's been tattooed on to the pale lines.

I feel my stomach stir at his response. He's growing less and less predictable with every passing second.

"Do you want a fate worse than death?" The words coming out of my lips are not my own. They are my father's. I remember him threatening a wolf that had betrayed us to the rogues when I was still a part of my pack. "Because that can be arranged."

"You make me laugh, Alaska." Hunter chuckles. "With your snide words. Thankfully, you won't be talking for much longer."

Something inside me explodes. An inferno bursts to life. An ocean surges through my veins, a tornado stirs inside of me, and lighting strikes directly into my ire.

My swords arcs across his body, slashing a bloody hole in his shirt. The navy coloured material doesn't change his appearance as his blood soaks through the shirt.

I stagger back, wondering what will happen. Is the wolf's bane strong enough to kill him all by itself? Or do I need to stab him through the heart?

Hunter's laugh echoes through my ears; I don't hear anything else except his indecisive laugher. It haunts me, and no matter how much I attempt to focus on the wind whistling irritably through the destroyed ruins of the kingdom, I can't. My werewolf senses are failing me.

"Are you kidding me?" Hunter mocks, glancing at his chest as the wound knits together before my very eyes. He shrugs his shoulders. He can smell the wolf's bane, but his lack of worry has my insides churning. Sweat begins to bead on my forehead and make my hair sticky. "Well, I guess I never did tell you my story."

I open my mouth, unable to contain my shock. What is he talking about?

Hunter efficiently notices my abnormal expression. "What?" he says blandly. "You think that I didn't know your pretty little blade is laced with wolf's bane?"

I gulp, a lump stuck in my throat. It refuses to go away.

"I—" I begin, but my words falter. What am I supposed to say? How else am I supposed to kill an immortal psychopath? I'm open to any suggestions.

I grit my teeth, willing to end this. My wrist flicks upwards, just nicking the edge of his knee, but the cut is merely a graze; nowhere deep enough to cause any damage at all. For some reason, the rogue isn't fighting back. He holds his ground and smiles.

I try again, the weapon rushing through the air with a whoosh as it slices it apart. This time, Hunter reacts to the blow and easily knocks it away with a fist. A deep gouge runs through the back of his hand like a valley, the river composed of scarlet liquid. He doesn't even flinch.

"My father wanted to make me stronger," he yells, striding towards me with elegant precision. His fisted hand comes out of nowhere, embedding itself in my stomach. "He wanted to make me the best."

All the air is expelled from my lungs by the blow, and I back away as my eyes cloud over with agony. But I don't allow myself to fall over. If I fall over, then I'm as good as dead.

Another punch lands in my abdomen before I can protect myself.

"He made me addicted to wolf's bane. Only in small doses, otherwise it would kill me, but it was enough," he yells in fury, but not at me; at his father. Then another blow lands near my heart. I feel the organ shudder at the bone-shattering punch. "Because he knew it would make me stronger—he knew it would make me the best.

"And now, if I don't take it, I'm dead," he explains, backing away for a second. "The wolf's bane makes me stronger than any creature. It makes me faster; better. Good luck trying to kill me, Alaska. You will not succeed, though, I'd like to see you try."

I almost choke as blood rises up my throat, spilling onto the ground. If I wasn't physically wounded, I would've been astonished that he has opened up to me about something so personal. Because information like that is dangerous in a world like ours. It's information that can—and will—get him killed.

I feel my hope deflate like a popped balloon. The wolf's bane slathered along the crisp blade of my sword can't work. And, to be honest, it was a stupid idea in the first place. Hunter is unlike any other werewolf on this earth, and where the poison would competently render us useless, Hunter will be stuck sitting on his throne of bones and ashes.

But I'm beyond caring. I don't need wolf's bane to kill him. Last time I checked, it's pretty hard to regrow a head.

When I lash out this time, my blade is met by Hunter's. I abstain from glance into his eyes, so I keep my gaze on the mixture of mud, blood, and snow beneath my feet. The sickly mix is unwelcoming.

I push forwards, the metal biting into my hand like a wild creature. My body roars with adrenaline, begging for me to shift. I push the thought away. I will be even weaker against Hunter's larger, overpowering wolf form.

Hunter abruptly lets his muscles go slack, and I find my weapon pressed up against is windpipe. My knee moves upwards to make contact with his groin. The blow hits hard, and I watch as Hunter gasps for a deep breath.

My legs move swiftly. I have been in this situation multiple times in training, which has not all gone in my favour, but this time I'm determined to win. For all those battles I have lost in preparation for this one, it was worth it.

Hunter falls face first into the mud, his hands not moving quick enough to break his fall. His body begins to move, but my foot holds him down to keep him from wriggling away. He is weaker than before, despite his recent top-up of wolf's bane. Maybe having too much is slowly poisoning him and turning his blood into venom. Is it eating him from the inside?

Will an overdose kill him?

I take in a huge inhale of oxygen, the air fresh in my lungs like I have just been reborn. This is it. The end.

I place both of my hands firmly around the hilt of my sword to get enough power to kill him. I'm ready to drive it through his heart when his legs kick out, cleanly knocking mine from under me.

This time, I'm the one in the mud. My hand falls in the thick, wet ground as I sit up. The top half of my white shirt is blackened by dirt, the cold temperature sending a chill down my spine.

I glance around, both of my hands empty. I must've released my sword when I fell. My right wrist throbs with every beat of my heart; it must be broken.

I grit my teeth. My hands claw at the mud, pushing me into a seated position. I know exactly what happens when someone is in this position in a fight. It's clear that the battle is drawing to a close, and I know that this time, I will not be victorious.

The cold of the mud below my shins is nothing compared to the frigid metal of Hunter's sword as he rests it against my windpipe in the blink of an eye. I wish I could rest my palms against it and shove it off, but his sword is also covered in wolf's bane, definitely from when our two weapons collided. Both situations mean death, but which one is less painful, I do not know.

You know how they say that your life flashes before your eyes when you're on the verge of death? Mine doesn't. All I'm left with is a blank canvas, stretching on into the horizon endlessly. My life has not even been worthy enough to be written into a novel.

The blade at my throat presses ever closer. Hunter must be aware of my refusal to push it away, and I hear him snigger. I've heard the unusual sound enough times to know what it means.

269

I can't let it end like this, I tell myself. Tears bleed into my eyes, distorting the world in a maroon hue.

My swords lies two feet away, and my hands consciously clench, pretending that they're holding it. But I know it's too far away, and as soon as I stretch out to reach for it, Hunter kicks it away. I definitely can't reach it now. He follows up by kicking me in the chin upwards, my teeth biting painfully into my gum and tongue. I land on the ground with my back exposed.

The blade is back under my throat. It pulses as I swallow.

"It was nice knowing you, Alaska." Hunter sighs. At least he takes no joy in my demise, as I would his.

I blink away the river of tears, formed from thoughts conjured up in my mind of Chase and Josh. I can't leave them. Not like this and Hunter's heart still beating.

"I wish I could say the same, arseh*le," I reply solemnly. I try to keep my voice emotionless, but it cracks, just like my soul. The groove is deep—irreparable.

The blade bites into my skin. And then falls out of Hunter's grasp.

I feel liquid splash onto the back of my exposed neck, and almost gag. Hunter's body is rigid and unmoving, and I quickly use the distraction to push his arms away from me. His sword falls onto my lap.

But instead of reaching for my weapon, I freeze. I can't move a muscle.

My eyes glaze over to a familiar set of eyes and the same silky black hair I had seen run past me earlier. But this time, her eyes are not filled with fear. They are filled with something much more dark and complex which I cannot even begin to decipher. And in her hand rests the hilt of a dagger, the blade buried into Hunter's skin.

"Harper!" I scream, half in fear, half in shock. Hunter can easily break her neck with the jolt of his fingers.

Hunter grabs up the wolf's bane sword from where it lies, and I am forced to watch in horror as he arcs it around his body without hesitation. With no choice, I pick up Hunter's sword, but I'm too slow.

My heart leaps to my throat. No. She can't die. Not for me. She's too young.But Harper steps back just in time, the blade slicing across her cheek, creating a shallow graze. At first, nothing happens. Her posture is strong, defiantly holding out as Hunter rises to his feet like a Phoenix being reborn from its ashes. He pulls the dagger from his back, eyes glowing a luminous silver as he snarls at the girl.

And that's when she falls to the ground, convulsing and sputtering frothing liquid from her mouth. All I can do is watch, powerless to the situation. She has sacrificed herself for me, and this time, I won't forgive myself.

Seconds pass, and she lies still.

"Harper!"

I suck in a laboured sob. I can still hear the faint pulsing of her struggling heart as it battles the wolf's bane in her bones, but I know the inevitable. Soon that sound will no longer exist. I try to run over to her body but my rage blinds me. I clutch Hunter's sword, only for it to be wrenched out of my grip. The man himself stands over me, hovering like an unwelcome ghost.

I lash out with my leg, the satisfying feeling of flesh beneath my foot. Hunter gasps, but it's not enough; it will never be enough. I kick again, aiming for his groin once more, but the kick misses completely. My vision is streaked with tears, making it nearly impossible to see. I attempt to wipe them away, but Hunter's quick to notice my distraction.

He gathers up the sword two metres from my feet, snarling like a hellhound. He knows what he has to do, but so do I. Instinct tingles in my fingertips, raring to sink my teeth deep into his flesh.

My legs involuntarily move towards my previous blade. It glitters in the sunlight, much too beautiful for an object so deadly.

271

I never reach it. Hunter latches on to my arm, using his heightened speed to stop me dead in my tracks.

I will never forget the smile riddled on his face. It distorts the mask he wears, peeling back at the edges to reveal the once innocent boy beneath. He used to be a child once—untampered with. It's the rogue life that has done this to him. It was power that made him into such a ferocious beast. That's why I have never wanted to be the queen of Arla. Why I sacrificed myself, allowing Chase to "take my life" to win the Alpha Trials. I know what power does to people—it corrupts them. It would've shattered me.

His sword surges straight towards my heart as I am unable to break his hold on my upper arm. It's over. This life will end, just like I have wanted it to so many times in the past.

I raise my head and feel the wind circulate around my body, ready to take my soul with it. I have always known the outcome of this battle, but I haven't accepted it, nor have I accepted death as a consequence. But now . . . now it doesn't seem so bad. When you die, the suffering ends. It's all over. No one needs to worry about you because they know that you are safe and in a place where no one can touch you.

I fight back, punching and kicking the air. I duck under the sword as Hunter continues to slash down at me, but he kicks my legs away, head smashing against the mud in a blaze of agony. Hunter places the tip of the sword on my breastbone. My head spins from dizziness.

I take my last breath.

And someone shoves hard against my shoulder, knocking me out of the way. I close my eyes, unable to see who it is, but I know what they've done: they've given me a fighting chance. A chance which I refuse to give away.

My body hits the ground, aching as I land next to my sword. The amber residue coating the blade of the sword stands out stark in contrast to the white and brown earth. The pigment is the only evidence of colour in this landscape filled with the cries of death.

I take it without blinking and rise to my feet whilst Hunter is preoccupied. My legs are weak, threatening to give way as I stagger towards the devil and the woman who stands on the other end of his sword.

The girl who knocked me out the way is unarmed, but she moves like a hurricane across the mud below her worn leather boots. Her brunette tresses shroud her face as she brings a shuddering punch into Hunter's angular nose. Even from where I am standing, I can hear the ringing crunch of breaking bone.

"Alaska!" the girl shouts, glancing back at me for a mere second. The azure of her eyes is enough to confirm who she is; Azra. "Get the sword!" she continues, turning back to her enemy. She crouches efficiently as metal swipes above her head. "Now!"

With her attention elsewhere, I nod. I know she doesn't see it, but I know what she has done for me. I know what she has done for the kingdom.

My hands shake as I pick up the weapon buried in a mound of brown snow. An engraved crescent moon on the hilt winks at me. I remember Chase being entrusted with it this morning, Logan's tight hands almost refusing to let it go, for it's the only family heirloom of hers that remains. In fact, my fingers are vibrating so much, alive with nerves, that the iron slips from my grasp. I catch it before it falls back into the icy snow.

I catch Harper's still body in the corner of my eye. I close my eyelids, forcing the world to turn black and forcing the tears to stay away. It feels like I'm holding back a tsunami, my skin threatening to split under the pressure.

I bite my tongue. It's the only action that manages to keep me from going insane with grief. Blood doesn't spill into my mouth, but I can still taste the lingering metallic tang at the back of my throat.

I blink once. I have to end this. Now.

273

Azra lunges forward, her beautiful face distorted into a veil of anger. I've never seen her so passionate about killing her opponent, but after everything the rogues had done to her, it does not surprise me. I help with her advance, swiping with my sword at every opportunity I get.

The three of us dance in an unconventional circle, Azra throwing punches while I manage to score Hunter's flesh with cuts and nicks.

Her eyes shift past Hunter as he backs away, stumbling over the debris littering the ground. It's the first time I've seen him do so.

Azra's fist connects with his head as I wrap all ten of my scarred fingers around the wolf's bane sword. It seems pointless to put so much faith in a weapon, but I have no choice. The girl advances, grabbing Hunter's forearm in a bid to shake the blade from his grasp.

Instead, Hunter pushes the warrior off with ease as though he is batting away a fly. Her face is a confused mess as she is forced backwards by his sheer strength. Her eyes are wide open. I'm not fast enough to catch up with the movements and gape as I watch the event play out in front of my eyes.

Hunter drives his sword through her abdomen.

"Azra!" I scream as her azure eyes fill with water. She doesn't have the energy to scream, her fingers twitching as they coil around the object embedded in her stomach. Her emotionless features waver, and the stench of fear and death fill my nostrils like a plague.

I can't breathe.

My lungs won't contract.

I refuse to blink.

"No," I murmur. "No, no, no, no, no!" Halfway through my cries of dismay, my voice turns to a gritty whine. It sounds like I've got something lodged in my throat.

274

My legs move forward without permission, muscles clenching despite my plea not to. I'm so blinded by rage, by grief, by fear, that I can't stop myself. My mind swells with too many emotions to separate. I can no longer tell love from hate; emptiness from longing. They all merge into a large flame of fury; a fire I can't extinguish. I don't think I want to.

My steps quicken. Hunter draws out his sword from Azra's chest, blood blotting her ripped shirt.

I don't hesitate to drive my sword straight through his heart.

Everything turns grey. Hunter doesn't turn around, and I don't want him to. His face will haunt my nightmares for the rest of my living life.

Unsure whether it'll work or not, I twist the blade, the clearing around us enhancing his cries of agony. He has to die this time, and I will burn his dying body if I have to. I'm not an animal, although it's written into my nature, but I have no remorse for this devil. I keep my mercy stored inside a small pocket of my heart, and it's firmly sealed shut for this monster.

Hunter makes a choking sound. His jaw clenches as he opens it to gasp for a breath of air. His arms flail out unnaturally, as though he is convulsing. Black blood splutters onto the ground, mixing with the muddy water to create a deadly concoction.

Finally, Hunter's legs give way. I take a gulp, finding the courage to walk silently and stand in front of him.

Blackened blood drips from his eyes like tears made of tar. Blood spills from his mouth, the colour contrasting the grotesque pigment of his skin.

"What?" Hunter chokes out, spluttering on his own words. He uses the last of his precious energy to wipe away the discoloured blood running down his face. He studies the residue like it's the first time he's seen the world in colour. "What did you do to me?" I have to strain to hear his distorted words.

I pull my lips into a tight line, squatting next to his face as his body begins to shake tremendously as it battles a losing fight against the poison in his system.

"Ever heard of an overdose?" I ask, holding my breath.

Hunter strains to look at me, his white face flushing crimson. He doesn't have enough energy to speak, let alone break his fall as his body topples onto the ground. His body convulses and shakes. His white hands scrape at his throat as it makes a horrific gurgling noise, the man choking on his own ebony blood. My sword sticks out of his back, pierced straight through his heart. His hand flops, fingers still vibrating as the life fades from his body. The fingers fall into Azra's lifeless hair as he slides into unconsciousness.

I rise from my squatting position, shifting my head to the side. My eyes narrow in disbelief, every single one of my limbs numb with relief. But I don't feel a huge weight lift off my shoulders, particularly with both Azra and Harper on the brink of death.

"For Azra," I hiss, my teeth clenched. "And Harper. And everyone else you've made suffer," I say coldly, finally allowing the tears to streak my eyes. The continuous fountain refuses to stop.

A breeze flows across the battlefield as I turn my back on the corpse, a fire in my bones.

"Burn in hell, arseh*le."

CHAPTER TWENTY-TWO
Fractured

"It's strange that they fear death. Life hurts a lot more than death. At the point of death, the pain is over."

- Jim Morrison

Hunter's dead eyes gaze up at the sky, black blood seeping into the fleshy crevices of his eye sockets. His cheeks have ceased to hold a single pigment of colour, lifeless and stone cold. Snow has begun to fall, settling on his flesh as though it's part of the landscape. His silver hair wavers in the breeze as I stagger to my knees beside Azra. The boy's eyelids refuse to close, still defying nature as he falls into darkness.

I can't find it within myself to feel sorry. Instead, I wrap my arms around my knees and bring them into my chest. The mud soaks through my leggings in less than a second, but the burning cold doesn't make me shiver like it normally does. Instead, I feel numb, like I'm unable to feel anything. I don't think I want to.

I bury my head in my knees, rocking back and forth as the tears drip steadily from my eyes. I thought the action would soothe me but it does nothing.

"Ali," a voice snaps me out of my temporary daze. A hand falls on my shoulder. I can't help but flinch away.

I press my face further into my legs in a bid to hide my ruined composure. Chase doesn't need to see me like this. It will shatter him.

"Alaska, you did it," he whispers. I feel his breath tickle my ear, his warmth enveloping me even though he's still too far away to feel completely safe. This time, I allow him to snake a strong arm around my body. Relief settles into my bones. "You did it. We won."

Those words sound so good to my ears. After Hunter had constantly undermined my hope, chanting that he would win, nothing makes my heart lift more than confirmation from Chase. We saved the kingdom, even if not all of us made it.

My fingers are itching to touch Chase's skin; to be with him. I want to run a hand through the soft strands of his dirty blonde hair, just to make sure that he's real. To ensure that I am still alive and breathing.

I shift my body, thrusting my arms tightly around Chase's broad chest before he can relax. For a second, his body tenses under my grip. He's unaware of the horrors that I've just witnessed, but I'm sure that he had spotted the two other casualties only meters away from my figure. It isn't hard to put two and two together. Then his arms fasten around me, pressing his ribcage into my chest.

"Azra," I let out with a choked sob, pushing myself away from my mate's chest to wipe the tears from my eyes. "I couldn't save her," I continue. Another tear rolls down my reddened cheek. "I couldn't save them."

Chase places both of his palms on my shoulders, prying me from the security of his body. I abruptly begin to shiver from deprived of his warmth. He places a firm kiss on my forehead.

Then he stills. I eye him curiously, but my attention has shortened and I soon find myself with my hands in the glacial snow. "Alaska?" he says slowly. I nod as a response, eyes flickering to his own. My mouth opens temporarily, but all that comes out is a

278

belated gasp. "They're still alive," he informs me, staggering to his feet as quickly as his wounded body will allow. "Listen."

Furrowing my eyebrows, I concentrate on my hearing. My eyes screw tightly shut, my eyeballs aching in the bid to pick up the faint flutter of a heartbeat. One second ticks by; nothing. Then another. That's when I hear it: the steady thump of a heartbeat—a lifeline. I zone into the noise, picking up the racing pulse as my eyes are forced open in shock.

I can't move. How has the wolf's bane not killed them already?

It takes Chase's soothing touch to snap me into action. I wave a hand at the two women. "Quick, take Azra," I instruct, much more bluntly than I anticipated. "I'll get Harper."

We both stagger to our feet in sync. I swiftly pick up Harper's body in my trembling arms. Despite my lack of physical strength due to how tired I am, I refuse to drop her.

I follow Chase as he heads through the castle doors, the cobblestone corridors swallowing us as Harper groans at every footfall. The shudders send jolts through my body, but I don't allow my arms to give way. She feels much too light; as though I can snap her in half.

Chase pushes aside another set of double doors, opening up to the large hall I was dragged through when I first met the late king. It was empty before, except for a lone pair of guards standing out against the grey background in bright scarlet uniform like sore thumbs. Now the grand hall is bustling, words roaring through my ears without consent.

The injured lie scattered across the floor. Other able-bodied people dash around and tend to their wounds. The number of wounded is small, but I am certain that it will grow. The war has barely just ended, and it will take days to get all of the injured in to be treated.

"Hey!" Chase shouts as he saunters over to a raised table in the corner of the room, not even caring to place a sheet under

Azra's body as she groans in protest. I continue to cradle Harper in my arms, finally spotting an empty area on the floor. I grab a strewn blanket and kick it into place before gently resting her onto the soft material. Her eyes are firmly shut. If I were human, I would've pronounced her dead.

Everyone passing the King barely gives him a glance. His knuckles clench in frustration, and I yearn to reach out and comfort him. But I can't do that when I'm breaking down inside, collapsing on to an already existent pile of rubble.

"Alaska?" a voice echoes from behind me, and I turn cautiously to see where the voice is coming from. The tears in my eyes distort her otherwise beautiful face, but I can tell it from anywhere. "What the hell happened?" Alex enquires, marching towards me as I stand up from beside Harper's crippled figure.

Alex suddenly takes a sharp breath as she spots Harper nestled in the white blanket on the ground.

"Harper," she whispers. Her voice cracks. "What happened?" the woman asks demandingly as she settles into a crouching position.

"She—" I don't know what to say. She stabbed Hunter in the back—literally—to save me because I can't even freaking fight, and now she's going to die because of it? Instead I whisper, "She saved my life."

Alex brings Harper up into her arms. Her eyes are covered. She brushes the girl's dark hair from her eyes, pressing a kiss onto her forehead.

"Why isn't she healing?" Alex mutters, the girl still clenched between her hands. It looks like she'll never let go.

I tentatively point to the cut on Harper's face. Black blood drips across her face in an enduring smear. My index finger wobbles as I do, shaking so intensely I can't stop. "She was cut with the wolf's bane sword," I state solemnly. The look on Alex's face makes my stomach drop. "I'm so sorry."

Alex's eyelashes flutter towards my face, inked with invisible tears. She presses a warm hand against my forearm, squeezing. "It's not your fault," she states. I almost throw up over her. How is it not my fault?

A guilty look passes across my face, and I turn away, only to glance up at Azra, much to my dismay. I know Alex noticed my action; she's been closely studying me for the past weeks. Her fingers grow lighter on the skin of my arm, leaving white fingerprints where she applied the pressure.

"Go help your friend," Alex says as calmly as she can. I know just how hard she's trying to stop her voice from shaking irrationally. "She needs you."

I nod, biting my wrist in an abnormal action to prevent more tears from rolling out of my eyes. I'm back standing on my unsupportive legs faster than I even thought possible, treading carefully between corpses and the injured. Some appear to be healing, gradually moving in torn garments of blood and dirt. But the condition of the others is worsening by the second. The heavy feeling of death hangs in the air.

I find Azra's raised deathbed a few meters away, although it takes me a minute to reach the wooden bench since I had to weave through crowd. Her skin is a deadly pastel compared to the ancient wood she rests on, which looks matte as it absorbs the light from the torches hanging around us. A trail of black blood runs from the corner of her left eye and down the side of her cheek like a scar. Her fingers lie slack by her sides, her chest rising and falling slower with every beat of her heart. The flesh is smothered with a concoction of crimson and coal dust.

I shake her softly as Chase presses both his palms into his forehead, blatantly frustrated that everyone else is too busy to give him a glance. The girl groans as a response, her pale pink lips parting as the noise escapes her mouth.

"Azra?" I call out to her, pushing greasy strands of hair from her forehead and out of her face. The strands are entwined

281

with sweat, the substance beading her skin as her body battles the wolf's bane. Her eyes flicker open, azure infiltrating my line of sight. I shiver as her boiling skin makes contact with me, latching her fingers around mine. The grip is almost too strong to bear but I can't let go for her sake.

"Hey," I whisper, bending my knees so that I'm hovering closer to her face, eyes level with the wooden ledge. She appears comfortable with the gesture.

Azra's lips curl into the beautiful smile I have grown to adore. Josh's best friend—my—best friend, is inevitably dying. My hearts sinks, knowing that there is nothing I can do to save her.

"Hey," she whispers back, the words practically inaudible. Her eyes rotate in their sockets, gazing up momentarily at the ceiling, then fastening a glare on Chase. It doesn't take a genius to work out who she's looking for.

She doesn't have the energy to move. The most she can manage to do is contract her bicep, resting a hand over the open wound on her chest. She was lucky; the sword missed her heart by a few inches, but the close proximity means that the wolf's bane will reach the major organ efficiently. When the bane poisons her heart, there's no going back.

The woman's eyebrows furrow. "Where's Josh?"

The boy in question is nowhere to be seen, but it's near impossible to identify anyone in the ever-growing swarm of people. My muscles clench as an deafening scream reverberates off the walls of the hall, splitting apart my eardrums as though they are nothing more than paper. All I can smell is death. All I can see is death. All I can hear is death.

Death. Death. Death.

With a gaping mouth and watering eyes, I find my eyes trailing over Azra's body. Death screams at me from every nook and cranny of her dying figure.

No, I scream inside my brain, the words empty. She will not die.

"I—" I stammer. "I don't know."

She grips my fingers even more tightly. Another black tear rushes across her face. Another incurable scar.

My eyes wander up to Chase, a hand still riddled in his hair. He appears more stressed than he had beforehand. He can feel the ache in my chest as prominently as I can.

Abruptly, Azra leans over the side of the bench. Her whole chest heaves as a plume of black blood emanates from her mouth, spilling onto the floor as she coughs restlessly. The liquid splatters on my leggings, sending a wave of heat through my legs, but I don't blink. I can't move.

"Chase!" I yell, unable to do anything but stare uselessly at the girl before me. I'm not a medical expert—I have only just recently learnt how to tie an effective tourniquet. My knowledge stops at the sheer mention of wolf's bane.

My mate turns around in a sudden panic, beckoning those nearest to him for help. When no one replies to his direct pleas, he resorts to raising his voice above the crowd.

"Help!" Chase's deep voice growls, but despite the power he is putting into the yell, it doesn't travel further than ten metres. All he gains are a few pairs of eyes glaring at him before returning to tend the wounded. "Someone, please!" This time, his words are quieter; hopeless.

Chase's status as king doesn't aid him in this situation. He told me once that he didn't want to worshipped as a ruler, just treated as fairly as the other citizens of Arla. It looks like he finally got what he wanted.

Unable to attract the attention of anyone willing to help, I find myself reaching for the bottom of Azra's shirt. Taking a second to gulp and push away the tears, Azra nods at me. I pull up the fabric to reveal a deep crevice of coal stained blood, trailing down her waist and dripping endlessly onto the floor. Her hand falls back over the skin, sinking into the darkness with disturbing ease.

"No," I mutter, my movements jerky. I don't know what to do. "No, this should've healed."

Azra smiles at me sympathetically. Her bloodied fingers run along my grey top, automatically grabbing my attention. "Alaska"—she sighs, blood pulsing from her wound like an endless tide—"it's okay," she continues, before doing the same gesture with her hand which she had done to me with Chase. His cobalt eyes dart around in confusion. "Don't, Chase. My time is up."

"Hey," I say, my voice bitter. I bite my tongue to avoid more from spilling out afterwards. "Don't you dare say that."

Azra's body is still. She barely has enough energy to breathe. "Please, Alaska," she whispers. "Don't make this harder than it already is." Even from where I'm standing, her azure irises appear faded; more of a shade of teal rather than their usual bright hue.

My hands visibly shake. Somewhere deep within the pit of my thoughts, I knew of her fate, but I don't allow myself to see it. She will live, no matter what.

"Chase!" I raise my voice. My thumb subconsciously rubs against Azra's smooth skin as I do so, as if my touch is keeping her soul trapped within her body. I don't want to admit it, but I'm afraid of letting go. "Go find Josh," I order. An image of Josh face down in the snow, blood belching from a wound in his chest creeps into my sight. If I had any energy, I would've screamed out in mental agony at the torment. For all any of us could know, he could be dead.

Chase holds eye contact, an invisible thread between us sparking like a strike of lightning. He knows how much this simple action will mean to me and Azra, and breaks away from the bench. I watch as his head merges into the swell of people, more and more flocking into the room by the second. The huge hall now feels tiny, the walls closing in as I struggle to stand upright.

Death. Death. Death.

I'm back crouching next to Azra's face in a blink. She's rolled over to her side, using the last of her energy to face me. I try my best to hold my concentration, but my breaking heart wants me to shut down. To wake up, as if the whole war—everything, including Josh, including Chase—has been a dream. A blip; nothing.

Except I don't wake up. When I come back to reality, Dylan is dead, my parents are long gone, Josh is missing, Chase is mentally scarred, and my other best friend is dying in my arms.

"Alaska," Azra speaks softly, the words trembling on her lips. The black surrounding her eyes like a makeup disaster is hard to ignore, but I try my best to concentrate on the bright blue of her irises. Her grip against my palm is immeasurably strong. "I'm sorry about everything I said."

I crease my eyebrows, taken over by a strange combination of fear and sorrow. "What do you mean?"

"When I said I didn't want you as a friend; that Josh was too good for you," she murmurs. The memory hits me like a train. I can't afford to think about Azra pressing me up against a wall in her final moments. "The truth is, my life has been so much better with you in it. I know what I said was wrong. It wasn't true.

"I need you to know that," she continues.

I squeeze her hand back. "I—" I start but my trembling lips can't even form words.

"Don't leave us," I manage to whisper, the words painfully scraping against my vocal chords. "Don't leave Josh."

Azra stares at the ceiling, as though she can see something I can't.

"I don't want to," she murmurs, pain blatant in her voice. I wish my touch could heal her, but I can't even take away her pain.

Wolf's bane—derived from the wolfsbane flower—is a strong poison. Werewolves are notoriously known not to get drunk. However, small doses of wolf's bane acts like what alcohol does to a human for werewolves. If the dose is too strong, the consumer

285

will be shown vivid hallucinations, conjured from the deepest depths of their mind, but that's only possible with a weak strain of wolf's bane.

The variety we have used, sourced from a locked cupboard in Logan's storeroom, is the deadliest in the species. Even a drop can render a werewolf dead within minutes.

Azra should already be dead, but I know that she's stronger than most. If anyone can battle against wolf's bane and survive, it's her.

"I wish I could stay," the woman continues. Her bottom lip trembles. I know how hard she's trying to stay strong and fearless in her last moments, but her shield is cracking. I can see the petrified girl lurking beneath like a shadow—permanent yet undesired. "I wish I could. For you and Josh. You both mean so much to me, and I . . . I can't thank you enough.

"But I'm going to a better place." She blinks. "I'm going to see my parents." Her words break into a whine. She's finally fractured, but she smiles at the thought of her parents. "I'm going to see them."

What should I tell her? Not to be stupid? That of course she'll survive this? Or be empathetic? Hold her hand whilst the life slips from the shell of her body?

Instead, I remain silent. My lips press a kiss against the back of her hand before resting my cheek on the skin. The action is new to me, but I remembered my father doing it when my mother was ill, to get her through the pain.

"I'm not scared, Alaska," she says. She's lying. "Everyone thinks that death is a terrible thing"—*That's because it is,* I scream inwardly—"But when you die, the pain, the suffering . . . It's all over. You don't have to worry about the deceased, because you know that they are safe; unreachable."

Her words bring a flood of stinging tears into my eyes. My throat is dry from the lack of water left in my body, but I'm too far gone to care.

She fastens her hand around my own. "You have to promise me something." She exhales. Her teeth are lined with black blood, staining the white enamel.

I nod cautiously. "Anything."

Azra bites her lip, her fleshy skin white against white. "Promise me that you'll tell Josh that I love him," she says solemnly. "And that I'm sorry."

I wipe away my tears with the corner of my top, but they are immediately replaced by fresh droplets. "I promise." Another squeeze of her hand.

A mop of brown hair catches the corner of my eye, matching pigmented eyes wandering over my back as they look past me and to the woman laid before me. His clothes are bloodied, a huge hole gaping in the side of his trouser. A long gash runs up the side of his leg, knitting together as a small amount of blood runs out of the incision.

In any other situation, I would be petrified that he's injured. But I don't have time to even feel remotely concerned or even relieved that Josh is safe. I can't when the crushing weight of Azra's death is hanging above my head like an axe.

I move out of the way in a blink, sliding my hand out of Azra's boiling grip. Josh immediately takes my place, barely giving me a second glance. His fingers hurriedly wrap around her own.

"I'm here," he speaks softly. The shattering tone in his voice forces my legs to wobble. "Oh God, Azra. I'm here."

Despite the current situation, Azra finds it within herself to smile. "Josh," she says breathily.

Josh's eyes are already swimming with tears. I stand two steps away from him, unsure of how to comfort both of my friends. Instead, I resort to Chase's touch. He walks over as the voices around me drown out the sound of my own breathing. He pulls me into his chest, resting a single hand on the back of my head. In an attempt to comfort me, he places a kiss on my forehead, but it's cold.

"I'm here, Azra," Josh repeats. "I'm here."

Azra continues to smile but it grows faint on her face. Her curled up posture makes her appear much smaller than she truly is.

"I'm sorry." Azra sighs, blinking rapidly to get the black liquid out of her eyes.

Josh tucks a strand of her hair behind her ear. "There's no need to be sorry."

"I didn't want it to end like this," she speaks truthfully. Her words are progressively getting softer with every fleeting second.

Josh shakes his head, refusing to accept the truth. He, just like the rest of us, is in denial. "This isn't the end," he insists.

Azra bows her head in a strained motion. Another bloodied drop runs from her eye, arcing gracefully into her mouth. "Josh, please. I know what's going to happen." The sentences, although quiet, are filled with an endless power that cracks me in two. "And it's okay—it's okay."

I can't see Josh's face, but I can imagine what it looks like. He is as easily confused as me, and I picture an emotional Josh with his eyebrows pinched together. At any other time, I would've laughed.

"How is it okay?" Josh retorts. His mouth hangs open in shock. He bends his knees, hovering closer to Azra's face than previously.

Azra ignores Josh's enquiry. Instead, she smiles at him, a fraction of her teeth glimmering in the low light. "I love you," she whispers. Her breaths are slowing down immensely, each rise of her chest a painfully straining to fill her lungs with enough oxygen to keep fighting.

Josh leans his head on the wooden bench, appearing disorientated. "I love you so much, Azra," he whispers as a response. "I love you, so you're not leaving me, okay? Do you understand? You. Are. Not. Leaving. Me."

I can swear that Azra chuckles at his remark.

"And whatever this is, you're going to fight it," he says defiantly, wiping away a black trail staining her cheeks. He knows what's happening to her, but the tense movements of his fingers lead me to believe that he doesn't want to accept the facts. He's always been one for fiction. "You're going to fight it because you're strong, and because I need you."

Azra closes her eyes, resulting in ferocious shaking from my best friend. I bury my face further into Chase's chest, trying to block out the horrors. To my dismay, my sight is clear, and I can't find it within myself to shut my eyes.

"I need you, Azra," Josh huffs as he continues to shake her. Eventually, she reopens her bright, electric blue orbs. "I love you."

Her lips are still shaped into a smile. I wish I could capture it; her happiness in that moment. I wish I could remember every detail of her face, so that I won't forget it over time. But I'm forgetful, and the only thing I seem to be mapping is the iridescence of her eyes.

Azra's hand shakes in Josh's.

Without warning, Azra screams at the top of her lungs, the noise enough to make my ears begin to ring endlessly. I push both of my hands over my ears in a bid to block out the wails, but it does nothing to halt the endless screaming.

Her muscles all immediately clench as her body grows rigid. Instead of her limbs appearing soft, they look frozen. The woman's chest expands and deflates rapidly as she attempts to force enough oxygen into her lungs.

The cracking and splintering of bones reverberates through the girl's screams. I gasp in horror when I realise that Azra is breaking Josh's hand with the sheer power of her grip. My best friend—as though defying the existence of pain and agony—doesn't flinch. I step away from Chase in a bid to aid the situation before me, but there is nothing I can do except endure the tormenting wails.

After ten seconds of Azra gritting her teeth so tightly that they might shatter, her limbs soften. Her body falls slack like a puppet torn from its strings. Azure eyes gaze up at the vast, high arched ceiling.

I can't hear her heart beating.

My body goes into shock, unable to tear my eyes from Azra's peaceful body. She doesn't move, her chest no longer rising and falling irregularly like it had previously done. Her fingers are slack around Josh's hand, having fallen from his grasp.

Perhaps I'm being paranoid. With so many heartbeats in one room, I could be mistaken.

She's not dead. She can't be. After everything she's been through, she doesn't deserve this.

I'm snapped back to reality by Josh's frantic murmuring, "Azra?" He gasps, cradling the side of her face. He shakes her but she doesn't respond. "Azra?"

I bring both of my hands up to my mouth as it splits open into a gasp. A sob heaves from my chest, the blood coating my fingers. I'm unable to do anything else.

I can't move. I don't blink.

No.

No. No. No.

"Azra?" Josh calls out one last time, his words a mumble as transparent tears slide down his face, reaching his jawline and sinking down into the crevice of his neck. "No," he cries out, despair laced within his voice.

"No, Azra, don't leave me. Please, don't-"

His voice is cut off by a round of sobs. Josh's head falls onto the wooden bench below Azra's corpse.

My gaze caged by her encapsulating azure eyes, my legs give way. Pain ricochets through my bones as I hit the cobblestone, but the agony is nothing compared to the weight of my shredded heart.

She's gone.

CHAPTER TWENTY-THREE
Void

"I always tell myself that I'm ok. I repeat it like a mantra. I'm ok. I'm ok.
I'm ok. I'm ok. Because I'm afraid that if I stop, even for a moment,
I will drown in all the reasons I am not."

- unknown

Josh's hands haven't stopped shaking. I don't think they ever will.

I don't know how long I've been on the floor for. Seconds stretch into minutes. Minutes stretch into hours, until my mind is a continuous tunnel of time. I don't know how long it's been since Azra's passing, but given her pale complexion and unmoving eyes, I know that it's been long enough. Long enough to confirm that she's dead. The only recollection I have of time is the trembling of Josh's hands. The broken hand that Azra gripped tightly appears partially healed, the bones knitting together as he refuses to blink.

I don't know how long it's been when Josh eventually breaks away from Azra's hand. Her fingers have stiffened around his, forcing Josh to pry himself out of her eternal hold. His back is in my face, but I fear that the emotions on his face will be too much for me to process, particularly when I find it impossible to read them in the first place.

We need each other, more than we have ever needed each other before. But with Azra gone, I feel a rift settle between us. Our friendship will never be the way it was before her demise.

The boy backs away, almost treading on my fingers. I pull them away as his boot lands exactly where my limb had been seconds ago. He doesn't know that I'm here; why should he? Why would he even care? A shattered finger is nothing compared to a soulless body.

Before I can get to my feet, Josh slips away into the crowd. Somehow, he manages to keep his face from turning in my direction. I stare at his ruffled hair and light footsteps. His figure sways, weak from the recent events. If I were him, I wouldn't be able to walk.

I place a hand on the floor, the glacial cobblestone biting my hands as I stagger to my feet. There is nothing graceful about my movements, and my body suffers for it. The wound where Hunter tore a hole straight through my body still aches. I can still feel the tissues healing as I move. My scars, mostly healed and covered with crusted blood, ache at the tiniest movement.

"Alaska?" Chase calls out to me as I use the wooden bench to steady my wavering body. I reel forwards, accidentally finding myself a metre away from Azra's face and her faded azure eyes. I shut mine in response, wishing that I could erase the last few hours from my mind completely.

I wave a hand at my mate. I don't want him to follow me. Josh is my friend, not his.

I feel the rejection weigh heavy on my heart. Although we can't share telepathic thoughts like stated in multiple human-made stories, we still share a faint connection of emotions. Whenever he's feeling distressed, I also feel the nauseous sensation rush through my blood uncontrollably.

But I don't let his emotions root me to the spot. I push myself from the wood, eyes still tightly shut until I'm able to stand without support. As soon as I open them, I spot a glimmer of

Josh's brunet hair in the orange light as he exits the hall at the other end of the room.

I follow the boy closely, using long strides in a bid to catch up with the taller teenager. But keeping up is harder than I anticipated. Although the disorganisation in the hall has somewhat diminished, the amount of wounded continues to grow. I almost trip over a corpse as I sidestep yet another medic rushing to find another patient to save.

Finally, I reach the corridor, only to find it empty. He must've passed through this hall minutes ago, especially with my disadvantage of trembling legs, along with the sick swelling at the back of my mouth.

I almost punch the wall in frustration but that will bring even more agony to this horrific day. I have already endured enough pain to last a lifetime.

"Sh*t," I murmur, rubbing my temples with my hands. My sweaty palms pull the hair out of my face, eyes open in thought. Where is he?

"Where are you, Josh?" I mutter inaudibly.

Of course, no one answers me. The silence in the corridor is unsettling, but as I pace down the narrow hallway without purpose, it becomes even heavier. With nothing to disrupt my thoughts, they all flow through my head at once. I have to stop and steady myself.

One thousand questions itch my brain, but I only allow one to surface: where the hell is Josh?

Then it clicks, switching on like a lightbulb, the darkness shredded by endearing light. There's only one place he can be, and I know the location like the white scars running down the back of my hand.

My pace picks up as I navigate through the castle. I still don't know my way around, but after living in the palace for a month, I have grown used to some of the endless corridors and winding staircases. It's like navigating a labyrinth, but I can only

293

remember patches in my disrupted memory. But this route will never leave me.

I find the room, flinging open the wooden door so harshly that the barricade swings and meets the wall with a reverberating crunch. It reminds me of the sound Josh's hand made when Azra shattered the bone.

There is only one tiny window in the room, with numerous items of clothing scattered across the floor in an array of blacks and greys. Azra and Josh have never been ones to dress in colour, just like me. It's one of the things that had made me feel welcomed when I first met them. Three beds—one of which I shared with Josh for a night during the Alpha Trials—equally spaced from each other, lie next to a chest of drawers.

I pry my eyes away from the small light staring through the window and the blood-stained snow beyond to the man before me.

Josh's chest heaves as he gazes out of the same window, his back still turned. I haven't seen his face for a while. The sensation makes the tips of my fingers tingle. Despite me slamming door, his attention is firmly plastered to the sight before him. I don't think he can find the courage to face me.

He will blame me for Azra's death. I know it, yet, I don't think I'll be able to handle the accusation if he follows through.

"Josh?" I call out to him, my voice rasping against my dry throat.

Only now does he turn around. Although the tears have appeared to stop flowing, his eyes are stained in a deep red hue from agitation. The tears have cut deep channels into his face, lighter skin peering out from under his already pastel-shaded complexion. His eyes are focused on the floor, unable to look at me. The gesture crushes my heart to sand.

"She's gone," Josh states, balling his hands into fists. I expect him to shout at me—to hurt me in ways I thought I could never be hurt—but he stays rooted to the spot. He is too weak to even move. "Alaska, Azra's gone, and she's never coming back."

I watch my vision blur as tears prick at the corner of my eyes. All I can do is take numerous steps towards him, before taking his fisted hands into my bloodied hold. I pry his fingertips away from his palms only to find that his claws have created deep gashes in the skin. I can only guess that it's to relieve the mental agony he is suffering.

I shake his hands, grabbing his attention. His head shifts abruptly to mine, but it still droops.

"Josh," I utter, squeezing one of his hands tightly. "I'm so sorry. I know how much she meant to you."

Josh sniffs, diverting his gaze once more. "It hurts so much," the boy whines. As an immediate response, I pull him into a tight hug despite the fact that he's a head taller than me. He rests his chin on my shoulder. We slot together with ease. I release his hands, sliding mine around his thin frame as he does the same. I can feel them shaking behind my back before he squeezes me so tightly, it feels like he's broken at least two of my ribs.

"Shh," I whisper, closing my eyes as a tear droplet escapes the threshold of my eye socket. "It's going to be okay."

Josh nods, but his body stiffens under my touch. Silences swarms the air, heavy and suffocating. The man's chest expands before he speaks once more.

"What happens if I forget her face?" he questions. The question itself shocks me. It's true that with time, you forget people's faces. I can barely remember my parents' faces, but Azra's and her crystal blue eyes remain as clear as day. "What happens when I'm fifty and I can't remember her?"

I'm shocked into silence. It takes everything within me to find the right words to say, but even then they might be the worst kind of words I can say.

"You won't." I pry my eyes open only to find Josh's scrutinising stare studying me. His deep mocha eyes remain as beautiful as they have always been. "You—We will never forget her. What she did . . ." I pause. "She saved us. She saved me. I will never forget that. I will never forget her. She'll always be with us."

Josh nods, stepping out of the hug. He uses the crook of his elbow to dry his tears, the grey material of his shirt saturated with tears.

They say that the sheer agony of losing someone—that the pain of letting someone slip through your fingers, powerless to their fate—heals over time. With years, the scars will scab over and dissipate, but never truly fade. But sometimes, the ache will only get worse with each passing second. I fear that Josh's scrutiny will only exacerbate his pain, as will mine. How can I live with myself when someone else has died in my place?

"She deserved so much better," I continue, taking Josh's hands again and refusing to let go. My thumb runs along his smooth skin in a bid to take away some of his pain, but I know that there is nothing I can do to ease the war raging inside him. "And you need to remember that I'll always be here for you, I promise," I mutter. It's something I can't truly promise, but some part of me hopes that he believes it.

Josh jerks his hands out of mine, as though my touch is toxic. I have no time to feel hurt before the words leave his mouth. "But you're not her."

The words sting, but I don't let them go deeper than the surface of my skin. He is in a dark place, and part of me wishes that he doesn't mean those words at all. But he's right; I'm not Azra. And no one ever will be, because she's dead.

She's dead.

I realise that's the first time I've admitted it to myself.

Yet again, I find myself stepping towards him as he takes a step back to give himself space. In response, he just shakes his head, warning me not to come any closer. I halt, crushing my hands into fists.

"You know what happened the day Azra's mother died?" Josh asks, practically shouting the question. I shudder at the sudden shift in his tone. He constantly moves the position of his legs, waving a hand in the air, clearly agitated. "She came to me, knowing that she was about to be executed. Not to Azra. To me.

"I didn't know why at first, but when she started weeping in my arms, it made sense," he continues. "She knew that it would make it so much harder for Azra to see her like that.

"But that wasn't the worst part." Josh pauses, licking his pastel lips. "The worst part was the promise she forced me to make. I promised her that I would do everything I could to protect Azra. I knew I would do that anyway, but I broke that promise, Alaska." He glares at me, his jaw taut and clenched in fury. "I don't break promises. And now she's gone!"

I can't stop his next actions. His trembling hands grab a vase on the side of my old bedside table. His muscles flex as he throws it at the far wall, the expensive sapphire and white china shattering into one thousand tiny fragments; irreparable like my heart.

Josh glances down at his hands, drawing his eyebrows together in confusion. His disorientated expression makes my stomach churn.

I'm too slow to react as his legs stumble backwards and he lands on what used to be Azra's bed. Despite the solid piece of furniture below him, he still wavers like the sea during a tormenting storm. He brings his knees into his chest, burying his face into his legs.

I move towards him immediately and sit beside him. My teeth brush my lips as I hold back yet another stream of ongoing tears. My heart was once uncorrupted. Now it's teeming with demons. I place my arm around his back. He relaxes under my touch this time, leaning into my chest as I hug him closer. I am never going to let him go. Josh is my only friend, and I'm not going to let him suffer more than he needs to.

"I loved her, Alaska," Josh mutters. The sound is muffled but still rings clear as day. "I loved her."

I cradle his head with my hand, his hair soft to the touch. "I know," is all I can say. "She's in a better place now."

"I knew her for ten years," Josh says into my chest. The tone of his voice threatens to tear me apart. He stammers, a soft chuckle escaping his lips. "I remember the first time we met and I couldn't even lift a sword. She-she knew that she wasn't supposed to talk to me—to her, I was an omega; nothing. But she didn't care. She always accepted me for who I was. A crazy, f*cked up boy with no sense of direction.

"And now that she's gone, it feels . . ." He pauses to find the right words. It's as if I can hear his brain clicking and whirring as he thinks. "It feels like that part of me no longer exists. Like there's a hole in my soul, which I will never be able to fill."

Josh bows his head, submerging into silence. My lips purse open, but my voice box has seemingly vanished.

Josh's sobbing continues, and we stay like that for what seems like hours. The daylight intensifies as Josh's relentless sobs die down. Dust motes float in the air like ghosts, refracting the luminescent light like one thousand miniature stars. All I can think about is the weight on my chest that will never be lifted.

Finally, Josh's muttering slices the silence apart like a knife. "She was my home," he states. This time, it's my turn to be confused. "She was-she was—"

Josh continues to mumble, abruptly sitting up and rifling a hand through his hair. He pries himself from the bed, glancing around the room with jerky movements. I watch in confusion as he gathers up a random top from the floor before scooping down to collect another item of clothing. It takes me a minute to figure out what he's doing.

The boy opens a drawer and pulls out a worn-out navy bag. It's empty, the sides caving in as he chucks it onto his bed. He once left it empty to come and share mine. That moment seems like a decade ago; as though the comfort he brought me that night doesn't belong in the aftermath of Azra's demise.

298

"Josh?" I call out to him, squatting down next to him as he empties the contents of the drawer into his bag. His hands work fast, flinging in the garments of clothing and the odd hunting knife without even batting an eyelash to think twice. "What're you doing?" I finally ask him.

Josh bites his lip, finally zipping up the stuffed human-made bag. The only item he keeps out of the confined material, and in his hands instead, is a picture. I gasp when I notice him and Azra standing beside a woman with the same soft features as Josh, but with blonde short-cropped hair and piercing hazel eyes. His mother. I don't know how he got the picture in the first place, but I don't pry for an answer.

He stands up, completely ignoring my question. I follow what he's doing.

My hand scrapes against his upper arm, pulling him to face me. "Josh!" I shout, snapping him back to reality. "What're you doing?"

The boy doesn't blink. "I need to get out of here," he says with a sigh, placing the blue bag firmly on his shoulder.

I shake my head furiously. "No," I say. "No. You're not leaving me."

Josh's chest heaves once more. This time, he's the one to place his empty hand in mine. He squeezes it tightly. "I have to," Josh whispers, tucking a loose strand of my hair behind my ear. It's a friendly gesture, nothing more. "Everything about this place reminds me of her. This room. The bright tapestries. Even you, Ali. I don't know how I'll be able to cope if I'm always thinking about her. Not right now."

My feet take a step towards him. "You will be able to cope, I promise. I'm here for you," I say, my voice coming out as a whine. "Just please stay. Please. We need you."

"Azra needed me." Josh nods glumly. "And I wasn't there for her."

He begins to turn away, his fingers slipping out of mine. I fasten my hold, pulling him back before he can slip from my life altogether.

"I need you," I say quietly, widening my eyes. I want him—need him—to see how much I care for him. But he's grieving, and all of my emotions are lost to him. I understand why he wants to pack up and disappear, but that will just leave me with Chase. As much as I like him, he doesn't understand me like Josh does.

Josh shakes his head once more. "No you don't, Ali," he replies, our eye contact so dangerous and invigorating I can hardly keep my focus on him. This might be the last time I see those perfect brown eyes. "You don't need anyone. You're strong, and don't you dare forget that."

I exhale, a tear escaping my eye for the last time. "Just-just promise me you'll come back," I stutter out.

Josh squeezes my hand for the last time. "I promise."

And with that, he slips his fingers out of my hand, the skin burning like fire until his touch is no longer present. Without his warming contact, I feel empty, dead, unloved—the list goes on—inside.

I watch him disappear out of the door, catching one last glimpse of his brunet hair as they catch the sunlight, dazzling like stars, and whisper under my breath, "Goodbye."

CHAPTER TWENTY-FOUR
End
"After all we've done, do we even deserve to survive?"
- Clarke Griffin, The 100

I've been standing in the throne room overlooking the aftermath of the rogue war for at least an hour, although time has once again slipped through my hands.

Without Josh, the only place I can find sanctuary is here, where everything reminds me of Chase. My fingers scrape at my fingernails in an attempt to rid all of the blood hidden beneath the nail. I washed my hands earlier vigorously—and with enough anger to beat Hunter over again—but faint scarlet lines still blemish my murdering fingers.

They're an ugly sight, but I pinch myself to stop my train of thought. My fingers are scarred, just like everyone else's. I'm no different to any other werewolf who has fought in the war, I'm just more recognised; I hate it.

Once upon a time, I was confident, but the war has stripped that away from me as easily as the snow has been smudged into ruby. Attention makes my skin crawl.

The creaking of a floorboard is the only sound I have heard—aside from the constant moans of pain slithering into my ears unwillingly from the hall beneath my feet—in the past hour. I turn around abruptly in curiosity.

My eyes wander over to two females, one figure half the size of the other standing next to her. I can't control my mouth as it falls open in shock. Not only is the younger girl standing; she's alive.

"Harper?" My legs stagger forward, stumbling over each other as I battle against the urge to sprint towards her and grab her up in my arms. I do it anyway. Without her consent, I fall on to my knees and pull her into an embrace.

My hand cradles the back of her head as it rests on my shoulder, unable to comprehend what is happening. She had clearly been cut by the wolf's bane sword, even if the dosage was low. She should be dead.

"Oh my God," I say in relief, the scent of stagnant blood and poison infiltrating my nostrils. My stomach threatens to empty itself at the strong odour, but luckily I haven't eaten enough to do so. I think that I have finally grown accustomed to the stench.

I flicker my eyes from Harper, to Iris—her mother—then to the throne situated at my side. My arms squeeze the girl's miniature frame just to be sure that this isn't a dream. I squeeze her again until she releases a belated gasp from her mouth.

Afraid that I've hurt her accidentally, I let go, only to reveal that her skin is much paler than I remember. Sweat still beads her forehead like stars, but she's okay—she's okay. As she licks her chapped lips and runs a hand subconsciously down her burned right arm, I exhale.

I hadn't even thought to check on her when I dashed after Josh, but at that point, I had already presumed her fate. I will never make the same mistake again. The cut on her face has vanished, a thin white scar the only thing claiming that it was once there. By some miracle, the wolf's bane hasn't killed her. She must have an immunity, because even the smell makes me gag.

My muscles ache as I stand firmly, locking my knees into place with a familiar click. My eyes come level with Iris's, hers puffy and red like mine. Black blood runs down the side of her cheek, most likely from Harper's cut when she was unconscious.

"What happened?" I ask immediately, too awestruck to embrace Iris. I divert my eyes to check that Harper is real one last time before jerking my head back into the correct position.

Iris opens her mouth but a whine comes out as she shakes her head. "We—" She pauses, then swallows. "We came to say goodbye."

I wince as my claws abruptly break through my skin. I don't know Iris well, but she feels like family, particularly after I rescued Harper from the fire. That day, an unbreakable bond was forged between us, and I'm not about to let that melt away into ashes.

The memories of that day haunt me, more so than the time when I was trapped in the rogue encampment, forced to talk one-on-one with a monster. The image of a man burning has been engraved into my head, and I doubt it will go away. It is permanent, like a tattoo. I hardly have time to even comprehend that she ignores my question, but I know what her answer will be.

My heart aches. They're leaving as well? I don't have many friends, or any family, but they are part of me. Iris and Harper leaving feels like part of my soul dethatching itself involuntarily.

"What?" Disbelief lines my voice.

Iris gulps once more, as though she's afraid of me. The thought is enough to set my brain alight with anxiety. "I don't want this life for her." Iris gestures her head towards Harper. The young girl slides her hand into her mother's, gazing upwards with beady eyes.

I slowly nod, my action delayed. I run my tongue along the bottom of my lip for no reason, but it somewhat calms me. Chase kissed these lips.

"I understand," I say, but my eyebrows are creased. Wherever these two will go, the overhanging threat of death and destruction will loom over them like the moon haunts all of us at night. My hand takes Iris's upper arm, clenching it. "Take care of her. She's a fighter."

Iris smiles faintly. It's a gesture I've never seen her do. "I will," she replies, shrugging off my hold. "You take care as well. I can never thank you enough for what you did, Alaska."

The last tear I will allow to slip out of my drying eyes runs down my face as I pull Iris into a hug before letting go. "Where will you go?" I enquire, intrigued.

Iris exhales, pulling Harper closer towards her legs. I could never be a mother. "There's a human town I visited once when our pack was on the move. Crescent Peak." I rattle my head for memories linked with the town name, but nothing sparks to life. I have never been to the human world, and I don't plan to go anytime soon. "There's currently no pack claiming the town, so we should be able to keep a low profile. Live a normal life."

A human life, I want to correct her. The thought of hiding my wolf stirs my stomach on their behalves, but I know that this is the right decision for them. It's away from all of the tragedy and all of the death.

"Sounds nice." I lower the volume of my voice, the reason unknown. I shrug my shoulders. "I guess this is goodbye."

Iris nods. "Goodbye, Alaska," the woman says, pulling Harper to me in a bid to pay her farewells. The young girl decides to hide behind her mother's back instead, tugging at her hand.

I smile as Iris shoots me a sympathetic smile, stepping back towards the unguarded door. But before she can disappear, I suddenly remember the remaining knife in my belt. I don't trust myself with the weapon and have no desire for it anymore. Giving it to Harper means that a piece of me can always be with her; protecting her. I know she's nine, but when she's older, the rusty piece of metal can be a reminder of the world she came from and survived.

I draw out the steel blade. My father had given it to me once, and although it's one of the only pieces I have left of him, it isn't permanent like his face. I rub the metal on my top to try and get it to shine more, but the difference isn't noticeable.

"Here," I say, handing the dagger to Harper handle first. She cautiously raises a hand before taking it. After all, she's nine and knows how to handle a weapon. Or at least, Iris does until Harper is old enough. She had proved that when she stood up to Hunter and stabbed him in the back.

To my surprise, Iris doesn't object. The gift of a weapon to a young werewolf was common and not at all abnormal. "This used to be my father's," I explain. The girl attempts to hand it back, thrusting it in my face, but I wave my hands frantically to tell her no. "I want you to have it." I pause, making sure that her dark mocha eyes are focused on my plain hazel ones. "Whenever you're in trouble, use it to protect yourself. I don't want you getting hurt."

The girl nods as Iris's smile grows, her cheeks bulging and making her face appear square. At first, I'm worried that it's a smile of distaste, but I soon realise that it's a smile of admiration.

"Thank you," Harper murmurs. The woman stretches out an inviting hand towards Harper, but the child hugs the dagger close to her chest and shakes her head, refusing to give up the weapon. Harper then steps back, tucking the blade into the waistband of her leggings. "I hope to see you again someday."

"I know I will," I beam back, the smile foreign on my grief-stricken features. I'm still smiling as the pair round the edge of the door. I watch anxiously as they merge into the corridor and cease to exist. Part of me wishes that they turn around and come back, just to spend one more minute with them. Just like I wish Josh had done the same.

But instead, they don't come back. And once again, I am left on my own with no one but Chase by my side.

☽

Chase turns up five minutes later, his face crooked with deliberation and stress. I have pondered where he is, but being the king I know that he has to oversee the dying and give hope to the living. His presence is a testimony to the remaining Arla citizens that we have won the war.

I run straight into his arms as soon as his cropped dirty-blond hair appear around the stone doorway, crushing my face into his chest. Right next to his beating, alive heart. The steady thumps vibrate through my bones, and I welcome the rhythmic beating.

Having Chase is more than I could ever ask for, especially the fact that he is alive. It could've easily been him in Deathmatch against Hunter instead of me; he could've easily ended up dead; like Azra. Like the other countless amounts of warriors who were slaughtered because of the brutality of rogues.

The man's muscles bulge as he leans down to kiss me on the top of my head. He doesn't complain about my windswept hair or the blood entwined with the dark fabric of my clothes. I almost exhale when he retreats, placing a hand on my cheek instead as I pull my face away from his chest. The thumping of his heart ceases. I feel numb without the reverberating sensation.

I press my cheek into the palm of his hand. I can't see whether it has dirt, blood, or both on it but I'm beyond the point of caring.

Chase pulls me closer, continuously gazing into my eyes. The gold flecks are lighter today, appearing luminescent like the sun. They swim in the fluctuating cobalt I have both loved and hated, but at this moment in time, they are the most stunning things I have ever seen.

I wish I can freeze this moment; stay in Chase's arms for the rest of my life. I know I will always be by his side, but with a crowd of people focusing on me, whispering about how I looked, or questioning my leadership skills. I hate the idea that one day, after all my efforts to survive and my bid to not to be queen, I will be anyway. I can't be. I don't know anything about leadership.

Some people are born to rule, some to stick to the sidelines. I was clearly chosen for the latter. I'm a murderer, not an idol.

"I'm sorry," Chase murmurs into my hair. It takes a snap second to figure what he's talking about. Or rather, who. Azra. "I know how much she meant to you, and I wish I could've done something to help."

I shake my head as a response. Not to patronise that he was almost utterly useless in the bid to save her life. To tell him that it isn't his fault. No matter what we had done, wolf's bane that strong couldn't be cured, and it had already twisted itself deep into the roots of Azra's body. She knew that her life was over the moment the sword so much as touched her. It's a miracle that Harper even survived such a small dosage. She must be slightly resistant to the substance.

I also shake my head because I don't want to be reminded of the heart-wrenching experience once more. Perhaps in a month—or even a year—I will be able to process what had happened to the alpha's daughter, but right now, I have to live in the moment. I have to live focusing on the living, otherwise I will be dragged down into my pool of sorrows by the dead.

The sky outside has turned into a veiled sunset, the mark to the end of a traumatic day. Ruby etches itself into the sky, grey hazes of water vapour obscuring part of the canvas as the sun plummets over the horizon. Pink infiltrates the edges of the clouds, lining them in orange. I sigh at the stunning sight, but my heart wavers purely at the shades of the sky.

The scarlet reminds me of the blood that still stains my open fists; lines across my palms like rivers. And whenever I see it, all I can picture is the flash of azure eyes and a mix of red and black; the pigment of blood as it ran down Harper's cheek while she was unconscious.

I gulp, remembering the King with his arms fastened around me and refusing to let me go. The scent of pine trees infiltrates my nostrils, defeating the stench of death. He needs to know how I feel. I need to tell him.

I push away from his chest with my hands, but the proximity is still close enough for his gentle breath to fan onto my face. "I—" I begin. It's going to be much harder to portray what I mean when Chase's head isn't as screwed up as mine. "I don't want to be your queen."

Chase's face turns into a mask of rejection. His lips part, jaw falling open as his lips begin to form words. I shush him before he has a chance to start his sentence.

"What I mean is that I don't want to lead the people," I state, playing with the hem of his shredded shirt. My eyes are wide, but I can't find enough courage within me to face my mate. I can already feel the rejection seeping into my heart. "Of course I want to be your mate, Chase, but I can't have people looking up to me. I don't want people asking me for advice when I can't even understand my own feelings. I just want to be your mate; nothing else."

Chase appears to have frozen. He doesn't move for a minute, unblinking in his stupor. I squeeze his arm gently until he nonchalantly bows his head. "That's okay." The corners of his mouth twitch into a gentle smile. "I understand."

I crease my brows in surprise. I didn't expect him to be so . . . accepting. "You do?"

Chase nods once more, this time the movement much more rapid. "You sacrificed yourself in the Alpha Trials so you wouldn't become queen. Why would you have changed your mind now?" he says, licking his lips. Perhaps he mimicked the habit from Josh. The thought of my best friend makes my chest ache. "I understand because it will make you happy. And right now, you need to be happy."

I blink away tears at the words. We have spent so long fighting a growing, consuming darkness, both in reality and in our minds, that we have forgotten what true happiness looks like. I rarely smile; I barely see Chase look comfortable in his own skin.

Silence stretches around us, entwining with the light breeze as it flutters through the open window. Beyond the cobblestone thresholds, the trees shake. Shadows etch themselves into every nook and cranny as the sun begins to disappear into the horizon. But the darkness is beautiful. I welcome it. It is not putrid, or diseased, like the darkness Hunter created.

"Josh left," I state, slicing apart a perfect moment.

Chase's strong arms tighten around me, eyes trained on mine. "He'll come back," he assures me, but I shake my head. I'm not so sure.

"I hope so," is all I can reply.

Chase's smile grows, the orange light emanating from the fading sun scattered across his face, making his skin appear sun-kissed. His cobalt eyes fade to a deep brown in the lack of light, watching my every movement with each click of his working brain.

The man abruptly leans in, placing a kiss on my lips. I welcome it immediately, our mouths fitting together perfectly like a jigsaw puzzle. Sparks ignite in my skin, trailing down my spine. I shiver at the overwhelming sensation, adrenaline flushing into my veins like a tsunami. I slide my hand into Chase's soft strands of hair. They remind me of the delicate webs spiders produced, but thicker. I tug on them, pulling him in closer to deepen the kiss.

Unlike the numerous other kisses we have shared, this is in the light of a world that has been swept of most evils. The crushing pain that once suffocated me no longer exists. I can finally breathe, even with Chase limiting my intake of oxygen.

Finally, we pull away. A smile cracks onto my face, so wide that my cheeks hurt. I haven't smiled like this in a very long time.

My mind goes back to the people we have lost along the way. An image of my parents forms first, their faces distorted by time. But they still remain beautiful and everlasting in my mind, permanently plastered in my memories like a vice.

Dylan comes next, with his crooked smile and handsome face. He was taken too soon, from a life where he could've prospered.

Finally, Azra, and her striking azure eyes. She will never be forgotten, her bravery a testimony to this world. I will make sure that everyone knows about the sacrifice she made, even if I have to show my face to thousands. They will forever live in my heart, locked away in a small pocket that only I can fathom. And the only thought that makes me feel relatively okay is that they are in a better place; untouchable.

But in this moment, I have to let go. Maybe for a few seconds. Maybe for my whole life. The dead are gone, and the living are still hungry for whatever power than can obtain. I will see them again in the future.

"I love you," Chase whispers, placing a soft kiss on my reddened cheek.

I slide my hand into his as I watch the final glimmer of the sun being consumed by the horizon slide away into the abyss of night. I part my lips, smiling inwardly as my body buzzes like a hurricane of fireflies.

"I-I love you, too," I whisper back.

EPILOGUE

*"I had it all wrong. Before I found you, I thought the only way
to hold on was to find something to live for. It isn't. To hold on,
you must find something you're willing to die for."*
- Evan Walker, The Fifth Wave

One year, two weeks, and seven days later.

Rogue. It's a word that's been circulating this world for as
long as I can remember. It's the word that keeps children up at
night, swarmed by nightmares of feral crimson eyes and yellowed
teeth. It's the word used to describe the beasts that walk this earth.
It also describes the beast that lives inside all of us, raring to get out
with each shuddering heartbeat.

I have a different opinion.

Yes, some rogues are bloodthirsty creatures stripped from
their very humanity. Rogues like Hunter. But in the end, rogue is
just another word for werewolf. I was once deemed a "rogue." I
was once frowned upon for my very existence.

But we are all rogues. We all have the capacity to do
terrible things, but only some of us have the nerve to follow
through.

Now, it's different. The once feared rogues no longer
patrol this earth, fleeing from the kingdom after Hunter's death. I
made sure that his body was burnt, where everyone could witness
the fall of an insecure and psychopathic leader. It didn't sadden me
to watch the flames engulf his body, eating away at his flesh as it

311

hungered for more than just a body to consume. That was my monster—the living one he created inside of me. And I destroyed it.

I almost trip as my feet stumble over the uneven cobblestone bricks beneath my feet. My arms pinwheel forwards, awkwardly hitting a woman to my left to regain my balance. Some things never change, like my inability to stay upright.

The courtyard is bustling, with stalls surrounding the four edges of the square patio. The steps to the castle are only ten meters away, but I have no desire to go and find my mate at this moment in time. He is busy keeping the kingdom in order and out of the human eye.

A man on my left waves a colourful piece of material in my face, wailing at the top of his voice. His words are lost amongst the crowd as I move forwards, weaving between people like an ant avoiding being squashed. I feel tiny as the swarms of people swallow me whole, straight into the belly of the moving beast.

I sigh, pushing past countless werewolves in my bid to get out of the square. I should've gone through the back door, but that would've taken twice as long. All I want is to be out of the city—to take a breath of fresh air and visit Azra's memorial.

My eyes flicker ahead to the sturdy grey walls enclosing the city before me. They tower above the tents, elongated shadows fork out across the emerald grass and brown mud as numerous pack members tend to their daily chores. Life has once again returned to "normal" in the city of Arla, though I never knew what it was like before the rogue war.

We told people to forget the tragedies that struck that day. Everyone was affected. Whether it was a close relative, friend, or pack member, everyone lost someone. I can still see the agony in people's eyes as they pass, seemingly dormant as they continue their day to day lives. Just like my pain, theirs will never dissipate.

As I near the looming iron gates, the crowd disperses, leaving me some arm room to walk comfortably. I exhale in relief as the rush of people thins out. The stalls are more sparse here as I enter pack territory. A few men and women give me side glances as my boots meet thick mud, squelching in the mix of melting snow and dirt.

My heart hammers at the very thought that they're watching me, but I shrug off their tedious stares. I have grown used to the attention, despite my lack of a leadership role. I'm the King's mate, but not his queen. I will never be a queen.

I squint my eyes in confusion as I notice that the great wrought iron doors are already open. I take a step back, my boots once against meeting solid stone. Why are the gates open? They're rarely open. Then again, pack members have to exit and enter the city and were allowed to do so as they please.

I pause, biting my bottom lip as I place my hands on my hips. I take in a deep breath, trying to reclaim the oxygen I was deprived from when I was weaving through the hordes of werewolves.

But all my thoughts about going outside the city cease to exist as a lone figure marches into the city. My sharp canines pierce the skin of my scarlet lips, drawing blood. The liquid splashes into my mouth, bitter on my tongue.

His hair is ruffled, the light breeze flowing through his silhouetted locks as the sun slices the horizon above the man's head. A rucksack hangs on his shoulders as he slouches, body rigid as he takes yet another laboured step forwards. The tall figure walks alone, his legs delicately supporting him as the other wolves surrounding him stop what they're doing to stare at him. Just like me, they know exactly who he is.

The boy finally steps up onto the courtyard, the once-busy bustlers pausing their conversations to stare, eyes flickering to monitor the scene before them. Before I can divert attention away from myself and the boy, the courtyard has fallen silent. Nothing exciting ever happens in Arla, let alone the return of an old face.

313

"Oh my God," I whisper under my breath, my hands shaking. They drop the flower I had collected this morning to place on Azra's grave. The violet-coloured plant flutters to the ground, twirling daintily in the breeze. I had never expected to see him again, especially after all this time.

There's no mistaking the man's sharp, square shoulders and his mop of brunet hair. He still wears the same battered beige boots, the fabric dusted with dried mud and the odd blade of grass. As he steps into the light and out of the shadow of the castle walls, I gasp, my throat tightening. His face is much thinner, his cheekbones prominent underneath the bronzed skin. The darker skin tone suits him, mocha eyes staring at me as his pale lips part. This time he doesn't lick them. I watch nervously as his hands unclench by his sides, shaking steadily as his eyes widen, finally landing on my shocked figure.

Before I can comprehend my actions, my legs sprint towards him. They have a will of their own as they leap over upturned rocks, still shifted out of place from the war. I don't look elegant in my endeavour, but I don't care. I don't care.

My arms embrace the boy, enclosing him in my everlasting grip. His arms waver at my side, hanging in the air as he gasps, winded.

After a second, his arms fasten around me. His chin rests on the crook of my shoulder, and I sigh as memories of past embraces flood back into my brain. His arms feel weaker than they were before, but his hold is almost suffocating, as is mine.

God, I've missed him.

"Josh," I say nostalgically as I pull away. Strands of my brunette tresses interlink with the wind, obscuring my view partially. They blow on to the boy's face, a smile etching itself onto the corners of his mouth. A smile that cracks me open, tears flooding into my blurred vision.

I haven't heard his voice in a lifetime. "What have I missed?"

314

The End

Do you like werewolf stories?
Here are samples of other stories
you might enjoy!

ASHLEY MICHELLE

His to Claim

CHAPTER 1

"—Shift."

I was jolted out of my daydreaming by the sound of a loud voice ringing in my ear. I turned around with raised brows to find Darlene, the shift manager of the small family-owned diner, staring at me expectantly with a tray of dirty dishes in one hand. I had clearly missed the important parts of whatever she had been saying to me.

A sheepish grin worked its way up my face. "What was that?"

She rolled her eyes and blew a stray hair out of her face. "I *said*, do you mind covering the end of my shift for me? My babysitter called. Apparently, Graham is running a pretty high fever."

I nodded my head. "Sure, no problem." It wasn't like I had any plans for the evening anyway, other than obsessively checking the mail. There were only two weeks left before graduation, and I was yet to hear from any of the colleges I had applied to.

Darlene let out a small sigh. "Thanks, Scarlett. I owe you."

I waved my hand. "Don't worry about it. I know how hard it is on you being left to take care of Graham while Troy is away. I'm happy to help lighten the load." Her husband had to travel a lot for his job, and that left Darlene with extra parenting duties.

She gave me a grateful smile as she turned away with the tray of dishes. "You're truly an angel, Scarlett."

I snorted at her comment. "I already agreed to cover you. You don't need to kiss my butt anymore, Darlene."

She gave me a playful wink before turning away, disappearing through the kitchen door. I slowly turned back around with a sigh. This was going to be a long night of nothing but the virtual emptiness of the diner.

I was happy when a familiar face shuffled through the front door of the diner, setting off the little bell that hung above the door. He lifted his hand to his head, ruffling his dark hair which was starting to look shaggy around the edges. This boy would look like a mountain man if it weren't for my constant influence in his life. He met my gaze briefly as he reached out and grabbed one of the cheaply made menus from an empty table. He flipped through the pages quickly before setting it back down.

I pulled the pen and pad from the front pocket of my stained apron. "What can I get you, Wyatt?"

He shrugged as he moved closer toward me. "I think a cup of coffee will be fine. It's been a long day."

"It's going to be a bit longer. Darlene asked me to cover the end of her shift," I commented with an apologetic smile. Wyatt had promised to pick me up after my shift ended while I was running out the door this morning.

He let out a sigh, running his hand through his hair. "Of course, she did. Well, there *is* a meeting tonight. Guess it's going to be extra long for both of us, sweetheart," he replied with a sarcastic grin as I poured him a cup of coffee and placed it on the counter in front of me.

Darlene approached us carrying her purse, her jacket slung over her arm. "You know the coffee here is shit, Wyatt. I don't know why you keep ordering it when you only ever have a sip and leave the rest."

Wyatt ignored her comment. The two of them were always at each other's throats for reasons unknown to me. He pressed his hands to the counter, breathing in deeply. His nose scrunched up a bit, and he looked over at me. "You smell." I frowned at my cousins greeting as he sat himself down on a stool at the breakfast counter, grabbing the coffee.

"Gee, you really know how to compliment a girl," I grumbled, my voice dripping with sarcasm. My cousin and I had a very close relationship, considering that my parents had taken him in after his father ran off and his mother got sick. He returned the favor when my parents died, taking me into his home and raising me like I was his kid sister.

"God, Wyatt..." Darlene remarked as she threw her arms into the sleeves of her jacket, pulling up the collar. "Even if a woman does stink, you shouldn't comment on it. And you wonder why you're still single."

Her words brought a smile to my face, and I gave him a sharp look. I snickered as I turned away from my cousin who was pouting at the blunt reprimand he had received. I could see Winston, our cook, slaving away over the grill through the small hole, singing along to some garbage being gurgled out of the old boom box he kept in the kitchen. The diner was my home away from home, and its motley crew was my self-created wolf pack even if they were only humans.

"Wyatt," she said his name in a flat tone. Darlene had never cared much for my cousin. Maybe it's because he had a knack for putting his foot in his mouth... or maybe because they had gone "grown-up" together and he'd been quite the fool back in his younger years.

"See you tomorrow, Scarlett. Thanks again," she called.

I turned around to give her a quick wave. "See ya, Darlene. Tell Graham I said hello and hope he feels better," I called back as she exited the front door, the bell ringing again.

Wyatt lifted his gaze to mine, staring at me expectantly with wide eyes as if he was waiting for something. I stared back at him, shifting my hands to my hips. "Why are you looking at me like that? Do I have something on my face?" I reached up with a hand and wiped it across my cheek, checking to see if there was any food splatter. It was a hazard of the job.

"Can't you feel it, Scarlett?" he asked me in a soft voice so that no one else could hear. Hell, if it weren't for my extra-sensitive senses I probably wouldn't have heard him either.

I narrowed my eyes in confusion at his question. "What are talking about? Are you feeling okay, Wyatt?" I reached out and placed my hand on his forehead. He pulled back with a furrowed brow and looked at me as if I had two heads.

"After all the complaining and whining I had to listen to from you... are you seriously telling me that you don't feel even the slightest bit different?" he asked a little louder in an exasperated tone, waving his hand in the air dramatically. I had no idea what he was going on about or why he seemed so upset.

I looked around the small room at the other patrons who seemed content to ignore his outburst. I leaned forward, stuffing my notepad back into the pocket of my apron. "I don't know why you think I should feel different, but I feel the same as I always do. Unless you want to count the fact that my feet feel like I've been walking barefoot on hot coals. These ten-hour shifts have been killing me," I whined at him.

He gave me a slow blink, shaking his head. "Seriously, Scarlett?"

"What?" I questioned with a tired tone.

"Your scent—"

I held up a hand, cutting off his thought mid-sentence.

"I know. I know. I smell, but in my defense, you would smell too if you worked with greasy food all day," I snapped at him, growing tired of the conversation he was having with me. If I wanted to be insulted, I'm sure I could easily find one of my peers to satisfy that need without a problem. Human or shifter, they were all eager to tear someone else down to elevate themselves.

He shook his head at me. "No, your scent has changed, Scarlett. Your wolf has matured. I can smell her on you now."

I stared at him blankly as I digested his words. Had my wolf finally reached maturity without me noticing? I searched my mind for a sign of my wolf's presence. I had been waiting for this moment since I hit puberty. Most of my peers had already matured, leaving me like an outsider when it came to the pack.

All shifters had to go through two stages of puberty: the natural human one and the beast underneath. It could happen at any time, but basically, it meant that the connection between human and wolf was fully formed. It wasn't until this happens that we were allowed to attend actual pack events. Most of my friends had already matured. I had been left in the group of late bloomers. Sometimes, it happened that a wolf never matured. These people were seen as Omegas. They were still a part of the pack, but they would never be considered true wolves.

I shifted back and forth on my feet, concentrating hard. "I don't feel any different."

Wyatt took a sip of his coffee. "You will trust me." He pulled the mug away from himself, peering down into the cup with a small look of disgust before setting it down. "But you know what this means?"

"What?" I questioned with a raised brow.

He met my gaze with a knowing look. "You don't have to wait in the car like the other pups during the meeting tonight. You're a true wolf now," he teased as he gave me a wolfish grin. I rolled my eyes at his comment, but on the inside, I felt a bubble of excitement.

* * *

I had only ever seen the pack house from the outside, having never been allowed to enter it before. I found myself getting anxious as I followed Wyatt down the dirt driveway and around the side of the house. In the back, there was another building, about the size of a guest house.

I could hear the sound of happy voices carried on the gentle evening breeze. My palms felt sweaty in the pockets of my sweatshirt as my nerves got the better of me. Wyatt gave me a grin as he opened the door. "So it begins."

I rolled my eyes at him as I walked past him into the large open room. The smells of other pack members overwhelmed me for a moment. My eyes scanned the crowd warily, looking for familiar faces. I found my gaze gravitating towards the front of the room where the stream of bodies seemed to be moving.

That was the first time I saw *him*.

He stood near the front, greeting people with a friendly smile. My heart hammered in my chest as I watched him from where I stood at the back of the room. I had no idea who he was, but I knew he was perfect. His dark hair was shaved close to his head as if it had been shaved bare at some point and was finally being allowed to grow out. My eyes followed the length of his body, taking in every part of him. He had a lean body that spoke of endurance-honed muscles.

Wyatt elbowed my side. "Don't just stand there, Scarlett. People are starting to look at us." He urged me to move forward. I had to force my feet to move from where I had been anchored. My whole world seemed to be shifting on its axis, and I couldn't be sure I was standing on solid ground anymore.

My heart was in my throat as I approached my mate—at least that was what my wolf was telling me. This perfect male specimen was our mate, the one that the Goddess had ordained for us at birth. But what if he hated me? What if I wasn't what he was expecting? Insecurities that I had never felt before began to flood my brain.

I dug my heels into the floor. "I can't do this. Let's go home."

Wyatt grabbed onto my elbow and led me on. "You're being ridiculous. We all had to go through this, Scarlett. Consider it your official initiation into the pack." I gritted my teeth as every step brought me closer to the finality of my situation.

The Alpha and his mate were standing together, greeting the other pack members as they filed into the room, grabbing seats for the meeting. I remembered them from the times they had visited my home when I was much younger, way back when my mother was still alive, and my father held a prominent position in the pack. They looked older and a little more worn down, but that had to be expected of people in their positions.

"Alpha Aaron," Wyatt spoke formally as he reached out a hand, a standard human greeting. I danced on the balls of my feet, wishing that I hadn't accepted Wyatt's offer to join him. I was still in my work uniform, smelling like grease and probably looking unkempt from the busy workday... not the way I wanted to make my first impression on the pack.

"Wyatt," he replied, shaking the hand that had been offered to him with a firm grip, "it is good to see you again."

Wyatt beamed at the acknowledgment, turning his eyes toward the female beside the Alpha, bowing his head. "Luna Victoria."

She gave him a kind smile. "Wyatt."

Alpha Aaron's dark gaze shifted in my direction, a smile still on his lips. "And who is this beauty?" he questioned, lifting a brow as he examined me further. My cheeks rushed with heat, and I felt the sudden urge to hide behind my cousin like I did back in my younger years where I would cling to my mother's leg.

Wyatt wrapped his arm around my shoulder, pulling me in protectively to his side, and that only made me feel more embarrassed. "This is my cousin, Scarlett."

Luna Victoria gave me a knowing glance as she leaned into her mate's side. "Sweetheart, it's Conrad and Elizabeth's daughter."

"Of course, she is," he replied as if he had already known. My lips twitched with the urge to smile when she looked at me with a playful eye roll at his expense. Alpha Aaron crossed his arms over his wide chest, leaning forward toward me. "I can see it now that I've gotten a closer look. You've got Conrad's eyes."

"And Elizabeth's beautiful face," Luna Victoria remarked. "If I recall correctly, your mother was a late bloomer as well." I felt my head sink a little lower at her comment.

"David..." Luna Victoria called, turning toward my mate with a smile, "come over here real fast."

She glanced back at me. "Conrad helped train David when he was a young boy. I'm sure he will be very interested in meeting you." I felt my nerves spike as he turned in our direction, and I realized that he wasn't an average member of the pack. This was *their* son, the next heir: an Alpha born male.

I wanted to run, but my feet kept me firmly rooted in place. I was afraid to look up from the ground. What would I see staring back at me? I swallowed hard, trying to prepare myself for what was about to happen.

His shoes came into view, and I felt my wolf stirring under my skin. Wyatt elbowed me in the side. "Scarlett..." he hissed under his breath in a warning tone. I lifted my face to meet his gaze with bated breath.

His dark eyes widened in surprise as we drank each other in. Something in my mind snapped. I could feel it all, everything everyone had tried to explain to me about having a wolf. Her emotions and thoughts surged through me as I watched the corners of his mouth lift upwards into a smile.. a heart-stopping smile that was meant for only me.

I felt my own lips begin to mimic his. There were nothing and no one else in the room for us at that moment. This is what it felt like to have a mate, and I knew he was feeling the same sensations by the look in his eyes.

The moment was broken when a tall dark-haired female placed a kiss on his cheek. "I'm sorry I'm late, David. My shift went into overtime. I had to help Doctor McCarthy deliver the Johnsons' twins. Those pups are going to be a handful. I can tell you that now." She finished with a soft chuckle of amusement.

I hadn't even seen her approach us I had been so lost in a different world. My smile faded quickly as my brows furrowed in confusion as I glanced between the two of them. He looked rather stiff as she grabbed hold of his hand with hers, turning her face in my direction.

"Hello. I don't think I've seen you before." She tilted her head to the side.

"That's because she's only just matured, Eva," Luna Victoria commented toward her, both of them sharing a look of understanding like two people who've already been through it.

"This must be very exciting for you then," she remarked with a bright smile, completely unaware of what had happened between me and the male she was holding onto as if he were hers. My wolf was growling possessively in my mind, struggling to free herself so that she could eliminate the competition.

"David, this is Scarlett," Luna Victoria introduced me. "Conrad's daughter," she supplied as if it were my own special title.

I felt like the rug had been pulled out from under my feet and I was falling without anyone to catch me. My stomach was in my throat, but I forced myself to speak. "Hi…" I replied in a tense voice, finding it hard to hold his gaze.

David pulled his hand free from Eva's grasp and took a step towards me. He lifted his hand slightly like he wanted to reach out to me, but he thought better of it, deciding to stuff it into the pocket of his slacks instead.

"It's nice to meet you, Scarlett." Goosebumps rose on my flesh, and I watched his pupils dilate a bit as he took in more of me.

"Your father was a great man. The pack lost a great warrior when he passed away. I lost a dear friend," he added, trying to keep things from getting strange in front of all the onlookers. None of them seemed to know what had transpired between the two of us.

I gave him a small smile that didn't reach my eyes. "Thank you." He looked like he wanted to say something more to me, his lips parted slightly. Alpha Aaron stepped forward, his dark eyes calculating as he glanced between myself and his son. I lowered my gaze to the ground, clenching my jaw tightly.

"Well, we should get this meeting going." He wrapped his arm around his mate and pulled her into his side. "It's wonderful to have another true wolf added to the pack."

Wyatt grabbed my elbow, and I tensed slightly at the touch. Now that I could connect to my wolf, the world seemed too overwhelming. Every sensation moved through me like an exploding bomb. I let him lead me away to some empty seats, but my mind was adrift as I looked around the room. I had matured and met my mate, only to find out that he already had someone at his side. How could I compete with her?

My gaze focused on the female in question, Eva. She was a fully matured female compared to myself, who was still growing into my body, which was mostly knees and elbows. She seemed kind, and she didn't waver under the gaze of all the people in the room. She looked like a queen. I certainly wasn't much compared to her. That was why she was the one standing on the stage, holding his hand.

I sunk down lower in my seat. I could hear Alpha Aaron's voice as he spoke to the group, but none of the words were able to pierce through my racing thoughts.

"We are happy to announce that the mating ceremony of Eva and David will be held at the end of next month," Alpha Aaron said with pride in his voice, clapping David on the back as he stood next to a smiling Eva, hand in hand. My heart dropped, and I sucked in a painful breath. This wasn't how things were supposed to go. I was his mate, not her.

I couldn't sit in that room for another moment and listen to any more words. I leaned over to Wyatt. "I need to go," I whispered. He looked over at me in confusion as I rose up out of my chair and hurried toward the exit. I didn't look back, but I felt David's eyes on me, my body heating up everywhere his gaze drifted to. It was getting hard to breathe as I pushed open the door and flung myself out into the night, letting the cool air wash over me.

I sucked in ragged breaths as I tried to overcome the ache in my chest. No one had warned me maturing would be so painful.

If you enjoyed this sample, look for
His to Claim
on Amazon.

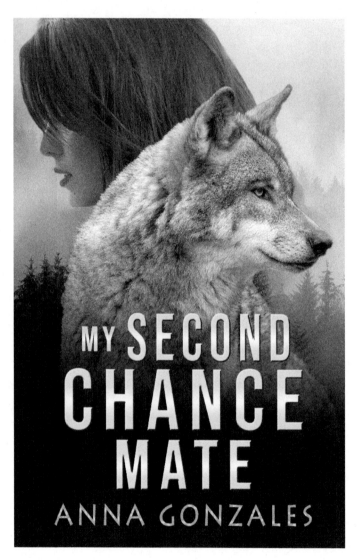

MY SECOND CHANCE MATE

ANNA GONZALES

CHAPTER ONE
Rejected but Moving On

HARMONY

    Waking up in the morning has never been easy for me and now it feels as if there's no point in doing it at all. I didn't always feel this way. I used to love life. I enjoyed hanging out with friends and even going to school. That changed the day I met my mate. What is a mate? It's supposed to be the best part of being a werewolf, which is what I am. We are born in human form and can transform into a wolf at the age of twelve. From that point on, it's a waiting game until we find our mate. A mate is a special someone who completes you; the one you was made for and vice versa. I should be happy to have found mine. Unfortunately, my story is unique and I don't mean that in a good way.

*   *   *

One Year Ago . . .

    I met him at the age of sixteen. He was everything I could've hoped for. Seventeen years old, 6"1', gorgeous gray eyes, dark black hair, nicely tanned skin, washboard abs, and strong long legs. Perfect, right? I thought so too. We found each other outside the airport baggage claim area. Our eyes met and it was electrifying. We moved towards one another as if pulled by some force until we were only a foot away.

"Mate," we both whispered. He reached out to touch my cheek and I leant into his palm. It felt right; like home. I was so happy that I closed my eyes to savor the moment when he suddenly tensed and dropped his hand. I opened my eyes to ask what was wrong just as he took a big step back. I stared at him in confusion and was about to ask what made him move away when the sound of a familiar voice made the words freeze on my lips.

"Babe, I see you've met my sister. Isn't she adorable?" My older sister, Megan, gushed as she gave me her usual too-tight, can't breathe type of hug.

"Did you say babe?" I asked.

"Yes, silly! Aiden, you didn't introduce yourself?" She laughed while playfully swatting his chest. "Harmony, meet the best thing to come out of this whole mandatory wolf camp that mom and dad sent me to. My boyfriend, Aiden James," she announced happily while grabbing his arm.

My wolf growled at the sight of her touching my mate, but I couldn't say anything right now. I love my sister. She's my best friend and she looked so happy. I couldn't do anything to ruin that. Don't get me wrong;I had some serious questions to ask but I would get my answers when the time was right. Even if I had to tie Aiden to a chair to do it. There was a satisfactory rumble from my wolf just by picturing it. I couldn't believe that, out of all people my sister could have met at this camp, she had to meet and fall in love with the one wolf meant for me.

The camp they attended was a first of it's kind. It was created for two types of wolves. The first was for someone like Aiden, a future alpha. These types of wolves would one day be the leaders of their pack and had to be taught to control their added power and authority so that it wouldn't be misused. The second was for wolves born from two werewolf parents who both carry the recessive gene. It causes their child to be born completely human, and my sister was one of those children. The whole thing was complicated enough as it is, and finding out I was the mate of a future alpha my sister was currently dating only added to the complication.

Aiden and I quickly exchanged hellos as if the spine tingling encounter between us never happened. We grabbed their bags and headed to the car. The ride was uncomfortable mainly because the love birds decided to share *the back seat and cuddle. I exchanged looks with Aiden a couple times in the mirror, and though he would smile at my sister, the looks he gave me seemed sad and resigned. His mood confused me but I expected to get an explanation soon.*

We made it to our pack house where they were having a big barbeque to welcome my sister and Aiden back. Aiden is the only nephew of our alpha, and because our alpha's mate is human, she could not conceive a child. Our law states that the next male in line would be the alpha's younger brother, Aiden's dad. However, he was killed by rogues when Aiden was thirteen so by law, Aiden is the next heir. It is strange that we never had the opportunity to meet before but that's due to the fact that Aiden's mother took him back to her pack shortly after his father's death. She was unable to deal with the memories of her lost mate that surrounded her wherever she went. Her story was sad and was still used today to teach young pups the ups and downs of mating.

After about an hour into the barbeque, my sister made a run to the store with our mom, and it finally gave me a chance to get Aiden alone. I dragged him to a clearing, a little far down from our pack house, and laid above him.

"So, what are we going to do? I love my sister to death but we're mates. We can't deny that. I don't want to hurt her but the pull I feel for you is so strong I can't ignore it," I started rambling.

"I can," he said.

I continued, not quite hearing him. "I mean, I know this is going to be difficult and create a lot of drama but I'm so happy I've found you a—"

He cut me off and repeated those two words, loud enough so I could hear them. "I can."

"You can? Can what?" I asked, confused.

"I can ignore it. This pull between us," he stated. He proceeded to rip my heart out of my chest with the rest of his words. "I never had a choice in many things in my life. I didn't choose to lose my dad, or have to leave my pack, or be put into the role of alpha but I chose your sister. I fell in love with her all on my own with no influence from anyone. I refuse to change how I feel just because my wolf wants me to. I want to be with the one I love because I say so and not because a bond is forcing me to."

I stared at him. I was shocked and hurt. "Are you saying what I'm thinking? Are you rejecting our bond?"

He sighed. "Look, I don't want to hurt you, Harmony. I spent time with your sister, and I got to know her and fell in love all on my own. If I'm with you, it's not by choice anymore but by fate. I refuse to let fate control anything else in my life. I'm sorry but that's just how it has to be."

To say I was hurt was an understatement. What came next was just anger. "You refuse? What about me? Do you know how long I've dreamed of meeting my mate and finally feeling the love only he can give me? Only you can give me? And now you tell me I can never feel that because fate has dealt you a cruel hand and you're rebelling? And so I'm the one who has to pay for your misfortune? I have never done anything in my sixteen years of life to deserve that, but does it matter to you? Obviously not!" I cried out.

"Look, Harmony. I—"

"No, you look. I'm sorry you had to go through all that but that's what I can be here for. I can help heal the pain you've been through and support you through the role that was forced onto you. No one will be able to understand you like I, your mate, can. Let me do this for you. For us," I pleaded.

"I just can't, Harmony. I've already chosen the future I want, and that future is with your sister," he replied firmly.

"What about our bond? It's going to be hard to fight it. My wolf is trying to get through, and I'm sure so is yours. How are you going to deny him?" I questioned.

Nothing. And I meant nothing could have saved me from the pain his answer caused. "Well, I'll fight him off until I completely mate with Megan. Once I mark her, he will be easier to control, and as more time passes, our bond will eventually weaken."

"True, but you forgot one important detail. Or maybe it's not so important to you since you won't be affected but what happens to the rejected mate, Aiden? What will happen to me? Let me remind you, being that I don't have a choice in the rejection," I lashed out in anger, "my wolf will weaken. When you mark Megan, I will feel as if my chest has been ripped open. You will have your love for Megan to help get you through the weakened bond, but I won't be able to find another wolf mate since we are only given one in our *lifetime. Even though the bond will deteriorate, I will still hurt every day. I will have to see you together and be reminded of my rejection time and time again. Is that really what you want for me? I know you feel something for me. I saw it at the airport. Are you absolutely sure this is what you want to do?"*

"It's what I want," he whispered. "I've thought about this my whole life."

I tried one last plea. "What about kids, Aiden? Megan is human. You won't be able to have a pup with her. How will you carry on your alpha line?"

"I'll deal with that when the problem arises."

"So you'll give up your mate and any future blood children just to spite fate?" I asked, hurt and shocked.

He nodded. "Yes. I'm really sorry. I just can't be with you." There was a hint of sadness in his voice.

"It's not that you can't. You just chose not to," I whispered in defeat. "So you're finally getting to choose for yourself, and that choice forces me into a life of pain and misery," I said as I looked him in the eyes. I thought I saw some indecision and pain, but it was quickly replaced by resignation and determination. I looked away as the tears started to fall. "Fine." I turned back to face him. "I will accept your rejection of the bond but only because like a mate should; I only want your happiness. You see, that's what mates are supposed to do: Protect each other, care for one another, and put each other first. I will endure the pain of the future for you, and I hope that it haunts you every night while you live your happily ever after with my sister." And with that said, I shifted into my light brown wolf and ran further into the darkness of the woods.

* * *

Shaking my head of the unwanted memories, I think about my life since then. I haven't done anything drastic to my appearance. I still wear my brown hair long and straight, no contacts cover my light green eyes, my full lips are still only covered in clear lip gloss, and I haven't changed from skinnys and tanks to ripped jeans and grungy t-shirts. No, the only change is my attitude.

The sweet carefree nature is gone. I now know how real life can be and it isn't a fairytale. My enthusiasm for life is gone. When you look into my eyes, you'll see emptiness that hides the constant pain.

I no longer live with my pack. Six months after my rejection, Aiden marked my sister and the pain was unbearable. I couldn't be around him and see him happy anymore. Yes, there were times when I was near him and could feel his wolf fighting for control but Aiden always pushed him back. I begged my parents to let me leave the pack and join my maternal aunt's pack— Her mate's pack in Hawaii, to be specific. My parents didn't understand why at first because I never told anyone about my rejection. I made up the excuse of it being hard to be around Aiden and Megan knowing I haven't found my mate yet. At least it was half true.

That's where I am now. A new pack, a new school, and hopefully, a new life. I should have an optimistic attitude, but I no longer have the illusion of happily ever after. Hope is something I seriously lack in the present. There is one good thing to come from all this.

"Harmony, get your lazy ass up so we can get to school. I don't want to miss all the fresh meat awaiting me. My game is on fire today. Just don't stare too hard at me 'cause you might be blinded by all this hotness."

There it is. My cousin Jared. He's the only one who knows about my rejection because, unlike my aunt and uncle, I can't hide the pain from him. He knows me too well, and it took all of my wolf strength to stop him from jumping on a plane to beat the crap out of Aiden. It's good though because he constantly takes my mind off of things with his crazy man whorish ways and wise remarks. His friends are awesome too. And are total eye candies. A few tried hitting on me when I was first introduced to the pack, but Jared gave all them death glares. He warned his player friends that I was completely hands off unless any of them were planning on putting a ring on my finger. I laughed at all the deathly ill expressions in the room after that announcement. Commitment is equal to a bad case of crabs in their minds. I can't wait 'til they meet their mates. It'll be fun watching them get tamed.

I get dressed in some black skinnys and an off-shoulder white top with a black tank underneath. I put my hair in a loose bun, gloss my lips, and slip into a pair of black gladiator sandals. As I'm tucking a fly away hair behind my ear, the opening of the front door announces Jace, Nate, and Brad's arrival. I make my way to their voices and find them in the kitchen as usual.

"Bro, I'm telling you. This year we're gonna score so much pu—"

"Lady in the room!" I shout, interrupting what I'm sure was gonna be one of Nate's more colorful terms for *vajayjay*.

"Right. Sorry, Harm. As I was saying, we're gonna score so much chicks because we're now seniors," Nate corrects himself excitedly.

"Well, I know I will, but I'm not too sure about you ugly mutts. Just don't stand too close to me and you'll have a chance since my sex appeal is just too massive," Jared boasts, a l in his usual arrogant self.

"Really, Jared? I know what's massive about you, and it's not your sex appeal or your weiner. Don't try to deny it. Our moms showered us together when we were little, and if I remember correctly, which I do, it was very, very, very tiny," I say, making sure I emphasized the size with my thumb and pointer fingers.

"Hey, that's because I haven't changed yet. Trust me. Massive isn't even a big enough word to describe it now," he argues, a tiny bit offended.

I cringe. "First of all, gross. And second, your ego is the only thing that's massive. I'm worried if you don't bring it down you might not be able to fit your fat head out the door."

"She's right. Besides, we all know my sexiness outshines all of you," Brad informs them.

"No way. I score the most ass . . . I mean chicks every year," Jace argues.

"That's only cause you don't have standards and will screw anything with two sets of lips," says Nate with a raised brow.

This sets off a whole new conversation about what's doable and what's not, followed by pushing and headlocks. These boys are too much and, even though I'm not excited about the day ahead, it promises to be entertaining.

If you enjoyed this sample, look for
My Second Chance Mate
on Amazon.

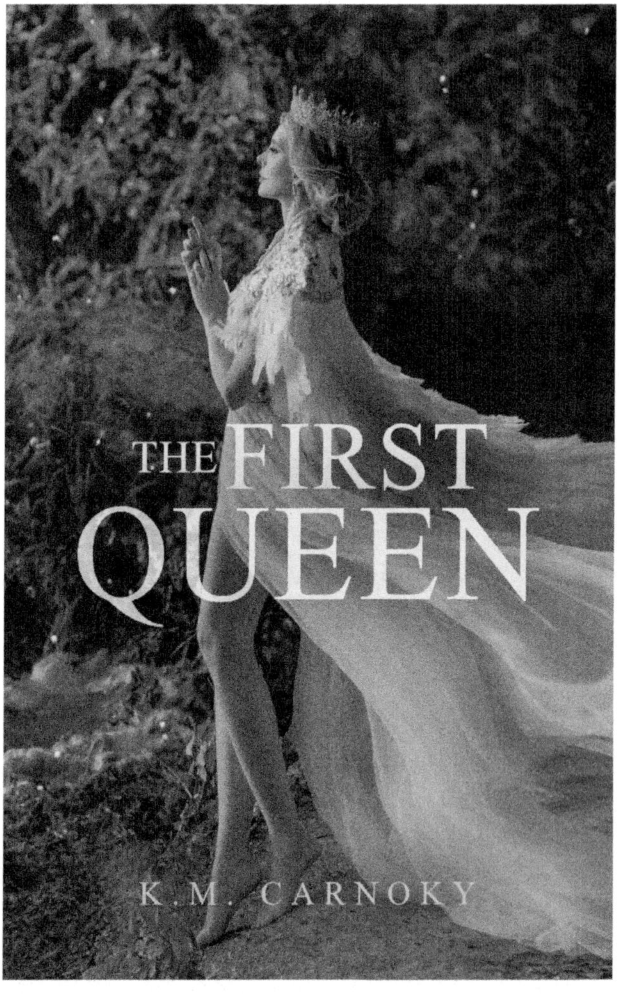
THE FIRST
QUEEN
K.M. CARNOKY

CHAPTER ONE

I hummed to myself as I untangled the horse's mane, contentment flowing through me. The tall workhorse basked in my attention. It was so still, it almost looked like it was already sleeping. While I worked away to remove all the knots he had accumulated in the past week, the sound of a soft snore filled the air. The coarse black hairs eventually started sliding through the old comb with ease, and I smiled to myself. Now, it was time for the rest of him, and the old gelding didn't mind. This was probably his favorite day of the week as he adored human contact, and because of that, he had earned the title of being my favorite creature. I bring him joy after long days of plowing the fields, and he makes me feel less lonely when the sun begins to set and I hadn't spoken to a single soul yet. The farm we lived in was miserable, and the old beast was hardly cared for considering his aging body, yet he always nickered to me and deeply enjoyed our quiet time together. I would whisper to him details from my day and watch those ears flicker back and forth. For a while, it would make me feel less alone. It seemed he was the only creature I could truly call a friend. And after losing my beloved Edna, a chicken, I wasn't prepared to befriend the other animals that could be eaten.

When I moved to fetch a brush for his filthy coat, I winced at the sound of my shackles and the soreness of my ankles. For the hundredth time, I regretted the actions that led me to this position. In my younger years, I had tried to run away from my owners too many times, and they would simply not have it anymore. They were both too tired and too old to be chasing after me and worrying every night about another escape attempt. So, now, this was my reality. My hands were free to work, but my legs were shackled together by a thick chain and locked with clamps. I could shuffle and bumble around at a slow pace, moving with little half-steps, but I couldn't get more than a couple hundred yards in an hour. At first, the shackles had been agony to wear, biting into the skin so angrily; now, there was just a constant ache and the occasional twinge that reminded me of my wrongs.

It could've been worse though, and I should be thankful for what freedom I did have. At least that's what I told myself as I began running the brush down the horse's coat with long sweeping motions. I could've been left on the street to die in the wretched winters. Or I could've been forced to work in a factory where the pollutants that floated through the air would fill my lungs until I died at the ripe age of twenty-five. Or, when I had initially been abandoned by my mother, I could've even been sold as a sex slave to some awful man with disgusting desires. Hell, I might've even encountered a werewolf when I was so young, barely six years old.

I shuddered at the possibilities. This was a much better reality than any of those. True, I was shackled, but my life still held brief moments of joy. Like the bond with old gelding, teaching myself to read using old picture books, and the plants that I managed to grow and sell in the markets. These were all things I had accomplished myself that wouldn't have been possible anywhere else.

Unfortunately, though I was safe from many threats now that I had been purchased, werewolves were still a very possible danger to everyone. Rich and poor. Married or single. No matter the societal status, we all bare the same fear. We were all the same to the beasts.

Werewolves had been discovered after a series of mistakes had led humans right into one of their tribes. I believe they called them packs. At first, the werewolves had been terrified of humans and everything had been fine then. We lived in a delicate balance for a time as no one was ready to confront the opposing group. But, within the past twenty years, werewolves had become more aggressive, and through various altercations, they came to realize that they held the upper hand. Werewolf men were usually larger than most human men, and the beasts they turned into were much stronger than the average wolf. The had the intelligence of a human paired with the snapping jaws and long claws of a wolf. Once they realized this, they began pillaging our communities, stealing our women, and killing indiscriminately. We were constantly teetering on the brink of war. It was a horrible reality, and every week, I would hear a story from the other village slaves about another woman who was kidnapped or a man who had been found lying in his own cold blood. It was disgusting and gruesome, but the werewolves were too strong to conquer.

The king at the time had tried to settle the whole dispute by marrying a werewolf woman, and the couple seemed quite pleased with both the match and the results. They even had a son who was now ruling with his wife, and the upper class seemed to love them. But I refused to be fooled. I had heard too many repulsive stories about their actions to believe that one romantic union had ceased their wretched ways. Werewolves were animals simply disguised as humans. They were violent and vicious creatures that had no moral sense whatsoever. And I knew I was not alone in my thinking; many humans still feared and loathed the current king. There was nearly constant chatter about uprisings. I was no fool. I knew which side to be on.

A loud clang startled me out of my thought process. The gelding was startled at the sound, tossing his head about and stamping his colossal hooves. I whirled around, nearly falling over my shackles to see my owner sneering at me, a pot of leftover potato water at his feet and a piece of stale bread floating in it.

He was an unattractive man, and his wife was hardly any better. They matched the farm in that regard. Unappealing to those who passed by and worn down. In fact, unattractive seemed to be too kind a word. They were both quite overweight with bulging guts, oily faces, and hair that was slowly thinning. Both of them frequently stank of alcohol; one of beer, the other of wine. Neither of them were particularly kind or compassionate, and they only gave me enough nutrients to make it to the next day. Even compared to the other village slaves, I was thin. I was frequently exhausted because of how little food I was given, though it hardly mattered to them. My sole purpose was to protect the animals from thieves who lurked in the dark at night, and so far, they hadn't lost a single creature.

"The first market of the season is next week. I will be taking your rhubarb with me."

"It's not ready," I grunted.

"It was ready at this time last year; you even had some wild lilies," he snapped, already becoming enraged.

"This year has been harder on them. It's been far too cold for them to grow so rapidly. The hyacinths haven't even sprouted," I countered, glaring at him.

"You watch your tongue."

"Or what? You'll get rid of me?" I challenged him. "You'll find someone else in the village that can successfully grow plants from another province in your soil? Please do."

"My God, you are more trouble than you're worth," he spat. "Why did the Lord punish me with such an ungrateful creature?"

His hand flexed by his side. I wondered if he was going to be brave enough to strike me. He had only done it a few times before, and though I could not physically fight him in shackles, I always found a way to get even.

"Then undo these shackles and I promise you'll never have to see me again." I looked him straight in the eye.

My owner stared at me for a while longer. I watched him back just as intensely, thinking that he was going to say something to me. Over the years, he had always complained about my sharp tongue, but he was never foolish enough to get rid of me. I was worth three times what he had paid for, and he was far too lazy to do the work himself.

Then, without a word, he turned around and walked away. And the only thing in the world that I envied about that man was the fact that he could walk without having to take small, shuffled steps and drag a heavy chain along with him.

I finished grooming the old plow horse before I sat myself down for my food.

The potato water would've been disgusting for many normal people, but I had grown used to the starchy flavor. I saved the stale bread for last so I could wash away the taste of dirt and potatoes that coated my mouth. Once I had eaten, I ignored the rumbling in my stomach, my body wanting for more, and slipped into an empty stall with clean straw. I could hear the rustling of all the other animals around me as they settled in for the night. I laid myself down on the straw, curling up to keep as much body heat as I could. Underneath my body, I could feel the hard edges of the books I kept hidden away. I had stolen them so long ago. I didn't recall how or why, but they had become my most treasured and old possessions. Then, for the hundredth time, I reminded myself that this whole situation could be much worse, and I fell asleep.

If you enjoyed this sample, look for
The First Queen
on Amazon.

AUTHOR'S NOTE

Thank you so much for reading *Alaska*! I can't express how grateful I am for reading something that was once just a thought inside my head.

I'd love to hear your thoughts on the book. Please leave a review on Amazon or Goodreads because I just love reading your comments and getting to know you!

Can't wait to hear from you!

Lotte Holder

AUTHOR'S NOTE

Lotte is an eighteen-year-old student studying Biology and Marine Biology from the rainy country of England. She started writing at the age of twelve, and has too many book ideas for her own good. Lotte was chosen as a runner-up for BBC Radio 2's 500 Word Short Story Contest in 2013, and was Shortlisted for a Watty Award in 2018. When she isn't writing, Lotte spends her time studying hard at university in the hopes to film the next Blue Planet. She also (admittedly) goes out too much for a university student, and misses her cat, Flame, when she's not at home in Kent.

Printed in Great Britain
by Amazon